I0655784

Terms and Concepts in Geomorphology Oceanography and Climatology

With Essential Diagrams and Illustrations

Dr Shrikant Karlekar

Diamond Publications

Terms and Concepts in Geomorphology, Oceanography and Climatology
(With Essential Diagrams and Illustrations)

Dr Shrikant Karlekar

First Edition : July, 2016

ISBN : 978-81-8483-667-7

©**Diamond Publications**

Cover Page :
Sham Bhalekar

Typesetting :
Aksharvel, Pune

Published by :
Diamond Publications
264/3 Shaniwar Peth, 302 Anugrah Apartment
Near Omkareshwar Temple, Pune - 411 030
☎ 020-24452387, 24466642

info@diamondbookspune.com
www.diamondbookspune.com

Sole Distributor :
Diamond Book Depot
661 Narayan Peth
Appa Balwant Chowk
Pune 411 030
Tel. - 24480677, 66020282

Preface

A number of new concepts, ideas and terms are being added to every branch of science since last few years. All these terms are not incorporated in the available conventional dictionaries.

These days, the subjects like Geomorphology, Oceanography and Climatology are rapidly expanding multi disciplinary subjects. They have a significant relationship with other disciplines like environmental science, hydrology and soil science.

Textbooks and reference books in these subjects do help in imparting, knowledge of fundamental concepts. Students appearing for competitive examinations however require an additional academic support in the form of definitions and short descriptions and their collection under one glossary. The concepts and ideas elaborated in the form of diagrams and illustrations are always more useful to them for the understanding of the subject.

This collection of terms and concepts in Geomorphology, Oceanography and Climatology (with essential diagrams and illustrations) is prepared with these requirements in mind. The terms and concepts included in this collection cover major part of the subject matter and are written in a manner such that they are easy to grasp and assimilate.

Care has been taken to ensure the inclusion of up-to-date information in the subjects. The entries are presented in alphabetical order and shown in the appropriate diagrams wherever required.

I am thankful to Shri. Dattatray Pashte of Diamond Publications for giving a whole-hearted support for the publication of this collection of Terms and Concepts in important branches of Earth Science.

Dr Shrikant Karlekar

Contents

Terms and Concepts
in Geomorphology,
Oceanography and Climatology

A

A Reach (of a stream), An uninterrupted part of a stream channel between two points; generally the two points are where readily recognizable tributary inflows occur, but can also include features such as meander bends, gorges, or a significant change in geology (which in turn could be the cause of a gorge or a waterfall). *(Fig. 54)*

aa lava flow, A type of basaltic lava flow dominated by aa lava and a characteristically rough, jagged, clinkery surface and a vesicular interior. *(Fig. 33)*

Ablation, The wasting and removal from a rock mass of material by physical processes such as wind erosion or by chemical processes, including dissolution of cementing agents followed by failure of rock material at the chemically altered surface. In glaciology, ablation is the removal of snow and ice from any mass of frozen water through processes of melting, sublimation and evaporation, wind erosion, and calving (such as failure at the snout of a glacier).

Abrasion, A form of mechanical weathering, is the reduction of rock fragments or rock surfaces by the wearing, grinding, or rubbing action of other rock particles or of the transport medium, particularly ice in glacial or periglacial environments. Particle-to-particle impact of the sediment load is the principal process of abrasion in streams and the cause of rounding of the sand and coarser stream sediment that comprises bed material. Aslo occurs in glaciers.

Abrupt climate Change, The nonlinearity of the climate system may lead to abrupt climate change, sometimes called rapid climate change, abrupt events or even surprises. The term abrupt often refers to time scales faster than the typical time scale of the responsible forcing.

Absolute humidity, The ratio of the mass of water vapor in a sample of moist air to a unit volume of the sample. It is expressed in grams per cubic meter and also called the vapor concentration.

Absorptance, In radiation transfer, the fraction of incoming radiation that is absorbed by a medium. The sum of this, the transmittance, and the reflectance must equal unity.

Absorption band, In atmospheric radiative transfer, a collection of absorption lines in a particular frequency interval.

Absorption line, In atmospheric radiative transfer, a discrete frequency at which an energy transition of an atmospheric gas occurs due to the absorption of incident solar radiation. The line width depends on broadening processes, the most important of which are natural, pressure (also known as collision) and Doppler broadening.

Absorption, A process by which incident radiation is taken into a body and retained without reflection or transmission. It increases either the internal or the kinetic energy of the molecules or atoms composing the absorbing medium.

Abyssal hill, Small hills found only in the deep sea which rise from the ocean basin floor with heights ranging from and widths from a few hundred meter to a few km. They are found along the seaward margin of most abyssal plains and originate from the spreading of mid-ocean ridges. They usually form two strips parallel to mid-ocean ridges. They generally decrease in height as one traverses away from the ridges as they gradually become covered with sediment and are replaced by abyssal plains.

Abyssal plain, Flat areas of the ocean basin floor which slope less than 1 part in 1000. These were formed by turbidity currents which covered the preexisting topography. Most abyssal plains are located between the base of the continental rise and the abyssal hills. The remainder are trench abyssal plains that lie in the bottom of deep-sea trenches. This latter type traps all sediment from turbidity currents and prevents abyssal plains from forming further seaward. Also defined as ''an extensive, flat, gently sloping or nearly level region at abyssal depths." *(Fig. 121)*

Abyssal Zone, This originally meant (before the mid-1800s) the entire depth area beyond the reach of fisherman, but later investigations led to its use being restricted to the deepest regions with a uniform fauna and low temperatures. Thus it was distinguished from the overlying bathyal or archibenthal zone with more varied fauna and higher temperatures. Eventually an underlying hadal zone was defined for areas in trenches and deeps below 6000-7000 m depth. The upper boundary of the abyssal zone ranges between 1000-3000 m, with the position of the 4° C isotherm generally considered the demarcation line. It is the world's largest ecological unit, with depths exceeding 2000 m comprising over three-quarters of the world ocean. *(Fig. 121)*

Abysspelagic zone, One of five vertical ecological zones into which the deep sea is sometimes divided. There is a pronounced drop in the number of species and the quantity of animals as one passes into this zone. It is separated from the overlying bathypelagic zone by the 4° C isotherm and from the underlying hadopelagic zone at about 6000 meters. The distinction between pelagic and benthic species can be difficult to ascertain in this zone.

Accelerated erosion, The erosion that occurs at a more rapid rate than is typical for a specified site or area. The term generally refers to human-induced land-surface disturbance, especially disruption of soil structure and destruction of natural soil cover by rock fragments and vegetation Most accelerated erosion is the result of human activity (agricultural, grazing, logging, surface mining, urban construction), but it also occurs naturally when a geomorphic threshold is exceeded by processes such as slope failure, avulsion, the effects of high-magnitude floods, fire, avalanche, or plant disease.

Accretion, A natural process of gradual sedimentation on channel features, especially channel bed and banks, or bottomland surfaces, including the flood plain and low-lying terraces.

Accretion, [sedimentology] The gradual increase or extension of land by natural forces acting over a long period of time, as on a beach by the washing up of sand from the sea or on a flood plain by the accumulation of sediment deposited by a stream.

Acoustic signature, A set of characteristics used to describe a sound signal. This may include sound echos from targets, radiated and ambient noise, with salient echo characteristics including target strength, spectral reflectivity versus frequency, doppler shift, doppler spread and target range extent.

Acoustic tomography, The inference of the state of the ocean from precise measurements of the properties of sound waves passing through it. This technique takes advantage of the facts that the properties of sound in the ocean are functions of temperature, water velocity and other salient oceanographic properties and that the ocean is nearly transparent to low-frequency sound waves.

Acoustical oceanograpy, The study of sound propagation in the ocean and its underlying sediments. This ranges from the earliest use of depth soundings to chart the ocean floor to the use of SONAR to locate schools of fish, underwater vehicles and ocean drifters to the most recent applications of acoustic tomography to infer large-scale properties of the ocean and the ocean floor.

Active channel, A short-term geomorphic feature subject to change by prevailing discharges; its upper limit is defined by a break in the relatively steep bank slope of the active channel to a more gently sloping surface beyond the channel edge. The break in slope normally coincides with lower limit of perennial vegetation so that the two features, individually or in combination, define the active-channel reference level.

Active layer, The layer of ground that is subject to annual thawing and freezing in areas underlain by permafrost

Active-channel shelf, A gently sloping riparian surface of an adjusted alluvial bottomland that normally extends from the break in slope of the channel banks that marks the active-channel edge to the higher bank slope that rises to the edge of the flood plain. It typically corresponds to a stage approximating mean discharge of perennial streams.

Actual evapotranspiration, The actual loss of water to the atmosphere, as a rate or volume, from a land surface through combined evaporation from the soil and transpiration of plants.

Adiabatic process, A process in which no external heat is gained or lost by the system. The opposite is called a diabatic process.

Adiabatic, Involving or allowing neither gain nor loss of heat.

Adjustment, The tendency of non-rigid landforms, such as stream channels, to change in size and shape in response to the changing effects (mostly fluxes) of water, sediment, dissolved solids, and organic matter that alter them or pass through them.

Adriatic Sea, A part of eastern basin of the Mediterranean Sea located between Italy and the

Balkan Peninsula. It is landlocked on the north, east and west, and is linked with the Mediterranean through the Otranto Strait to the south. The Adriatic is a rectangular basin oriented in a NW-SE direction with a length of about 800 km and width of about 200 km. *(Fig. 143)*

Advection, Transport of water or air along with its properties (e.g., temperature, chemical tracers) by the motion of the fluid. Regarding the general distinction between advection and convection, the former describes the predominantly horizontal, large-scale motions of the atmosphere or ocean, while convection describes the predominantly vertical, locally induced motions.

Aegean Sea, A marginal sea in the eastern Mediterranean Sea centered at approximately 25° E and 38° N. It is located between the Greek coast to the west, the Turkish coast to the east, and the islands of Crete and Rhodes to the south. It contains more than 2000 islands forming small basins and narrow passages with very irregular coastline and topography. The northern part of the Aegean is also known as the Thracian Sea, and the southern part between the Cretan Arc and the Kiklades Plateau (defined as the 400 m isobath) as the Cretan Sea. It contains an extended plateau (Thermaikos, Samothraki, Limnos and Kyklades) as well as the deep basins the North Aegean Trough (1600 m maximum depth), the Chios Basin (1160 m) and the Cretan Sea (two depressions in the east 2561 m and 2295 m deep). It covers an area of 20,105 km_2, has a volume of 74,000 km_3, and a maximum depth of 2500 m. *(Fig. 143)*

Aerosols, A collection of airborne solid or liquid particles, with a typical size between 0.01 and 10 um that reside in the atmosphere for at least several hours. Aerosols may be of either natural or anthropogenic origin. Aerosols may influence climate in several ways: directly through scattering and absorbing radiation, and indirectly by acting as cloud condensation nuclei or modifying the optical properties and lifetime of clouds. *(Fig. 160)*

Afforestation, Planting of new forests on lands that historically have not contained forests.

Age of tide, The delay, usually a day or two, between full and new moons (when the equilibrium semi-diurnal tide is maximum) and the following spring tides.

Aggradation, The building-up of the Earth's surface by deposition; specifically, the accumulation of material by any process in order to establish or maintain uniformity of grade or slope; also called accretion. The raising or elevating of a bottomland surface through the process of alluvial deposition; conceptually it is the vertical component of accretion and is most frequently applied to sediment deposition on a channel bed, bar or other near-channel surfaces, flood plain, or, less often, low-lying alluvial terrace.

Aggregation, A Process that significantly alters the sizes, characteristics and abundances of suspended particles in the ocean.

Aguaje, A condition observed annually in the coast water off Peru in which the water is discolored red or yellow and there is a significant loss of marine life. It typically occurs from April through June and is probably caused by an increase in water temperatures via the importation of warmer waters by ocean currents. This causes the death of temperature sensitive marine organisms such as dinoflagellatcs, which may in turn kill other organisms via the release of toxins. The annual nature of this phenomenon makes it distinct from the El Nino phenomenon occurring in the same region. This is also known as salgaso or aqua enferma.

Agulas Basin, An ocean basin located off the southern tip of Africa at about 43° S in the South Atlantic Ocean. It includes the Agulhas Abyssal Plain.

Agulhas Current, The western boundary current in the Indian Ocean south of 30° S. The southern Agulhas Current flows southwestward as a narrow jet along a steep continental slope, and is normally pinned to within 10-15 km of its mean position at latitudes 28.5-34°S. Large meanders - called the Natal pulse - can sometimes occur within this region. These extend an average of 170 km offshore with downstream propagation rates of about 21 cm s_{-1}, with the rates decreasing to 5 cm s_{-1} as the continental shelf broadens near 34°S. At this point the current separates from the coast and continues southwestward along the Agulhas Bank, where many meanders, plumes and eddies exist. *(Fig. 146)*

Air mass, A widespread body of air, the approximately homogeneous properties of which (1) have been established while that air was situated over a particular region of the Earth's surface, and (2) undergos specific modifications while in transit away from the source region.

Air-sea interaction, The processes that involve the trasnfer of energy, matter, and momentum between the atmosphere and the ocean.

Airy wave, A theory of waves of small amplitude in water of arbitary depth that is also known as linear wave theory.

Aland Sea, A part of the Baltic Sea bordered by the Gulf of Bothnia to the north, the Gulf of Finland to the east, and the part of the Baltic Sea to the south.

Alas, A type of thermokarst depression with steep sides and a flat, grass-covered floor, found in thermokarst terrain, produced by thawing of extensive areas of very thick and exceedingly ice-rich permafrost.

Alaska Coastal Current, A narrow, high-speed, westward flow which extends for more than 1000 km along the coast of Alaska. *(Fig. 145)*

Alaska Current, The eastern limb of the counterclockwise-flowing subpolar gyre in the North Pacific. *(Fig. 145)*

Albcdo, The fraction of solar radiation reflected by a surface or object, often expressed as a percentage. Snow-covered surfaces have a high albedo, the surface albedo of soils ranges from high to low, and vegetation-covered surfaces and oceans have a low albedo. The Earth's planetary albedo varies mainly through varying cloudiness, snow, ice, leaf area and land cover changes. The proportion of incident radiation reflected by a surface. About 30% of the incoming solar energy is reflected back to space from the earth, of which 25% is reflected by clouds and 5% by the surface or by atmospheric molecules or suspended particles. The clouds and atmospheric gases and particles absorb 25% of the incident radiation with the remainder absorbed at the surface.

Alboran Sea, The westernmost basin of the Mediterranean Sea. The Alboran Sea extends from the Gibraltar Strait to the Alboran Islands, an area between about 35° and 38° N and 6° N and the Equator. It abuts the Balearic Sea to the east. *(Fig. 143)*

Algerian Current, A current that flows eastward along the Algerian coast in the Mediterranean Sea. *(Fig. 143)*

Alkalinity, A measure of capacity of mutually occuring water to neutralize acids and is primarily the result of dissolved salts of weak acids; bicarbonate is a principal form of alkalinity owing to chemical reactions of carbon dioxide dissolved in water with calcium carbonate and other soil components.

Allometric growth, The word is derived from the study of Allometry, the recognition that the proportional sizes of rates of growth of parts of organisms are comparable and often quantifiable; e.g. the measurement of increase in stream-channel width and depth with increase in discharge of the stream.

Alluvial aquifer, A partially saturated deposit of alluvium that yields water to wells; most alluvial aquifers are unconfined and are composed of channel and flood-plain sediment; the water that partially saturates an alluvial aquifer is largely derived from the stream that transported and deposited the sediment.

Alluvial cone, A semi-conical type of alluvial fan with very steep slopes; it is higher, narrower, and steeper (e.g., > 40% slopes) than a fan, and composed of coarser, and thicker layers of material deposited by a combination of alluvial episodes and to a much lesser degree, landslides (e.g., debris flow). Coarsest materials tend to concentrate at the cone apex. *(Fig. 50)*

Alluvial fan, A wedge-shaped deposit of recent stream alluvium (erosion products) or poorly consolidated rock debris that radiates outward and downslope as, in plan view, an open fan from a site draining an area of high relief or topography, such as the mouth of a mountain valley, onto a gentler slope, typically a pediment or an alluvial plain. The deposit is thickest at the fan apex, near the valley mouth, and thins to a feather edge at the distal edge of the fan. Active alluvial fans are surfaces of net deposition whereas inactive alluvial fans generally exhibit erosion and stream incision at the apex, the depth of incision decreasing with distance downslope to the distal edges of the fan. *(Fig. 52)*

Alluvial plain remnant , An erosional remnant of an alluvial plain which retains the surface form and alluvial deposits of its origin but was not emplaced by, and commonly does not grade to a present-day stream or drainage network.

Alluvial plain, A large assemblage of fluvial landforms (braided streams, terraces, etc.,) that form low gradient, regional ramps along the flanks of mountains and extend great distances from their sources. A general, informal term for a broad flood plain or a low-gradient delta. *(Fig. 51)*

Alluvial, Pertaining to material or processes associated with transportation and/or subaerial deposition by concentrated running water.

Alluvium – Unconsolidated, clastic material subaerially deposited by running water, including gravel, sand, silt, clay, and various mixtures of these. A general term for sediment deposited in a streambed, on a flood plain or other bottomland feature, delta, or at the base of a mountain during comparatively recent geologic time.

Alpine glacier, Any glacier in a mountain range except an ice cap or ice sheet. It usually originates in a cirque and may flow down into a valley previously carved by a stream. *(Fig. 85)*

Alpine, Characteristic of, or resembling the European Alps, or any lofty mountain or mountain system, especially one so modified by intense glacial erosion as to contain cirques, horns, etc. (e.g., alpine lake) An ecological community term for high-elevation plant communities.

Altimetry, A technique for measuring the height of the sea, lake or river, land or ice surface with respect to the centre of the Earth within a defined terrestrial reference frame. More conventionally, the height is with respect to a standard reference ellipsoid approximating the Earth's oblateness, and can be measured from space by using radar or laser with centimetric precision at present. Altimetry has the advantages of being a geocentric measurement, rather than a measurement relative to the Earth's crust as for a tide gauge, and of affording quasi-global coverage.

Amphidrome, A stationary point around which tides rotate in a counterclockwise (clockwise) sense in the northern (southern) hemisphere, i.e. the point about which the cotidal lines radiate. The vertical range of the tide increases with distance away from the amphidrome, with the amphidrome itself the spot where the tide vanishes to zero (or almost zero). This is also called an amphidromic point. *(Fig. 140)*

Amundsen Abyssal Plain, One of the three plains that comprise the Pacific-Antarctic Basin (the others being the Bellingshausen and Mornington Abyssal Plains). It is located at around 150° W.

Amundsen Sea, A marginal sea of Antarctica centered at about 112° W and 73° S. It sits between the Bellingshausen Sea to the east and the Ross Sea to the west, with the Antarctic Circle serving as the northern boundry.

Anabranch, A separate channel that has diverged from the main channel and rejoins the stream at some downstream site. An anabranch is a discrete, semi-permanent channel that may be of equal or smaller size as the main channel, thereby distinguishing it from channel braids that are not discrete and may be highly ephemeral.

Anadyr Current, A surface current that flows along the northwestern side of the Bering Sea and on through the Bering Strait. It is mostly seasonally invariant with a velocity of about 0.3 m/s.

Analog, In signal processing this refers to a continuous physical variable which bears a direct relationship to another variable so that one is proportional to the other. An example would be the mercury level in a thermometer and its relation to the temperature, both of which vary continuously on the macroscopic level. Contrast with digital.

Andaman Sea, A body of water in the northeastern corner of the Indian Ocean that lies to the west of the Malay Peninsula, the north of Sumatra, the east of the Andaman Islands, and the south of the Irrawaddy Delta in Burma. It stretches about 650 km from west to east and 1200 km from north to south.

Angle of repose, The maximum departure from horizontal, expressed as an angle, at which a slope formed of loose, cohesionless sediment retains stability. The angle of repose is a function of the frictional properties of the sediment and the angularity of the sediment grains. It varies from about 30 degrees for coarse, rounded particles to about 39 degrees for angular particles of sand, and is typically 32 to 34 degrees for dry sand of dunes.

Angola Basin, An ocean basin located to the west of Africa at about 15° S in the south-central Atlantic Ocean. It is demarcated to the north by the Guinea Ridge, south of which lies the Angola Abyssal Plain which is fed by the Congo Canyon, the largest in the eastern Atlantic. This has also been known as the Buchanan Deep.

Angola Current The eastern part of a cyclonic gyre centered around 13° S and 4° E that is driven by the South Equatorial Countercurrent in the Atlantic Ocean.

Angola-Benguela Front, A front, often abbreviated as ABF, caused by the confluence of the south-ward flowing Angola Current and the northward flowing Benguela Current near 16° S off the African coast. This can be identified in the temperature of the upper 50 m and in the salinity to at least 200 m.

Angular momentum, The product of mass times the perpendicular distance from the axis of rotation times the rotation velocity. The angular momentum about the Earth's axis of rotation can be expressed as the sum of the angular momentum of the solid Earth's rotation plus the angular momentum of zonal air motion relative to the surface of the Earth.

Anisotropic, Descriptor for a physical property (e.g. density, etc.) that varies depending on the direction in which it is measured.

Annual flood series, A list of annual floods measured at a streamflow gage site for the period of record or a selected part of the period of record.

Annual flood, The maximum instantaneous discharge, expressed in cubic meters per second ($m_3 s_{-1}$), that occurs at a stream site.

Annular drainage pattern, A drainage pattern in which subsequent streams follow a roughly circular or concentric path along a belt of weak rocks, resembling in plan view, a ring-like pattern where the bedrock joints or fracturing control the parallel tributaries. It is best displayed in streams draining a maturely dissected granitic or sedimentary structural dome or basin where erosion has exposed rimming sedimentary strata of greatly varying degrees of hardness.

Anthropogenic feature, An artificial feature on the earth's surface (including those in shallow water), having a characteristic shape and range in composition, composed of unconsolidated earthy, organic materials, artificial materials, or rock, that is the direct result of human manipulation or activities; can be either constructional (e.g., artificial levee) or destructional (e.g., quarry).

Anthropogenic, Resulting from or produced by human beings.

Anthroscape, A human-modified "landscape" of substantial and permanent alterations (removal, additions, or reorganization) of the physical shape and /or internal stratigraphy of the land, associated with management for habitation, commerce, food or fiber production, recreation, or other human activities that have substantively altered water flow and sediment transport across or within the regolith.

Anticline, (a) A unit of folded strata that is convex upward and whose core contains the stratigraphically oldest rocks, and occurs at the earth's surface. In a single anticline, beds forming the opposing limbs of the fold dip away from its axial plane. (b) A fold, at any depth, generally convex upward whose core contains the stratigraphically older rocks. *(Fig. 26)*

Anticyclone, An atmospheric pressure distribution in which there is a high central pressure relative to the surroundings. This term was selected to imply the possession of characteristics opposite to those found in a cyclone or depression. As such, the circulation about the center of an anticyclone is clockwise (counter-clockwise) in the northern (southern) hemisphere, and the weather is generally quiet and settled. *(Fig. 203)*

Anticyclonic, The direction of rotation around a center of high pressure. This is clockwise in the northern hemisphere and counter-clockwise in the southern.

Antidune, A transient sand wave or dune that moves upstream by processes in which erosion of sand particles occurs on the downstream slope of the bedform followed by deposition of the sand particles on the next upstream slope. *(Fig. 71)*

Aquiclude, A nearly impermeable rock body that can absorb water very slowly and hence can only release the absorbed water to springs or seeps very slowly. Where an aquiclude is at or near a lowland surface, swampy conditions may occur owing to the inability of surface water to infiltrate readily. *(Fig. 110)*

Aquifer, Any rock body or geologic deposit of alluvium or similar rock debris that is partially or fully saturated with ground water and has properties of permeability and porosity that enable it to yield the ground water to a well or spring at a rate significantly high to fulfill a specified purpose. Aquifers are grouped as unconfined those controlled by near-surface gravitational and atmospheric-pressure conditions and artesian, those that are poorly connected to the land surface due to an impermeable layer separating it from the land surface. *(Fig. 110)*

Aquifuge, An impermeable rock body that cannot absorb water and hence cannot release water to springs or seeps very slowly; where an aquifuge is at or near a lowland surface. Swampy conditions may occur owing to the inability of surface water to infiltrate.

Aquitard, A body of rock or sediment that retards but does not prevent the flow of water to or from an adjacent aquifer. It does not readily yield water to wells or springs but may serve as a storage unit for groundwater. *(Fig. 111)*

Arabian Sea, A regional sea, centered at approximately 65° E and 15° N, that is bounded by Pakistan and Iran to the north, Oman, Yemen and the Somali Republic to the west, India to the east, and the greater Indian Ocean to the south. The southern boundary, from an oceanographic point of view, runs from Goa on the Indian coast along the west side of the Laccadive Islands to the equator, and thence slightly to the south to near Mombasa on the Kenyan coast. It covers an area of about 7,456,000 km$_2$.

Archaeology, A science involving the study and understanding of both recent-past and ancient people and cultures through the excavation of sites of habitation and the recovery of artifacts, It requires the application of disciplines including soil science, paleontology, hydrology, geomorphology, chemistry, and sedimentology, and the use of analytical techniques such as the identification of clays and rock fragments, particle-size analysis, and dating by radiocarbon analysis.

Archipelagic plain, A gentle slope with a generally smooth surface of the sea floor, characteristically found around groups of islands or seamounts.

Arctic domain, A hydrographic division sometimes used in the North Atlantic Ocean to distinguish it from the polar domain to the north and the Atlantic domain to the south. In this region upper layer waters are relatively cold (0 to 4°C) and saline (34.6 to 34.9). The most significant indication that this domain is not just a smooth transition Zone between the polar and Atlantic domain is that the waters are markedly denser than either of the surface source water masses.

Arctic Ocean, The smallest and most poorly studied of the oceans on earth. It covers an area of 14 million square km that is divided by three submarine ridges, i.e. the Alpha Ridge, the Lomonosov Ridge, and an extension of the mid- Atlantic ridge. It is also nearly landlocked, covered year-round by pack ice, and one-third of its area is continental shelf containing marginal seas. The marginal seas of the Arctic are the Beaufort Sea, the Chukchi Sea, the East Siberian Sea, the Laptev Sea, the Kara Sea and the Barents Sea. An important climatic function of the Arctic and its adjacent seas is the production of the dense water than drives the global transports of heat and fresh water between the high latitude North Atlantic and the Pacific.

Arête, (from the French term for fishbone) A sharp-edged, serrated ridgeline feature of a high alpine area sculpted by progressive back erosion of steep bedrock walls above two or more cirques formed by the glaciers occupying the cirques. It is a feature generally separating two glaciated peaks and bounded on both sides by cirques. *(Fig. 89)*

Argentine Basin, An ocean basin located in the western South Atlantic Ocean off the coast of Argentina. It is separated from the Brazil Basin to the north by the Rio Grande Rise and includes the Argentine Abyssal Plain.

Arid, refers to a climatic zone that receives average precipitation of less than 250 mm annually.

Armoring, The winnowing of fine particles from the uppermost bed sediment of a stream, Channel, resulting in a bed - surface layer of generally gravel to boulder sizes that are resistant to scour. Since armoring occurs at specific flow rate, the armor layer may be susceptible to removal by higher flow and sedimentation during lower flow. Armoring occurs on hillslopes by similar winnowing processes of eolian removal of fine sediment, or by a variety of related processes that result in the concentration of coarse sediment or rock particles as a surface veneer.

Arroyo, A gully or small channel, generally in arid and semiarid areas in which streamflow occurs inconsistently or infrequently and, except during periods of streamflow, is directly underlain by unsaturated alluvium. They typically have a rectangular to steeply sided trapezoidal cross section, banks a meter or more in height formed of fine-grained, poorly consolidated over-bank sediment, and a nearly flat, sandy bed. Synonyms are ephemeral-stream channel, dry wash, and wadi.

Artifact, An artificial (human-derived) object or material (e.g., brick, concrete, metal, plastic, or treated wood), commonly larger than 2 mm in diameter, made and deposited in association with habitation, manufacturing, excavation, or construction activities.

Artificial collapsed depression, A collapse basin, commonly a closed depression, which is the direct result of surficial subsidence associated with subsurface mining (e.g., long-wall mining).

Artificial drainage pattern, Human-made networks of drainage structures (ditches, canals, etc.) built primarily to lower or control the local water table in low lying, flat topography such as glacial lakebeds, broad flood plains, low coastal plains, or marshes most commonly in humid climates. Irrigation ditches found in arid and semiarid climates, which bring water into the fields, should not be confused with drainage structures.

Artificial levee, An artificial embankment constructed along the bank of a watercourse or an arm of the sea, to protect land from inundation or to confine streamflow to its channel.

Ash field, A land area covered by a relatively thick or distinctive, surficial deposit of volcanic ash (air fall) that can be traced to a specific source and has well defined boundaries. An ash field can be distinguished from adjacent landforms or land areas based on ash thickness, mineral composition, and physical characteristics. Soils within an ash field form solely or predominantly within the ash deposit.

Ash flow, A highly heated mixture of volcanic gases and ash, traveling down the flank of a volcano or along the surface of the ground; produced by the explosive disintegration of viscous lava in a volcanic crater, or by the explosive emission of gas-charged ash from a fissure or group of fissures. The solid materials contained in a typical ash flow are generally unsorted and ordinarily include volcanic dust, pumice, scoria, and blocks in addition to ash. (Also called a *pyroclastic* flow) *(Fig. 37)*

Ash, [volcanic] Unconsolidated, pyroclastic material less than 2 mm in all dimensions. Commonly called volcanic ash.

Asia Minor Current, A meandering current flowing westward and then northward along the Turkish coast and the Southeastern coast of Rhodes. It borders the northwest part of the Rhodes gyre, and originates as part of the mid-Mediterranean jet branching to the north. There is a major branch in the AMC in the region of the Rhodes and Karpathos Straits. Both branches intrude into the south Aegean Sea and meander in the northeastern Cretan Sea as a continuation of the AMC. The branches carry warm and saline Levantine waters within the upper 300-400 dbar layer

Aspect, The orientation or the compass direction in which a landform or surface faces (the north-facing slope of a mountain has a northerly aspect).

Atlantic domain, One of three regions into which the North Atlantic Ocean is sometimes divided for the purposes of describing water mass formation processes in the region, with the other two being the (northward lying) arctic domain and the polar domain. Surface source water masses from the Atlantic domain (called Atlantic Water (AW), are carried into the arctic domain by the Norwegian Atlantic Current and, to a much smaller extent, by the North Icelandic Irminger Current.

Atlantic period, A post-LGM European climate regime. This refers to the period from about 6000-3000 BC that spans most of the warmest postglacial times. It is also known as the Postglacial Climatic Optimum. It was preceded by the Boreal period and followed by the Sub-Boreal period.

Atlantic-Indian Basin, One of three major basins in the Southern Ocean. It extends from its western border with the Pacific-Antarctic Basin at the Scotia Ridge and Drake Passage (at about 70° W) to its eastern border with the Australian-Atlantic Basin at the Kerguelan Plateau (about 75° E). It consists of the Enderby and Weddell Abyssal Plains and is bounded to the north below 4000 m by the Mid-Atlantic and South-West Indian Ridges except for deeper connections into the Argentine Basin in the western Atlantic and into the deep basins of the western Indian Ocean.

Atmosphere, The gaseous envelope surrounding the Earth. The dry atmosphere consists almost entirely of nitrogen (78.1% volume mixing ratio) and oxygen (20.9% volume mixing ratio), together with a number of trace gases, such as argon (0.93% volume mixing ratio), helium and radiatively active greenhouse gases such as carbon dioxide (0.035% volume mixing ratio) and ozone. In addition, the atmosphere contains the greenhouse gas water vapour, whose amounts are highly variable but typically around 1% volume mixing ratio. The atmosphere also contains clouds and aerosols. *(Fig. 166)*

Atmospheric boundary layer, The atmospheric layer adjacent to the Earth's surface that is affected by friction against that boundary surface, and possibly by transport of heat and other variables across that surface. The lowest 10 metres or so of the boundary layer, where mechanical generation of turbulence is dominant, is called the surface boundary layer or surface layer.

Atmospheric tide, Those oscillations in any atmospheric field whose periods are integral fractions of either a lunar or a solar day. These differ from ocean tides in several ways, one of which is that atmospheric tides are excited not only by the tidal gravitational potential of the sun and moon but also (and to the larger extent) by daily variations in solar heating. Another difference is that the atmosphere is a spherical shell and thus there are no coastal boundaries to worry about. Finally, the response of the atmosphere to tidal forcing is by means of internal gravity waves rather than the barotropic surface waves of the sea.

Atoll, A coral reef appearing in plan view as roughly circular, and surmounted by a chain of closely spaced, low coral islets that encircle or nearly encircle a shallow lagoon in which there is no land or islands of non-coral origin; the reef is surrounded by open sea. One of three geomorphologically distinct types of coral reefs, the other two being fringing reefs and barrier reefs. An atoll is an annular reef formed around a subsiding volcanic island. *(Fig. 156, 157)*

Australasian Mediterranean Sea, The region on either side of the equator between the islands of the Indonesian archipelago. This has the most complicated topography of any of the regional seas of the world, consisting of a series of deep basins with limited interconnections, each characterized by its own type of bottom water of great age. The basins comprising this include the Banda, Sulawesi (formerly Celebes), Molucca, Halmahera, Serman, Sulu, Flores, Java and Sawu Seas, with the Banda being the largest and deepest.

Australian-Antarctic Basin, One of three major basins in the Southern Ocean. It extends from its eastern boundary with the Pacific-Antarctic Basin at the longitude of Tasmania (at about 145° E) to the Kerguelan Plateau (at about 75° E). The South-East Indian Ridge separates it from the Indian Ocean at depths greater than 4000 m except for a gap in the Ridge at 117° E.

Authigenic, One of three major components of deep sea sediments, the other two being detrital and biogenic. Authigenic minerals are those formed by spontaneous crystallization within the sediment or water column, and make up only a small fraction of the total sediment volume. The most important of this type of sediment is the iron-manganese oxide material formed by reduction of these metals deep in the sediment column.

Autotrophic, Self-nourishing organisms with the ability to synthesize organic molecules from CO_2 using either photosynthesis or chemosynthesis.

Avalanche chute, The central, channel-like corridor, scar, or depression along which an avalanche has moved. An eroded surface marked by pits, scratches, and grooves.

Avalanche, A volume of snow, ice, soil, or rock fragments, or more commonly a mixture of them, that moves very rapidly down a slope by gravity. The term is most typically applied to the sudden movement of snow and ice in mountainous areas, but very poorly sorted deposits resulting from similar slope failures of de-stabilized soil and near-surface rock material, as a debris avalanche, are widespread in high-relief areas.

Avulsion, A rapid change in the course or position of a stream channel, especially by incision (erosion) of lowland alluvium, to bypass a meander and thereby shorten channel length and increase channel gradient. Avulsion commonly occurs during floods but also can occur by normal processes of lateral migration of a stream channel during non-flood discharges.

Axial stream, (a) The main stream of an intermontane valley, flowing in the deepest part of the valley and parallel to its longest dimension. (b) A stream that follows the axis of a syncline or anticline.

Azoic zone, Term used to describe the part of the deep sea thought lifeless in the mid-19th century. It was thought that the abyss was filled with a thick layer of 4°C (since sea water thought to be densest at that temperature), motionless water which, combined with the tremendous pressures and absence of sunlight, virtually guaranteed an absence of life.

Azores Current, The northern branch of the subtropical gyre in the North Atlantic Ocean.

B

Back-barrier beach, A narrow, elongate, intertidal, sloping landform that is generally parallel with the shoreline located on the lagoon or estuary side of the barrier island, or spit.

Back-barrier flat, A subaerial, gently sloping landform on the lagoon side of the barrier beach ridge composed predominantly of sand washed over or through the beach ridge during tidal surges; a portion of a barrier flat.

Backshore, That part or zone of a beach profile that extends landward from the sloping foreshore to a point of either vegetation development or a change of physiography, e.g. a sea cliff or a dune field. The upper or inner, usually dry, zone of the shore or beach, lying between the high-water line of mean spring tides and the upper limit of shore-zone processes; it is acted upon by waves or covered by water only during exceptionally severe storms or unusually high tides. It is essentially horizontal or slopes gently landward, and is divided from the foreshore by the crest of the most seaward berm. *(Fig. 79)*

Backslope, The hillslope profile position that forms the steepest and generally linear, middle portion of the slope. In profile, backslopes are commonly bounded by a convex shoulder above and a concave footslope below. They may or may not include cliff segments (i.e., free faces). Backslopes are commonly erosional forms produced by mass movement, colluvial action, and running water.

Backswamp deposit, Lamina of silt and clay deposited in the flood basin between valley sides or terraces and the natural levees of a river. *(Fig. 74)*

Backswamp, A flood-plain landform. Extensive, marshy or swampy, depressed areas of flood plains between natural levees and valley sides or terraces.

Backwater, Any volume of water that is backed up or prevented from moving downslope or downstream by any barrier obstructing movement; in hydrology, backwater often is the slowing or reversal of flow in a stream or tributary upstream from its confluence with another stream that is at flood stage.

Backwearing , Slope erosion that causes the parallel retreat of an escarpment or the slope of a hill or mountain or the sideways recession of a slope without changing its general slope; a process contributing to the development of a pediment.

Badlands, A landscape which is intricately dissected and characterized by a very fine drainage network with high drainage densities and short, steep slopes with narrow interfluves. Badlands develop on surfaces with little or no vegetative cover, overlying unconsolidated or poorly cemented materials (clays, silts, or in some cases sandstones) sometimes with soluble minerals such as gypsum or halite. A semi-technical term referring to a very rugged topography of badly eroded, soft, relatively flat-lying sedimentary rocks that are deeply incised by rills and gullies. Badlands generally occur in areas of arid or semiarid climate that sustain short-duration but high-intensity thundershowers, have steep side slopes that support little or no vegetation, exhibit virtually no soil development, and yield large amounts of sediment to runoff and streamflow following rainfall.

Baffin Bay, A large sea located between the Canadian Archipelago and the Labrador Sea. It is about 1000 km and 400 km. Most of Baffin Bay is deeper than 1500 m, but deep water exchange with the Labrador Sea is restricted by a sill in Davis Strait with a depth of 670 m. A mobile ice cover forms during winter and moves southward under the prevailing winds. Icebergs calved from glaicers in southern and western Greenland drift across the bay and southward in the Baffin Current to southern latitudes. A significant oceanographic feature of Baffin Bay is the North Water, a partially open water area in the northern part where complete ice cover would be expected under prevailing climatological conditions.

Baguio, The local name given to tropical cyclones in the phillipines, especially those occurring from July to November.

Bajada, A group of coalesced alluvial fans, generally deposits of numerous streams draining and eroding parts of the same mountain range, that form a broad band along and downslope from a mountain front. Bajadas are composites of many alluvial fans, their surfaces are of irregular shape. Bajadas are most common in arid and semiarid areas and were named for landforms adjacent to mountain ranges of the southwestern United States and northern Mexico. *(Fig. 107)*

Balearic Sea, One of the seas that comprise the western basin of the Mediterranean Sea which is sometimes called the Catalan Sea. It lies between the Iberian coast and the Balearic Islands (Ibiza, Mallorca, , Menorca) in the northwestern Mediterranean. It is separated from the Tyrrhenian Sea to the east by Sardinia and Corsica and abuts the Alboran Sea to the west. The bathymetry is dominated by the Balearic Abyssal Plain, which covers over 30,000 square miles, covering the majority of the basin floor at depths ranging from 2700-2800 m. This is bordered to the northwest by the Rhone Fan, a large sedimentary cone. *(Fig. 143)*

Bali Sea, regional sea which is part of the Australasian Mediterranean Sea in the southwest Pacific Ocean. It is classified as a distinct sea for navigational purposes but is usually grouped with the Flores Sea for oceanographic purposes. It is centered at around 116° E and 8.5° S and is bordered by Bali and Sumbawa to the south and Madura to the west, and abuts the Java Sea to the north and the Flores Sea to the east. The Bali Sea covers an area of about 45,000 km, and has a greatest depth of 1590 m.

Baltic Sea, A dilution basin type of mediterranean sea that is connected to and experiences limited, in-termittent water exchange with the North Sea. It comprises several parts separately known as the Gulf of Bothnia, the Aland Sea, the Gulf of Finland, the Gulf of Riga, Kattegat and Skagerrak. It has a mean depth is about 57 m, an area of about 370,000 km$_2$, and a volume of about 20,000 km$_3$, and is one of the largest brackish water bodies in the world. About 17% of its area is shallower than 10 m. The / Baltic Sea depression is essentially a long fjord in the north-south direction (1500 km) with an average width of 230 km. The topography divides it into a series of relatively deep basins, with maximum depths ranging from 105-459 m.

Baltica, A paleogeographic area during the late Precambrian and early Paleozoic that comprised north-western Europe, including most of what are now the U.K., Scandinavia, European Russian and Central Europe. It formed the southeastern margin of the Iapetus Ocean and was moved by the subduction of that ocean (during the Caledonian erogenic event) such that it made contact with North America and Greenland during the Silurian and Early Devonian.

Banda Sea, A regional sea in the Australasian Archipelago covering approximately 470,000 square kilometers and centered at about 126° E and 5° S. It consists of several basins and troughs interconnected by sills whose depths are mostly greater than 3000 m.

Bank material, The sediment of which the mostly sloping sides, or banks, of a stream channel are formed; like bed material, it is generally reflective of the size range of the total sediment load of the stream, may be partly residual, but for regime channels is mostly indicative of the suspended-load transported by streams during non-flood periods.

Bank storage, The process by which water, during periods of above-normal streamflow, infiltrates into and saturates typically aerated bank sediment (alluvium) higher than the normal stream surface; as the flow event recedes and stream stage declines, bank-storage water seeps from the alluvium and reenters the stream.

Bank, An elevation of the sea floor, over which the depth of water is relatively shallow, but sufficient for safe surface navigation. It typically refers to a sloping margin of a natural, stream-formed, alluvial channel that confines discharge during non-flood flow; within the earth sciences, designation of a right or left bank is done when looking in the downstream direction.

Bankful stage, A fluvial-geomorphic term. It is the water-surface level at the tops of alluvial-stream banks that corresponds to the level of adjacent flood-plain surfaces, Bankfull stage is the level at which bankfull discharge occurs, the upper limit of channel capacity. Although bankfull stage can refer to various channel-bank levels, it generally applies to alluvial-stream channels (1) having sizes and shapes adjusted to recent fluxes of water and sediment, (2) that are principal conduits for discharges moving through a length of alluvial bottomland, and (3) that are bounded by flood plains upon which water and sediment spill when the flow rate exceeds that of bankfull discharge.

Bankfull discharge A hydrologic term, is the flow rate (m_3 s_{-1}) when the stage (height) of a stream is coincident with the uppermost level of the banks — the water level at channel capacity, or bankfull stage. Thus, the concept of bankfull discharge, which often approximates the mean annual flood for perennial streams, includes the flood plain as a unique, identifiable geomorphic surface, all higher surfaces of alluvial bottomlands being terraces, and acknowledgement that bankfull discharge occurs only when stream stage is at flood-plain level.

Bar and channel topography, A local-scale topographic pattern of recurring, small, sinuous or arcuate ridges separated by shallow troughs irregularly spaced across low-relief flood plains(slopes generally 2 –6 %); the effect is one of a subdued, sinuously undulating surface that is common on active, meandering flood plains. Micro-elevational differences between bars and channels generally range from <0.5 to 2 m and are largely controlled by the competency of the stream. The ridge-like bars often consist of somewhat coarser sediments compared to the finer textured sediments of the micro-low troughs. *(Fig. 75)*

Bar, (a) [streams] A general landform term for a ridge-like accumulation of sand, gravel, or other alluvial material formed in the channel, along the banks, or at the mouth of a stream where a decrease in velocity induces deposition; e.g., a channel bar or a meander bar. (b) [coast] A generic landform term for any of various elongate offshore ridges, banks, or mounds of sand, gravel, or other unconsolidated material submerged at least at high tide, and built up by the action of waves or currents, especially at the mouth of a river or estuary, or at a slight distance offshore from the beach. *(Fig. 83)*

Bar, A unit of pressure equal to the pressure of 29.530 in. or 750.062 mm of mercury under the standard conditions of 0° C temperature and 9.80665 m/s$_2$ gravitational acceleration.

Bar, A small, sinuous or arcuate, ridge-like lineation on a flood plain and separated from others by small channels or troughs; caused by fluvial processes and common to flood plains and young alluvial terraces; a constituent part of *bar and channel topography*. In-channel sediment of relatively coarse bed material, typically coarse sand through cobbles in size, that is generally deposited during the recession of a high flow and is mostly exposed during periods of low flow. The upper surface of bars of perennial streams is typically equivalent to a stage of about 40-percent flow duration.

Barat, The local name given to strong, northwesterly squalls on the north coast of the island of Celebes that occur most frequently from December to February.

Barchan dune, A crescent-shaped dune with tips extending leeward (downwind), making this side concave and the windward (upwind) side convex. Barchan dunes tend to be arranged in chains extending in the dominant wind direction. *(Fig. 102, 83)*

Barents Sea, One of the seas found on the Siberian shelf in the Arctic Mediterranean Sea. It is located between the White Sea to the west and the Kara Sea to the east and adjoins the Arctic Ocean proper to the north.

Baroclinic, Descriptive of an an atmosphere or ocean in which surfaces of pressure and density intersect at some level or levels. The state of the real atmosphere and ocean, as opposed to barotropic. In a baroclinically stratified fluid total potential energy can be converted to kinetic energy.

Barotropic flow, In oceanography, depth-independent circulation due to changes in surface elevation.

Barotropic, Descriptive of a hypothetical atmosphere or ocean in which surfaces of pressure (isobaric surfaces) and density (isentropic surfaces) coincide at all levels, as compared to baroclinic. In a state of barotropic stratification, no potential energy is available for conversion to kinetic energy.

Barrier beach, A narrow, elongate, coarse-textured, intertidal, sloping landform that is generally parallel with the beach ridge component of a barrier island or spit and adjacent to the ocean. *(Fig. 80)*

Barrier cove, A subaqueous area adjacent to a barrier island or submerged barrier beach that forms a minor embayment or cove within the larger basin.

Barrier flat, A relatively flat, low-lying area, commonly including pools of water, separating the exposed or seaward edge of a barrier beach or barrier island from the lagoon behind it. An assemblage of both deflation flats left behind migrating dunes and /or storm washover sediments; may be either barren or vegetated.

Barrier island, A long, narrow, sandy island, that is above high tide and parallel to the shore that commonly has dunes, vegetated zones, and swampy or marshy terrains extending lagoonward from the beach. *(Fig. 80)*

Barrier layer, In physical oceanography, the layer between the thermocline and the halocline. It is called this because of its effect on the mixed layer heat budget due to the temperature at the bottom of the barrier layer being zero, which excludes heat loss to the underlying water via mixing. It is defined as the difference between the thickness of the isothermal layer and the mixed layer (determined by a defined change in density), with the isothermal layer generally being greater than or equal to the mixed layer depth.

Barrier reef, One of three geomorophologically distinct types of coral reefs, the other two being fringing reefs and atolls. Barrier reefs are separated from land by a lagoon usually formed by coastal subsidence. *(Fig. 80)*

Barronco or Barranco, A Spanish term applied to incised channels of the water-deficient southwestern United States, refers to a deep, rectangular to steep-sided trapezoid shaped ravine or arroyo in partially consolidated bottomland alluvium; barroncos are indicative of an erosive drainage network and are maintained by channel-bed erosion and the collapse of the arroyo walls during brief periods of ephemeral streamflow..

Base flow, Sustained, low, or fair-weather flow of a stream. The base flow ($m^3 s^{-1}$) generally is derived from ground-water inputs to the stream channel.

Base level, The lowest level or elevation for which a stream of flowing water hypothetically can effect erosion. The ultimate base level is the sea surface or slightly lower, but as a geomorphic concept, base level refers to more transient conditions such as an erosion-resistant dike over which a stream flows and is unable to alter during a short interval of geologic time.

Base slope, A geomorphic component of hills consisting of the concave to linear slope (perpendicular to the contour) which, regardless of the lateral shape is an area that forms an apron or wedge at the bottom of a hillside dominated by colluvial and slope wash processes and sediments (e.g., colluvium and slope alluvium). Distal base slope sediments commonly grade to, or interfinger with, alluvial fills, or gradually thin to form pedisediment over residuum.

Basin floor, A general term for the nearly level, lower-most part of intermontane basins (i.e., bolsons, semi-bolsons). The floor includes all of the alluvial, eolian, and erosional landforms below the piedmont slope.

Basin, (a) Drainage basin. (b) A low area in the Earth's crust, of tectonic origin, in which sediments have accumulated. (c) A general term for the nearly level to gently sloping, bottom surface of an intermontane basin (bolson). Landforms include playas, broad alluvial flats containing ephemeral drainageways, and relict alluvial and lacustrine surfaces that rarely, if ever, are subject to flooding. Where through-drainage systems are well developed, flood plains are dominant and lake plains are absent or of limited extent. Basin floors grade mountainward to distal parts of piedmont slopes.

Basin, A depression, in the sea floor, more or less equidimensional in plan and of variable extent.

Batholith, A large, generally discordant plutonic rock body exposed at the land surface, with an aerial extent > 40 sq. mi. (100 km2) and no known bottom. (Fig. 34)

Bathyal zone, The marine ecologic zone that lies deeper than the continental shelf but shallower than the deep ocean floor, i.e. those depths corresponding to the locations of the continental slope and rise. The depth range is from 100-300 m down to 1000-4000 m depending on such variables as the depth of the shelf break, the depth of light penetration, and local physical oceanographic conditions.

Bathymetry, The measurement and charting of the spatial variation of the ocean depths.

Bathypelagic zone, One of five vertical ecological zones into which the deep sea is sometimes divided. This is the zone starting from 100 to 700 m deep (coinciding with the upper limit of the psychrosphere) at the 10° C isotherm. The number of species and populations decreases greatly as one proceeds into the bathypelagic zone where there is no light source other than bioluminescence, temperature is uniformly low, and pressures are great. This overlies the abyssopelagic zone and is overlain by the mesopelagic zone. This is the lowest of the three vertical sections of the pelagic part of the ocean, the other two being the upper eu photic and the middle mesopelagic.

Bauxite, An off-white to dark red brown weathered detritus or rock composed of aluminum oxides (mainly gibbsite with some boehmite and diaspore), iron hydroxides, silica, silt, and especially clay minerals. Bauxite originates in tropical and subtropical environments as highly weathered residue from carbonate or silicate rocks and can occur in concretionary, earthy, pisolitic, or oolitic forms.

Bay [coast], (a) A wide, curving open indentation, recess, or arm of a sea or lake into the land or between two capes or headlands, larger than a cove [coast], and usually smaller than, but of the same general character as, a gulf. (b) A large tract of water that penetrates into the land and around which the land forms a broad curve. By international agreement a bay is a water body having a baymouth that is less than 24 nautical miles wide and an area that is equal to or greater than the area of a semicircle whose diameter is equal to the width of the bay mouth. Any terrestrial formation resembling a bay of the sea, as a recess or extension of lowland along a river valley or within a curve in a range of hills.

Bay bottom, The nearly level or slightly undulating central portion of a submerged, low-energy, depositional estuarine embayment characterized by relatively deep water (1.0 to >2.5 m).

Bay of Bengal, The northeastern arm of the Indian Ocean, located between peninsular India and Burma. It covers about 2,200,000 sq. km and is bordered on the north by the Ganges and Brahmaputra River deltas, on the east by the Burmese peninsula and the Andaman and Nicobar Islands, on the west by India proper and Ceylon, and on the south by the Indian Ocean proper. The average depth is around 3000 m with maximum depths reaching over 400 m in the southern parts.

Beach Berm, The nearly horizontal portion of a beach formed by the deposition of sediment by receding waves. A beach may have more than one berm. *(Fig. 80, 81)*

Beach face, The sloping section of a beach profile below the beach berm which is normally exposed to the action of the wave swash. *(Fig. 79)*

Beach plain, A continuous and level or undulating area formed by closely spaced successive embankments of wave-deposited beach material added more or less uniformly to a prograding shoreline, such as to a growing compound spit or to a cuspate foreland.

Beach ridge, A low, essentially continuous mound of beach or beach-and-dune material heaped up by the action of waves and currents on the backshore of a beach, beyond the present limit of storm waves or the reach of ordinary tides, and occurring singly or as one of a series of approximately parallel deposits. The ridges are roughly parallel to the shoreline and represent successive positions of an advancing shoreline. *(Fig. 81)*

Beach sands, Well sorted, sand-sized, clastic material transported and deposited primarily by wave action and deposited in a shore environment.

Beach terrace, A landform that consists of a wave-cut scarp and wave-built terrace of well-sorted sand and gravel of marine and lacustrine origin.

Beach, (a) A gently sloping zone of unconsolidated material, typically with a slightly concave profile, extending landward from the low-water line to the place where there is a definite change in material or physiographic form (such as a cliff) or to the line of permanent vegetation (usually the effective limit of the highest storm waves); a shore of a body of water, formed and washed by waves or tides, usually covered by sand or gravel. (b) the relatively thick and temporary accumulation of loose water-borne material (usually well-sorted sand and pebbles) accompanied by mud, cobbles, boulders, and smoothed rock and shell fragments, that is in active transit along, or deposited on, the shore zone between the limits of low water and high water. (Fig. 79)

Beaded stream pattern, A characteristic pattern of small streams in areas underlain by ice wedges. The course of the stream channel is controlled by the pattern of the wedges, with beads (pools) occurring at the junctions of the wedges.

Beaufort Sea, The marginal sea consisting of the waters off the northern coast of Alaska and Canada. This is bounded to the east by Banks Island of the Canadian Arctic

Archipelago and on the west by the Chukchi Sea. The bathymetric characteristics include the narrowest continental shelf found anywhere in the Arctic Ocean. This shelf is dissected by three submarine valleys, the largest of which is 45 km wide, and drops off rapidly to the Beaufort Deep, whose maximum depth is 3940 m. Although it is geographically identified as a separate entity, the Beaufort Sea is oceanographically an integral part of the Arctic Ocean and as such can't be described in isolation.

Bed load, or sediment discharged as bed load, The sediment that is moved by saltation, rolling, or sliding on or near the stream bed, essentially in continuous contact with it.

Bed material, The sediment of which the mostly horizontal bed of a stream channel is formed; it is generally reflective of the size range of the total sediment load of the stream, in many cases may be partly residual, but is mostly indicative of the bed-load sizes transported by the stream.

Bed, [stratigraphy] The layer of sediments or sedimentary rocks bounded above and below by more or less well-defined bedding surfaces. The smallest, formal lithostratigraphic unit of sedimentary rocks. The designation of a bed or a unit of beds as a formally named lithostratigraphic unit generally should be limited to certain distinctive beds whose recognition is particularly useful. Coal beds, oil sands, and other layers of economic importance commonly are named, but such units and their names usually are not a part of formal stratigraphic nomenclature.

Bed, or stream bed, The bottom surface of a water course, generally of a stream channel, upon which water and sediment move during periods of discharge.

Bedded, Formed, arranged, or deposited in layers or beds, or made up of or occurring in the form of beds; especially said of a layered sedimentary rock, deposit, or formation.

Bedding plane, A planar or nearly planar bedding surface that visibly separates each successive layer of stratified sediment or rock (of the same or different lithology) from the preceding or following layer; a plane of deposition. It often marks a change in the circumstances of deposition, and may show a parting, a color difference, a change in particle size, or various combinations. A term commonly applied to any bedding surface even when conspicuously bent or deformed by folding. *(Fig. 35)*

Bedrock, A general term for the solid rock that underlies the soil and other unconsolidated material or that is exposed at the surface.

Benguala Current, A current that flows northward along the west coast of southern Africa between about 15 and 35° S. This is the eastern limb of the subtropical gyre circulation system in the South Atlantic Ocean. *(Fig. 144)*

Benthic, Organisms that are attached to or resting on bottom sediments, as opposed to pelagic.

Benthos, One of three major ecological groups into which marine organisms are divided, the other two being the nekton and the plankton. The benthos are organisms and communities found on or near the seabed. This includes those animals (zoobenthos) and plants (phytobenthos) living on (epifauna) or in (endofauna) marine substrata as well as those that swim in close proximity to the bottom without ever really leaving it. In terms of size, this is generally divided into three categories: meiobenthos, the organisms that pass through a 0.5 mm sieve; macrobenthos, those that are caught by grabs or dredges but retained on the 0.5 m sieve; and epibenthos, those organisms than live on rather than in the seabed. Those in the latter category are usually larger.

Bering Sea, A marginal sea located on the northern rim of the Pacific Ocean centered at approximately 58° N and 160° W. It is surrounded by Alaska to the east, Siberia to the west and northwest, and the Aleutian Island arc to the south. It has an area of about 2,300,000 km$_2$ and a volume of about 3,700,000 km$_3$. The bathymetry is about equally divided between a vast shelf to the northeast that is at most 200 m deep and the Aleutian Basin where depths range from 3800-3900 m over most of the region.

Bering Strait, A narrow ocean passage separating the North American and Asian continents.

Berm crest, The seaward limit of a beach berm. *(Fig. 80)*

Berm, [beach] A low, impermanent, nearly horizontal or landward-sloping shelf, ledge, or narrow terrace on the backshore of a beach, formed of material thrown up and deposited by storm waves; it is generally bounded on one side or the other by a beach ridge or beach scarp. Some beaches have no berms, others have one or several. *(Fig. 80)*

Beveled base, The lower portion of a canyon wall or escarpment marked by a sharp reduction in slope gradient from the precipitous cliff above, and characteristically composed of thinly mantled colluvium (i.e., < 1 m) and / or carapaced with a thin surficial mantle of large rock fragments from above, which overly residuum of less resistant rock (e.g., shale) whose thin strata intermittently outcrop at the surface.

Beveled cut, A bank or slope portion of a cut excavated into unconsolidated material (regolith) or bedrock as in a roadcut, whose slope gradient has been mechanically reduced to a subdued angle (e.g., to < 33 %) to increase slope stability, reduce erosion, or to facilitate revegetation.

Bioacoustical oceanography, The application of underwater acoustics to investigations of biological patterns and processes in the sea.

Biogenic, One of three major components of deep sea sediments, the other two being authigenic and detrital. Biogenic consists mainly of calcite and opal produced as the hard parts of organisms and eventually precipitated. Calcite is formed by coccoliths (plants) and foraminifera (animals) and opal by diatoms and radiolarians (animals).

Biological oceanography, The study of life in the oceans and how the physical and chemical properties of the ocean are influenced by marine life. The basic goal is to examine the distribution, abundance, and production of marine species and to obtain a basic understanding of the processes controlling them. Compare to chemical, geological and physical oceanography.

Biological pump, The transformation, via photosynthesis in the ocean surface layer by plant cells (primarily phytoplankton), of dissolved inorganic carbon (DIC) into biogenic carbon, including, for example, the $CaCO_3$ in shells of coccolithophorids.

Biomass, The total mass of living organisms in a given area or volume; dead plant material can be included as dead biomass.

Biome, A biome is a major and distinct regional element of the biosphere, typically consisting of several ecosystems (e.g. forests, rivers, ponds, swamps within a region). Biomes are characterised by typical communities of plants and animals.

Biosphere (terrestrial and marine), The part of the Earth system comprising all ecosystems and living organisms, in the atmosphere, on land (terrestrial biosphere) or in the oceans (marine biosphere), including derived dead organic matter, such as litter, soil organic matter and oceanic detritus.

Bioturbation, of soil and subsoil. The physical rearrangement of sediment particles forming the soil and subsoil fabric by churning, stirring, or disruption through organic or biophysical processes of resident lifeforms; included types of bioturbation, or faunal and floral soil disturbance, are the effects of worms, rodents, and ungulates, as well as root expansion and, in forested areas, sediment movement due to treefall. *(Fig. 43)*

Bioturbation, The stirring of sediment by animal life.

Black carbon (BC), Operationally defined aerosol species based on measurement of light absorption and chemical reactivity and/or thermal stability; consists of soot, charcoal and/or possible light-absorbing refractory organic matter.

Black Sea, A mediterranean *sea,* centered at approximately 35° E and 44° N, that is the world's largest inland water basin. It has an area of about 461,000 km_2 and a volume of 537,000 km_3 with a mean depth of around 1200-1300 m, although depths greater than 2000 m are common in the central basin. The western part of the Black Sea is a wide shelf that gradually narrows to the south and breaks at around 100-150 m. In the rest of the basin the shelf doesn't exceed 10-15 km in width. It is connected to the Marmara Sea via the narrow (760 m wide) and shallow (27.5 m maximum depth) Bosporus Strait, and further connects to the Mediterranean Sea via the long and narrow Dardanelles. It is also connected to the Sea of Azov to the north. *(Fig. 143)*

Blind valley, A valley, commonly in karst, that ends abruptly downstream at the point at which its stream disappears underground. *(Fig. 87)*

Block field, A continuous surface cover of large angular to subangular rocks derived from a source of well jointed bedrock either beneath or upslope from the block covering. The blocks are generally dislodged by frost action and form a layer greater than one or two clast thicknesses (as opposed to a rock veneer, which has a thickness no greater than two clast thicknesses). A block field can occur on a steep slope if the source rock is exposed along a high ridge or similar topographic feature, whereas the term felsenmeer refers to a block field that occurs on a flat or gently sloping surface that is derived from an underlying source

Block glide, The mass movement process, associated sediments (block glide deposit), or resultant landform characterized by a slow type of slide, in which largely intact units (blocks) of rock or soil slide downslope along a relatively planar surface, such as a bedding plane, without any significant distortion of the original mass; a type of translational rock slide.

Block lava flow, A lava flow dominated by block lava.

Block lava, Lava having a surface of angular blocks; it is similar to aa lava but the fragments are larger and more regular in shape, somewhat smoother, and less vesicular. .

Block stream, An accumulation of boulders or angular blocks, with no fine sizes in the upper part, overlying solid or weathered bedrock, colluvium, or alluvium, and lying below a cliff or ledge from which rock fragments originate. Block streams usually occur at the heads of ravines as narrow bodies that are more extensive downslope than along the slope. They may exist on any slope angle, but ordinarily not steeper than 90 percent slope (approx. 40 degrees).

Blocking anticyclone, An anticyclone that remains nearly stationary for a week or more at middle to high latitudes, so that it blocks the normal eastward progression of high- and low-pressure systems.

Blowout, A saucer-, cup-, or trough-shaped depression formed by wind erosion on a preexisting dune or other sand deposit, especially in an area of shifting sand, loose soil, or where protective vegetation is disturbed or destroyed; the adjoining accumulation of sand derived from the depression, where recognizable, is commonly included. Commonly small, some blowouts may be large (kilometers in diameter).

Bluff, A high bank or bold headland, with a broad, precipitous, sometimes rounded cliff face overlooking a plain or body of water, especially on the outside of a stream meander; e.g., a river bluff.

Bog , Waterlogged, spongy ground, consisting primarily of mosses, containing acidic, decaying vegetation such as sphagnum, sedges, and heaths that may develop into peat.

Bohol Sea, A small sea centered in the Philippines at about 124° E and 9° S. It is surrounded by the islands of Mindanao to the southeast and Negros, Bohol and Leyte to the northwest. It is connected to the Sulu Sea to the west via a passage between Negros and Mindanao, the Visayan Sea to the north via the Tanon Strait, the Camotes Sea to the north via the Bohol Strait and a passage between Bohol and Leyte, and to the Leyte Gulf to the northeast via the Surigao Strait. Prominent geographic features include the islands of Siquijor and Camiguin and Sogod (in Leyte), Gingoog, Macajalar and Iligan (in Mindanao) Bays. This has also been called the Mindanao Sea.

Bolson, A term applied to an internally drained (closed) intermontane basin in arid regions where drainages from adjacent mountains converge toward a central depression. Bolsons are often tectonically formed depressions. According to Peterson, a bolson can include alluvial flat, alluvial plain, beach plain, barrier beach, lake plain, sand sheet, dune, and playa landforms. The piedmont slope above a bolson includes erosional (pediments) and older depositional surfaces (fans) that adjoin the mountain front. A semi-bolson is an externally drained (open) bolson. *(Fig. 108)*

Bolson, or **playa basin,** A drainage basin of an arid to semiarid area with interior drainage toward the playa; it is the surface area that contributes excess precipitation, as runoff, to the playa. *(Fig. 108)*

Borderland, A region adjacent to a continent, normally occupied by or bordering a shelf and sometimes emerging as islands, that is irregular or blocky in plan or profile, with depths well in excess of those typical of a shelf.

Boreal period, A post-LGM European climate regime. This refers to the period from about 7000-6000 BC when temperatures continued to rise, e.g. the colder seasons of the year gradually became milder (although probably with some dry and frosty winters) and the summers became generally warmer than today. It was preceded by the Pre-Boreal period and followed by the Atlantic period.

Bottomland, That part of an alluvial valley formed of and underlain by alluvium that has been transported by and deposited by the stream flowing through the valley reach; bottomlands may include the channel bed and one or more terraces.

Boulder, The sediment defined to be of particle diameter greater than 256 mm in diameter.

Box canyon, (a) A narrow gorge or canyon containing an intermittent stream following a zigzag course, characterized by high, steep rock walls and typically closed upstream by a similar wall, giving the impression, as viewed from its bottom, of being surrounded or "boxed in" by almost vertical walls. (b) A steep-walled canyon heading against a cliff a dead-end canyon.

Brackish water, The water on or beneath a land (or water) surface that accumulates as a result of natural processes of precipitation and which contains dissolved solids (mostly salts) of concentration intermediate between that of fresh water and salt water; the concentration of dissolved solids in brackish water is sufficient to cause deleterious effects by ingestion of living organisms adapted to a dependency on fresh water.

Braided stream, A channel or stream with multiple channels that interweave as a result of repeated bifurcation and convergence of flow around inter-channel bars, resembling (in plan view) the strands of a complex braid. Braiding is generally confined to broad, shallow streams of low sinuosity, high bed load, non-cohesive bank material, and a steep gradient. At a given bank-full discharge, braided streams have steeper slopes and shallower, broader, and less stable channel cross sections than meandering streams. A wide, relatively horizontal channel bed over which water during low flows forms an interlacing pattern of splitting into numerous small conveyances that again coalesce a short distance downstream; the conveyances, or sub-channels, lack channel characteristics, are highly ephemeral, and thereby are distinguishable from anabranches. *(Fig. 70)*

Brazil Basin, An ocean basin located off the eastern coast of Brazil in the west-central Atlantic Ocean. It is bounded to the north by the Belem (formerly Para) Rise, at which end there is also a broad depression called the Recife (formerly Pernambuco) Abyssal Plain.

Brazil Current, A western boundary current that forms the western limb of the subtropical gyre in the South Atlantic Ocean. This current is conspicuously weak as compared with other western boundary currents. The BC is not only comparatively weak but also much weaker than might be expected from observed wind fields. *(Fig. 144)*

Breached anticline, A structurally-controlled landscape or landform typically underlain by sedimentary rocks in which an anticline crest has been eroded such that the former crest has become a canyon or valley flanked by inward-facing erosional scarp slopes or cliffs and outward-facing dip slopes. When used as a landscape term, the associated landforms include cuestas and strike valleys.

Break, (a) [slopes] An abrupt change or inflection in a slope or profile (as in "a break in slope") such as knickpoint, shoulder, escarpment. (b) [geomorphology] A marked variation of topography, or a tract of land distinct from adjacent land, or an irregular or rough piece of ground.

Breaker zone, The portion of the nearshore zone where waves arriving from offshore become unstable and break. *(Fig. 79)*

Breaklands, An assemblage of very steep (e.g. 60-90 %), high relief slopes flanking major rivers and streams in mountainous terrain that form the walls of a v-shaped river valley. Breaklands are characterized by colluviated slopes of which the majority of the ground surface drains directly to a large axial stream at the base, and the remainder consists of shallowly incised, parallel drainageways. Breaklands have shallow to very deep soils, substantial rock outcrop, and more frequent fires than lower-gradient mountain slopes above;

Breccia, A coarse-grained, clastic rock composed of angular rock fragments (larger than 2 mm) commonly bonded by a mineral cement in a finer-grained matrix of varying composition and origin. The consolidated equivalent of rubble.

Brook, [streams] Generally a very small, ephemeral stream, especially one that issues from a spring or seep and conducts less water volume and over shorter distances than a creek.

Bucket temperature, The surface temperature of the ocean as measured by a bucket thermometer. This can also be the temperature measured by immersing a surface thermometer into a freshly drawn bucket of water.

Bucket thermometer, A thermometer with an insulated container around the bulb. It is used to measure ocean temperatures by lowering it on a line, allowing it to equilibrate with the temperature of the surface water, withdrawing it along with the water surrounding it, and reading the temperature. The water serves both as insulation for the thermometer (after withdrawal) and as a sample for a salinity determination.

Burden, The total mass of a gaseous substance of concern in the atmosphere.

Burial mound, A pile, hillock, or human-made hill, composed of debris or earth heaped up to mark a burial site.

Buried soil, Soil covered by an surface mantle of new soil material, typically to depths exceeding 50 cm; recent surface deposits < 50 cm thick are generally considered as part of the ground soil.

Buried, Landforms, geomorphic surfaces, or paleosols covered by younger sediments (e.g., eolian, glacial, and alluvial).

Butte, An isolated, generally flat-topped hill or mountain with relatively steep slopes and talus or precipitous cliffs and characterized by summit width that is less than the height of bounding escarpments, commonly topped by a caprock of resistant material and representing an erosion remnant carved from flat-lying rocks. *(Fig. 105)*

Buys Ballot's law, A synoptic meteorology rule stating that if, in the northern hemisphere, an observer stands with his back to the wind, pressure is lower on his left hand than on his right, while in the southern hemisphere the converse is true. This is basically a restatement of the fact that winds blow clockwise around a depression in the northern hemisphere and anticlockwise in the southern hemisphere.

C

C3 plants, Plants that produce a three-carbon compound during photosynthesis, including most trees and agricultural crops such as rice, wheat, soybeans, potatoes and vegetables.

C4 plants, Plants that produce a four-carbon compound during photosynthesis, mainly of tropical origin, including grasses and the agriculturally important crops maize, sugar cane, millet and sorghum.

Cabbeling, In physical oceanography, a phenomenon that occurs when two water masses with identical densities but different temperatures and salinities mix to form a third water mass with a greater density than either of its constituents. This is hypothesized to be a major cause of sinking in high northern lattitudes.

Caibbean Sea, The largest marginal sea of the Atlantic Ocean, with a surface area of 2.52 x 10^6 km^2 and a volume of 6.48 x 10^6 km^3 (twice that of the Mediterranean Sea). The north and eastern boundaries are the Greater and Lesser Antilles, and the southern extent is bounded by the irregular coasts of Venezuela, Colombia and Panama. The western boundary is Central America. It is located between 8-22°N latitude and 60-

89°W longitude, i.e. about 3000 km east to west and 1500 km south to north. The average depth of the Caribbean is 4400 m.

Calcareous ooze, A fine-grained, deep-sea deposit of pelagic origin containing more than 30% calcium carbonate derived from the skeletal material of various plankton. It is the most extensive deposit on the ocean floor but restricted to depths less than about 3500 m due to the carbon compensation depth. *(Fig. 153)*

Calcareous, containing calcium carbonate or another, usually insoluble, calcium salt.

Calcrete, A calcium-rich type of duricrust, is a near-surface pedogenic accumulation, usually less than a meter in thinckness, of secondary precipitates of calcium carbonate and other calcium or silica salts. Calcrete is typical of a semiarid climate and forms a poorly permeable to nearly impermeable layer or crust binding silt, sand, and gravel of poorly developed mineral soils. Because calcrete formation reduces soil permeability and porosity, infiltrating rainfall may be temporarily perched on its top, providing soil moisture to vegetation.

Caldera ,A large, more or less circular depression, formed by explosion and/or collapse, which surrounds a volcanic vent or vents, and whose diameter is many times greater than that of the included vent, or vents. A collapsed or partially-collapsed seamount, commonly of annular shape. *(Fig. 36)*

Caliche, A general term for a prominent zone of secondary carbonate accumulation in surficial materials in warm, subhumid to arid areas. Caliche is formed by both geologic and pedologic processes. Finely crystalline calcium carbonate forms a nearly continuous surface-coating and void-filling medium in geologic (parent) materials. Cementation ranges from weak in non-indurated forms to very strong in types that are indurated. Other minerals (carbonates, silicates, sulfates) may be present as accessory cements. Most petrocalcic and some calcic horizons are caliche.

California Current, The eastern limb of the clockwise flowing subtropical gyre in the North Pacific. The California Current flows equatorward throughout the year offshore from California from the shelf break to about 1000 km from the coast. The current is strongest at the surface and extends over the upper 500 m of the water column, with seasonal mean speeds of about 10 cm s^{-1}. It carries relatively colder fresher subarctic water equatorward. Within about 300 km of the coast, some of the fresher water in the upper 20 m is associated with the Columbia River plume.

Canary Basin, An ocean basin located to the west of the Canary Islands in the eastern North Atlantic Ocean. This is bound to the north by the Azores Rise and is mostly composed of the madeira Abyssal Plain, although a smaller depression called the Seine Abyssal Plain is also found there. This has also been called the Monaco Deep.

Canyon bench, One of a series of relatively narrow, flat landforms occurring along a canyon wall and caused by differential erosion of alternating strong and weak horizontal strata; a type of structural bench.

Canyon wall , The steep to near vertical slope between a canyon bottom and higher, adjacent hillslopes, mountain slopes, or summits. Canyon walls are generally dominated by rock outcrop and/or bedrock within the soil profile. Canyon walls commonly include cliffs or ledges, and may include a beveled base cut into less resistant rocks (e.g., shale). In large canyons, canyon walls may be vertically interrupted by nearly level or gentle slopes of canyon benches.

Canyon, A relatively narrow, deep depression with steep sides, the bottom of which generally deepends continuously, developed characteristically on some continental slopes.

Canyonlands, A deeply and extensively dissected landscape composed predominantly of relatively narrow, steep-walled valleys with small flood plains or valley floors; commonly with considerable outcrops of hard bedrock on steep slopes, ledges, or cliffs, and with broader summits or interfluves than found in badlands. Side slopes exhibit extensive erosion, active back-wearing, and relatively sparse vegetation.

Capacity of a stream, Synonymous with competence, or stream competence, refers to the ability of a current of water (or wind) to transport specified particle sizes of sediment.

Cape Basin, An ocean basin located to the west of South Africa at about 35° S in the South Atlantic Ocean. This includes the Cape Abyssal Plain which is fed by the Orange River. This has also been called the Walvis Basin.

Cape Horn Current (CMC), A current found south of approximately 42°S along the coast of Chile. The west wind drift of the subtropical gyre veers south and becomes the Cape Horn Current at this latitude. The lower salinity and higher oxygen values found in the upper part of the current as it moves south indicate interaction with the estuarine circulation in the complex fjords along the coast.

Cape Verde Basin, An ocean basin located at about 15° N off the west coast of Africa in the North Atlantic Ocean. It includes the Cape Verde Abyssal Plain, separated from the Madeira Abyssal Plain to the north by a belt of abyssal hills, and the Gambia Abyssal Plain. This has also been known as the North African Trough, the Chun Deep, and the Moseley Deep.

Capillary fringe, A zone of the subsurface that is continuous with the overlying zone of saturation, contains capillary interstices (some or all of which are filled with water), and in which the pressure is less than atmospheric.

Capillary Wave, A wave on a ocean surface for which the restoring force is surface tension.

Caprock, (a) A hard rock layer, usually sandstone, lava, or in arid environments, limestone, that lies above shale or other less resistant bedrock or sediments; specifically a rock layer that forms relatively level, resistant topmost strata that holds up hills, ridges, mesas, etc., and commonly forms cliffs or escarpments. Also spelled "cap rock". (b) A hard rock layer, usually sandstone, overlying the shale above a coal bed.

Captured stream, A stream whose course has been diverted into the channel of another stream by natural processes. *(Fig. 73)*

Carbon Compensation depth, The level in the ocean below which the solution rate of calcium carbonate exceeds its deposition rate.

Carbon cycle The term used to describe the flow of carbon (in various forms, e.g., as carbon dioxide) through the atmosphere, ocean, terrestrial biosphere and lithosphere.

Carbon Cycle, The cycling of carbon in the form of carbon dioxide, carbonates, organic Compounds, etc. between various reservoirs, e.g. the atmosphere, the oceans, land and marine biota and, on geological time scales, sediments and rocks.

Carbon dioxide (CO_2), A naturally occurring gas, also a by-product of burning fossil fuels from fossil carbon deposits, such as oil, gas and coal, of burning biomass and of land use changes and other industrial processes. It is the principal anthropogenic greenhouse gas that affects the Earth's radiative balance. It is the reference gas against which other greenhouse gases are measured and therefore has a Global Warming Potential of 1. This is the most important of the greenhouse gases with an atmospheric concentration of 353 ppm (in 1990), up from an estimated 260-290 in pre-industrial times (pre-1880). This gas plays a very large part in the natural carbon cycle, with the amount of carbon taken out of the atmosphere each year by plant photosynthesis being almost perfectly balanced by the amount put back into the atmosphere by the processes of animal respiration and plant decay. The chief natural sources the burning of coal, oil and natural gas, the so-called fossil fuels, and the cutting down and burning of forests, with the latter contributing about a third as much as the former.

Carbon-14 dating, A radioisotope dating method wherein a radioactive isotope of carbon, also called radiocarbon, is used to date materials containing carbon.

Carbonate pump, The name given to the cycling of $CaCO_3$ in the ocean. Plants and animals living in the euphotic zone have $CaCO_3$ skeletons (tests) which they precipitate from dissolved calcium and carbonate ions.

Caribbean Current, One of two downstream branches into which the confluence of the Guiana Current and the North Equatorial Current split when encountering the Lesser Antilles. The Antilles Current flows northward along the eastward side of the Antillean Island Arc to eventually merge into the Florida Current, while the Caribbean Current flows west-northwesterly through the various passages between the Windward Islands of the Lesser Antilles.

Carrbonaceous aerosol, Aerosol consisting predominantly of organic substances and various forms of black carbon

Carrying capacity, (of a watershed, landscape, drainage network, lake, or ground-water system) The production, through natural biophysical processes, of ecosystem services that each can yield without sustaining loss in function; for a grassland the carrying capacity might be the annual growth of grass that can support grazing by herbivores without environmental damage, whereas the carrying capacity of a ground-water system is the rate at which water can be extracted from wells, and replaced by natural recharge, without a reduction in volume of the ground-water reservoir.

Catchment, is a synonym for drainage basin, but the term often has the connotation of a smaller area than that of a drainage basin (a sub-basin). *(Fig. 53)*

Catena (from the Latin word for chain), A soil association of a limited area derived from common parent material or source rocks that provide it with characteristics distinguishing it from other soil associations of the larger area or drainage basin.

Catena, A sequence of soils across a landscape, of about the same age, derived from similar parent material, and occurring under similar climatic conditions, but have different characteristics due to variations in relief and in drainage.

Cation exchange capacity (of a colloidal material) The excess of oppositely charged ions in proximity to a charged clay or mineral surface (or layer) that can be exchanged for other cations; it is usually expressed in milliequivalents of cations that can be exchanged in a soil or sediment sample with a dry weight of 100 grams.

Cave, Any natural subsurface macro opening, or chamber, or series of openings or chambers; caves form through a variety of processes in most rock types but most commonly are the result of solution of carbonate rocks, particularly limestone, by the movement of ground water or erosion by sea waves. *(Fig. 76)*

Central South Equatorial Current, One of three distinct branches into which the South Equatorial Current splits in the western South Atlantic.

Centripetal drainage pattern. A drainage pattern in which the streams converge inward toward a central depression; generally indicative of a structural basin, volcanic crater, caldera, breached dome, bolson, or the end of an eroded anticline or syncline.

Channel erosion, The detachment and transport, possibly followed quickly by re-deposition, of soil particles or channel-bed material by concentrated flow in areas of open-channel flow.

Channel island, A landform that rises above and is surrounded by stream passageways and which persists a sufficient time so that persistent vegetation can develop if adequate moisture is available.

Channel, (a) The hollow bed where a natural body of surface water flows or may flow. The deepest or central part of the bed of a stream, containing the main current and occupied more or less continuously by water. (b) The bed of a single or braided watercourse that commonly is barren of vegetation and is formed of modern alluvium. Channels may be enclosed by banks or splayed across and slightly mounded above a fan surface and include bars and mounds of cobbles and stones. (c) Small, trough-like, arcuate or sinuous channels separated by small bars or ridges, caused by fluvial processes; common to flood plains and young alluvial terraces; a constituent part of bar and channel topography.

Channel, A natural, or constructed, passageway or depression of perceptible linear extent containing continuously or periodically flowing water and sediment, or a connecting link between two bodies of water.

Channel-geometry method, A technique of indirectly estimating streamflow characteristics by recognizing that the size of an alluvial channel is indicative of the water conveyed through it, and that the shape of the channel is largely the result of the sediment transported by the stream.

Charcoal, Material resulting from charring of biomass, usually retaining some of the microscopic texture typical of plant tissues; chemically it consists mainly of carbon with a disturbed graphitic structure, with lesser amounts of oxygen and hydrogen.

Chenier plain, A mud-rich strand plain, occupied by cheniers and intervening mud flats with marsh and swamp vegetation. *(Fig. 82)*

Chenier, A long, narrow, vegetated marine beach ridge or sandy hummock, 1 to 6 m high, forming roughly parallel to a prograding shoreline seaward of marsh and mud-flat deposits, enclosed on the seaward side by fine-grained sediments, and resting on foreshore or mud-flat deposits. It is well drained, often supporting trees on higher areas. Widths range from 45 - 450 m and lengths may exceed several tens of kilometers.

Chert, A hard, extremely dense or compact, dull to semivitreous, cryptocrystalline sedimentary rock, consisting dominantly of interlocking crystals of quartz less than about 30 mm in diameter; it may contain amorphous silica (opal). It sometimes contains impurities such as calcite, iron oxide, or the remains of siliceous and other organisms. It has a tough, splintery to conchoidal fracture and may be white or variously colored gray, green, blue, pink, red, yellow, brown, and black. Chert occurs principally as nodular or concretionary segregations in limestones and dolomites.

Chezy equation, A empirical formula relating stream velocity, V, to controlling variables R, hydraulic radius and energy slope, S: $V = C (RS)^{1/2}$, in which C (which is analogous to the Manning coefficient, n) is a constant of proportionality.

Chinook, A regional name in alpine areas of North America for vertical, cyclonic-induced, foehn winds; chinook winds typically occur in the winter, result from the downslope movement of relatively warm, dry air, and often are especially strong in valleys of east-flowing mountain streams. Chinook winds can be quite strong, and can be very damaging and erosive, causing snapping and uprooting of trees and eolian entrainment of soil and sediment particles as coarse as fine gravel.

Chlorinity, The mass of silver required to precipitate completely the halogens in 0.3285234 kg of sample seawater.

Chlorofluorocarbon (CFC), Any of a group of exceptionally stable compounds containing carbon, fluorine, and chlorine, which have been used especially as refrigerants and aerosol propellants. CFCs are climatically significant for their ability to break down ozone molecules in the atmosphere. There are several kinds of CFCs, the most common being CFC-11, CFC-12, CFC-113, CFC-114 and CFC-115, They are also significant as a greenhouse gas since, molecule for molecule, they are 10,000 times more efficient in trapping heat in the atmosphere than carbon dioxide.

Chronology, Arrangement of events according to dates or times of occurrence.

Cinder cone, A conical hill formed by the accumulation of cinders and other pyroclastics, normally of basaltic or andesitic composition. Slopes generally exceed 20 percent.

Cinders, Unconsolidated, juvenile, vitric, vesicular pyroclastic material; individual fragments are 2.0 mm or more in at least one dimension with an apparent specific gravity (including vesicles) of more than 1.0 and less than 2.0 g/cm3.

Cirque floor, The comparatively level bottom of a cirque, thinly mantled with till and consisting of glacially scoured knolls and hillocks separated by depressions, flat areas and small lakes (tarn); commonly it is bounded by a slightly elevated rock lip at its exit. *(Fig. 65, 68)*

Cirque headwall, The glacially-scoured, steep and arcuate side or wall of a cirque, dominated by rock outcrop, rubble, and colluvium. *(Fig. 86, 89)*

Cirque platform, A relatively level or bench-like surface formed by the coalescence of several cirques.

Cirque, A deep, steep-walled, bowl-shaped (or partial bowl-shaped) depression formed by glacial erosion of bedrock in the uppermost snow-accumulation high alpine areas; cirques of lower-relief alpine areas may have walls of moderate steepness and relatively shallow bowl-like depressions. *(Fig. 86, 88, 89)*

Clast, An individual constituent, grain, or fragment of sediment or rock, produced by the mechanical weathering (disintegration) of a larger rock mass.

Clastic, Pertaining to rock or sediment composed mainly of fragments derived from preexisting rocks or minerals and moved from their place of origin. The term indicates sediment sources that are both within and outside the depositional basin.

Clay, (as used in sedimentology as opposed to mineralogy) A fluvial sediment defined to be of particle diameter no greater than 0.002 mm; some systems define the upper size limit to be 0.004 mm.

Claypan, A dense, compact, slowly permeable layer in the subsoil, with a much higher clay content than overlying materials from which it is separated by a sharply defined boundary. Claypans are usually hard when dry, and plastic and sticky when wet.

Cliff, Any high, very steep to perpendicular or overhanging face of rock or earth; a precipice.

Climate change, Climate change refers to a change in the state of the climate that can be identified (e.g., by using statistical tests) by changes in the mean and/or the variability of its properties, and that x'persists for an extended period, typically decades or longer. Climate change may be due to natural internal processes or external forcings, or to persistent anthropogenic changes in the composition of the atmosphere or in land use.

Note that the Framework Convention on Climate Change (UNFCCC), in its Article 1, defines climate change as: 'a change of climate which is attributed directly or indirectly to human activity that alters the composition of the global atmosphere and which is in addition to natural climate variability observed over comparable time periods'. The UNFCCC thus makes a distinction between climate change attributable to human activities altering the atmospheric composition, and climate variability attributable to natural causes.

Climate prediction, A climate prediction or climate forecast, the result of an attempt to produce an estimate of the actual evolutions of the climate in the future, for example, at seasonal, interannual or long-term time scales. Since the future evolution of the climate system may be highly sensitive to initial conditions, such predictions are usually probabilistic in nature.

Climate projection, A projection of the response of the climate system to emission or concentration scenarios of greenhouse gases and aerosols, or radiative forcing scenarios, often based upon simulations by climate models. Climate projections are distinguished from climate predictions in order to emphasize that climate projections depend upon the emission/concentration/ radiative forcing scenario used, which are based on assumptions concerning, for example, future socioeconomic and technological developments that may or may not be realised and are therefore subject to substantial uncertainty.

Climate scenario, A plausible and often simplified representation of the future climate, based on an internally consistent set of climatological relationships that has been constructed for explicit use in investigating the potential consequences of anthropogenic climate change, often serving as input to impact models. Climate projections often serve as the raw material for constructing climate scenarios, but climate scenarios usually require additional information such as about the observed current climate. A climate change scenario is the difference between a climate scenario and the current climate.

Climate sensitivity, Refers to the equilibrium charige in the annual mean global surface temperature following a doubling of the atmospheric equivalent carbon dioxide concentration. Due to computational constraints, the equilibrium climate sensitivity hi a climate model is usually estimated by running an atmospheric general circulation model coupled to a mixed-layer ocean model, because equilibrium climate sensitivity is largely determined by atmospheric processes. Efficient models can be run to equilibrium with a dynamic ocean.

Climate shift or climate regime shift, An abrupt shift or jump /in mean values signalling a change in regime. Most widely used in conjunction with the 1976/1977 climate shift that seems to correspond to a change in El Nifio-Southem Oscillation behavior.

Climate system, The climate system is the highly complex system consisting of five major components: the atmosphere, the hydrosphere, the cryosphere, the land surface and the biosphere, and the interactions between them. The climate system evolves hi time under the influence of its own internal dynamics and because of external forcings such as volcanic eruptions, solar variations and anthropogenic forcings such as the changing composition of the atmosphere and land use change.

Climate variability, Climate variability refers to variations in / the mean state and other statistics (such as standard deviations, the occurrence of extremes, etc.) of the climate on all spatial and temporal scales beyond that of individual weather events. Variability may be due to natural internal processes within the climate system (internal variability), or to variations in natural or anthropogenic external forcing (external variability). See also Climate change.

Climate, Climate in a narrow sense is usually defined as the average weather, or more rigorously, as the statistical description in terms of the mean and variability of relevant quantities over a period of time ranging from months to thousands or millions of years. The classical period for averaging these variables is 30 years, as defined by the World Meteorological Organization. The relevant quantities are most often surface variables such as temperature, precipitation and wind. Climate in a wider sense is the state, including a statistical description, of the climate system. Different averaging periods, such as a period of 20 years, are also used. The characteristics and variability of weather at a site or specified area; included are precipitation, temperature, humidity, and derivative elements such as barometric pressure, wind velocity, dew point, and measures of cloud cover. Climate is one of the basic controls of soil and landscape development, the movement of water, erosion, and vegetation.

Climate, Traditionally defined in terms of the mean atmospheric conditions at the earth's surface. A Set of averaged quanitities completed with higher moment statistics (such as variances, covariances, correlations, etc.) that characterize the structure and behaviour of the atmosphere, hydrosphere, and cryosphere over a period of time.

Climatology, The science or study of climate, including its effects on the physical and biological resources of the area of interest; it is a quantitative description of the spatial and temporal variability of climate characteristics over areas of land and water.

Climbing dune, A dune formed by the piling-up of sand by wind against a cliff or mountain slope; very common in arid regions with substantial local relief and strong, prevailing winds.

Closed depression, A generic name for any enclosed area that has no surface drainage outlet and from which water escapes only by evaporation or subsurface drainage; an area of lower ground indicated on a topographic map by a hachured contour line forming a closed loop.

Cloud condensation nuclei, Airborne particles that serve as an initial site for the condensation of liquid water, which can lead to the formation of cloud droplets.

Cluster, (as applied to issues of bed load and the formation of small-scale bed forms in the surface layer of gravel-bed alluvial channels) Either a discrete or individually organized grouping or interconnected structures comprised of a network of bed-material or bed-load particles that rises above the level of areas of adjacent channel bed; clusters occur in any part of a channel, including near the edge, near the thalweg, and on bars. The dynamics of clusters (which are loosely subdivided and named by shape, such as pebble, line, comet, ring, and heap), that is processes of their formation, are not well understood.

Coastal dune, (including coastal dune field) An accumulation, or concentration, of beach sand primarily by wave-action sorting processes as a low, small-scale mound, ridge, or, more commonly, a complex (field, or zone) of mounds and ridges along coastlines of oceans, seas, and other large water bodies; if active they may be bare, or, if inactive, they may be partially to fully vegetated. Coastal dunes are subject to translocation, without a basic loss of scale or structure, by wave action or wind.

Coastal marl, An earthy, unconsolidated deposit of gray to buff-colored mud of low bulk density (dry) composed primarily of very fine, almost pure calcium carbonate formed in subaqueous settings that span freshwater lacustrine conditions to saline intertidal settings formed by the chemical action of algal mats and organic detritus . Coastal marl can be quite pure or it can be finely disseminated throughout living root mats (e.g., mangrove roots) and / or organic soil layers.

Coastal plain, A low, generally broad plain that has as its margin an oceanic shore and its strata horizontal or gently sloping toward the water, and generally represents a strip of recently prograded or emerged sea floor.

Cobble (as fluvial sediment) Sediment defined to be of particle diameter between 64 and 256 mm in diameter.

Cockpit karst, A karst landscape dominated by subsurface drainage and serrate or star-shaped depressions (cockpits) that range widely in size and density but typically are considerably larger than sinkholes (dolines), and are separated by intermediate residual hills with concave side slopes; a common type of tropical karst

Cockpit, A crudely star-shaped, closed depression (i.e., large sinkhole) in tropical karst having an inverted conical or slightly concave floor, with an irregular or serrate perimeter formed by subsidiary solution channels and corridors into adjacent hills, and surrounded by residual hills with steep, concave side slopes; the dominant type of closed depression in cockpit karst.

Cohesiveness, A strength-imparting property of fine-grained sediment, generally clay, by which individual particles cohere or bond together by electrochemical forces of the particle surfaces.

Col, A high, narrow, sharp-edged pass or saddle through a divide or between two adjacent peaks in a mountain range; especially a deep pass formed by the headward erosion and intersection of two cirques.

Collapse sinkhole, A type of sinkhole that is formed by collapse of a cave within the underlying soluble bedrock (e.g., limestone, gypsum, salt).

Collapsed lake plain, A lake plain formed on, and bounded by, glacial ice and subsequently "let down" or collapsed by the melting of underlying ice resulting in contortion or folding of the sediments and sedimentary structures. Lacustrine sediments cap present topography.

Collapsed outwash plain, An outwash plain which forms on glacial ice (inside the glacial margin), and is subsequently let down or collapsed when the underlying ice melts, resulting in contortion or folding of the sediments and sedimentary structures to the extent that little of the original plain or its gradient remain. Outwash sediments commonly cap present-day topography.

Colluvial apron, A landform with a concave to planar surface composed of a thick wedge-shaped deposit of colluvium and/or slope alluvium that forms the base (footslope) of a bluff, escarpment or steep slope .

Colluvial, Pertaining to material or processes associated with transportation and/or deposition by mass movement (direct gravitational action) and local, unconcentrated runoff (overland flow) on side slopes and/or at the base of slopes.

Colluvium, A layer, generally less than 3 meters in thickness, of unconsolidated and heterogeneous weathering products (soil material and sediment) and rock fragments deposited following sheet erosion by unconcentrated surface runoff and by gravitational processes, especially soil creep, other types of mass wasting, physical weathering, and bioturbation; colluvium generally occurs as a blanket of poorly sorted sediment and rock fragments on the lower parts of hillslopes underlain by bedrock.

Comminution, is the process of reducing a mass to small, fine particles by impact, abrasion, or soil dynamics; as a geomorphic or hydrologic process, comminution occurs through particle interaction in flowing water or glacial ice, and in archaeology the term is applied to taphonomic (fossilization) processes in which charcoal, bone, or shell becomes pulverized and disseminated following deposition and burial by physical weathering, mass movement such as creep, bioturbation, and pedogenesis.

Competence, The ability of a current of water or wind to transport sediment, emphasizing the particle size rather that the amount, measured as the diameter of the largest particle transported; it depends, therefore, on the critical shear stress, which is a function of the hydraulic radius of the stream channel and the energy slope.

Complex landslide, A category of mass movement processes, associated sediments (complex landslide deposit), or resultant landforms characterized by a composite of several mass movement processes none of which dominates or leaves a prevailing landform. Numerous types of complex landslides can be specified by naming the constituent processes evident.

Complex response, (as applied to geomorphology) The tendency of natural drainage systems that receive water and sediment from a complex assortment of landforms (such as hillslopes, terraces, and flood plain) to respond accordingly in complex, often difficult to anticipate, manners following disturbance such as rejuvenation. The concept is based on the recognition that any change modifying a system, whether natural or imposed, induces change elsewhere that may progress sequentially from a landform or process to others.

Composite science, The complex disciplines, including geomorphology, ecology, soil science, hydrology, and archaeology, that are composed of distinct parts of other types of study but which have specific and generally agreed-upon goals requiring various scientific and technological approaches of investigation to meet those objectives. A goal of geomorphology, for example, is a genetic interpretation of landforms, and techniques of physics, chemistry, biology, and engineering Ask writer employed to develop interpretations.

Cone karst, A variety of kegel karst topography, common in the tropics (e.g., Puerto Rico, Pacific Basin Islands) characterized by steep-sided, cone-shaped residual hills and ridges separated by star-shaped depressions, broader valleys, or lagoons. These hills and ridges have steep, convex side slopes and rounded tops that are dissected into secondary karst surfaces with shafts and various forms of karren microfeatures.

Conformity, The mutual and undisturbed relationship between adjacent sedimentary strata that have been deposited in orderly sequence with little or no evidence of time lapses; true stratigraphic continuity in the sequence of beds without evidence that the lower beds were folded, tilted, or eroded before the higher beds were deposited.

Conglomerate, A coarse-grained, clastic sedimentary rock composed of rounded to subangular rock fragments larger than 2 mm, commonly with a matrix of sand and finer material; cements include silica, calcium carbonate, and iron oxides. The consolidated equivalent of gravel.

Conservation terrace, An earthen embankment constructed across a slope for conducting water from above at a regulated flow to prevent accelerated erosion and to conserve water.

Constructional, [geomorphology] Said of a landform that owes its origin, form, position, or general character to depositional (aggradational) processes, such as the accumulation of sediment (e.g., alluvial fan, volcanic cone).

Continental glacier, A glacier of considerable thickness completely covering a large part of a continent or an area of at least 50,000 square km, obscuring the underlying surface, such as the ice sheets covering Antarctica or Greenland. Continental glaciers occupied northern portions of the coterminous USA and Alaska in the past (e.g., Pleistocene) and usage commonly implies former continental glacier conditions.

Continental margin, The zone, generally consisting of shelf, slope and continental rise, separating the continent from the deep sea floor or abyssal plain; occasionally a trench may be present in place of a continental rise. *(Fig 119)*

Continental rise, A gentle slope rising from the oceanic depths towards the foot of a continental slope. *(Fig. 118)*

Continental slope, The relatively steep slope usually found between the continental shelf and the abyssal plain. Continental slopes range from 3 to 6° in slope (with 4° being about average), range in depth from 100-300 m to 1400-3200 m, range in width from 20-100 km, and occupy about 8.5% of the ocean floor if the 2000 m contour is taken as the deeper border. The continental shelf and slope are said to comprise the continental margin. *(Fig. 118, 119)*

Continental Zone, In physical oceanography, a region in the Southern Ocean between the Southern Front and the continent of Antarctica. It is characterized hydrographically by a water mass of uniform temperature and low salinity in the upper 500 m. The CZ is one of four distinct surface water mass regimes in the Southern Ocean, the others being (to the north) the Antarctic Zone (AZ), the Polar Front Zone (PFZ) and the Subantarctic Zone (SAZ).

Continuous permafrost, Permafrost occurring everywhere beneath the exposed land surface throughout a geographic region.

Control, (as applied to a gaging station (streamgage)) The physical feature(s), either sectional, channel, or flood plain, that directly defines the slope of the stage-discharge relation at the streamgage. The control defines the relative hydraulic stability of a stream bed, channel, or flood plain. At low flows the sectional control is usually at or immediately downstream from the measurement section of the gage; a typical stable natural control is bedrock or consolidated alluvium that is not subject to scour or deposition. Typical unstable natural controls are sand and gravel riffles and point bars, which are subject to shifting both by scour and deposition. Examples of an artificial control are a weir, flume, or low cement dam. At channel and flood-plain flows, the control is defined by the shape and roughness of the channel and flood-plain cross-sections.

Convection, Vertical motion driven by buoyancy forces arising from static instability, usually caused by near-surface cooling or increases in salinity in the case of the ocean and near-surface warming in the case of the atmosphere. At the location of convection, the horizontal scale is approximately the same as the vertical scale, as opposed to the large contrast between these scales in the general circulation. The net vertical mass transport is usually much smaller than the upward and downward exchange.

Convergence, (used in a geomorphic context) A term to acknowledge that some landforms with outwardly similar characteristics developed from a narrow range of similar process sets causing the landforms and thus may have quite different internal or structural characteristics. When used in a hydrologic context, convergence, or convergent flow, refers to a contraction of flow paths as surface runoff traverses a concave slope or as ground water moves from a relatively unrestricted flow path to one of greater restriction.

Conveyance, (as applied to hydrology and fluvial geomorphology) A measure of the amount of water that can pass through a stream-channel section without spilling onto higher surfaces as flood flow.

Cooscillating tide, The tide created in an estuary caused by the ocean tide at the entrance to the estuary acting as a driving force.

Coral bleaching, A phenomena wherein coral reefs bleach as a result of high temperatures or other environmental stresses, e.g. pollution episodes. Observations indicate that since 1979 bleaching episodes have coincided with El Nino events and suggest that the scale of bleaching since 1979 is unprecedented Since 1870.

Coral island, (a) A relict coral reef that stands above sea level and surrounded by water (e.g., Florida Keys). Carbonate sands rich in coral and shell fragments generally mantle the underlying flat coral platform. (b) An oceanic island formed from coral accumulations lying atop or fringing volcanic peaks or platforms.

Coral limestone, An informal term for massive limestone composed primarily of coral and coral fragments commonly associated with marine islands or coral reefs in tropical or subtropical waters.

Coral reef, A limestone structure found in relatively shallow water composed of corals, organisms that secrete limestone foundations to provide structural support and protection. There are three geomor-phologically distinct types of coral reefs, fringing reefs, barrier reefs, and atolls, although there are gradations between these types. All these types have the same basic biological structure and result from the same processes of accretion. *(Fig. 154, 155, 156, 157)*

Coral Sea, A marginal sea located in the southwest Pacific centered at about 155° E and 14°s off of the northeast coast of Australia. It is also bordered by the Solomon Islands and Papua New Guinea to the north and west, New Caledonia and the New Hebrides Islands to the east, and abuts the Tasman Sea to the south. The bathymetry is essentially composed of the Solomon Basin to the northwest, the Coral Sea Basin in the center, and the New Hebrides basin to the east. It has a mean depth of about 2400 m with a maximum depth of 9140 m in the New Britain Trench. The shallowest parts are found on the continental shelf off of Queensland.

Coriolis effect, The denotes the effect of the Coriolis force to deviate a moving body perpendicular to its velocity. *(Fig. 184, 185)*

Coriolis force, The force which, acting on a given mass, produces the Coriolis acceleration. It is a fictitious force introduced to facilitate the application of Newton's second law of motion to a rotating reference frame. *(Fig. 185, 186)*

Corrosion, The water-related chemical erosion of rocks and inorganic soil material by dissolution and similar weathering processes including oxidation, hydrolysis, carbonation, and hydration; the older, less specific term, corrasion, is loosely synonymous.

Cosmogenic Isotopes, Rare isotopes that are created when a high-.energy cosmic ray interacts with the nucleus of an in situ atom. They are often used as indications of solar magnetic activity (which can shield cosmic rays) or as tracers of atmospheric transport, and are also called cosmogenic nuclides.

Cotidal line, Lines joining the points where high water occurs at the same time. The lines show the lapse of time between the moon's transit over a reference meridian (usually the Greenwich meridian) and the occurence of high water for any point lying on the time. *(Fig. 140)*

Country rock, A general term for the non-igneous rock surrounding an igneous intrusion.

Cove, (a) A small, narrow sheltered bay, inlet, creek or recess in an estuary, often inside a larger embayment. (b) A small, often circular, wave-cut indentation in a cliff; it usually has a restricted or narrow entrance. (c) A fairly broad, looped embayment in a lake shoreline. (d) A shallow tidal river, or the backwater near the mouth of a tidal river. A walled and rounded or cirque-like opening at the head of a small steep valley. A smooth-floored, somewhat oval-shaped "valley" sheltered by hills or mountains.

Crag and tail, An elongate hill or ridge of subglacially streamlined drift, having at the stoss end (up-ice) a steep, often precipitous face or knob of ice-smoothed, resistant bedrock (the "crag") obstructing the movement of the glacier, and at the lee end (down-ice) a tapering, streamlined, gentle slope (the "tail") of intact, weaker rock and / or drift protected by the crag; also called lee-side cone. *(Fig. 92)*

Craton, A part of the earth's crust that has attained stability, and has been minimally deformed for a prolonged period. The term is now restricted to continental areas of largely Precambrian rocks.

Creek , [streams] A general term used throughout the USA (except New England), Canada, and Australia for a small, intermittent stream that is larger than a brook but smaller than a river.

Creep, (as applied to geomorphology) A process of mass movement by which soil and rock gradually and slowly move by deformation caused by gravitational stress; the process is continuous, or nearly so, and irreversible, resulting in the movement of sediment and rock fragments to lower sites on the landscape and the availability of the sediment and rock fragments for addition to fluvial-sediment loads. Creep also includes glacial processes of deformation of snow and ice.

Crest, A geomorphic component of hills consisting of the convex slopes (perpendicular to the contour) that forms the narrow, roughly linear top area of a hill, ridge, or other upland where shoulders have converged to the extent that little or no summit remains; dominated by erosion, slope wash and mass movement processes and sediments (e.g., slope alluvium, creep). Commonly, soils on crests are more similar to those on side slopes than to soils on adjacent interfluves. *(Fig. 115)*

Crevasse filling, A short, straight ridge of stratified sand and gravel believed to have been deposited in a crevasse of a wasting glacier and left standing after the ice melted; a variety of kame. May also occur as long, sinuous ridges and linear complexes of till or drift.

Crevasse, [geomorphology] (a) A wide breach or crack in the bank of a river or canal; especially one in a natural levee or an artificial bank. (b) A wide, deep break or fissure in the Earth after an earthquake. [glaciology] A deep, nearly vertical fissure, crack, or rift in a glacier or other mass of land ice. *(Fig. 88)*

Critical flow, (in open channels] Occurs when flow rate is at a maximum for the energy (d -/v^2/2a) in which d is water depth, v is water velocity, and g is the acceleration due to gravity) of the water; critical flow occurs only when the Froude number is 1.0.

Critical shear stress, (in fluvial geomorphology and hydraulic) The lowest required value of shear stress applied by flowing water to initiate motion of individual particles of specified size (diameter) along the bed of a stream.

Cross-bedding, (a) Cross-stratification in which the cross-beds are more than 1 cm in thickness. (b) A cross-bedded structure; a cross-bed.

Cross-lamination, (a) Cross-stratification characterized by cross-beds that are less than 1 cm in thickness. (b) A cross-laminated structure; a cross-lamina.

Cross-stratification, Arrangement of strata inclined at an angle to the main stratification. This is a general term having two subdivisions; cross-bedding, in which the cross-strata are thicker than 1 cm, and cross-lamination, in which they are thinner than 1 cm. A single group of related cross-strata is a set and a group of similar, related sets is a coset.

Cryoplanation, The reduction and modification of a land surface by processes associated with intensive frost action, such as solifluction, supplemented by the erosive and transport actions of running water, moving ice, and other agents.

Cryosphere, That part of the climate system consisting of the ice fields of Antarctica and ice fields of Antarctica and Greenland, other continental snow and ice fields, sea ice and permafrost. At present the Antarctic ice sheet holds 89.3% of the total global ice mass, with the Greenland ice sheet holding 8.6% and mountain glaciers and permafrost holding 0.76% and 0.95%, respectively. The remaining 0.39% is distributed among seasonal snow and sea ice. The component of the climate system consisting of all snow, ice and frozen ground (including permafrost) on and beneath the surface of the Earth and ocean.

Cryoturbate , A mass of soil or other unconsolidated earthy material moved or disturbed by frost action, and usually coarser than the underlying material; especially a rubbly deposit formed by solifluction.

Cryoturbation, A collective term used to describe all soil movements due to frost action, characterized by folded, broken and dislocated beds and lenses of unconsolidated deposits.

Cryptogamic crust, A type of microbiotic crust consisting of a thin, biotic layer at the ground surface composed predominantly of cryptogams (i.e., algae, lichen, mosses, lichens and liverworts); most commonly found in semiarid or arid environments.

Cuesta valley, An asymmetric depression adjacent to a cuesta that lies parallels to the strike of the underlying strata; a type of strike valley. It's formed by differential erosion of weaker strata interbedded with, or stratigraphically adjacent to more resistant rocks. It may or may not contain a local drainage network but commonly lies above and is unconnected to the regional drainage system.

Cuesta, An asymmetric ridge capped by resistant rock layers of slight to moderate dip, commonly less than 10° (approximately < 15 percent); a homocline type produced by differential erosion of interbedded resistant and weak rocks. A cuesta has a long, gentle slope on one side (dip slope), that roughly parallels the inclined beds, and on the opposite side has a relatively short, steep or cliff-like slope (scarp slope) that cuts the tilted rocks.

Current meter A device to measure velocity at a point within the flow field of a stream of water; the device, consists of a vertical rod with attached cups that are free to rotate at a rate corresponding to the water velocity.

Current, A flow of water within the sea which is coherent at least in a time-averaged sense.

Curve number, (An index of the runoff potential on a land surface in response to rainfall. It is the maximum possible difference between the effective rainfall and the direct storm runoff depths. Curve numbers range from 0 (no runoff under any condition) to 100 (all rainfall of any event results in runoff).

Cut , A passage, incision, or space from which material has been excavated, such as a road cut or a railroad cut.

Cut and fill, A process of leveling, whereby material eroded from one place by waves, currents, streams, or winds is deposited nearby until the surfaces of erosion and deposition are continuous and uniformly graded; especially lateral erosion on the concave banks of a meandering stream accompanied by deposition within its loops.

Cutbank , A slope or wall portion of a cut excavated into unconsolidated material (regolith) or bedrock, as in a borrow pit. It may stand nearly vertical resulting from collapse as the base is undercut during excavation or by erosion, or it may be reduced by subsequent erosion to a more subdued angle by slope wash.

Cutoff , [streams] The new and relatively short channel formed when a stream cuts through a narrow strip of land and thereby shortens the length of its channel.

Cutter, [karst] A dissolution groove or trench formed along vertical bedrock fractures beneath soil and usually buried beneath regolith with little or no ground surface expression, commonly wider than a solution fissure (widths commonly range from 0.5 to 3 meters) and tapering down to a crack or a bedrock floored trench.

Cyclone, A atmospheric pressure distribution in which there is a low central pressure relative to the surroundings. The circulation around the center is anticlockwise (clockwise) in the northern (southern) hemisphere. *(Fig. 200, 201)*

Cyclonic, The direction of rotation around a center of low pressure. This is counter-clockwise in the northern hemisphere and clockwise in the southern. The term originates from the circulation observed around tropical cyclones. *(Fig. 198, 199)*

D

Datum, any point or surface to which other landscape points can be related, both horizontally and vertically, to locate the points on the earth's surface, typically for purposes of topographic mapping.

Dead Sea, The Dead Sea is a large and deep terminal lake, situated in the lowest section of the Jordan Rift Valley between Israel and Jordan. As a terminal lake, the level of the Dead Sea is determined by the balance between evaporation, rain and runoff (the last including the inflow of subsurface springs). Historical records indicate that throughout its existence, the water level of the Dead Sea oscillated significantly.

Debris , Any surficial accumulation of loose material detached from rock masses by chemical and mechanical means, as by decay and disintegration. It consists of rock clastic material of any size and sometimes organic matter.

Debris avalanche, The mass movement process, associated sediments (debris avalanche deposit), or resultant landform characterized by a very rapid to extremely rapid type of flow dominated by the sudden downslope movement of incoherent, unsorted mixtures of soil and weathered bedrock which, although comparatively dry, behave much as a viscous fluid when moving.

Debris fall, The mass movement process, associated sediments (debris fall deposit), or resultant landform characterized by a rapid type of fall involving the relatively free, downslope movement or collapse of detached, unconsolidated material which falls freely through the air (lacks an underlying slip face); sediments have substantial proportions of both fine earth and rock fragments; common along undercut stream banks.

Debris flow, The downslope mass movement, by either inertial or viscous processes at velocities greater than those of creep or solifluction, of a non-Newtonian slurry of a plastic mixture of water and generally coarse, poorly sorted sediment; debris-flow slurries, depending on the particle-size distribution of the sediment, typically vary from 50 to 80 percent sediment by volume. *(Fig. 48)*

Debris slide, The mass movement process, associated sediments (debris slide deposit), or resultant landform characterized by a rapid type of slide, composed of comparatively dry and largely unconsolidated earthy material which slides or rolls downslope (does not exhibit backward rotation) and resulting in an irregular, hummocky deposit somewhat resembling a moraine. *(Fig. 48)*

Debris spread, The mass movement process, associated sediments (debris spread deposit), or resultant landform characterized by a very rapid type of *spread* dominated by lateral movement in a soil and rock mass resulting from liquefaction or plastic flow of underlying materials that may be extruded out between intact units; sediments have substantial proportions of both fine earth and rock fragments. *(Fig. 48)*

Debris topple , The mass movement process, associated sediments (debris topple deposit), or resultant landform characterized by a localized, very rapid type of *topple* in which large blocks of soil and rock material literally fall over, rotating outward over a low pivot point; sediments have substantial proportions of both fine earth and rock fragments. Portions of the original material may remain intact, although reoriented, within the resulting debris pile.

Deep convection, In physical oceanography, the sinking of surface waters to form deep water masses, a process of fundamental importance for ocean climate and the maintenance of a stably stratified world ocean. There are two main types of deep convection, the physics of which are very different. The first is convection near an open boundry, which involves the formation of a dense water mass which reaches the bottom of the ocean by descending a continental slope. The second type is open-ocean deep convection, Where the sinking occurs far from land and is predominantly vertical.

Deflation basin, A topographic basin excavated and maintained by wind erosion which removes unconsolidated material and commonly leaves a rim of resistant material surrounding the depression. Unlike a blowout, a deflation basin does not include adjacent deposits derived from the basin.

Deflation, (a form of erosion) The entrainment and transport of fine (mostly clay, silt, fine sand), dry, generally unconsolidated, sediment from a source deposit by the action of wind turbulence; the re-deposited sediment may be concentrated as eolian dunes (sand) or loess (clay, silt, and very fine sand). *(Fig. 97)*

Degenerate amphidromic point, An amphidromic point whose center or nodal point appears to be located over land rather than water.

Degradation, The lowering of a bottomland surface through the process of erosion; conceptually it is the opposite of the vertical component of aggradation and is most frequently applied to sediment removed from a channel bed or other low-lying parts of a stream channel.

Delta plain, The level or nearly level surface composing the land-ward part of a large delta; strictly, a flood plain characterized by repeated channel bifurcation and divergence, multiple distributary channels, and interdistributary flood basins.

Delta, A body of alluvium, nearly flat and fan-shaped, deposited at or near the mouth of a river or stream where it enters a body of relatively quiet water, usually a sea or lake. A fan-shaped landform of fluvial sediment deposited at and beyond the mouth of a stream, usually a river, as it debouches into a body of standing or low-velocity water, generally an ocean or lake, or some other water body of reduced or stagnant flow. As a delta continues to form and grow outward from the mouth of the stream into the standing water, channel gradient is minimized and the stream typically separates into a complex of relatively straight channel distributaries that are poorly capable of carrying the coarser fractions of their total sediment loads to the distal edge of the delta. *(Fig. 62)*

Dendritic drainage pattern, A common drainage pattern in which the tributaries join the gently curving mainstream at acute angles, resembling in plan view the branching habit of an oak or chestnut tree; it is produced where a consequent stream receives several tributaries which in turn are fed by smaller tributaries. It indicates streams flowing across horizontal rock strata and homogenous soil typified by the landforms of soft sedimentary rocks, volcanic tuff, old dissected coastal plains, or complex crystalline rocks offering uniform resistance to erosion. *(Fig. 69)*

Dendrochronology, The dating of past events, including climate fluctuations, through the counting of annual tree rings and analysis of the sizes and structure of the rings; the application of dendrochronology to geomorphology, sometimes termed dendrogeomorphology, is the use of dendrochronological techniques to interpret and date earth-surface processes and resulting landforms.

Denudation, The sum of the processes that result in the wearing away or the progressive lowering of the earth's surface by various natural agencies that include weathering, erosion, mass wasting, and transportation. *(Fig.42)*

Deposit, Either consolidated or unconsolidated material of any type that has accumulated by natural processes or by human activity.

Deposition, The constructive process of accumulation into beds or irregular masses of loose sediment or other rock material by any natural agent; it is especially the mechanical settling of sediment from suspension or tractive movement in water.

Depression, Any relatively sunken part of the Earth's surface; especially a low-lying area surrounded by higher ground. A closed depression has no natural outlet for surface drainage (e.g., a sinkhole). An open depression has a natural outlet for surface drainage.

Deranged drainage pattern, A distinctively disordered drainage pattern of nonintegrated streams which indicates a complete lack of underlying structural and bedrock control, resulting from a relatively young landscape having a flat or undulating topographic surface and a high water table. It is characterized by relatively few, irregular streams with few, short tributaries, that flow into and out of depressions containing swamps, bogs, marshes, ponds, or lakes; interstream areas are swampy. Regional streams may meander through the area but do not influence its drainage. These drainage patterns commonly occur on young, thick till plains, end moraines, flood plains, and coastal plains.

Desert pavement, A natural, residual concentration or layer of wind-polished, closely packed gravel, boulders, and other rock fragments, mantling a desert surface. It is formed where wind action and sheetwash have removed all smaller particles or where rock fragments have migrated upward through sediments to the surface. It usually protects the underlying, finer-grained material from further deflation.

Desert, A generic term describing an area of low precipitation relative to evaporation; typically, the term desert applies to areas receiving less than 250 mm mean annual precipitation, but areas of higher precipitation are also considered deserts if evaporation rates are high. Owing to low precipitation, very cold areas, such as Antarctica, may be classed as deserts.

Desertification, Land degradation in arid, semi-arid, and dry ' Sub-humid areas resulting from various factors, including climatic variations and human activities. The United Nations Convention to Combat Desertification defines land degradation as a reduction or loss in arid, semi-arid, and dry sub-humid areas, of the biological or economic productivity and complexity of rain-fed cropland, irrigated cropland, or range, pasture, Forest and woodlands resulting from land uses or from a process or combination of processes, including processes arising from human activities and habitation patterns, such as (i) soil erosion caused by wind and/or water; (ii) deterioration of the physical, chemical and biological or economic properties of soil; and (iii) long-term loss of natural vegetation.

Destructional, [geomorphology] Said of a landform that owes its origin, form, position, or general character to the removal of material by erosion and weathering (degradation) processes resulting from the wearing-down or away of the land surface.

Detachment, The process of separation of transportable particles from a soil or soft-rock layer, usually by running water, raindrop impact, or wind.

Detrital, The most voluminous of three major components of deep sea sediments, the other two being authigenic and biogenic. Detrital material is derived from the mechanical and chemical fragmentation of continental materials, most of which is in the form of alumino-silicate minerals. It is transported chiefly by rivers into coastal waters and by the wind onto the sea surface.

Detritus, A general collective term for loose mineral and rock that is broken or worn off by mechanical means, as by disintegration or abrasion.

Diagnesis, The chemical, physical, and biological changes sediment undergoes after it is initially de- posited. This includes such processes as compaction, cementation, reworking, authigenesis, replace- ment, crystallization, leaching, hydration, bacterial action, and formation of concretions that normally occur at temperatures and pressures characteristic of surface conditions. Weathering and metamorphic processes are usually excluded from this category.

Diagnostic, In numerical modeling, an equation is diagnostic if the present value of a dependent variable is calculated from the present value(s) of one or more dependent variables.

Diatom ooze, A soft, siliceous, deep-sea deposit of which more than 30% is composed of silica-rich diatom cell walls. This type of siliceous ooze (another of which is radiolarian ooze) predominates in high latitudes around the coast of Antarctica and in the North Pacific, but is overwhelmed by sediment of continental origin in the North Atlantic. This type of ooze covers about 9% of the sea floor. *(Fig. 152)*

Diatomite, A light-colored, soft, siliceous sedimentary rock consisting chiefly of opaline diatom frustules deposited in a lacustrine or marine environment. Diatomite has a number of uses owing to its high surface area, absorptive capacity, and relative chemical stability but the term is generally reserved for deposits of actual or potential commercial value.

Diatoms, Silt-sized algae that live in surface waters of lakes, rivers and oceans and form shells of opal. Their species distribution in ocean cores is often related to past sea surface temperatures.

Differential heating, The difference in how land and water surfaces absorb heat, with water having a higher heat capacity than land. The same amount of solar radiation will heat the same area of ground more than it will the ocean. The heat absorbed by the ocean will be distributed over a greater vertical extent than on land due to mixing in the water column. These factors lead to the difference between land and ocean temperatures being greatest in the summer when the amount of solar radiation is the highest, with the land being warmer than the ocean. In the winter the ocean surface is warmer than the land, although the differential isn't as great as in winter. Diurnal variations in differential heating lead to the phenomenon known as a sea breeze, while long term (i.e. over weeks to months) variations lead to prevailing winds often called monsoons.

Dike, [intrusive rocks] A tabular igneous intrusion that cuts across the bedding or foliation of the country rock. *(Fig. 34)*

Dip slope, A slope of the land surface, roughly determined by and approximately conforming to the dip of underlying bedded rocks; (i.e., the long, gently inclined surface of a cuesta).

Dip, [structural geology] The maximum angle that a structural surface, (e.g., a bedding or fault plane) makes with the horizontal, measured perpendicular to the strike of the structure and in the vertical plane; used in combination with "dip" to describe the orientation of bedrock strata.

Direct tide, A tide which is in phase with the apparent motion of the attracting body, whether it be the sun or the moon. It has its local maximums directly under the tide-producing body and on the opposite side of the earth.

Discharge, (as hydrologic term of streamflow) The movement downstream per unit length of channel of a volume of water; water discharge is given in volume per unit time, typically cubic meters per second (m_3s_{-1}). As a sedimentology term, discharge is the movement of a mass of sediment per unit length of channel in a specified time interval; technically it is expressed in watts per meter ($W\ m_{-1}$), but informally it is viewed as mass per unit time.

Discontinuity, [stratigraphy] Any interruption in sedimentation, whatever its cause or length, usually a manifestation of nondeposition and accompanying erosion; an unconformity.

Discontinuous permafrost, Permafrost occurring in some areas beneath the exposed land surface throughout a geographic region where other areas are free of permafrost.

Disintegration moraine, A drift topography characterized by chaotic mounds and pits, generally randomly oriented, developed in supraglacial drift by collapse and flow as the underlying stagnant ice melted. Slopes may be steep and unstable and there will be used and unused stream courses and lake depressions interspersed with the morainic ridges. Characteristically, there are numerous abrupt, lateral and vertical changes between unconsolidated materials of differing lithology.

Dispersion, The dependence of wave velocity on the frequency of wave motion. The name comes from the fact that waves starting at the same place will, if they have different frequencies, move away at different speeds and thus disperse or spread out.

Dissected breaklands, Very steep slopes flanking major rivers and streams in mountainous terrain and dominated by deeply incised, sub-parallel to dendritic, chute-like drainageways that occupy > 50 % of the ground surface. Dissected breakland slopes are dominated by hillslope elements that grade to secondary drainageways, rather than directly to the axial stream; a type of breakland.

Dissected plateau, A land area (landscape) produced by significant stream erosion and incision of a plateau such that only a small part of the plateau surface is at or near the original summit level. Much of the area occurs as hillslopes, or if incision is sufficient and relief is > 1000 feet, as mountain slopes.

Dissolved load, The part of the total stream load that is carried in solution, such as chemical ions yielded by erosion of the landmass during the return of precipitation to the oceans; also called dissolved solids and solution load.

Dissolved solids, All mineral material in solution in surface or ground waters; the amount of dissolved solids is a measure of the quality of the water and is generally expressed as milligrams per liter. The regulatory acronym for dissolved solids is TDS (total dissolved solids). Distinctions between estuaries are usually made based on the prevailing physical oceanographic con-ditions (principally the salinity distribution) which are governed by the geometry of the estuary, the magnitude of fresh water flow into the estuary, and the magnitude and extent of the tidal motion. The four principal categories into which estuaries are divided using these criteria are well mixed, stratified, arrested salt wedge and fjord entrainment estuaries, although a single estuary can vary seasonally from one type to another.

Distal, (sedimentology) Said of a sedimentary deposit consisting of fine clastics and deposited farthest from the source area.

Distributary, (as a fluvial-geomorphic term) The spitting of a stream channel into two or more segments that leave the main channel and do rejoin it, as generally occurs on deltas; less commonly the term is used to characterize the individual channels of an alluvial fan that split from a main, up-slope, channel and again coalesce downslope.

Disturbance, Any short-term alteration, natural or imposed, of the land surface that results in a change of geomorphic, hydrologic, or biological processes from a state of approximate equilibrium to one of relative instability; time scales of disturbance generally vary from years to centuries.

Ditch, An open and usually unpaved (unlined), channel or trench excavated to convey water for drainage (removal) or irrigation (addition) to or from a landscape; smaller than a canal; some ditches are modified natural waterways.

Diurnal temperature range, The difference between the maximum and mininimum temperature during a 24-hour period.

Diurnal, 1. Generally, occuring once a day. 2. Descriptive of a tide that has only one high and one low water per day, as opposed to semidiurnal.

Divergence, (in a geomorphic contex) A term to acknowledge that some landforms with characteristics measurably different among each other are the end, or final, results of a narrow range of similar process sets causing the landforms. When used in a hydrologic context, divergence, or divergent flow, refers to a broadening or expansion of flow paths as surface runoff traverses a convex slope or as ground water moves from a restricted flow path to one of less restriction.

Divide, A summit area or tract of high ground, which can vary from broad to narrow, or a line of separation that constitutes a watershed boundary between adjacent drainage basins; a divide separates surface waters that flow naturally in one direction from those that flow in a different or opposite direction.

Dolomite, [mineral] A common rock-forming rhombohedral carbonate mineral: $CaMg(CO3)2$. [rock] A carbonate sedimentary rock consisting chiefly (more than 50 percent by weight or by areal percentages under the microscope) of the mineral dolomite.

Dome, (a) An uplift or anticlinal structure, either circular or elliptical in outline, in which the rocks dip gently away in all directions. A dome may be small (e.g., a salt dome) or many kilometers in diameter. (b) A landform that is a smoothly rounded rock mass such as a rock-capped mountain summit that roughly resembles a building dome. *(Fig. 36)*

Dominant discharge, The discharge of a stream that is associated with the maximum sediment-transport rate for specified magnitude and frequency of flow; as such it is a theoretical discharge representing the single flow rate of a stream that accomplishes the most geomorphic work during an extended period of time. The term is an extension of the bankfull-discharge concept and is commonly inferred to be the maximum flow that the channel of an adjusted perennial stream can convey without causing spillage onto the flood plain.

Double tide, Either a high water consisting of two maximums of about the same height separated by a relatively small depression or a low water consisting of two minimums separated by a relatively small elevation. This has also been called a double high water, an agger, and a gulder.

Drainage basin, An area of land surface, upslope from a specified channel site to topographic divides separating the basin from adjacent drainage basins, over which water that results from precipitation moves and converges through a system of channels to the specified channel site. *(Fig. 53)*

Drainage density, The ratio of the combined stream lengths of a drainage basin to the basin area (km km$_{-2}$); drainage density is indicative of the facility by which excess rainfall moves from an upland surface. High values of drainage density are indicative of high transfer efficiency and therefore of high peak discharge.

Drainage network, The system of channels and other paths of conveyance for water and sediment moving downslope through a drainage basin. *(Fig. 53)*

Drainage pattern, The configuration or arrangement, in plan view, of stream courses in an area, including gullies or first-order channelized flow areas, higher order tributaries, and main streams. Drainage pattern is related to local geologic materials and structure, geomorphologic features, and geomorphic history of an area. Major drainage pattern types include dendritic, trellis, artificial, etc. Also called drainage network. *(Fig. 69)*

Drainageway, (a) A general term for a course or channel along which water moves in draining an area. (b) [soil survey] a term restricted to relatively small, roughly linear or arcuate depressions that move concentrated water at some time, and either lack a defined channel (e.g., head slope, swale) or have a small, defined channel (e.g., low order streams).

Dredge spoils, Unconsolidated, randomly mixed sediments composed of rock, soil, and/or shell materials extracted and deposited during dredging and dumping activities. Dredge spoils lie unconformably upon natural, undisturbed soil or regolith and can form anthropogenic landforms (e.g., dredge spoil bank).

Dredged channel, A roughly linear, deep water area formed by a dredging operation for navigation purposes.

Dredge-deposit shoal , A subaqueous area, substantially shallower than the surrounding area that resulted from the deposition of materials from dredging and dumping (modified from Demas 1998).

Drift, A term with different meanings depending on whether the topic is caves, coastal studies, geophysics, hydraulics, or surface-water hydrology; as applied to glacial geology and geomorphology, drift is rock debris of any size deposited by ice of a glacier or sediment-laden meltwater flowing from a glacier. Related terms are outwash and till.

Dropstone, An oversized stone (compared to the matrix sediments) in laminated sediment that depresses the underlying laminae and can be covered by "draped laminae". Most dropstones originate through ice-rafting; another source is floating tree roots.

Drought, In general terms, drought is a' prolonged absence or marked deficiency of precipitation', a 'deficiency that results in water shortage for some activity or for some group', or a 'period of abnormally dry weather sufficiently prolonged for the lack of precipitation to cause a serious hydrological imbalance' ie:Drought has been defined in a number of ways. Agricultural drough trelates to moisture deficits in the topmost 1 metre or so of soil (the root zone) that affect crops, meteorological drought is mainly a prolonged deficit of precipitation, and hydrologic drought is related to below-normal streamflow, lake and groundwater levels. A megadrought is a long-drawn out and pervasive drought, lasting much longer than normal, usually a decade or more.

Drumlin, A low, smooth, elongated oval hill, mound, or ridge of compact till that has a core of bedrock or drift. It usually has a blunt nose facing the direction from which the ice approached and a gentler slope tapering in the other direction. The longest axis is parallel to the general direction of glacier flow. Drumlins are products of streamline (laminar) flow of glaciers, which molded the subglacial floor through a combination of erosion and deposition. *(Fig. 95)*

Drumlin field, Groups or clusters of closely spaced drumlins or drumlinoid ridges, distributed more or less en echelon, and commonly separated by small, marshy tracts or depressions (interdrumlins). *(Fig. 95)*

Drumlinoid ridge, A rock drumlin or drift deposit whose form approaches but does not fully attain that of a classic drumlin, even though it seemingly results from similar processes of moving ice.

Dry wash, A channel in which streamflow occurs inconsistently or infrequently and, except during periods of streamflow, is directly underlain by unsaturated alluvium; dry washes are most common in arid and semiarid regions and typically have a rectangular to steeply sided trapezoidal cross section, banks a meter or more in height formed of fine-grained, poorly consolidated over-bank sediment, and a nearly flat, sandy bed. Synonyms are ephemeral-stream channel, arroyo (northern Mexico and southwestern United States), and wadi (southwestern Asia, Arabian peninsula, and northern Africa).

Dump, An area of smooth or uneven accumulations or piles of waste rock, earthy material, or general refuse that without major reclamation are incapable of supporting plants.

Dune lake, (a) A lake occupying a deflation basin as in a blowout on a dune. (b) A lake occupying a basin formed by the blocking of a stream by sand dunes migrating along a shore.

Dune slack, A damp depression or trough between dunes in a dune field or dune ridges on a shore, caused by intersecting the capillary fringe of the local water table; a moist type of interdune.

Dune traces, A series of linear to semi-concentric micro-ridges and intervening troughs, on the floor of a dune slack or interdune that were exposed by deflation or dune migration. The ridges are remnant bases of slip face lamina held together by soil moisture and /or cemented by evaporites.

Dune, (including dune field) An accumulation, or concentration, by depositional processes of water or wind as a low, small-scale mound, ridge, or, more commonly, a complex (field, or zone) of mounds and ridges, of loose, well sorted granular material (generally sand) that, if active, may be bare or, if inactive, partially to fully vegetated; dunes are subject to translocation, without a basic loss of scale or structure, by the action of streamflow, waves, or wind. *(Fig. 79)*

Duricrust, An accumulation of mineral precipitates at or near the land surface of generally semiarid areas; a calcium-rich duricrust is a calcrete and a silica-rich duricrust is termed a duripan.

Dynamic height, In oceanography, this refers to the pressure associated with a column of water. Horizontal variations of this (due to horizontal variations in temperature and salinity) are mapped to determine what is called the dynamic topography and its corresponding geostrophic flow field in the ocean. Dynamic topography In oceanography, a field of horizontally varying dynamic heights in the ocean, analogous to, for example, a topography field on land. This is also called geopotential topography.

Dynamic topography, In oceanography, a field of horizontally varrying dynamic hights in the o lean, analogous of, for example, a topography of field on land. This is alos called geopotential topography.

E

Earth pillar , A tall, conical column of unconsolidated to semi-consolidated earth materials (e.g., clay till, or landslide debris) produced by differential erosion and usually capped by a flat, hard rock fragment that shields the underlying, softer material from erosion. It can measure up to 6-20 m in height, and its diameter is a function of the width of the protective boulder.

Earth spread , The mass movement process, associated sediments (earth spread deposit), or resultant landform characterized by a very rapid type of spread dominated by lateral movement in a soil mass resulting from liquefaction or plastic flow of underlying materials that may be extruded out between intact units.

Earth topple , The mass movement process, associated sediments (earth topple deposit), or resultant landform characterized by a localized, very rapid type of topple in which large blocks of soil material literally fall over, rotating outward over a low pivot point; sediments < 2 mm predominate. Portions of the original material may remain intact, although reoriented, within the resulting deposit.

Earthflow, The mass movement process, associated sediments (earthflow deposit), or resultant landform characterized by slow to rapid flow dominated by downslope movement of soil, rock, and mud (more than 50% of the particles are < 2 mm), and whether saturated or comparatively dry, behaves as a viscous fluid when moving. *(Fig. 48)*

East Arabian Current, A strong northeastward flowing current along the Saudi Arabian coast. It is part of the monsoonal circulation in the area and as such exists from about April through October, being fully established by mid-May with velocities ranging form 0.5-0.8 m/s. It is also part of a strong coastal upwelling system during those months when it flows strongest.

East Indian Current, A seasonal and northward flowing current found in the western part of the Bay of Bengal from about January until October. The weak and variable currents found early strengthen with the Northeast Monsoon, exceeding 0.5 m/s by March and ranging from 0.7-1.0 m/s through May and June. This current flows counter to the wind, apparently as an extension of the North Equatorial Current, although a convincing dynamical explanation has yet to be offered. The northward flow gradually weakens with the advent of the Southwest Monsoon, with the currents to the north and close to the shelf beginning to reverse in September. By late October, the East Indian Current has completely reversed into the East Indian Winter Jet.

East Indian Winter Jet, A seasonal southwestward flowing western boundry current found in the western Bay of Bengal from late October through around late December. It has velocities consistently above 1m/s as it flows southwestward, eventually turing west and following topographic contours as it passes Sri Lanka and feeds all its waters into the Arabian Sea. In late December its northern part fades, eventually to become the East Indian Current, and the southern part merges with the developing North Equatorial Current.

Ebb current, The tidal current existing during any time the height of the tide is decreasing. These generally flow in a seaward direction. This has been erroneously called ebb tide.

Ebb interval. The interval between the transit of the moon over a meridian and the time of strength of ebb of the following tide.

Echo sounder, An instrument used to determine ocean depth by measuring the time needed for a sound wave to travel from the ship to the ocean floor and return. The first reliable acoustical sounding machine was built by A. Behm in 1919, who called it an echo sounder. An echo sounder consists of three main components : the sound transmitter, the sound receiver, and a device to measure time.

Ecohydrology Branch of natural science that describes interactions between ecosystems and hydrologic processes by considering how those processes affect the distributions, functions, and dynamics of biota, and by identifying feedbacks from biota to the hydrologic cycle.

Ecosystem, A system of living organisms interacting with each other and their physical environment. The boundaries of what could be called an ecosystem are somewhat arbitrary, depending on the focus of interest or study. Thus, the extent of an ecosystem may range from very small spatial scales to, ultimately, the entire Earth.

Eddy heat flux, In physical oceanography, the total meridional heat transport due to mesoscale eddies. This has also been used to refer to the correlation of time-dependent fluctuations of velocity and temperature across a section, which is not indicative of the total heat transport due to eddies. Eddies can also induce a thermally driven, overturning cell in subtropical gyres that is analogous to the Ferrel cell in the atmosphere.

Edge wave, A wave which travels parallel to a coastline with crests normal to the coastline. The height of the wave diminishes rapidly offshore.

Effective precipitation That portion of rainfall, generally measured in millimeters (mm), resulting in runoff and sustaining soil moisture available for plant growth; owing to elevated rates of evapotranspiration, effective precipitation in arid and semiarid regions is generally lower than it is in high-latitude areas with the same measured precipitation but lower evapotranspiration.

El Nino, A term originally applied as a description of an annual weak warm current running Southward along the coast of Peru and Ecuador during the Christmas holiday, i.e. the Spanish word for "the boy christ-child" is Nino. a The name El Nino eventually became associated with unusually large warmings that occur every few years and effect large changes on the local, regional, and even global climate. It gradually became known that the coastal warming was part of a much larger warming of the upper waters of the Pacific extending as far as the international date line. There is an associated atmospheric phenomenon called the Southern Oscillation, with the combined changes in atmosphere and ocean termed El Nino/Southern Oscillation or ENSO, with El Nino properly referring the warm phase of ENSO. A typical El Nino event begins in the nothern spring or sometimes summer, peaks from November to January in and ends the following summer. The opposite phase is similarly called La Nina, i.e. Spanish for "the girl," and features a basinwide cooling in the tropical Pacific. The entire system is called El Nino in many if not most popular accounts. *(Fig. 190)*

El Nino-Southern Oscillation (ENSO), The term El Nino was initially used to describe a warm-water current that periodically flows along the coast of Ecuador and Peru, disrupting the local fishery. It has since become identified with a basin-wide warming of the tropical Pacific Ocean east of the dateline. This oceanic event is associated with a fluctuation of a global-scale tropical and subtropical surface pressure pattern called the Southern Oscillation. This coupled atmosphere-ocean phenomenon, with preferred time scales of two to about seven years, is collectively known as the El Niflo-Southern Oscillation (ENSO). It is often measured by the surface pressure anomaly difference between Darwin and Tahiti and the sea surface temperatures in the central and eastern equatorial Pacific. During an ENSO event, the prevailing trade winds weaken, reducing upwelling and altering ocean currents such that the sea surface temperatures warm, further weakening the trade winds. This event has a great impact on the wind, sea surface temperature and precipitation patterns in the tropical Pacific. It has climatic effects throughout the Pacific region and in many other parts of the world, through global teleconnections. The cold phase of ENSO is called La Nina. *(Fig. 190, 191)*

Elevation, [survey] The height of a point on the earth's surface relative to mean sea level (msl).

Eluviation The hydrologic process by which water percolates downward and out of a soil zone, moving dissolved solids, colloids, and organic material from the surface through the A horizon into the B horizon; precipitation of dissolved solids, especially as carbonate minerals, in the B horizon may be an important process of calcrete formation.

Emission scenario, A plausible representation of the future development of emissions of substances that are potentially radiatively active (e.g., greenhouse gases, aerosols), based on a coherent and internally consistent set of assumptions about driving forces (such as demographic and socioeconomic development, technological change) and their key relationships

Emissivity, The ratio of the emittance from a body to that of a black body emitter at the same temperature, i.e. the degree to which a real body approaches a black body radiator.

Emittance, The rate at which radiation is emitted from a unit area.

End moraine , A ridge-like accumulation that is being or was produced at the outer margin of an actively flowing glacier at any given time; a moraine that has been deposited at the outer or lower end of a valley glacier. *(Fig. 88)*

Energy balance, The difference between the total incoming and total outgoing energy. If this balance is positive, warming occurs; if it is negative, cooling occurs. Averaged over the globe and over long time periods, this balance must be zero. Because the climate system derives virtually all its energy from the Sun. Zero balance implies that, globally, the amount of incoming solar radiation on average must be equal to the sum of the outgoing reflected solar radiation and the outgoing thermal infrared radiation emitted by the climate system. A perturbation of this global radiation balance, be it anthropogenic or natural, is called radiative forcing. *(Fig. 169)*

Entrainment The process by flowing water or air, or by the mixing of water or air between opposing currents, of mobilizing sediment by picking up particles and transporting them in suspension, as suspended load, and along the channel or other surface of transfer, as bed (or traction) load; rates of hydrologic entrainment depend on stream power (the product of discharge and water-surface slope) and the sizes of the sediment particles.

Eocene, An epoch (from 35.4 to 56.5 million years ago) of the Tertiary Period of geologic time that follows the Paleocene and precedes the Oligocene epoch; also the corresponding (time-stratigraphic) "series" of earth materials.

Eolian (or aeolian) The entrainment processes of erosion and sediment transport, deposition, and translocation (mainly sorting) by wind; eolian features include wind-blown sand forming dune fields, atmospherically deposited silt and fine sand (loess) and volcanic ash (tuff), and erosional landforms such as yardangs. *(Fig. 99)*

Eolian deposit, [soil survey] Sand, silt or clay-sized clastic material transported and deposited primarily by wind, commonly in the form of a dune or a sheet of sand or loess. Conventionally, primary volcanic deposits (e.g., tephra) are handled separately.

Eolian dune, (including **eolian dune field**) An accumulation, or concentration, by depositional processes of wind as a low, small-scale mound, ridge, or, more commonly, a complex (field, or zone) of mounds and ridges, of loose, well sorted granular material (generally sand) that, if active, may be bare or, if inactive, partially to fully vegetated; eolian dunes are subject to translocation, without a basic loss of scale or structure, by the action of wind.

Eolian sands, [soil survey] Sand-sized, clastic material transported and deposited primarily by wind, commonly in the form of a dune or a sand sheet.

Ephemeral gully, A gully, typically in an agricultural field, that develops due to water erosion during a growing season but which is subject to removal by any primary tillage operation.

Ephemeral stream, Streamflow within a normally dry channel; the streamflow occurs inconsistently or infrequently and, except during periods when the ephemeral streamflows occur, the channel bed is directly underlain by unsaturated alluvium.

Ephemeral-stream channel, A channel in which streamflow occurs inconsistently or infrequently and, except during periods of streamflow, is directly underlain by unsaturated alluvium or rock; ephemeral-stream channels are most common in arid and semiarid regions and typically have a rectangular to steeply sided trapezoidal cross section, banks a meter or more in height formed of fine-grained, poorly consolidated over-bank sediment, and a nearly flat, sandy bed. Synonyms are dry wash, arroyo (northern Mexico and southwestern United States), and wadi (southwestern Asia, Arabian Peninsula, and northern Africa).

Epiclastic, Pertaining to any clastic rock or sediment other than pyroclastic. Constituent fragments are derived by weathering and erosion rather than by direct volcanic processes.

Epicontinental sea, A shallow sea on a wide portion of a continental shelf or in the interior of a continent. The former type is also known as a shelf sea.

Epilimnion, The layer of water above the thermocline in a fresh water lake, as opposed to the hypolimnion. This is equivalent to the mixed layer in the ocean.

Epipelagic zone, One of five vertical ecological zones into which the deep sea is sometimes divided. The epipelagic zone extends from the surface downward as far as sunlight penetrates during the day. It is a very thin layer, less than 100 meters thick in the eastern parts of the oceans in regions of upwelling and high productivity and up to 200 meters thick in clear subtropical areas. The endemic species of this zone either do not migrate or perform only limited vertical migrations, although there are many animals that do invade the epipelagic zone from deeper layers during the night or pass their early development stages in the photic zone. The epipelagic zone overlies the mesopelagic zone.

Equatorial Countercurrent, In physical oceanography, a subsurface eastward flow that is about 100-200 m thick and 200-300 km wide. It is centered approximately on the equator, and its core lies just beneath the base of the mixed layer in the top of the equatorial thermocline. Such a current is found in all three oceans, although it appears to be a seasonal phenomenon in the Indian Ocean.

Equatorial trough, A region of lower pressure located between the subtropical highs on each side of the equator. Within this zone the trade wind airstreams from either hemisphere meet causing ascending motion and large amounts of precipitation. It constitutes the equatorward, ascending portions of the Hadley mean meridional circulation cells of both hemispheres.

Equatorial undercurrent, In physical oceanography, a subsurface eastward flow centered approximately on the equator whose core lies just beneath the base of the mixed layer in the top of the equatorial thermocline. The flow generally ranges from 100-200 m thick and 200-300 km in width. Such a current is found in all three oceans, although it appears to be a seasonal phenomenon in the Indian Ocean. In the Atlantic its core is around 100 m deep with speeds exceeding 1.2 m/s, between extreme positions 90 km on either side of the Equator on a 2-3 week time scale.

Equifinality, (in a geomorphic context) A term to recognize that some landforms, such as braided stream channels, are the end, or final, results of a wide range of possible process sets yielding the observed landform; the concept of geomorphic equifinality is roughly analogous to the biological concept of convergent evolution, which is an acknowledgement that initially dissimilar species, if subjected to similar environmental conditions over long time periods, may develop closely similar physical and behavioral characteristics. As applied to watersheds, a range of different disturbances, both intrinsic and extrinsic, may ultimately yield similar down-basin landforms; a braided stream channel is one of many examples.

Equilibrium tide, The hypothetical tide which would exist if the ocean responded instantly to the tide producing forces and formed an equilibrium surface. The effects of friction, inertia, and the irregular distribution of land masses are ignored. *(Fig. 136)*

Equilibrium, (as a means of characterizing a geomorphic feature) To the balance between inputs and outputs, mostly water, dissolved solids, and sediment (including specific particle sizes), that must be attained to achieve stability. Because fluxes of matter and energy are never constant in natural landscapes, the term equilibrium, when applied to geomorphic systems, is generally modified by "dynamic" or "quasi", implying that the feature or process is time-integrated and adjusted to the range of inflows and outflows typical of the system. The term is often used synonymously with geomorphic stability.

Equivalent barotropic, An atmospheric state in which the temperature gradients are such that the isotherms are parallel to the isobars.

Equivalent potential temperature, In meteorology, the equivalent temperature of an air sample when it is brought adiabatically to a pressure of 1000 mb. It is a conservative property for both dry and saturated adiabatic processes.

Ergodic hypothesis, The assumption that a process is statistically stationary, and therefore ensemble averaging is equivalent to averaging over time.

Eroded fan remnant, All, or a portion of an alluvial fan that is much more extensively eroded and dissected than a fan remnant; sometimes called an erosional fan remnant . It consists primarily of eroded and highly dissected sides (eroded fan-remnant sideslopes) dominated by hillslope positions (shoulder, backslope, etc.), and to a lesser extent an intact, relatively planar, relict alluvial fan "summit" area best described as a tread.

Erodibility, An expression of the susceptibility of a surface to the erosion process; thus, it is the ease by which sediment, rock, or especially soil is detached and entrained, generally by rainsplash, surface flow, or wind. Erodibility, in quantitative terms, is the loss in mass per unit area of a sediment, rock, or soil surface that results from application of a known external energy or shear.

Erosion pavement, A surficial lag concentration or layer of gravel and other rock fragments that remains on the soil surface after sheet or rill erosion or wind has removed the finer soil particles and that tends to protect the underlying soil from further erosion.

Erosion remnant, A topographic feature that remains or is left standing above the general land surface after erosion has reduced the surrounding area; e.g., a monadnock, a butte, or a stack.

Erosion surface, A land surface shaped by the action of erosion, especially by running water.

Erosion, The process of detachment and transport of soil particles by the erosive agents of raindrop impact and surface runoff from rainfall.

Erosivity, An expression of the capacity of rainfall to detach particles from a soil surface and initiate the erosion process; it should not be confused with erodibility, which expresses the susceptibility of soil, sediment, or rock to erosion processes. Research has demonstrated that the erosivity (of rainfall) for an individual storm approximates the product of the energy of the storm and its maximum 30-minute intensity.

Erratic, A rock fragment carried by glacial ice, or by floating ice (ice-rafting), and subsequently deposited at some distance from the outcrop from which it was derived, and generally, though not necessarily, resting on bedrock or sediments of different lithology. Fragments range in size from a pebble to a house-size block. *(Fig. 96)*

Escarpment, A relatively continuous and steep slope or cliff produced by erosion or faulting and that topographically interrupts or breaks the general continuity of more gently sloping land surfaces. The term is most commonly applied to cliffs produced by differential erosion. *(Fig. 115)*

Escarpment, (undersea feature) A elongated, characteristically linear, steep slope separating horizontal or gently sloping sectors of the sea floor in non-shelf areas; also abbreviated to scarp.

Esker, A long, narrow, sinuous and steep-sided ridge composed of irregularly stratified sand and gravel deposited as the bed of a stream flowing in an ice tunnel within or below the ice (subglacial) or between ice walls on top of the ice of a wasting glacier, and left behind as high ground when the ice melted. Eskers range in length from less than a kilometer to more than 160 kilometers, and in height from 3 to 30 meters. *(Fig. 95)*

Estuarine deposit, Fine-grained sediments (very fine sand, silt and clay) of marine and fluvial origin commonly containing decomposed organic matter, laid down in the brackish waters of an estuary; characteristically finer sediments than deltaic deposits.

Estuarine subaqueous soils, Soils that form in sediment found in shallow-subtidal environments in protected estuarine coves, bays, inlets, and lagoons.

Estuary, (as a geomorphic feature) The funnel-shaped river-valley reach where the river deboucnes into a marine environment. Most estuaries are continental-margin stream valleys that were formed by typical fluvial processes at a time, generally glacial, of lowered sea level. Owing to glacial retreat and rise in sea level, the valley of the formerly free-flowing near-coast river became flooded as an estuary of a mixture of fresh river water and saline marine water. A semi-enclosed body of water having a free connection with the open sea and within which sea water is measurably diluted with fresh water derived from land drainage. The term has traditionally been applied to the lower reaches of rivers into which sea water intrudes and mixes with fresh water as well as to bays, inlets, gulfs and sounds into which several rivers might empty and in which the mixing of fresh and salt water occurs. *(Fig. 63)*

Eulerian velocity, That velocity which would be measured by a current meter at a fixed point. Compare and contrast to Lagrangian velocity and Stokes velocity

Euphotic zone, In the ocean, the sunlit layer from the surface to the depth of 1% light level wherein most of the primary productivity takes place. The depth varies geographically and seasonally and can range from a few meters in turbid, highly productive waters near the shore to around 200 m in tropical waters. The ocean average is around 100 m. It is a zone with sharp gradients in illumination, temperature and salinity, and overlies the aphotic zone. It is also known as the photic zone.

Eustatic, Descriptive of global sea level variations due to absolute changes in the quantity of seawater, the most recent significant examples of which have been caused by the waxing and waning of continental ice sheets during glaciation cycles.

Eutrophic, A situation in which the increased availability of nutrients such as nitrate and phosphate (e.g. from the use of agricultural fertilizers and the combustion of fossil fuels) stimulates the growth of plants such that the oxygen content is depleted and carbon sequestered. It is hypothesized that this might serve as a negative feedback to an increase in atmospheric CO_2.

Eutrophication, The process by which water, generally ponded or stagnant, becomes enriched in dissolved nutrients and deficient in dissolved oxygen; typically, the process occurs when runoff from fertilized fields transports phosphates into the water body, thereby causing algal blooms and a consequent depletion of dissolved oxygen.

Evaporation, The conversion of water to a gaseous or vapor state.

Evapotranspiration, The combined process of evaporation from the Earth's surface and transpiration from vegetation. The loss of water from any surface by the combined processes of evaporation and transpiration; actual evapotranspiration, the actual rate of water loss to the atmosphere is a concept often used by hydrologists for water-balance studies, whereas potential evapotranspiration, a threoretical water loss under conditions of continuous saturation, is used especially by climatologists. *(Fig. 167)*

Everglades, A large expanse of marshy land, covered mostly by grasses, e.g., the Florida Everglades.

Exceedance probability, The probability, or likelihood, that the peak discharge of a designated flood event will exceed a specified discharge within some standard period of time, generally a water year.

Exchangeable sodium percentage, The percent of the cation exchange capacity of soil or sediment that is due to sodium.

Exfoliation, The process by which concentric scales, plates, or shells of rock, from less than a centimeter to several meters in thickness, are successively spalled or stripped from the bare surface of a large rock mass. It often results in a rounded rock mass or dome-shaped hill.

Exhumed, Formerly buried landforms, geomorphic surfaces, or paleosols that have been re-exposed by erosion of the covering mantle.

Expansion reach, (of a stream or channel) A length of the stream or channel in which the width increases to the degree that flow spreads over the widened section of channel bed, causing a corresponding increase in cross-sectional area of the flow and reductions in flow depth and velocity. Owing to lowered velocity as a stream enters an expansion reach, the ability of flow to transport coarse sediment is diminished and deposition as bars or other in-channel features occurs. For this reason, channel islands commonly form in expansion reaches.

Extramorainal, Said of deposits and phenomena occurring outside the area occupied by a glacier and its lateral and end moraines.

Extrusive, Said of igneous rocks and sediments derived from deep-seated, molten matter (magma), deposited and cooled on the earth's surface (e.g., including lava flows and tephra deposits). *(Fig. 38)*

F

Faceted spur, The inverted V-shaped end of a ridge that has been truncated or steeply beveled by steam erosion (e.g., meander scar or bluff), glacial truncation, or fault scarp displacement.

Facies, [stratigraphy] A distinctive group of characteristics that distinguish one group from another within a stratigraphic unit; the sum of all primary lithologic and paleontological characteristics of sediments or sedimentary rock that are used to infer its origin and environment; the general nature of appearance of sediments or sedimentary rock produced under a given set of conditions; e.g., contrasting river-channel facies and overbank-flood plain facies in alluvial valley fills.

Fall, – (a) A category of mass movement processes, associated sediments (fall deposit), or resultant landforms (e.g., rockfall, debris fall, soil fall) characterized by very rapid movement of a mass of rock or earth that travels mostly through the air by free fall, leaping, bounding, or rolling, with little or no interaction between one moving unit and another. (b) The mass of material moved by a fall.

Falling dune, An accumulation of sand that is formed as sand is blown off a mesa top or over a cliff face or steep slope, forming a solid wall, sloping at the angle of repose of dry sand, or a fan extending downward from a re-entrant in the mesa wall.

Falling tide, That interval of the tidal cycle between a high water and the following low water. This is also known as ebb tide.

Fan apron, A sheet-like mantle of relatively young alluvium and soils covering part of an older fan piedmont (and occasionally alluvial fan) surface, commonly thicker and further down slope (e.g., mid-fan or mid-fan piedmont) than a fan collar. It somewhere buries an older soil that can be traced to the edge of the fan apron where the older soil emerges as the land surface, or relict soil. No buried soils should occur within a fan apron mantle itself.

Fan collar, A landform comprised of a thin, short, relatively young mantle of alluvium along the very upper margin (near the proximal end or apex) of a major alluvial fan. The young mantle somewhere buries an older soil that can be traced to the edge of the collar where the older soil emerges at the land surface as a relict soil.

Fan piedmont ,The most extensive landform on piedmont slopes, formed by: 1) the lateral, downslope, coalescence of mountain-front alluvial fans into one generally smooth slope with or without the transverse undulations of the semi-conical alluvial fans, and: 2) accretion of fan aprons.

Fan remnant , A general term for landforms that are the remaining parts of older fan-landforms, such as alluvial fans, fan aprons, inset fans, and fan skirts, that either have been dissected (erosional fan-remnants) or partially buried (nonburied fan-remnants). An erosional fan remnant must have a relatively flat summit that is a relict fan-surface. A nonburied fan-remnant is a relict surface in its entirety.

Fan skirt, The zone of smooth, laterally-coalescing, small alluvial fans that issue from gullies cut into the fan piedmont of a basin or that are coalescing extensions of the inset fans of the fan piedmont, and that merge with the basin floor at their toeslopes. These are generally younger fans which onlap older fan surfaces.

Fan, [geomorphology] (a) A gently sloping, fan-shaped mass of detritus forming a section of a low-angle cone commonly at a place where there is a notable decrease in gradient; specifically an alluvial fan (not preferred – use alluvial fan). (b) A fan-shaped mass of congealed lava that formed on a steep slope by the continually changing direction of flow.

Fanglomerate, A sedimentary rock consisting of waterworn, heterogeneous fragments of all sizes, deposited in an alluvial fan and later cemented into a firm rock.

Fanhead trench, A linear depression formed by a drainageway that is incised considerably below the surface of an alluvial fan.

Fault, A discrete surface (fracture) or zone of discrete surfaces separating two rock masses across which one mass has slid past the other. *(Fig. 28)*

Fault block, A displaced crustal unit, formed during block faulting, that is bounded by faults, either completely or in part, and behaves as a coherent unit during tectonic activity.

Fault line, The trace of a fault plane on the ground surface or on a reference plane.

Fault zone, A fault that is expressed as a zone of numerous small fractures or of breccia or fault gouge. A fault zone may be as wide as hundreds of meters.

Fault-block mountains, Mountains that formed primarily by block faulting, and commonly exhibit asymmetrical rotation and vertical displacement from a horizontal plane by large, coherent fault-block units hinged along fault lines; common in , but not limited to, the Basin and Range region of the western USA. The term is not applied to mountains formed by thrust-faulting.

Fault-line scarp, A steep slope or cliff formed by differential erosion along a fault line, as by the more rapid erosion of soft rock on the side of a fault as compared to that of more resistant rock on the other side; e.g., the eastern face of the Sierra Nevada in California.

Felsenmeer, A type of block field, a continuous surface cover of large angular to subangular rocks derived from an underlying source of well jointed bedrock; the blocks are generally dislodged by frost action and form a layer greater than one or two clast thicknesses (as opposed to a rock veneer, which has a thickness no greater than two clast thicknesses).

Felsic rock, A general term for igneous rock containing abundant, light-colored minerals (granite, etc); also applied to those minerals (quartz, feldspars, feldspathoids, muscovite) as a group.

Fen, Waterlogged, spongy ground containing alkaline decaying vegetation, characterized by reeds, that develops into peat. It sometimes occurs in sinkholes of karst regions.

Ferrel cell, A mid-latitude mean atmospheric circulation cell for weather proposed by Ferrel in the 19th century, In this cell the air flows poleward and eastward near the surface and equatorward and westward at higher levels. This is now known to disagree with reality, although it is sometimes used to describe a mid-latitude circulation identifiable in mean meridionaln wind patterns. *(Fig. 182)*

Fill, (a) Human-constructed deposits of natural earth materials (e.g., soil, gravel, rock) and waste materials (e.g., tailings or spoil from dredging) used to fill a depression, to extend shore land into a body of water, or in building dams. (b) Soil or loose rock used to raise the surface level of low-lying land, such as an embankment to fill a hollow or ravine in roads construction.

Filled marshland , A subaerial soil area composed of fill materials (construction debris, dredged or pumped sandy or shell-rich sediments, etc.) deposited and smoothed to provide building sites and associated uses (e.g., lawns, driveways, parking lots). These fill materials are typically 0.5 to 3 m thick and have been deposited unconformably over natural soils.

Fissure vent, An opening in earth's surface of a volcanic conduit in the form of a crack or fissure rather than a localized crater; a roughly linear crack or area along which lava, generally mafic and of low viscosity, wells up to the surface, usually without any explosive activity. The results can be an extensive lava plateau.

Fjord, The term fjord, has been rather loosely applied to geological structures developed by glacial erosion and partly filled with seawater. Its original Norwegian usage also included freshwater lakes and, more recently, the term 'fjord-lake' has been used to describe lakes in glacially carved valleys, but we shall here be strictly concerned only with semi-enclosed coastal inlets. The same coastal structures have been alternatively called sounds, inlets or arms. Several features characteristic of most fjords are,

- there is usually a river discharging into the head, with the head used to describe the inland termination of the fjord (and the mouth the seaward opening) .

- they are steep sided and deep (often deeper than the adjacent continental shelf);

- they are usually long relative to their width;

- they typically possess one or more submarine sills which define the deep basin(s) of the fjord and which may be remnant moraines; *(Fig. 128)*

Flat, [geomorphology] (a) Said of an area characterized by a continuous surface or stretch of land that is smooth, even, or horizontal, or nearly so, and that lacks any significant curvature, slope, elevations, or depressions. (b) An informal, generic term for a level or nearly level surface or small area of land marked by little or no local relief.

Flood plain, A strip of relatively smooth land bordering a stream incision, built of sediment carried by the stream and dropped in slackwater beyond the influence of the swift current of the channel; the level of the flood plain is generally about the stage of the mean annual flood, and therefore one and only one flood-plain level can occur in a limited reach of bottomland. *(Fig. 67)*

Flood, Any climatically controlled, relatively high streamflow that overtops the natural or artificial banks in any reach of a stream, thereby being of geomorphic significance; where a flood plain exists, a flood is any flow that spreads over or inundates the flood plain.

Flood-frequency curve, is a graph showing recurrence intervals of floods plotted as the abscissa and the magnitudes of the floods plotted as the ordinate.

Flood-plain landforms, A variety of constructional and erosional features produced by stream channel migration and flooding, e.g., backswamp, braided stream, flood-plain splay, meander, meander belt, meander scroll, oxbow lake, and natural levee.

Flood-plain playa, A landform consisting of very low gradient, broad, barren, axial-stream channel segments in an intermontane basin. It floods broadly and shallowly and is veneered with barren fine-textured sediment that crusts. Commonly, a flood-plain playa is segmented by transverse, narrow bands of vegetation, and it may alternate with ordinary narrow or braided channel segments.

Flood-plain splay, A fan-shaped deposit or other outspread deposit formed where an overloaded stream breaks through a levee (natural or artificial) and deposits its material (often coarse-grained) on the flood plain.

Flood-plain step, An essentially flat, terrace-like alluvial surface within a valley that is frequently covered by flood water from the present stream (e.g., below the 100 year flood level); any approximately horizontal surface still actively modified by fluvial scour and/or deposition (i.e., cut and fill and/or scour and fill processes). May occur individually or as a series of steps.

Flood-tidal delta, A largely subaqueous (sometimes intertidal), crudely fan-shaped deposit of sand-sized sediment formed on the landward side of a tidal inlet. Flood tides transport sediment through the tidal inlet and into the lagoon over a flood ramp where currents slow and dissipate . Generally, flood-tidal deltas along microtidal coasts are multi-lobate and unaffected by ebbing currents .

Flood-tidal delta flat, The relatively flat, dominant component of the flood-tidal delta. At extreme low tide this landform may be exposed for a relatively short period .

Flood-tidal delta slope, An extension of the flood-tidal delta that slopes toward deeper water in a lagoon or estuary, composed of flood channels, inactive lobes (areas of the flood-tidal delta that are not actively accumulating sand as a result of flood tides), and parts of the terminal lobe of the flood-tidal delta.

Floodway, (a) A large-capacity channel constructed to divert floodwaters or excess streamflow from populous, flood-prone areas, such as a bypass route bounded by levees. (b) The part of the flood plain kept clear of encumbrances and reserved for emergency diversion of floodwaters.

Floor, [geomorphology] (a) A general term for the nearly level, lower part of a basin or valley; (not preferred) refer to basin floor, valley floor. (b) The bed of any body of water; e.g., the nearly level surface beneath the water of a stream, lake, or ocean.

Flow, A category of mass movement processes, associated sediments (flow deposit) and landforms characterized by slow to very rapid downslope movement of unconsolidated material which, whether saturated or comparatively dry, behaves much as a viscous fluid as it moves. Types of flows can be specified based on the dominant particle size of sediments [i.e., debris flow (e.g., lahar), earthflow (creep, mudflow), rockfall avalanche, debris avalanche].

Flow duration, The percentage of time that a specified discharge is equaled or exceeded.

Flow till, A till that may be either subglacial or supraglacial in origin. Flow till displays secondary transport, sorting, and/or fabric modification by plastic mass flow. Flow till exhibits weak stratification and sorting and may contain distorted layers indicative of lateral displacement and soft sediment deformation. The secondary flow processes obliterate most of the original fabric and clast orientations in the till.

Flow-duration curve, A cumulative-frequency curve that shows the percentage of time that specified discharges are equaled or exceeded.

Fluorescence, The re-emission of light energy at a lower frequency by an absorber illuminated with optical energy. The response is usually immediate and on order 1 to 3% of the incident intensity.

Fluorometer, A device used to measure the concentration of chlorophyll in sea water. It does this by mimicking the sun and emitting a flash of light at a specific wavelength and causing the phytoplankton present to fluoresce at another wavelength. The light emitted by the plankton is measured and converted to a chlorophyll measurement via a calibration obtained from discrete measuremets of known quantities of chlorophyll.

Flute, [glacial] A lineation or streamlined furrow or ridge parallel to the direction of ice movement, formed in newly deposited till or older drift. They range in height from a few centimeters to 25 m, and in length from a few meters to 20 km.

Fluve, A roughly linear or elongated depression (topographic low) of any size, along which water flows, at some time.

Fluvial system, An idealized representation of a watershed into zones of (1) erosion and sediment entrainment, (2) transfer of sediment, and (3) deposition of sediment.

Fluvial, Included are stream processes (fluvial processes), fluvial landforms, such as fluvial islands and bars, and biota living in and near stream channels. Common usage is often extended by geomorphologists to hydrologic processes on hillslopes.

Fluviokarst , A karst landscape dominated by both 1) karst features (deranged and subsurface drainage, blind valleys, swallow holes, large springs, closed depressions, and caves), generally limited to low-lying interfluve areas, and 2) surface drainage by large rivers, with associated fluvial features (adjacent stream terraces) and sediments (alluvium), that commonly maintain their surface courses and are fed by underground tributaries.

Fluviomarine bottom, The nearly level or slightly undulating, relatively low-energy, depositional environment with relatively deep water (1.0 to >2.5 m) directly adjacent to an incoming stream and composed of interfingered and mixed fluvial and marine sediments (fluviomarine deposits).

Fluviomarine deposit – Stratified materials (clay, silt, sand, or gravel) formed by both marine and fluvial processes, resulting from non-tidal sea level fluctuations, subsidence and/or stream migration (i.e., materials originally deposited in a nearshore environment and subsequently reworked by fluvial processes as sea level fell). Compare – estuarine deposit, lacustrine deposit, lagoonal deposit, marine deposit, overbank deposit. SW

Fluviomarine terrace , A constructional coastal strip, sloping gently seaward and/or down valley, veneered or completely composed of fluviomarine deposits (typically silt, sand, fine gravel).

Fly ash, All particulate matter that is carried in a gas stream, especially in stack gases at a coal-fired plant for the generation of electric power; also name given to sediments from the same source, stock piled in settling ponds or spoil piles.

Fold, A curve or bend of a planar structure such as rock strata, bedding planes, foliation, or cleavage. *(Fig 25)*

Foothills, A steeply sloping upland composed of hills with relief of 30 up to 300 meters and fringes a mountain range or high-plateau escarpment.

Footslope, The hillslope profile position that forms the concave surface at the base of a hillslope. It is a transition zone between upslope sites of erosion and transport (shoulder, backslope) and downslope sites of deposition (toeslope).

Foredune, A coastal dune or dune ridge oriented parallel to the shoreline, occurring at the landward margin of the beach, along the shoreward face of a beach ridge, or at the landward limit of the highest tide, and more or less stabilized by vegetation.

Foreshore, The sloping portion of a beach profile that lies between a berm crest (or, in its absence, the upper limit of wave swash at high tide) and the low water mark of the backrush of the wave swash at low tide. This term has been used synonymously with beach face, although the foreshore can also contain some of the flat portion of the profile below the beach face. *(Fig. 79)*

Fosse, A long, narrow depression or trough-like hollow between the edge of a retreating glacier and the wall of its valley, or between the front of a moraine and its outwash plain.

Fossil fuel emissions, Emissions of greenhouse gases (in particular carbon dioxide) resulting from the combustion of fuels from fossil deposits such as oil, gas and coal.

Fourier analysis, The determination of the harmonic components of a complex waveform, i.e. the terms of a Fourier series that represents the waveform.

Fracture zone, (undersea feature) "An extensive linear zone of irregular topography, mountainous or faulted, characterized by steep-sided or asymmetrical ridges, cleffs, troughs or escarpments.

Free atmosphere, The atmospheric layer that is negligibly affected by friction against the Earth's surface, and which is above the atmospheric boundary layer.

Free face, [geomorphology] A geomorphic component of hills and mountains consisting of an outcrop of bare rock that sheds rock fragments and other sediments to, and commonly stands more steeply than the angle of repose of, the colluvial slope immediately below; most commonly found on shoulder and backslope positions, and can comprise part or all of a nose slope or side slope. *(Fig 115)*

Free face, The part of a hillside or mountainside consisting of an outcrop of bare rock (scarp or cliff) that sheds colluvium to slopes below and commonly stands more steeply than the angle of repose of the colluvial slope (e.g., talus slope) immediately below. *(Fig. 115)*

Freeze-thaw cycle, (as applied to rock and soil weathering) The process by which capillary water occupies the pores, fractures, joints, or crevices of near-surface rocks or rock fragments and freezes in lowered air temperature; owing to expansion as water turns to ice, pressure is exerted on the pore, fracture, joint, or crevice sides, pushing them apart and causing a form of physical weathering.

Fresh water, (in contrast to brackish water or salt water) Water (or ice) on or beneath a land (or water) surface that accumulates as a result of natural processes of precipitation; fresh water contains dissolved solids (mostly salts) of insufficient concentration to cause deleterious effects by ingestion of living organisms other than those adapted to sea water or similar supplies of water with high concentrations of dissolved solids.

Freshwater marl, A soft, grayish to white, earthy or powdery, usually impure calcium carbonate precipitated on the bottoms of present-day freshwater lakes and ponds largely through the chemical action of algal mats and organic detritus, or forming deposits that underlie marshes, swamps, and bogs that occupy the sites of former (glacial) lakes. The calcium carbonate may range from 90% to less than 30%. Freshwater marl is usually gray; it has been used as a fertilizer for acid soils deficient in lime.

Fringe-tidal marsh, Narrow salt marsh adjacent to a relatively higher energy environment.

Fringing reef, One of three main geomorphological types of coral reefs, the other two being barrier reefs and atolls. These are formed close to shore on rocky coastlines by the growth of corals and associated hydrozoans, alcyonarians and calcareous algae. Fragments of limestone derived from such bioherms are welded together by the encrusting calcareous algae as well as by the deposition of interstitial calcium carbonate cement, the latter brought about by geochemical reactions and possibly bacterial action. The zone of living corals is separated from the shore by a shallow reef flat where reduced circulation, periods of tidal emersion, and the accumulation of sediments inhibit coral growth. *(Fig. 154, 156)*

Frost shattering, The mechanical disintegration, splitting, or breakup of a rock or soil caused by the pressure exerted by freezing water in cracks or pores, or along bedding planes.

Froude number, A dimensionless index to characterize the type of flow, or tranquility of flow, in a channel or similar hydraulic structure;

Frozen ground, Soil or rock in which part or all of the pore water is frozen. Frozen ground includes permafrost. Ground that freezes and thaws annually is called seasonally frozen ground.

Fully developed sea, A hypothesized situation in wave prediction methods in which storm duration and fetch are both long enough such that energy is being dissipated internally and radiated away at the same rate at which it is being transferred from the wind to the water in the form of waves. In a fully developed sea a steady state of maximum wave development is achieved.

Furrow, A linear or arcuate opening left in the soil after a plow or disk has opened a shallow channel at the soil surface. A shallow channel cut in the soil surface, usually between planted rows for controlling surface water and soil loss, or for conveying irrigation water.

G

Gage height, (as determined for a gaging station) The water-surface elevation, or stage, relative to an arbitrary datum.

Gaging station, (also referred to as a streamgage) A specified site on a stream, channel, canal, lake, or reservoir where systematic observations of streamflow or related hydrologic data are collected.

Gap, A sharp break or opening in a mountain ridge, or a short pass through a mountain range.

General circulation model, Generally a three-dimensional time-dependent model of the atmosphere and/or ocean circulation.

General circulation, The large-scale motions of the atmosphere and the ocean as a consequence of differential heating on a rotating Earth, which tend to restore the energy balance of the system through transport of heat and momentum.

Geodesy, A branch of applied mathematics which determines by observation and measurement the exact positions of points and the figures and areas of large portions of the earth's surface, the shape and size of the earth, and the variations of terrestrial gravity.

Geoid, A hypothetical, global, and continuous sea-level surface perpendicular to the direction of gravity at all points. The equipotential surface (i.e., having the same gravity potential at each point) that best fits the mean sea level (see relative sea level) in the absence of astronomical tides; ocean circulations; hydrological, cryospheric and atmospheric effects; Earth rotation variations and polar motion; nutation and precession; tectonics and other effects such as post-glacial rebound. The geoid is global and extends over continents, oceans and ice sheets, and at present includes the effect of the permanent tides (zero-frequency gravitational effect from the Sun and the Moon). It is the surface of reference for astronomical observations, geodetic levelling, and for ocean, hydrological, glaciological and climate modelling, in practice, there exist various operational definitions of the geoid, depending on the way the time-variable effects mentioned above are modelled. *(Fig. 2)*

Geomorphic component, A fundamental, three dimensional piece or area of a geomorphic setting (i.e., hills, mountains, terraces, flat plains) that has unique and prevailing kinetic energy dynamics and sediment transport conditions which result in their characteristic form, patterns of sedimentation and soil development.

Geomorphic surface, A mappable area of the earth's surface that has a common history; the area is of similar age and is formed by a set of processes during an episode of landscape evolution. A geomorphic surface can be erosional, constructional or both. The surface shape can be planar, concave, convex, or any combination of these.

Geomorphic threshold, A critical characteristic or condition of a landscape or geomorphic system that, if rendered unstable by some measure of disturbance exceeding the critical level of stability, change within the system, often as a sequence of responses, is induced. Geomorphic responses to an external stress exceeding a threshold are termed extrinsic, whereas those occurring because on-going change within a system has caused a threshold to be exceeded are termed intrinsic.

Geomorphology, The science that treats the general configuration of the earth's surface; specifically the study of the classification, description, nature, origin, and development of landforms and their relationships to underlying structures, and of the history of geologic changes as recorded by these surface features. The term is especially applied to the genetic interpretation of landforms.

Geomorphology, The study of landforms including, in recent times especially, investigations into the processes that cause and alter the landforms.

Geopotential surface, A surface to which the force of gravity is everywhere perpendicular and equal. No work is necessary for the displacement of mass along a potential surface as long as no other forces act in addition to gravity. This can also be defined as a surface of equal dynamic height below the level of the sea surface, using the ideal sea surface level as a reference surface with the potential value 0. This has also been called a potential surface or a level surface.

Geopotential, The potential energy per unit mass of a body due to the Earth's gravitational field as referred to an arbitrary zero reference level. A unit of geopotential is the potential energy acquired by a unit mass on being raised a unit distance in a gravitational field of unit strength.

Geostrophic adjustment, The mutual adaptation of mass and momentum toward a steady geostrophic state in rotating fluids. The adjustment problem was first considered by Rossby [1938], who derived the geostrophically balanced steady end state for an ocean to which momentum is impulsively imparted. The end state always possesses less energy than the initial state, a fact due to the end state being achieved through decaying inertial oscillations which disperse energy away in pulses of Poincare waves.

Geostrophic current, A current resulting from geostrophy. Analogous to the geostrophic wind concept in meteorology.

Geostrophic force, A virtual force used to account for the change in direction of the wind relative to the Earth's surface. It results from the Earth's rotation and the Coriolis force.

Geostrophic method, A method for determining the relative geostrophic flow field in the ocean from the distribution of density in the ocean. An absolute geostrophic flow field can additionally be found with iditional assumption of a level of no motion.

Geostrophic turbulence, The large amplitude motion of the energy-containing eddifis in the oceans and the atmosphere.

Geostrophic velocity, Those velocities exhibited by geostrophic currents due to geostrophy.

Geostrophic wind, The result of geostrophy in the atmosphere. Analogous to the geostrophic current in oceanography. *(Fig. 187)*

Geostrophic winds or currents, A wind or current that is in balance with the horizontal pressure gradient and the Coriolis force, and thus is outside of the influence of friction. Thus, the wind or current is directly parallel to isobars and its speed is inversely proportional to the spacing of the isobaric contours. *(Fig. 187)*

Geostrophy, The balance between the Coriolis force and the horizontal pressure gradient that determines the first order circulation patterns in the open ocean. This balance is expected to hold for most latitudes but to break down near the equator where the local vertical component of the Coriolis force vanishes, although comparisons between geostrophic estimates and direct measurements have shown it to hold within fractions of a degree from the equator. Geostrophy allows the large scale flow of the oceans to be determined by mapping the horizontal pressure distribution, although such solutions are degenerate in that they only allow the current fields to be determined relative to an absolute reference level.

Geyser basin, A valley that contains numerous springs, geysers, and steam fissures fed by the same ground-water flow.

Geyser cone, A low hill or mound built up of siliceous sinter around the orifice of a geyser.

Geyser, A type of hot spring that intermittently erupts jets of hot water and steam, the result of ground water coming in contact with rock or steam hot enough to create steam under conditions preventing free circulation; a type of intermittent spring. *(Fig. 31)*

Giant ripple, A ripple that is more than 30 m in length; it usually exhibits superimposed megaripples.

Glacial drainage channel, A channel formed by an ice-marginal, englacial, or subglacial stream during glaciation.

Glacial groove, A deep, wide, usually straight furrow cut in bedrock by the abrasive action of a rock fragment embedded in the bottom of a moving glacier; it is larger and deeper than a glacial striation, ranging in size from a deep scratch to a small glacial valley.

Glacial lake, (a) A lake that derives much or all of its water from the melting of glacier ice, fed by meltwater, and lying outside the glacier margins (e.g., proglacial lake) or lying on a glacier (e.g., ice-walled lake, ice-floored lake) and due to differential melting. (b) A lake occupying a basin produced by glacial deposition, such as one held in by a morainal dam. (c) A lake occupying a basin produced in bedrock by glacial erosion (scouring, quarrying); e.g., cirque lake, fjord. (d) A lake occupying a basin produced by collapse of outwash material surrounding masses of stagnant ice. *(Fig. 70)*

Glacial, The conditions, processes, features, and landforms of those areas with adequate precipitation and sufficiently low temperatures that snow and ice accumulates, or formerly accumulated, to a thickness that deformation and the flow, or movement, of glacial ice occurs.

Glacial-marine sedimentation, The accumulation of glacially eroded, terrestrially derived sediment in the marine environment. Sediment may be introduced by fluvial transport, by ice rafting, as an ice-contact deposit, or by eolian transport.

Glacial-valley floor, The comparatively flat bottom of a mountain valley predominantly mantled by till but which can grade from glacial scour (scoured rock outcrop) near its head to a thick mantle of till, and ultimately merging with alluvium or colluvium further down valley. Some glacial-valley floors descend downstream in a series of scour-derived steps which may contain sequential tarn lakes

Glacial-valley wall, The comparatively steep, glacially scoured, concave sides of a u-shaped, mountain valley mantled by colluvium with little or no till.

Glaciation, The formation, movement and recession of glaciers or ice sheets. A collective term for the geologic processes of glacial activity, including erosion and deposition, and the resulting effects of such action on the earth's surface.

Glacier outburst flood, A sudden, often annual, release of meltwater from a glacier or glacier-damned lake sometimes resulting in a catastrophic flood, formed by melting of a drainage channel or buoyant lifting of ice by water or by subglacial volcanic activity; also called jokuhlaup.

Glacier, A large mass of ice formed wholly or mostly on land by the compaction and recrystallization of snow, possibly with ice additions from the freezing of meltwater or rainfall, that creeps slowly downslope by gravity-induced deformational processes; glaciers have permanence measured in periods exceeding decades or centuries and range in size and environment from small alpine glaciers of high-elevation or high-relief areas to flowing ice sheets that are sub-continental in areal scale and that can move on very low slopes. A mass of land ice that flows downhill under gravity (through internal deformation and/or sliding at the base) and is constrained by internal stress and friction at the base and sides. A glacier is maintained by accumulation of snow at high altitudes, balanced by melting at low altitudes or discharge into the sea. *(Fig. 90)*

Glaciofluvial deposit, Material moved by glaciers and subsequently sorted and deposited by streams flowing from the melting ice. The deposits are stratified and may occur in the form of outwash plains, valley trains, deltas, kames, eskers, and kame terraces.

Glaciokarst, Karst in glaciated terrain developed on bedrock susceptible to dissolution (e.g., limestone), thinly mantled (e.g., < 5 - 30 m) with drift and characterized by surficial, closed depressions formed by post-glacial, subsurface karstic collapse (e.g., sinkholes)

rather than by glacial processes (e.g., ice-block melt-out).

Glaciolacustrine deposit, Material ranging from fine clay to sand derived from glaciers and deposited in glacial lakes by water originating mainly from the melting of glacial ice. Many are bedded or laminated with varves or rhythmites.

Glaciomarine deposit, Glacially eroded, terrestrially derived sediments (clay, silt, sand, and gravel) that accumulated on the ocean floor. Sediments may be accumulated as an ice-contact deposit, by fluvial transport, ice-rafting, or eolian transport. *(Fig. 152)*

Gleying, A process of soil genesis, commonly of well weathered clay horizons, in which the soil becomes mottled, generally in a tightly layered manner, caused by partial oxidation and reduction of ferric-iron compounds due to fluctuating ground-water levels (intermittent episodes of saturation and aeration). The amount of time indicated by gleying is indefinite but often it is interpreted to suggest that the gleyed zone dates from sediment deposited in a slough or similar depression of a flood-plain surface of a paleo-landscape.

Global dimming, Global dimming refers to perceived widespread reduction of solar radiation received at the surface of the Earth from about the year 1961 to around 1990.

Global surface temperature, The global surface temperature is an estimate of the global mean surface air temperature. However, for changes over time, only anomalies, as departures from a climatology, are used, most commonly based on the area-weighted global average of the sea surface temperature anomaly and land surface air temperature anomaly.

Global Warming Potential (GWP), An index, based upon radiative properties of well-mixed greenhouse gases, measuring the radiative forcing of a unit mass of a given well-mixed greenhouse gas, in the present-day atmosphere integrated over a chosen time horizon, relative to that of carbon dioxide. The GWP represents the combined effect of the differing times these gases remain in the atmosphere and their relative effectiveness in absorbing outgoing thermal infrared radiation. The Kyoto Protocol is based on GWPs from pulse emissions over a 100-year time frame.

Globigerina ooze, A type of calcareous ooze composed of the shells of unicellular creatures called globigerina that live in the waters of warmer ocean regions. These oozes are seldom found above 5000 m depth and cover about 35% of the surface of the sea floor. *(Fig. 152)*

Gorge, (a) A narrow, deep valley with nearly vertical, rocky walls, smaller than a canyon, and more steep-sided than a ravine; especially a restricted, steep-walled part of a canyon. (b) A narrow defile or passage between hills or mountains. *(Fig. 64)*

Graben, An elongate trough or basin bounded on both sides by high-angle, normal faults that dip towards the interior of the trough. It is a structural form that may or may not be geomorphically expressed as a rift valley. *(Fig. 27)*

Gradient wind, A wind that theoretically exists as a balance between the pressure gradient, Coriolis, and centrifugal forces. It blows along curved isobars with no tangential acceleration. In the case of rotation around a high/low pressure area the centrifugal force is in the same/opposite direction as the pressure gradient force and leads to an increase/decrease in wind speed compared to that calculated for the geostrophic wind resulting from a balance between the Coriolis and pressure gradient forces. *(Fig. 184, 185)*

Gradientm (as applied to stream channels) The rate of elevation change between two specified sites of horizontal distance measured along the thalweg of the channel. It is generally expressed as a non-dimensional number (m m$_{-1}$).

Granitoid, A preliminary term (for field use) for a plutonic rock with Q (quartz) between 20 and 60 (%). A general term for all phaneritic igneous rocks dominated by quartz and feldspars.

Gravel pit, A depression, ditch or pit excavated to furnish gravel for roads or other construction purposes; a type of burrow pit.

Gravel, (as fluvial sediment) sediment defined to be of particle diameter between 2 and 64 mm in diameter. *(Fig. 39)*

Gravitational acceleration, The acceleration with which a body would freely fall under the action of gravity in a vacuum. This actually varies with the distance from the center of the Earth as well as with geographical location (due to the inhomogeneities in the solid Earth), but the internationally adopted value is 9.80665 m/s$_2$ or 32.1740 ft/s$_2$.

Great Salinity Anomaly, A low salinity and temperature event that propagates around the North Atlantic. The first event identified as such - and now called GSA '70s - was a freshening of the upper 500-800 m that propagated around the North Atlantic subpolar gyre over a period of about 14 years. It left the region of Iceland in the mid-to-late 1960s and returned to the Greenland Sea in 1981-1982. The second event occurred in the 1980s and is called GSA '80s. Belkin et al. [1998] compare and contrast the two events, identifying two GSA modes.

Greenhouse effect, Greenhouse gases effectively absorb thermal infrared radiation, emitted by the Earth's surface, by the atmosphere itself due to the same gases, and by clouds. Atmospheric radiation is emitted to all sides, including downward to the Earth's surface. Thus, greenhouse gases trap heat within the swface-troposphere system. This is called the greenhouse effect. Thermal infrared radiation in the troposphere is strongly coupled to the temperature of the atmosphere at the altitude at which it is emitted. In the troposphere, the temperature generally decreases with height. Effectively, infrared radiation emitted to space originates from an altitude with a temperature of, on average, -19°C, in balance with the net incoming solar radiation, whereas the Earth's surface is kept at a much higher temperature of, on average, +14°C. An increase in the concentration of greenhouse gases leads to an increased infrared opacity of the atmosphere, and therefore to an effective radiation into space from a higher altitude at a lower temperature. This causes a radiative forcing that leads to an enhancement of the greenhouse effect, the so-called enhanced greenhouse effect. Short-wave solar radiation can pass through the clear atmosphere relatively unimpeded, but long-wave radiation emitted by the warm surface of the Earth is partially absorbed and then re-emitted by a number of trace gases in the cooler atmosphere above. Since, on average, the outgoing long-wave radiation balances the incoming solar radiation, both the atmosphere and the surface will be warmer than they would be without the greenhouse gases.

Greenhouse gas (GHG) Greenhouse gases are those gaseous constituents of the atmosphere, both natural and anthropogenic, that absorb and emit radiation at specific wavelengths within the spectrum of thermal infrared radiation emitted by the Earth's surface, the atmosphere itself, and by clouds. This property causes the greenhouse effect. Water vapour (H_2O), carbon dioxide (COJ, nitrous oxide (N2O), methane (CH4) and ozone (O3) are the primary greenhouse gases in the Earth's atmosphere. Moreover, there are a number of entirely human-made greenhouse gases in the atmosphere, such as the halocarbons and other chlorine- and bromine-containing substances. Those gases that contribute to the greenhouse effect by trapping heat within the earth's atmosphere. The chief greenhouse gases are carbon dioxide and water vapor. Other potentially important trace gases are chlorofluorocarbons, methane, ozone, and nitrous oxide.

Greenland Sea, The regional sea in the North Atlantic Ocean which comprises the waters in the Greenland Basin. The average depth is about 2866 m.

Greensands, An unconsolidated, near-shore marine sediment containing substantial amounts of dark greenish glauconite pellets, often mingled with clay or sand (quartz may form the dominant constituent); prominent in Cretaceous and Tertiary coastal plain strata. Has been commercially mined for potassium fertilizer. The term is loosely applied to any glauconitic sediment

Groove, A small, natural, narrow drainageway on high angle slopes which separate tertiary spur ridges or mini-interfluves and is a constituent part of rib and groove topography; common in well dissected uplands.

Grorss Primary Production (GPP), The amount of energy fixed from the atmosphere through photosynthesis.

Ground moraine, (a) Commonly an extensive, low relief area of till, having an uneven or undulating surface, and commonly bounded on the distal end by a recessional or end moraine. (b) A layer of poorly sorted rock and mineral debris (till) dragged along, in, on, or beneath a glacier and deposited by processes including basal lodgment and release from downwasting stagnant ice by ablation. *(Fig. 90)*

Ground soil, Any soil at the present-day land surface and actively undergoing pedogenesis, regardless of its history (i.e., relict, exhumed).

Ground temperature, The temperature of the ground near the surface (often within the first 10 cm). It is often called soil temperature.

Ground water, Water in the subsurface that saturates the rocks and sediment in which it occurs; the upper surface of ground-water saturation is commonly termed the water table.

Grounding line/zone, The junction between a glacier or ice sheet and ice shelf, the place where ice starts to float.

Ground-water reservoir, A saturated body of ground water having loosely definable spatial limits. Among the goals of ground-water hydrology is the objective of determining the volumes of water in ground-water reservoirs.

Grus, The fragmental products of in situ granular disintegration of granite and granitic rocks, dominated by inter-crystal disintegration.

Guiana Basin, An ocean basin located off the Venezuela, Guiana and Brazilian coasts in the west-central Atlantic Ocean. This comprises the western Demerara Abyssal Plain and the eastern Ceara Abyssals Plain, separated by the Amazon abyssal cone. This has been called the Makaroff Deep.

Guinea Current, The part of the cyclonic gyre that forms the Guineau Dome that flows northwestward along the west African coast.

Gulf of California, A water body separating Baja california from the Mexican mainland. It is connected to the Pacific Ocean through a southern opening between 20-23°N. The principal mechanisms forcing the Gulf are Pacific Ocean circulation, the tides, the fluxs of heat and moisture exchanged with the atmosphere, and the wind.

Gulf, A relatively large part of an ocean or sea extending far into the land, partly enclosed by an extensive sweep of the coast, and opened to the sea through a strait (e.g., Gulf of Mexico); the largest of various forms of inlets of the sea. It is usually larger, more enclosed, and more deeply indented than a bay. *(Fig. 126)*

Gully erosion, The displacement of soil or soft rock particles by running water that forms distinct, narrow incisements that are larger and deeper than rills and that usually carry water only during and immediately after heavy rain or the melting of ice or snow.

Gully, A small hollow or channel worn in earth or unconsolidated material, as on a hillside, by running water and through which water runs only after a rain or the melting of ice or snow; it is larger than a rill and smaller than a stream channel.

Gut [channel], A tidal stream connecting two larger waterways within a lagoon, estuary, or bay.

Guyot (undersea feature), A seamount having a comparatively smooth flat top; also called tablemount

Gypsite, An earthy gypsum (CaSO4'''2H2O) variety that contains various quantities (i.e., < 50%) of soil material, silicate clay minerals, and sometimes other salts (e.g. NaCl); found only in arid or semiarid regions as secondary precipitation concentrations or efflorescence associated with rock gypsum or gypsum-bearing strata.

Gyre, Basin-scale ocean horizontal circulation pattern with slow flow circulating around the ocean basin, closed by a strong and narrow (100-200 km wide) boundary current on the western side. The subtropical gyres in each ocean are associated with high pressure in the centre of the gyres; the subpolar gyres are associated with low pressure.

Hadley Cell, A part of the atmospheric circulation system extending from the Equator to 30° latitude on both sides of the Equator. It is a thermally-driven system which heated air rises at the Equator, flows poleward, cools and descends at subtropical latitudes, and then flows back towards the Equator. This description was suggested by Hadley in the 18th century. *(Fig. 182)*

Hadley Circulation, A direct, thermally driven overturning cell in the atmosphere consisting of poleward flow in the upper troposphere, subsiding air into the subtropical anticyclones, return flow as part of the trade winds near the surface, and with rising air near the equator in the so-called Inter-Tropical Convergence Zone.

Half graben, An elongate, structural trough or basin bounded on one side by a normal fault. It may or may not produce a topographic basin.

Halocarbons, A collective term for the group of partially halogenated organic species, including the chlorofluorocarbons (CFCs), hydrochlorofluorocarbons (HCFCs), hydrofluorocarbons (HFCs), halons, methyl chloride, methyl bromide, etc. Many of the halocarbons have large Global Warming Potentials. The chlorine-and bromine-containing halocarbons are also involved in the depletion of the ozone layer.

Halocline, A relatively sharp change in salinity with depth.

Hanging valley, A tributary valley whose floor at the lower end is notably higher than the floor of the main valley in the area of glaciation. *(Fig. 91)*

Hard-water effect, The tendency of the dissolved inorganic carbon in many "hard-water" lakes to be in disequilibrium with atmospheric CO2 owing to a short residence time. A result is that radiocarbon in the water, carbonate minerals formed in the water, and organisms living in the water, is deficient relative to that of the atmosphere, thereby yielding computed ages older than the true ages. Similarly, streams that receive significant amounts of ground water with substantial subsurface residence times contain dissolved carbon that also is deficient relative to atmospheric radiocarbon, and radiocarbon dates derived from the water and its biota are greater than the true ages.

Harmonic, A frequency that is a simple multiple of a fundamental frequency. A second harmonic, for example, would have twice the frequency of the fundamental.

Head slope, A geomorphic component of hills consisting of a laterally concave area of a hillside, especially at the head of a drainageway, resulting in converging overland water flow (e.g., sheet wash); head slopes are dominated by colluvium and slope wash sediments (e.g., slope alluvium); contour lines form concave curves. Slope complexity (downslope shape) can range from simple to complex. Headslopes are comparatively moister portions of hillslopes and tend to accumulate sediments (e.g., soils with over-thickened, dark epipedons) where they are not directly contributing materials to channel flow.

Head, (a) The source, beginning, or upper part of a stream. (b) The upper part or end of a slope or valley.

Headcut, A type of knickpoint, is a vertical or near-vertical face, or drop, on the bed of a stream channel that interrupts the channel gradient and, through processes of channel erosion, progressively moves up-channel.

Headland – (a) An irregularity of land, especially of considerable height with a steep cliff face, jutting out from the coast into a large body of water (usually the sea or a lake); a bold promontory or a high cape. (b) The high ground flanking a body of water, such as a cove. (c) The steep crag or cliff face of a promontory. *(Fig. 127)*

Head-of-outwash, A sloping and sometimes high relief landform composed predominantly of glaciofluvial sediment that delimits a former ice-margin of a relatively static, rapidly wasting glacier. A steep ice-contact slope forms the ice-proximal face of the landform; a more gently sloping surface dips away on the distal slope, if not slumped.

Headwall, A steep slope at the head of a valley; e.g., the rock cliff at the back of a cirque. [anthropogenic] A sheer slope or cliff face at the head of an excavation; e.g., the rock cliff at the active face of a mine, pit, or quarry, from which material has been extracted; also called a highwall.

Heat capacity, The heat capacity of a body is the product of its mass and its specific heat.

Hemipelagic, Opertaining to continental margins and the adjacent abyssal plains

Herbaceous peat, An accumulation of organic material, decomposed to some degree that is predominantly the remains of sedges, reeds, cattails and other herbaceous plants.

Heterotrophic respiration, The convertion of organic matter to carban dioxide by organisms other than plants.

High hill, A generic name for an elevated, generally rounded land surface with high local relief, rising between 90 meters (approx. 300 ft.) to as much as 300 m (approx. 1000 ft.)

above surrounding lowlands.

High pressure center, A region of relatively high barometric pressure. These are characterized by subsidence at altitude and by divergence near the surface. They predominate at 30 and 90° latitude where the global generation circulation patterns exhibit downward motion. This type of circulation feature is also known as an anticyclone and as such rotates clockwise/counterclockwise in the norther/southern hemisphere. High pressure systems are generally characterized by clear skies and fair weather since cloud development is impeded therein, and winds are also generally light.

Highmoor bog, A bog, often on the uplands, whose surface is covered by sphagnum mosses which, because of their high degree of water retention, make the bog more dependent upon precipitation than on the water table. The bog often occurs as a raised peat bog or blanket bog.

Hill, (undersea feature) An isolated (or group of) elevations(s), smaller than a seamount. A generic term for an elevated area of the land surface, rising at least 30 m (100 ft.) to as much as 300 meters (approx. 1000 ft.) above surrounding lowlands, usually with a nominal summit area relative to bounding slopes, a well-defined, rounded outline and slopes that generally exceed 15 percent. A hill can occur as a single, isolated mass or in a group. A hill can be further specified based on the magnitude of local relief: *low hill* (30 – 90 m) or *high hill* (90 - 300 m). Informal distinctions between a hill and a mountain are often arbitrary and dependent on local convention.

Hillock, A generic name for a small, low hill, generally between 3 – 30 m in height and slopes between 5 and 50% (e.g., bigger than a mound but smaller than a hill); commonly considered a microfeature.

Hillslope terrace, A raised, generally horizontal strip of earth and/or rock bounded by a down-slope berm or retaining wall, constructed along a contour on a hillslope to make land suitable for tillage and to prevent accelerated erosion; common in steep terrain, both archaic (e.g., Peru) and modern (e.g., Nepal).

Hillslope, A generic term for the steeper part of a hill between its summit and the drainage line, valley flat, or depression floor at the base of the hill. *(Fig. 115)*

Hillslope-profile position, Discrete slope segments found along a transect line that runs perpendicular to the contour, beginning at a divide and descending to a lower, bounding stream channel or valley floor; a discrete piece of a two-dimensional cross profile of a hill. Positions are commonly separated from one another by inflection points along the line. In descending elevational order, the hillslope-profile positions of a simple hillslope include summit, shoulder, backslope, footslope, and toeslope. Not all of these segments (positions) are necessarily present along a particular hillslope. Complex hillslopes include multiple sequences or partial sequences, or partial sequences. *(Fig. 115)*

Hogback, A sharp-crested, symmetric ridge formed by highly tilted resistant rock layers; a type of homocline produced by differential erosion of interlayered resistant and weak rocks with dips greater than about 25° (or approximately > 45 % slopes). *(Fig. 109)*

Hole, (undersea feature) A small local depression, often steep sided, in the sea floor.

Holocene, The Holocene geological epoch is the latter of two Quaternary epochs, extending from about 11.6 ka to and including the Present. *(Fig. 3)*

Homoclinal ridge, A homocline that forms an asymmetric ridge with a dip slope commonly between 10 to 25° (15 to 45 %). A homoclinal ridge has steeper dip than a cuesta, but lower dip than a hogback.

Homoclinal, Pertaining to strata that dip in one direction with a uniform angle.

Homocline, A general term for a series of rock strata that dip in one direction with a uniform angle; e.g., one limb of a fold, a tilted fault block, or an isocline.

Horn, [glacial geology] A high, rocky, sharp pointed, steep-sided, mountain peak with prominent faces and ridges, bounded by the intersecting walls of three or more cirques that have been cut back into the mountain by headward erosion of glaciers.

Horse latitudes, The belts of variable, light winds and fine weather associated with the subtropical anticy-clones The name originated with the historical sailing practice of throwing the horses being transported to America or the West Indies overboard when these latitudes were reached and the light winds caused the voyage to be overly extended.

Horst, An elongate block that is bounded on both sides by normal faults that dip away from the interior of the horst. It is a structural form and may or may not be expressed geomorphically. *(Fig. 27)*

Hot spring, A natural, geothermally heated spring whose temperature is above that of the human body. *(Fig. 31)*

Hudson Bay, A large inland Arctic sea exceeding 1 million square kilometers in area, connected to the Arctic Ocean at its northern end through Foxe Basin. It can be characterized as shallow, with a mean depth of less than 150 m.

Humidity mixing ratio, The ratio of the mass of water vapor in a sample of moist air to the mass of dry air with which it is associated.

Hummock, An imprecise, general term for a rounded or conical mound or other small elevation. A slight rise of ground above a level surface. A small, irregular knob of earth (earth hummock) or turf (turf hummock). Neither type of hummock is diagnostic of permafrost, but both are most common in subpolar or alpine regions. Both require vegetative cover.

Humus, A complex mixture of brown to dark brown components of soil organic matter, mostly amorphous and colloidal substances, that are decomposed to the extent that the sources of the material cannot be identified.

Hydraulic conductivity, A measure of the ease by which a fluid, generally water, will pass through a porous medium, often soil or rock.

Hydraulic geometry, (for a given cross section of a stream channel) The graphical relations among plots of hydraulic characteristics (width, depth, velocity, gradient, roughness coefficient, particle sizes) as simple power functions of river discharge; hydraulic-geometry pertains to the water in a channel as opposed to the geometry of the channel. Hydraulic-geometry relations can be developed both for the at-a-station condition and the downstream-direction condition.

Hydraulic gradient, The gradient (often termed slope) of the energy grade line - the line representing the sum of kinetic and potential energy along the flow path; for uniform flow, the hydraulic gradient and the slope of the water surface are equal. An analogous term of ground-water hydrology is potentiometric surface.

Hydraulic radius, (R, of a stream channel) The ratio of its cross-sectional area, A, to its wetted perimeter, WP : R = A/WP

Hydrochlorofluorocarbon, (HCFC) A class of chemicals being used to replace CFCs since they deplete stratospheric ozone to a much lesser extent than CFCs.

Hydrofluorocarbon, (HFC) A class of chemicals being used to replace CFCs. They do not contain chlorine or bromine and therefore do not deplete ozone in the stratosphere

Hydrograph, The graphical representation of a hydrologic variable, such as the stage of a stream or the water level in a well, as a function of time; a hydrograph for runoff (streamflow) is a graph of the time-rate distribution of flowing water passing a site on the landscape, generally at a stream channel and often for a specific flow or runoff event. *(Fig. 204)*

Hydrography, The study of the physical features of water bodies like oceans and lakes (in analogy to geography being the study of the physical features on land). Oceanic features of interest include the location and spatial extent of water masses as identified by their characteristic properties such as salinity, temperature and micronutrient concentrations.

Hydrologic budget, A quantitative accounting of the various components of water or stored in drainage basins or watersheds; when the amount of water entering a system equals that leaving or stored in the system, the hydrologic budget is assumed, over reasonably long time periods, to be in balance.

Hydrologic cycle, The cycle of water movement (in the liquid, solid, and vapor phases) from the atmosphere to land, surface-water, and ground-water bodies, including movement among land and water bodies, before returning to the atmosphere. *(Fig 192)*

Hydrological cycle, The importance of the oceanic component of the hydrologic cycle is evidenced by estimates indicating that 86% of global evaporation and 78% of precipitation occur over the ocean. The global water reservoirs are the ocean, the land, and the atmosphere, holding 1,400,000,000 km$_3$, 59,000,000 km$_3$, and 16 km$_3$ of water, respectively. *(Fig. 46)*

Hydrology, That part of the earth sciences that is concerned with the origin, circulation, distribution, and properties of water; important elements of hydrology include the measurement effluxes of water (as streamflow, ground-water discharge, etc.) and the manners by which the fluxes affect the landscape (erosion, plant growth, etc.).

Hydrometeor, Any condensed water particle in the atmosphere of size much larger than individual water molecules, e.g. fog, cloud, some hazes, rain and snow.

Hydrometer, A bulb that indicates the specific gravity of a water-sediment mixture by the height at which it floats above the mixture surface; the hydrometer is commonly used to compute concentrations of fluvial sediment too fine to fall from suspension, and to determine particle sizes of fine sediment in soils.

Hydroperiod, The annual or otherwise repeatable period of time, typically expressed in days or weeks, during which either alluvium underlying a bottomland area is persistently saturated or the bottomland area is covered by water

Hydrosphere, The component of the climate system comprising liquid surface and subterranean water, such as oceans, seas, rivers, fresh water lakes, underground water, etc.

Hyporheic zone, The ill-defined volume of sediment, adjacent to and beneath an alluvial stream channel, through which ground water moves roughly parallel to streamflow. Water of the hyporheic zone generally is readily exchangeable with stream water, receiving water as bank storage through influent reaches of channel and yielding water as seepage through effluent reaches.

Hypsometric curve, A plot of the percentage of elevation and depth distribution on the continents and oceans, i.e. the representation of the statistical distribution of elevations over the entire planet. *(Fig. 117)*

Hypsometry, The study of the elevation and depth distribution on the continents and oceans.

I

Iapetus Ocean, A paleogeographic term for the ocean that lay between Baltica and Laurentia during the late Precambrian and early Paleozoic. It was subducted during the early Paleozoic and is thought to have disappeared completely by the Late Silurian-early Devonian (around 400 Ma).

Iberia Basin, An ocean basin located to the west of Spain in the eastern North Atlantic Ocean. This is connected to the West Europe Basin to the north via the Theta Gap and includes the Tagus Abyssal Plain and the Horseshoe Abyssal Plain. This has also been called the Spanish Basin

Ice age, An ice age or glacial period is characterised by a long-term reduction in the temperature of the Earth's climate, resulting in growth of continental ice sheets and mountain glaciers (glaciation). *(Fig. 4)*

Ice cap, A dome shaped ice mass, usually covering a highland area, which is considerably smaller in extent than an ice sheet.

Ice core, A cylinder of ice drilled out of a glacier or ice sheet.

Ice sheet, A mass of land ice that is sufficiently deep to cover most of the underlying bedrock topography, so that its shape is mainly determined by its dynamics (the flow of the ice as it deforms internally and/or slides at its base). An ice sheet flows outward from a high central ice plateau with a small average surface slope. The margins usually slope more steeply and most ice is discharged through fast-flowing ice streams or outlet glaciers, in some cases into the sea or into ice shelves floating on the sea. There are only three large ice sheets in the modern world, one on Greenland and two on Antarctica, the East and West Antarctic Ice Sheets, divided by the Transantarctic Mountains. During glacial periods there were others.

Ice shelf, A floating slab of ice of considerable thickness extending from, the coast (usually of great horizontal extent with a level or gently sloping surface), often filling embayments in the coastline of the ice sheets. Nearly all ice shelves are in Antarctica, where most of the ice discharged seaward flows into ice shelves. An ice sheet that extends over the sea and floats on the water. These range in thickness from a few hundred to over 1000 meters and are connected to land at coastal grounding lines and where they flow around islands. They calve icebergs at their seaward fronts and gain mass by flow from grounded ice sheets and glaciers and from new snow accumulation. Iceberg calving is the primary ablation process with melting providing a secondary mechanism. Ice shelves are key indicators of climate change.

Ice stream, A stream of ice flowing faster than the surrounding ice sheet. It can be thought of as a glacier flowing between walls of slower-moving ice instead of rock.

Ice wedge, A massive, generally wedge-shaped body with its apex pointing downward, composed of foliated or vertically banded, commonly white, ice.

Iceberg, A massive piece of ice of greatly varying shape, more than 5 m above sea-level, which has broken away from a glacier (or an ice shelf), and which may be afloat or aground. Icebergs may be described as tabular, dome-shaped, sloping, pinnacled, weathered or glacier bergs (an irregularly shaped iceberg). Icebergs are not a form of sea ice, as they originate on land.

Iceland Sea, A marginal sea located in the North Atlantic Ocean. It is roughly defined as the waters lying to the west of Jan Mayen Ridge at about 7° W. It adjoins the waters of the

Norwegian Sea to the east, the Greenland Sea to the north, Denmark Strait to the west, and the North Atlantic Ocean to the south. The average depth of theis region is about 1128 m.

Ice-rafting, The transportation of rock fragments of all sizes on or within icebergs, ice floes, or other forms of floating ice.

Igneous rock, Rock formed by cooling and solidification from magma, and that has not been changed appreciably by weathering since its formation; major varieties include plutonic (i.e., intrusive) and volcanic (i.e., extrusive) rocks. Examples: andesite, basalt, granite. *(Fig. 38)*

Illuviation, The movement of soluble and fine-grained material downward with descending soil water into sites of the B horizon, where deposition or re-precipitation of the dissolved minerals occur; illuviation is a specific form of eluviation.

Impact crater, A generally circular or elliptical depression formed by hypervelocity impact of an experimental projectile or ordinance into earthy or rock material.

In situ data, Data associated with reference to measurements made at the actual location of the object or material measured, by contrast with remote sensing (i.e., from space).

Indian monsoon, The seasonal reversal of the wind direction along the shores of the Indian Ocean, especially in the Arabian Sea. The winds blow from the southwest during half of the year and from the northeast during the other half. The reversal of direction (form that due to the normal Zonal circulation pattern) is due to the effects of differential heating as the Himalayan plateau heats up during the summer, causing the air to rise and be replaced by the warm, moist air from over the Indian Ocean.

Indicator species, (as applied to plant ecology) A plant whose natural presence on a particular surface, soil, or landform is indicative of that surface, soil, or landform.

Indirect aerosol effect, Aerosols may lead to an indirect radiative forcing of the climate system through acting as cloud condensation nuclei or modifying the optical properties and lifetime of clouds.

Industrial revolution, A period of rapid industrial growth with far reaching social and economic consequences, beginning in Britain during the second half of the eighteenth century and spreading to Europe and later to other countries including the United States. The invention of the steam engine was an important trigger of this development. The industrial revolution marks the beginning of a strong increase in the use of fossil fuels and emission of, in particular, fossil carbon dioxide. In this report the terms pre-industrial and industrial refer, somewhat arbitrarily, to the periods before and after 1750, respectively.

Infiltration rate, (of porous rock or a soil) The rate, often expressed in mm sec^{-1}, at which the rock or soil can absorb water provided to it from the surface by rainfall or snowmelt;

infiltration rate replaces the previous term, infiltration capacity, which was the maximum rate at which infiltration could occur.

Infiltration, The movement of water, from rain, snowmelt, runoff, and storage, from the land surface through the air-soil interface and into the soil zone.

Infrared, That part of the electromagnetic radiation spectrum from approximately 0.75 to 1000 *m*. This is between the visible and microwave regions of the spectrum. It is further divided into the near (0.75 to 1.5 m), intermediate (1.5 to 20 m), and far (20 to 1000 m) ranges. Most of the energy emitted by the Earth and its atmosphere is at infrared wavelengths, and it is generated almost entirely by large-scale intramolecular processes. The tri-atomic gases such as water vapor, CO_2, and ozone absorb infrared radiation and play important roles in the propagation of infrared radiation in the atmosphere. *(Fig. 162)*

Inland sea, A sea surrounded by land and connected to the open ocean by one or more narrow straits. Examples include the Baltic Sea, the Red Sea, and the Black Sea.

Inlet, A short, narrow waterway connecting a bay, lagoon, or similar body of water.

Inselberg, (German, meaning island hill or island mountain), A rock prominence surrounded and partially submerged by unconsolidated to loosely consolidated sediment mostly of fluvial origin; inselbergs are common where bedrock segments of mountain blocks, relative to the land surface, have become separated or detached from the main mountain block through alluvial-fan deposition around the bedrock segment. A prominent, isolated, residual knob, hill, or small mountain, usually smoothed and rounded, rising abruptly from an extensive lowland erosion surface in a hot dry region; generally bare and rocky although the lower slopes are commonly buried by colluvium. *(Fig. 100)*

Inshore, The zone or portion of a beach profile extending seaward from the foreshore to just beyond the breaker zone.

Insolation, The amount of solar radiation reaching the Earth by latitude and by season. Usually insolation refers to the radiation arriving at the top of the atmosphere. Sometimes it is specified as referring to the radiation arriving at the Earth's surface. *(Fig. 163)*

Instability, (of geomorphic processes and landforms) A condition of imbalance between inflows and outflows of matter through or over a landscape feature. As a geomorphic concept, instability is often expressed as some state of dynamic- or quasi-equilibrium, signifying that geomorphic processes and landforms are almost always in a condition of dis-equilibrium and are almost always adjusting to regain relative stability; an objective if applying the term is to determine the degree to which a process or landform deviates from stability or equilibrium.

Instrumental data, This refers to data, e.g. temperatures, rainfall amounts, atmospheric pressure, etc., that have been gathered via direct measurement as opposed to proxy data.

Integrated drainage, A general term for a drainage pattern in which stream systems have developed to the point where all parts of the landscape drain into some part of a stream system, the initial or original surfaces have essentially disappeared and the region drains to a common base level. Few or no closed drainage systems are present.

Interbasin exchange, The active exchange of waters and/or water mass propertiese: between basins.

Interbedded, Said of beds lying between or alternating with others of different character; especially said of rock material or sediments laid down in sequence between other beds, such as "interbedded" sands and gravels.

Interdrumlin, The concave to relatively flat bottomed, roughly linear depressions ranging from small saddles or swales to small valleys that separate drumlins or drumlinoid ridges in drumlin fields. Streams, if present, have not had a dominant impact on the formation of the depression.

Interdune valley, A broad interdune area consisting of a low-lying, relatively flat surface commonly found between very large dunes, and which lies in close proximity to the local groundwater table (if present).

Interdune, The relatively flat surface, whether sand-free or sand-covered, between dunes.

Interferometer, A device, e.g. imaging radar, that uses two different paths for imaging and deduces information from the coherent interference between the two signals. Paths with spatial and temporal differences have been used to measure, respectively, terrain height and ocean currents.

Interfluve, The area between sites of concentrated flow, particularly stream channels but including gullies and, at a smaller scale, even rills, for which interrill area may be a preferred term.

Interglacials, The warm periods between ice age glaciations. The previous interglacial, dated approximately from 129 to 116 ka, is referred to as the Last Interglacial.

Intermittent stream, Intermittently or seasonally flowing water in a natural, intermittent-stream channel; the flow of an intermittent stream typically is derived from wet-season runoff or snowmelt, and the surface of an intermittent stream, or the bed of the channel upon which flow occurs, typically is higher than the level of the zone of saturation in the adjacent water-bearing alluvium or rocks. This characteristic is fundamentally different from that of an ephemeral-stream channel, which at most times is separated from the zone of saturation by a variable thickness of unsaturated alluvium or rock.

Intermontane basin, A generic term for wide structural depressions between mountain ranges that are partly filled with alluvium and called "valleys" in the vernacular. Intermontane basins may be drained internally (bolsons) or externally (semi-bolson).

Internal tide, Internal waves somehow excited at or near tidal periods. It is generally accepted that these are generated by energy scattered from surface to internal tides by bottom roughness,

Internal wave, A gravity wave propagating in the interior of the ocean with typical spatial and temporal scales of kilometers and hours. The amplitudes are on the order of 10 meters, much larger than their surface counterparts.

Intertidal, The coastal environment between mean low tide and mean high tide that alternates between subaerial and subaqueous depending on the tidal cycle.

Intertropical Convergence Zone, A narrow low-latitude zone in which air masses originating in the northern and southern hemispheres converge and generally produce cloudy, showery weather. Over the Atlantic and Pacific it is the boundary between the northeast and southeast trade winds. The mean position is somewhat north of the equator, but over the continents the range of motion is considerable. Often abbreviated as ITCZ. *(Fig. 168)*

Intramorainal, said of deposits and phenomena occurring within a lobate curve of a moraine (e.g., within the area occupied by a glacier).

Intrusive, Denoting igneous rocks derived from molten matter (magmas) that invaded pre-existing rocks and cooled below the surface of the earth.

Ionian Sea, One of the seas that comprise the eastern basin of the Mediterranean Sea. It is surrounded by Italy, Hellas, Libya and Tunisia, and has a volume of $10.8 \times 10_4$ km$_3$. It connects to the Cretan Sea via the Kithira (160 m deep, 33 km wide) and Antikithira (700 m deep, 32 km wide) Straits, the Levantine Sea via the Cretan Passage, the western Mediterranean via the Strait of Sicily, and the Adriatic Sea via Otranto Strait (780 m deep, 75 km wide). *(Fig. 143)*

Irish Sea, A marginal sea located between Ireland and Wales. It extends from the Mull of Galloway in the north to a line connecting St. David's Head (in Wales) to Carnsore Point (in Ireland) in the south.

Irminger Current, A branch of the North Atlantic Current that curves north near Iceland, where a minor part of it splits to flow north along the west coast of Iceland and the major part curves to the west and joins the southward flowing East Greenland Current. Both branches ultimately rejoin the North Atlantic Current.

Irradiance, The radiant energy that passes through a unit horizontal area per unit time coming from all directions above it.

Irrigation, The application of water, by means of canals, pipes, sprinklers, or controlled flooding, onto a land surface to augment the water that otherwise would be inadequate to promote growth of crops or other vegetation.

Isallobar, A contour line on a weather map that signifies the location of equal changes of pressure over a specified period.

Isallobaric wind, A theoretical wind component originating from the spatial non-uniformity of local rates of change of pressure.

Isentropic coordinates, The replacement of the z coordinate in an x-y-z coordinate system with the potential temperature. This can be done when horizontal scales are large compared to vertical scales, i.e. when the hydrostatic approximation can be made.

Island, (a) An area of land completely surrounded by water. (b) An elevated area of land surrounded by swamp, or marsh, or isolated at high water or during floods.

Isohaline, A contour of constant salinity.

Isohyet, A line, or contour on an isohyetal map, that connects points of equal precipitation; isohyets and isohyetal maps generally refer to amounts of mean annual precipitation (as examples, 50 mm or 100 mm), but also can be generated for other periods of time such as months, seasons, or the duration of a single storm.

Isopleth, A general term referring to lines drawn on a map or chart to display the distribution of any element, each line being drawn through places at which the element has the same value, for example, isohaline, isobar, etc. Isogram is sometimes used as a synonym.

Isopycnal, A contour of constant density.

Isostasy, The tendency of the crust of the earth (i.e. the lithosphere) to maintain a near equilibrium state in relation to the denser, underlying asthenosphere or upper mantle. For example, a continental block might sink or rise due to the presence or absence of an ice sheet in a process called glacial isostatic adjustment. Isostasy refers to the way in which the lithosphere and mantle respond visco-elastically to changes in surface loads. When the loading of the lithosphere and/or the mantle is changed by alterations in land ice mass, ocean mass, sedimentation, erosion or mountain building, vertical isostatic adjustment results, in order to balance the new load. *(Fig. 8 and 9)*

Isostere, A line on a chart joining points of equal specific volume, the volume of unit mass.

Isotach, A line or contour of constant wind speed. An alternative is isovel.

Isotherm, A contour of constant temperature.

Isotope stage, A division of a deep-sea core on the basis of oxygen isotope ratios. There have been 19 isotope stages since the reversal of the Earth's magnetic field 700,000 years ago.

Isotope, Each of two or more varieties of a particular chemical element which have different numbers of neutrons in the nucleus, and therefore different relative atomic masses and different nuclear (but the same chemical) properties.

J

Japan Sea, A marginal sea of the western Pacific Ocean bounded on the east by the Japanese islands, the west and southwest by Korea, and the north and northwest by the former Soviet Union. It is connected to the East China Sea in the south, the Okhotsk Sea in the north, and the Pacific Ocean in the east via narrow passages whose sill depths don't exceed 100 m. It comprises the Japan Basin (with depths exceeding 3500 m) north of about 40° N, and the Yamato Basin (with depths around 2500 m) south of 40° N, the the basins separated by the Yamato Ridge. The dimensions are are about 1600 by 900 km, an area of 978,000 km$_2$, the average depth 1750 m, and a maximum depth of about 3700 m.

JavaSea, A shallow body of water located in the southwestern part of the Australasian Mediterranean Sea. Centered at about 114° E and 5° S, it has average depths of around 40-50 m, and an area ranging from 367,000 to 433,000 km$_2$ depending on where the boundaries are specified. It is connected to the Sulawesi Sea to the northeast by the Makassar Strait, adjoins the Flores Sea to the east, connects to the South China Sea to the northwest via the Karimata Strait, and abuts the Ball Sea to the south and Kalimantan to the north. It is sometimes grouped together with the shelf sector of the South China Sea as the SundaSea, and also variously spelled as Jawa Sea.

Jet stream, A well-defined core of strong wind, ranging from 200-300 miles (320-480 km) wide with wind speeds up to 200 mph (320 kph), that occurs in the vicinity of the tropopause.

Joint, A surface of actual or potential fracture or parting in a rock, without displacement; the surface is usually planar and often occurs with parallel joints to form part of a joint set.

K

Kamchatka Current, One of two currents (the other being the Alaskan Stream) in the northwest Pacific that combine to form the Oyashio Current.

Kame moraine, (a) An end moraine that contains numerous kames. (b) A group of kames along the front of a stagnant glacier, commonly comprising the slumped or erosional remnants of a formerly continuous outwash plain built up over the foot of rapidly wasting or stagnant ice.

Kame terrace, A terrace-like ridge consisting of stratified sand and gravel 1) deposited by a meltwater stream flowing between a melting glacier and a higher valley wall or lateral moraine, and 2) left standing after the disappearance of the ice. It is commonly pitted with "kettles" and has an irregular ice-contact slope.

Kame, A low mound, knob, hummock, or short irregular ridge, composed of stratified sand and gravel deposited by a subglacial stream as a fan or delta at the margin of a melting glacier; by a supraglacial stream in a low place or hole on the surface of the glacier; or as a ponded deposit on the surface or at the margin of stagnant ice.

Karst cone, A conically-shaped residual hill in karst with a rounded top and relatively steep, convex (e.g., parabolic) side slopes, commonly in tropical climates.

Karst drainage pattern, A drainage pattern that lacks an integrated drainage system associated with soluble rocks with little or no surface drainage but a considerable underground, internal drainage system; characteristic of karst landscapes underlain by limestone, gypsum, or salt.

Karst lake, A large area of standing water in an extensive closed depression in soluble bedrock (e.g., limestone) and commonly is directly connected to and controlled by the subsurface karst drainage network.

Karst tower, An isolated, separate hill or ridge in a karst region consisting of an erosional remnant of limestone or other sedimentary rocks with vertical or near-vertical, convex side slopes and commonly surrounded by an alluvial plain, lagoon, or deep rugged ravines.

Karst valley, A closed depression formed by the coalescence of multiple sinkholes; an elongate, solutional valley. Its drainage is subsurface, diameters range from several hundred meters to a few kilometers, and it usually has a scalloped margin inherited from the sinkholes. It may have nominal, local channel flow (small streams), sequential sinkhole inlets (springs) and outlets (swallow hole, etc.).

Karst, A kind of topography formed in limestone, gypsum, or other soluble rocks by dissolution, and that is characterized by closed depressions, sinkholes, caves, and underground drainage. Various types of karst can be recognized depending upon the dominant surface features: karst dominated by closed depressions (*sinkhole karst* – temperate climates; *cockpit karst* – humid tropical climates), closed depressions and large rivers (*fluviokarst*), bare rock dominated by dissolution joints (*pavement karst*), tropical cone-, tower- or domed-hills (*kegel karst*), or karst thinly mantled with glacial drift (*glaciokarst*), etc. A type of topography or large-scale landform characterized by numerous collapse structures visible at the surface as spring or cave openings and sinkholes, and in the subsurface as caves and smaller solution openings that provide underground drainage; the closed depressions and collapse structures that dot a karst landscape are the result of chemical weathering by dissolution of carbonate rocks, principally limestone and dolomite, and less commonly of evaporate rocks, especially gypsum and anhydrite, in areas of arid and semiarid Climate.

Karstic marine terrace, A relict, wave-cut terrace or solution platform formed across soluble bedrock (e.g., limestone), and subsequently subaerially weathered by solution resulting in prominent karst features (e.g., sinkholes, karst valleys, solution pipes, etc.); a type of marine terrace, extensive across the Florida peninsula. Dunefields and sand sheets of reworked coastal / fluviomarine sands are common capping materials.

Karstic, Having the attributes of karst.

Katabatic wind, A phenomenon that originates with a layer of cold air forming near the ground on a night with clear skies and a low pressure gradient. If the ground is sloping, the air close to the ground is colder than air at the same level but at some horizontal distance. The result is downslope gravitational flow of the colder, denser air beneath the warmer, lighter air. This occurs on the largest scale as the outflowing winds from Greenland and Antarctica. Contrast with anabatic wind.

Kelvin wave, A type of coastally trapped wave motion where the velocity normal to the coast vanishes everywhere. The wave is nondispersive and propagates parallel to the shore with the speed of shallow water gravity waves, The profile perpendicular to shore either decays or grows exponentially seaward depending on whether the wave propagates with the coast to its right or left (in the northern hemisphere). For vanishing rotation, the decay or growth scale becomes infinite and the Kelvin wave reduces to an ordinary gravity wave propagating parallel to the coast. The dynamics of a Kelvin wave are such that it is exactly a linearized shallow water gravity wave in the longshore direction and exactly geostrophic in the cross-shore direction.

Kerguelan Plateau, A ridge located at approximately 75° E in the Southern Ocean that impedes the flow of the Antarctic Circumpolar Current at depths below 2000 m. Most of this broad plateau is between 2000 and 3000 m deep with some flow occurring below 3000 m in a narrow gap between itself and Antarctica.

Kettle – A steep-sided, bowl-shaped depression commonly without surface drainage (closed depression) in drift deposits, often containing a lake or swamp, and formed by the melting of a large, detached block of stagnant ice that had been wholly or partly buried in the drift. Kettles range in depth from 1 to tens of meters, and with diameters up to 13 km. *(Fig. 95)*

Kinematic viscosity The ratio of the viscosity coefficient to density of a liquid, is a measure of the ability of streamflow to entrain and transport sediment.

Knickpoint, Any interruption or break of a channel gradient, especially a headcut site of abrupt change or inflection in the longitudinal profile of a stream channel or its valley. *(Fig. 67)*

Knight Inlet, A fjord located on the west coast of Canada approximately 300 km north of Vancouver. It exhibits the characteristic steep sides, deep basins, and sills of a fjord estuary, and first reaches inland eastward from the mouth to Sallie Point and after an abrupt turn reaches sinuously northward to the head. Two sills - on 64 m deep at the mouth and the other 68 m deep about 72 km from the head -separate the inlet's 120 km length into two basins. The outer basin has a maximum depth of 250 m and the inner basin 540 m.

Knob, (a) A rounded eminence, a small hill or mountain; especially a prominent or isolated hill with steep sides. (b) A peak or other projection from the top of a hill or mountain. Also, a boulder or group of boulders or an area of resistant rocks protruding from the side of a hill or mountain.

Knoll, (undersea feature) An elevation somewhat smaller than a seamount and of rounded profile, characteristically isolated or as a cluster on the sea floor;

Knoll, A small, low, rounded hill rising above adjacent landforms.

Knot, A speed of 1 nautical mph. It is equal to 1.15 mph or 1.85 kph and used in navigation and meteorology.

Kuroshio Current, A western boundary current located in the western North Pacific Ocean. The Kuroshio begins where the North Equatorial Current approaches the Philippines and continues northward east of Taiwan. It then crosses a ridge between Kyushu and the Okinawa Islands, responding by forming the East China Sea meander, and proceeds through the Tokara Strait, after which it takes a sharp turn to the left (north). *(Fig. 142, 145)*

Kymatology, The science of waves and wave motion.

L

Labrador Basin, A ocean basin situated between Labrador, Greenland and Newfoundland. It underlies the Labrador Sea as well as most of the Irminger Sea.

Labrador Current, A current that flows southward over the continental shelves and slopes of Labrador and Newfoundland from Hudson Strait at 60° N to the Tail of the Grand Banks of Newfoundland at 43°N. It was first described by Smith et al. [1937] as a continuation of the Baffin hland Current, which transports the cold and relatively low salinity waters flowing out of Baffin Bay, and the warmer and more saline waters of a branch of the West Greenland Current. It appears as two branches at Hamilton Bank on the southern Labrador Shelf, a small inshore stream carrying about 15% of the transport and the main stream over the upper continental slope carrying about 85%. *(Fig. 142)*

Labrador Sea, A part of the north Atlantic recognized as a separate body of water for hydrographic pur-poses although not officially recognized as such. The southern boundary is a line from the southern tip of Greenland to Cape St. Charles on the coast of Labrador and the northern boundary the 66° N latitude line that joins Greenland and Baffin Island north of the Arctic Circle.

Lacustrine deposit, Clastic sediments and chemical precipitates deposited in lakes.

Lacustrine, Any feature formed or caused by the processes of a lake; thus, a body of lacustrine sediment (lake beds) is typically one of mostly fine fluvial sediment that dropped from suspension as and while the silt-laden streamflow was ponded as lake water.

Lacustrine, Pertaining to a lake or lakes, or of plants and animals growing in or inhabiting lakes.

Lagoon [relict] – A nearly level, filled trough or depression behind the longshore bar on a barrier beach and built by a receding pluvial or glacial lake.

Lagoon bottom, The nearly level or slightly undulating central portion of a submerged, low-energy, depositional estuarine basin characterized by relatively deep water (1.0 to >2.5 m).

Lagoon channel, A subaqueous, sinuous area within a lagoon that likely represents a relict channel (paleochannel) that is maintained by strong currents during tidal cycles.

Lagoon, A shallow stretch of salt or brackish water, partly or completely separated from a sea or lake by an offshore reef, barrier island, sandbank or spit. *(Fig. 127, 130)*

Lagoonal deposit, Sand, silt or clay-sized sediments transported and deposited by wind, currents, and storm washover in the relatively low-energy, brackish to saline, shallow waters of a lagoon.

Lahar deposit, Unconsolidated volcaniclastic material emplaced as mudflows on or near the flanks of a volcano.

Lahar, The landform and sediments (i.e., lahar deposit) emplaced by, and the process associated with, a mudflow composed mainly of volcaniclastic debris on or near the flank of a volcano. Sediment composition includes pyroclastic material, primary lava-flow blocks and fragments, and nonvolcanic material. Thick lahar deposits may have crude (poorly sorted) upward-fining strata. A lahar is initially unconsolidated material, but through cementation and compression can become bedrock.

Lake plain, A nearly level surface marking the floor of an extinct lake filled by well-sorted, generally fine-textured, stratified deposits, commonly containing varves.

Lake terrace, A narrow shelf, partly cut and partly built, produced along a lake shore in front of a scarp line of low cliffs and later exposed when the water level falls.

Lake, An inland body of permanently standing water fresh or saline, occupying a depression on the Earth's surface, generally of appreciable size (larger than a pond) and too deep to permit vegetation (excluding subaqueous vegetation) to take root completely across the expanse of water.

Lakebed [relict], The flat to gently undulating, exposed ground underlain or composed of fine-grained sediments deposited in a former lake.

Lakebed, The bottom of a lake; a lake basin.

Lakeshore, The narrow strip of land in contact with or bordering a lake; especially the beach of a lake.

Lamella – A thin (< 7.5 cm thick), discontinuous or continuous, generally horizontal layer of fine material (especially clay and iron oxides) that has been pedogenically concentrated (illuviated) within a coarser (e.g., sandy), eluviated layer (several centimeters to several decimeters thick).

Lamina, The thinnest recognizable layer (commonly < 1 cm thick) of original deposition in a sediment or sedimentary rock, differing from other layers in color, composition, or particle size. Plural=laminae; Several laminae constitute a bed.

Laminar flow, (as a hydrologic term) The water movement (flow) in which the lines of flow are essentially constant and in which flow direction at all sites remains nearly unchanged through time; laminar flow is typical of most ground-water movement whereas most concentrated flows of stream channels are turbulent.

Land surface air temperature, The surface air temperature as measured in well-ventilated screens over land at 1.5 m above the ground.

Land use and Land use change, Land use refers to the total of arrangements, activities and inputs undertaken in a certain land cover type (a set of human actions). The term land use is also used in the sense of the social and economic purposes for which land is , managed (e.g., grazing, timber extraction and conservation). Land use change refers to a change in the use or management of land by humans, which may lead to a change in land cover. Land cover and land use change may have an impact on the surface albedo, evapotranspiration, sources and sinks of greenhouse gases, or other properties of the climate system and may thus have a radiative forcing and/or other impacts on climate, locally or globally.

Landform, Any physical, recognizable form or feature on the earth's surface, having a characteristic shape, internal composition, and produced by natural causes; a distinct individual produced by a set of processes. Landforms can span a large size (e.g., *dune* encompasses a number of feature including *parabolic dune*, which is tens-of-meters across and *seif dune*, which can be up to a 100 kilometers across. Landforms provide an empirical description of the earth's surface features.

Landscape, A broad or unique land area comprised of an assemblage or collection of landforms that define a general geomorphic form or setting (e.g., mountain range, lake plain, lava plateau, or loess hill) Landforms within a landscape are spatially associated, but may vary in formation processes and age.

Landslide, A general, encompassing term for most types of mass movement landforms and processes involving the downslope transport and outward deposition of soil and rock materials, caused by gravitational forces and which may or may not involve saturated materials. Names of landslide types generally reflect the dominant process and/or the resultant landform. The main operational categories of mass movement are *fall* (rockfall, debris fall, soil fall), *topple* (rock topple, debris topple, soil topple), *slide* (rotational landslide, block glide, debris slide, lateral spread), *flow* [rockfall avalanche, debris avalanche, debris flow (e.g., lahar), earthflow, (creep, mudflow)], and *complex landslides.* (*Fig. 47, 48*)

Land-surface form, The description of a given terrain unit based on empirical analysis of the land surface rather than interpretation of genetic factors. Surface form may be expressed quantitatively in terms of vertical and planimetric slope-class distribution, local and absolute relief, and patterns of terrain features such as interfluve crests, drainage lines, or escarpments.

Lapilli, Nonvesicular or slightly vesicular pyroclastics, 2.0 to 76 mm in at least one dimension, with an apparent specific gravity of 2.0 or more g/cm3.

Lapse rate, The rate of change of an atmospheric variable, usually temperature, with height. The lapse rate is considered positive when the variable decreases with height.

Lapse rate, The rate of decrease of temperature with height. This can be either an environmental or a process lapse rate. An environmental lapse rate is a static measure of the state of the environment, e.g. finding the rate of temperature decrease by measuring the vertical temperature profile in some way. A process lapse rate, on the other hand, gives the temperature associated with some action or process, e.g. a rising or sinking air parcel.

Last Glacial Maximum (LGM), The Last Glacial Maximum refers to the time of maximum extent of the ice sheets during the last glaciation, approximately 21 ka. This period has been widely studied because the radiative forcing and boundary conditions are relatively well known and because the global cooling during that period is comparable with the projected warming over the 21st century.

Latent heat, The quantity of heat absorbed or emitted, without change of temperature, during a change of state (from solid to liquid or from liquid to gas) of a unit mass of a material. It is a hidden heat (i.e. it can't be sensed by humans) that doesn't occur until phase changes ocur. An example is the evaporation of liquid water cloud droplets cooling the air by removing heat and storing it as latent heat.

Lateral moraine, A ridge-like moraine carried on and deposited at the side margin of a valley glacier. It is composed chiefly of rock fragments derived from valley walls by glacial abrasion and plucking, or colluvial accumulation from adjacent slopes. (*Fig. 91*)

Lateral spread, A category of mass movement processes, associated sediments (lateral spread deposit), or resultant landform characterized by a very rapid *spread* dominated by lateral movement in a soil or fractured rock mass resulting from liquefaction or plastic flow of underlying materials; also called spread. Types of lateral spreads can be specified based on the dominant particle size of sediments (i.e., debris spread, earth spread, rock spread.

Laurasia, The name given to a hypothetical northern hemisphere supercontinent consisting of North America, Europe, and Asia north of Himalayas prior to breaking up into its separate components. It was formed in the early Mesozoic by the rifting of Pangaea along the line of the North Atlantic Ocean and the Tethys Sea. The southern hemisphere analogue was called Gondwanaland and both comprised a hypothetical single supercontinent called Pangaea before their splitting up. *(Fig. 10 and 23)*

Laurentia, The Precambrian craton of central eastern Canada. It forms the ancient core of Canada, the remainder having been accreted via orogeny.

Lava dome, A rounded or irregular mound, hill or small mountain composed of lava congealed over a volcanic vent on the flanks or within a crater or caldera. Typically composed of silica-rich volcanic rocks (e.g., rhyolite, dacite) with admixtures of obsidian, agglomerate, volcanic breccia, etc. The lava may be uniform or varied in color and texture; also called a resurgent dome.

Lava field, An area covered primarily by lava flows whose terrain can be rough and broken or relatively smooth; it can include vent structures (e.g., small cinder cones, spatter cones, etc.), surface flow structures (e.g., pressure ridges, tumuli, etc.) and small, intermittent areas covered with pyroclastics.

Lava flow unit, A separate, distinct lobe of lava that issues from the main body of a lava flow; a specific outpouring of lava, a few centimeters to several meters thick and of variable lateral extent that forms a subdivision within a single flow. A series of overlapping lava flow-units together comprise a single lava flow. Also called flow unit.

Lava flow, A solidified body of rock formed from the lateral, surficial outpouring of molten lava from a vent or fissure, often lobate in form.

Lava plain, A broad area of nearly level land, that can be localized but is commonly hundreds of square kilometers in extent, covered by a relatively thin succession of primarily basaltic lava flows resulting from fissure eruptions.

Lava plateau, A broad elevated tableland or flat-topped highland that may be localized but commonly is many hundreds or thousands of square kilometers in extent, underlain by a thick succession of basaltic lava flows resulting from fissure eruptions (e.g., Deccan Plateau).

Lava trench, A natural surface channel in a lava flow that never had a roof, formed by the surficial draining of molten lava rather than by erosion from running water; also called lava channel.

Lava tube, A natural, hollow tunnel beneath the surface of a solidified lava flow through which the lava flow was fed; the tunnel was left empty when the molten lava drained out.

Lava, A general term for a molten extrusive, also the rock solidified from it.

Ledge, (a) A narrow shelf or projection of rock, much longer than wide, formed on a rock wall or cliff face, as along a coast by differential wave action on softer rocks; erosion is by combined biological and chemical weathering. (b) A rocky outcrop; solid rock. (c) A shelf-like quarry exposure or natural rock outcrop.

Lee – Said of a side or slope that faces away from an advancing glacier or ice sheet, and facing the downstream ("down-ice") side of a glacier and relatively protected from its abrasive action.

Lentic, A still or sluggish water such as lakes, ponds, and swamps; lentic species are organisms that live in still or sluggish water.

Levee, (natural) of a stream channel. A broad, low ridge or embankment of coarse silt and sand that is deposited by a stream on its flood plain and along either bank of its channel; natural levees are formed by reduced velocity of flood flows as they spill onto flood-plain surfaces and can no longer transport the coarse fraction of the suspended-sediment load. Especially along meandering streams, natural levees may be of mappable areal extent; they tend to be relatively thin bands of silt and sand sloping gently down-valley from the down-valley bank of the channel from that portion of a meander crossing the valley floor.

Levee, (undersea feature) A depositional natural embankment bordering a canyon, valley or seachannel on the ocean floor. An artificial or natural embankment built along the margin of a watercourse or an arm of the sea, to protect land from inundation or to confine streamflow to its channel.

Leveled land, A land area, usually a field, that has been mechanically flattened or smoothed to facilitate management practices such as flood irrigation; as a result the natural soil has been partially or completely modified (e.g., truncated or buried).

Limestone, A sedimentary rock consisting chiefly (more than 50 percent) of calcium carbonate, primarily in the form of calcite. Limestones are usually formed by a combination of organic and inorganic processes and include chemical and clastic (soluble and insoluble) constituents; many contain fossils. *(Fig. 112)*

Limonite, A general "field" term for various brown to yellowish brown, amorphous- to-cryptocrystalline hydrous ferric oxides that are an undetermined mixture of goethite, hematite, and lepidocrocite formed by weathering and iron oxidation from iron-bearing rocks and minerals.

Lincoln Sea, A part of the Arctic Mediterranean Sea located on the Greenland-Canadian-Alaskan shelf. It is situated northeastward of Ellesmere Island and northwest of northern Greenland.

Lithification, The conversion of unconsolidated sediment into a coherent and solid rock, involving processes such as cementation, compaction, desiccation, crystallization, recrystallization, and compression. It may occur concurrently with, shortly after, or long after deposition.

Lithologic, Pertaining to the physical character of a rock.

Lithosphere, The upper layer of the solid Earth, both continental and-ticeanic, which comprises all crustal rocks and the cold, mainly elastic part of the uppermost mantle. Volcanic activity, although part of the lithosphere, is not considered as part of the climate system, but acts as an external forcing factor.

Little Ice (Age), A return to colder climatic conditions beginning in about 1450 and ending around 1890. This was an era of moderate, renewed glaciation that followed the warmest known part of the Holocene. It was marked by the advance of valley glaciers in the Alps, Alaska, Swedish Lapland and New Zealand far beyond their present limits as well as by snow on the high mountains of Ethiopia where it is now unknown. The evidence points to two main cold stages, each lasting about a century, during the seventeenth and nineteenth centuries. Regional timings of the cold periods differed and thus some doubts have been raised as to the global nature of this phenomenon.

Little Ice Age (LIA), An interval between approximately AD 1400 and 1900 when temperatures in the Northern Hemisphere were generally colder than today's, especially in Europe.

Loam, A porous, permeable soil comprised of similar proportions of clay, silt, and sand; loams generally contain humus (decomposed organic matter) and may have a minor amount of gravel.

Local relief, (a) An informal term referring to the prevailing difference in elevation between drainageways or local depressions and adjacent elevated landforms (on a local scale). (b) A generic term referring to the collective, relative differences in elevation of a land surface on a broad scale.

Loess bluff, A bluff composed of a thick deposit of coarse loess, formed immediately adjacent to the edges of flood plains, as along the Mississippi River valley or China.

Loess, A wind-deposited accumulation of terrestrial clastic sediment generally of coarse-clay to fine-sand sizes but mostly silt; loess bodies tend to be highly erodible, unstratified, and are mostly derived by deflation and re-deposition of fine, quartzitic sediment from poorly protected surfaces of till, glacial outwash, fluvial-overbank and lake-bed deposits, and deserts.

Lombok Strait, A strait located at 155°37'E-116°02'E and 8°20'S-8°50'S between the islands of Lombok and Bali in the Australasian Mediterranean Sea. This is one of many possible and the second largest of the passages for throughflow from the Pacific to the Indian Ocean, and connects the western Flores Sea to the Indian Ocean. The strait spans a length of about 60 km with a north-south orientation. It is about 40 km wide and 1000 m deep at its northern opening, but only 18 km wide and 300 m deep at the sill in the southern opening.

Longitudinal dune, A long, narrow sand dune, usually symmetrical in cross profile, oriented parallel to the prevailing wind direction; it is wider and steeper on the windward side but tapers to a point on the lee side. It commonly forms behind an obstacle in an area where sand is abundant and the wind is strong and constant. Such dunes can be a few meters high and up to 100 km long. *(Fig. 103)*

Longshore bar [relict], A narrow, elongate, wave-built sand ridge that originally rose near to, or barely above, the surface of a body of water, and extended generally parallel to the shore but was separated from it by an intervening trough.

Longshore bar, A low, elongate sand ridge, built chiefly by wave action, occurring at some distance from, and extending generally parallel with, the shoreline. They are submerged at least by high tides and are typically separated from the beach by an intervening trough.

Longshore bar, A ridge of sand running roughly parallel to the shoreline which may become exposed at low tide. There can be a series of these running parallel to one another at different water depths.

Longshore trough, An elongated depression extending parallel to the shoreline and any longshore bars that are present and, like the longshore bars, there may be more than one present.

Lotic, The moving water, especially streamflow; lotic species are organisms that live in moving water.

Low hill , A generic name for an elevated, generally rounded land surface with low local relief, rising between 30 m (100 ft.) to as much as 90 m (approx. 300 ft.) above surrounding lowlands.

Low marsh, The flat, usually bare ground situated seaward of a salt marsh and regularly covered and uncovered by the tide; e.g., a mud flat.

Low pressure center, In meteorology, a region of relatively low barometric pressure. These are characterized by upward moving air at altitude and convergence near the ground. These predominate in midlatitudes, i.e. around 40-50°. These are also known as cyclones and as such rotate clock-wise/counterclockwise in the southern/northern hemisphere. Low pressure systems are generally characterized by clouds, precipitation, and occasionally thunderstorms, all of which are facilitated by the upward movement of moist air from near the ground.

Lower high water interval (LHWI), The time interval between the transit of the moon over either the local or Greenwich meridian and the next lower high water (LHW). This is generally used when the diurnal inequality is large.

Lower high water, (LHW) The lower of two high waters on a day when the tide is neither predominantly diurnal nor predominantly semidiurnal but rather intermediate to either (a situation sometimes called a mixed tide).

Lower low water (LLW), The lower of two low waters on a day when the tide is neither predominantly diurnal nor predominantly semidiurnal but rather intermediate to either (a situation sometimes called a mixed tide).

Lower low water interval (LLWI), The time interval between the transit of the moon over either the local or Greenwich meridian and the next lower low water (LLW). This is generally used when the diurnal inequality is large.

Lowland, An informal, generic, imprecise term for low-lying land or an extensive region of low-lying land, especially near a coast and including the extended plains or country lying not far above tide level.

Lysocline, The upper portion of the transition zone in sediments between supersaturated (shallow) and undersaturated (deep) sediments in the ocean. The transition is between the burial and dissolution of $CaCO_3$ sediments.

Maar, A low relief, broad volcanic crater formed by multiple, shallow explosive eruptions. It is surrounded by a crater ring in the form of low ramparts of gently dipping (i.e., < 25 degrees), well-bedded tephra; may be partially or completely filled by water.

Mafic rock, A general term for igneous rock composed chiefly of one or more ferromagnesian, dark-colored minerals; also said of those minerals.

Main scarp, The steep surface on undisturbed ground at the upper edge of a landslide, caused by movement of displaced material away from the undisturbed ground; it is visible a part of the surface of rupture (slip surface).

Mainland cove, A subaqueous area adjacent to the mainland or a submerged mainland beach that forms a minor recess or embayment within the larger basin.

Mangrove swamp, A tropical or subtropical marine swamp formed in a silty, organic, or occasionally a coralline substratum and characterized by abundant mangrove trees along the seashore in a low area of salty or brackish water affected by daily tidal fluctuation but protected from violent wave action by reefs or land.

Manning equation, An empirical formula relating stream velocity to controlling variables; when channel width and depth are included, the simplified formula (in metric units) is expressed in terms of discharge, $Q = [1/n]G_{1/2} WD_{5/3}$ in which n is the roughness coefficient, G is channel gradient, W is channel width, and D is mean channel depth. For hydraulic computations, the formula is usually expressed as $Q =$, in which n is the roughness coefficient, A is cross-sectional area, R is hydraulic radius, and S is the energy slope of the reach.

Marine deposit, Sediments (predominantly sands, silts and clays) of marine origin; laid down in the waters of an ocean. *(Fig. 151, 152, 153)*

Marine lake, An inland body of permanently standing brackish or saline water, occupying a depression on the Earth's surface whose water level is commonly influenced by ocean tides through subterranean cavities connecting to nearby lagoons; generally of appreciable size (larger than a pond) and too deep to permit emergent vegetation to take root completely across the expanse of water. Such water bodies can have unique biota.

Marine palynology, The study of pollen deposits in marine records.

Marine snow, Oceanic particles which are amorphous, heterogeneous aggregates greater than 500 mm and composed of detrital material, living organisms and inorganic matter.

Marine terrace, A constructional coastal strip, sloping gently seaward, veneered by marine deposits (typically silt, sand, fine gravel).

Marl, A generic term loosely applied to a variety of materials, most of which occur as an earthy, unconsolidated deposit consisting chiefly of an intimate mixture of clay and calcium carbonate formed commonly by the chemical action of algae mats and organic detritus (periphyton); specifically an earthy substance containing 35 to 65 % clay and 65 to 35 % calcium carbonate mud; formed primarily under freshwater lacustrine conditions, but varieties associated with more saline environments and higher carbonate contents also occur.

Marsh , Periodically wet or continually flooded areas with the surface not deeply submerged. Covered dominantly with sedges, cattails, rushes, or other hydrophytic plants.

Mass balance (of glaciers, ice caps or ice sheets), The balance between the mass input to the ice body (accumulation) and the mass loss.

Mass movement, A generic term for any process or sediments (mass movement deposit) resulting from the dislodgment and downslope transport of soil and rock material as a unit under direct gravitational stress. The process includes slow displacements such as creep and solifluction, and rapid movements such as landslides, rock slides, and falls, earthflows, debris flows, and avalanches. Agents of fluid transport (water, ice, air) may play an important, if subordinate role in the process. Any downslope transfer, through gravitational (inertial) and generally water-facilitated (viscous) processes, of near-surface soil and rock material; rates of mass movement range from very slow creep to nearly instantaneous slope failure. *(Fig. 47, 48, 49)*

Mass wasting, The failure and movement by gravity of a volume of soil, alluvium, rock, or ice to a downslope site storage; is the result of the process of mass movement. *(Fig. 47)*

Mean annual flood, The average flood discharge (m_3 s_{-1}) for a specified period or number of years.

Mean meridional circulation, An average circulation feature or cell defined to consist of the zonal-mean meridional and vertical velocities. In the tropics and subtropics this mean meridional circulation cell is known as the Hadley cell and in midlatitudes as the Ferrel cell.

Mean sea level (MSL), A concept defined differently in the fields of tidal analysis and geodesy. In tidal analysis, MSL means the still water level averaged over a period of time such as a month or year so periodic changes in sea level due to, e.g. the tides, are also averaged out. MSL values are measured with respect to the level of benchmarks on land, and as such a change in an MSL can result from either a real change in sea level or a change in the height of the land on which the tide gauge is located (e.g. from isostatic rebound). In geodesy, MSL usually means the local height of the global Mean Sea Surface (MSS) above a level reference surface called the geoid.

Mean specific mass balance, The total mass balance per unit area of the glacier. If surface is specified (specific surface mass balance, etc.) then ice flow contributions are not considered; otherwise, mass balance includes contributions from ice flow and iceberg calving. The specific surface mass balance is positive in the accumulation area and negative in the ablation area.

Meander belt, Area of an alluvial bottomland defined by lines, on both sides of the zone of activity, drawn tangentially along the points of maximum horizontal extent of the various meanders in a sequence of meanders. The zone within which migration of a meandering channel occurs; the flood plain area included between two imaginary lines drawn tangential to the outer bends of active channel loops. Landform components of the meander-belt surface are produced by a combination of gradual (lateral and down-valley) migration of meander loops and avulsive channel shifts causing abrupt cut-offs of loop segments. Landforms flanking the sinuous stream channel include: point bars, abandoned meanders, meander scrolls, oxbow lakes, natural levees, and flood-plain splays. Meander belts may not exhibit prominent natural levee or splay forms. Flood plains of broad valleys may contain one or more abandoned meander belts in addition to the zone flanking the active stream channel. *(Fig. 60)*

Meander scar, (a) A crescent-shaped, concave or linear mark on the face of a bluff or valley wall, produced by the lateral erosion of a meandering stream which impinged upon and undercut the bluff; if it's no longer adjacent to the modern stream channel it indicates an abandoned route of the stream. (b) An abandoned meander, commonly filled in by deposition and vegetation, but still discernable. *(Fig. 61)*

Meander scroll, One of a series of long, parallel, close fitting, crescent-shaped ridges and troughs formed along the inner bank of a stream meander as the channel migrated laterally down-valley and toward the outer bank.

Meander, (of a stream) One of a series of regular, sharp, freely developing, and sinuous curves, bends, loops, turns, or windings in the course of a stream; the process of stream meandering is a means of channel-gradient adjustment through sorting of stored sediment by erosion at the outside of a bend and deposition, as a point bar, at the inside of the bend. *(Fig. 60)*

Meandering channel, The term "meandering" should be restricted to loops with channel length more than 1.5 to 2 times the meander wave length. Meandering stream channels commonly have cross sections with low width-to-depth ratios, cohesive (fine-grained) bank materials, and low gradient. At a given bank-full discharge, meandering streams have gentler slopes, and deeper narrower, and more stable channel cross sections than braided streams. *(Fig. 60)*

Mechanical (or physical) weathering, The reduction of rock fragments and rock surfaces by physical processes including abrasion, shattering by particle impact, expansion of crevices by roots, frost action, or salt-crystal growth, and gravitational effects such as slope failure and other forms of mass movement. Mechanical weathering affects the physical condition of the rock or rock fragment; the chemistry of the rock is unaltered.

Medial moraine, (a) An elongate moraine carried in or upon the middle of a glacier and parallel to its sides, usually formed by the merging of adjacent and inner lateral moraines below the junction of two coalescing valley glaciers. (b) A moraine formed by glacial abrasion of a rocky protuberance near the middle of a glacier and whose debris appears at the glacier surface in the ablation area. (c) The irregular ridge left behind in the middle of a glacial valley, when the glacier on which it was formed has disappeared.

Median valley, (undersea feature) The axial depression of the mid-oceanic ridge system.

Medieval Warm Period (MWP), An interval between AD 1000 and 1300 in which some Northern Hemisphere regions were warmer than during the Little Ice Age that followed.

Mediolittoral zone, The second (from the surface) of seven zones into which the benthos has been divided. In this zone organisms are more or less regularly emerged and submerged, usually by the action of the tides. Species are here adapted to resist prolonged emersion and are generally incapable of living if continually emerged.

Mediterranean sea, A generic term used to describe a class of ocean basins that have limited Communication with the major ocean basins and in which the circulation is dominated by thermohaline forcing. This causes a circulation that is the reverse of that found in the major basins, i.e. it is driven by salinity and temperature differences and only modified by wind action. Mediterranean seas exhibit the dynamics of estuaries rather than those of open oceans. Examples include the Arctic Mediterranean Basin, Australasian Mediterreanan Basin, and of course the Mediterranean Sea. * Mediterranan seas can be further distinguished by their balance of precipitation and evaporation. If evaporation exceeds precipitation, the deep vertical convection occurs and the water below the sill depth is frequently renewed. The open ocean connection features inflow in the upper layer and outflow in the lower layer since the inflow is driven by the freshwater loss in the upper layer. This is called a concentration basin.

Mediterranean Sea, A semi-enclosed basin containing many of the characteristics found in the open ocean, e.g. deep and intermediate water formation, jets, eddies, and intense air-sea interaction. It is an evaporation basin with the most significant heat loss occuring in the northern portion, particularly in the Gulfe de Lion and northern Adriatic Sea were deep water is formed.

Melt-out till, A till that may be either subglacial or supraglacial in origin. Melt-out till forms by slow melting of debris-rich stagnant ice, but without secondary flow processes. The fabric and clast orientations, imparted by ice processes, remain mostly intact.

Mesa, An isolated, flat-topped landform that stands distinctly above the adjacent land area and is bounded by steep slopes or cliffs; and is generally capped by erosion-resistant, nearly horizontal rock (often lava). Mesas and buttes have similar forms and isolated occurrence. A mesa has a summit area broader than the bounding cliff height. Mesas are most common in arid and semiarid regions, but are not climatically restricted. *(Fig. 105, 106)*

Mesopelagic zone, One of five vertical ecological zones into which the deep sea is sometimes dividend. This is the uppermost aphotic zone from 200 to 1000 m deep where little light penetrates and the temperature gradient is even and gradual with little seasonal variation. This zone contains an oxygen minimum layer and usually the maximum concentrations of the nutrients nitrate and phosphate. This overlies the bathypelagic zone and is overlain by the epipelagic zone.

Metadata, Information about meteorological and climatological data concerning how and when they were measured, their quality, known problems and other characteristics.

Metamorphic rock, Rock of any origin altered in mineralogical composition, chemical composition, or structure by heat, pressure, and movement at depth in the earth's crust. Nearly all such rocks are crystalline. Examples: schist, gneiss, quartzite, slate, marble. *(Fig. 40)*

Metasediment, A sediment or sedimentary rock that shows evidence of having been subjected to metamorphism.

Meteoric water, Water produced by or derived from the atmosphere. Meteoric waters start as precipitation in the hydrologic cycle, and the source thereof is evaporation from oceanic surfaces.

Meteorite crater, An impact crater formed by the falling of a large meteorite onto the earth's surface.

Meteorological equator, The latitude of the mean annual position of the equatorial trough. This is located at about 5° N rather than on the geographical equator.

Meteosat, A geostationary meteorological satellite.

Microbiotic crust , A thin, surface layer (crust) of soil particles bound together primarily by living organisms and their organic byproducts; thickness can range up from < 1 cm up to 10 cm; aerial coverage of the ground surface can range from 10 to 100 %. Crusts stabilize loose earthy material. Other types of surface crusts include chemical crusts (e.g., salt crusts) and physical crusts (e.g., raindrop-impact crust).

Microfeature, Small, local, natural forms (features) on the land surface that are too small to delineate on a topographic or soils map at commonly used map scales (e.g., 1:24,000 to 1:10,000). Examples include earth pillar, patterned ground, frost boil.

Microhigh, A generic microrelief term applied to slightly elevated areas relative to the adjacent ground surface; differences in relief range from several centimeters to several meters. Cross-sectional profiles can be simple or complex and generally consist of gently rounded, convex tops with gently sloping sides.

Microlow, A generic microrelief term applied to slightly lower areas relative to the adjacent ground surface (e.g., shallow depression); differences in relief range from several centimeters to several meters. Cross-sectional profiles can be simple or complex and generally consist of subdued, concave, open or closed depressions with gently sloping sides.

Microrelief , Slight variations in the height of a land surface that are too small or intricate to delineate on a topographic or soils map at commonly used map scales (e.g., 1:24,000 through 1:10,000). Examples include microhigh, microslope, and microlow.

Microslope, A generic microrelief term applied to areas of nominal surface relief (slightly sloping to level), relative to the adjacent ground surface; differences in overall local relief range from several centimeters to several meters. Cross-sectional profiles can be simple or complex and generally consist of low and gently rounded, convex tops (microhigh), gently sloping to level sides (microslope), and depressional low areas (microlow).

Minor scarp , A steep surface on the displaced material of a landslide, produced by differential movements within the sliding mass.

Miocene, An epoch of the Tertiary Period of geologic time (approximately 5.2 to 23 million years ago) that immediately follows the Oligocene and precedes the Pliocene Epoch.

Mistral, A northwesterly or northerly wind which blows offshore along the north coast of the Mediterranean from the Ebro to Genoa. In the region of its chief development its characteristics are its frequency, its strength, and its dry coldness. It is most intense on the coasts of Languedoc and Provence, especially near the Rhone delta. Its speeds are usually around 40 knots, but can reach over 75 knots in the delta.

Mitigation, A human intervention to reduce the sources or enhance the sinks of greenhouse gases.

Moat, (undersea feature) An annular depression that may not be continuous, located at the base of many seamounts, oceanic islands and other isolated elevations.

Monadnock, An isolated hill or mountain of resistant rock rising conspicuously above the general level of a lower erosion surface in a temperate climate representing an isolated remnant of a former erosion cycle in an area that has largely been beveled to its base level.

Monocline, (a) A unit of folded strata that dips from the horizontal in one direction only, is not part of an anticline or syncline, and occurs at the earth's surface. This structure is typically present in plateau areas where nearly flat strata locally assume steep dips caused by differential vertical movements without faulting. (b) A local steepening in an otherwise uniform gentle dip.

Monsoon, A periodic wind caused by the effects of differential heating, with the largest and most notorious being the Indian monsoon found in the Indian Ocean and southern Asia. The word is thought to have originated from the Arabic word mausim meaning season. *(Fig. 188, 189)*

Moraine, (a) A mound, ridge, or other topographically distinct accumulation of unsorted, unstratified glacial drift, predominantly till, deposited primarily by the direct action of glacier ice, in a variety of landforms. (b) A general term for a landform composed mainly of till that has been deposited by a glacier; a kame moraine is a type of moraine similar in exterior form to other types of moraines but composed mainly of stratified outwash materials. Types of moraine include: disintegration, end, ground, kame, lateral, recessional, and terminal. *(Fig. 91, 94)*

Mornington Abyssal Plain, One of three plains that comprise the Pacific-Antarctic Basin (the others being the Amundsen and the Bellingshausen Abyssal Plains. It is located at around 85-95° W.

Moss peat, An accumulation of organic material that is predominantly the remains of mosses (e.g., sphagnum moss).

Mound – (a) A low, rounded natural hill of unspecified origin, generally < 3 m high and, composed of earthy material. (b) A small, human-made hill, composed either of debris accumulated during successive occupations of the site (e.g., tell) or of earth heaped up to mark a burial site (e.g., burial mound). (c) A structure built by colonial organisms (e.g., termite mound).

Mountain range, A single, large mass consisting of a succession of mountains or narrowly spaced mountain ridges, with or without peaks, closely related in position, direction, orientation, formation, and age; a component part of a mountain system.

Mountain slope, A part of a mountain between the summit and the foot.

Mountain system, A group of mountain ranges exhibiting certain unifying features, such as similarity in form, structure and alignment, and presumably originating from the same general causes; especially a series of mountain ranges belonging to an orogenic belt.

Mountain valley, Any small, externally drained V-shaped depression (in cross-section) cut or deepened by a stream and floored with alluvium, or a broader, U-shaped depression modified by an alpine glacier and floored with either till or alluvium, that occurs on a mountain or within mountains. Several types of mountain valleys can be recognized based on their form and valley floor sediments (i.e., *V-shaped valley*, *U-shaped valley*).

Mountain, A generic term for an elevated area of the land surface, rising more than 300 meters above surrounding lowlands, usually with a nominal summit area relative to bounding slopes and generally with steep sides (greater than 25 percent slope) with or without considerable bare-rock exposed. A mountain can occur as a single, isolated mass or in a group forming a chain or range. Mountains are primarily formed by tectonic activity and/or volcanic action and secondarily by differential erosion.

Mountainbase, A geomorphic component of mountains consisting of the lowermost area, consisting of the strongly to slightly concave colluvial apron or wedge at the bottom of mountain slopes; composed of long-transport colluvium and slope alluvium sediment. It can extend out onto more level valley areas where it ultimately interfingers with, is buried by alluvium or is replaced by re-emergent residuum.

Mountainflank, A geomorphic component of mountains consisting of the side area of mountains, characterized by very long, complex backslopes with comparatively high slope gradients and composed of highly-diverse, colluvial sediment mantles, complex near-surface hydrology, mass movement processes and features (e.g., creep, landslides); rock outcrops or structural benches may be present. The mountainflank can be subdivided by the general location along the mountainside (i.e., upper third, middle third, or lower third mountainflank).

Mountaintop, A geomorphic component of mountains consisting of the uppermost, comparatively level or gently sloped area of mountains, characterized by relatively short, simple slopes composed of bare rock, residuum, or short-transport colluvial sediments. In humid environments, mountaintop soils can be quite thick and well developed.

Mozambique Current, A western boundary current that flows south-southwestward between the African coast and Madagascar from about 10 to 35° S. The flow has been estimated at about 6 Sv near 15° S increasing to 15 Sv near 20° as the northward looping East Madagascar Current turns back towards the south and joins it. This combined flow eventually becomes the major part of the Agulhas Current. *(Fig. 146)*

Mud flat, A relatively level area of fine grained material (e.g., silt) along a shore (as in a sheltered estuary) or around an island, alternately covered and uncovered by the tide or covered by shallow water, and barren of vegetation.

Mud pot, A type of hot spring containing boiling mud, usually sulfurous and often multicolored, as in a paint pot. Mud pots are commonly associated with geysers and other hot springs in volcanic areas.

Mudflow, The mass movement process, associated sediments (mudflow deposit), or resultant landform characterized by a very rapid type of earthflow dominated by a sudden, downslope movement of a saturated mass of rock, soil, and mud (more than 50 % of the particles are < 2 mm), that behaves as much as a viscous fluid when moving.

Mudstone, (a) A blocky or massive, fine-grained sedimentary rock in which the proportions of clay and silt are approximately equal. (b) A general term that includes clay, silt, claystone, siltstone, shale, and argillite, and that should be used only when the amounts of clay and silt are not known or cannot be precisely identified. *(Fig. 39)*

Natural levee, A long, broad low ridge or embankment of sand and coarse silt, built by a stream on its flood plain and along both sides of its channel, especially in time of flood when water overflowing the normal banks is forced to deposit the coarsest part of its load. It has a gentle slope away from the river and toward the surrounding floodplain, and its highest elevation is closest to the river bank.

Neap tide, The tides produced when the gravitational pull of the Sun is in quadrature, i.e. at right angles to, with that of the Moon. These occur twice a month at about the times of the first and last quarters. In these situations the gravitational pull of the Sun/Moon produces high/low water or vice-versa, and as such the differences between high and low tides are unusually small, with both the high tide lower and the low tide higher than usual. The tidal height is about 0.375 that of maximum during neap tides.

Nearshore zone [relict] , A former nearshore zone now subaerially exposed due to isostatic rebound or glacial lake drainage. Commonly a raised beach marks the former landward edge of a relict nearshore zone and relict longshore bars may exist in offshore positions. Surficial sediments may display evidence of wave and current action such as sorting or particle-size discontinuities.

Nearshore zone, A subaqueous marine or lacustrine landform area that generally parallels the shore and extends seaward or lakeward from the low water line to beyond the breaker zone including longshore bars. In the nearshore zone, waves steepen, break, and reform during passage to the beach. Sediment transport occurs both along and perpendicular to the shore via wave and current action.

Nearshore zone, A zone extending from the upper limit of a beach to the offshore. In terms of the beach profile, it consists of (progressing seawards) the backshore, foreshore and inshore. In terms of the wave and current regimes, it consists of (again progressing seawards) the swash zone, surf zone and breaker zone. *(Fig. 79)*

Nekton, One of three major ecological groups into which marine organisms are divided, the other two being the benthos and the plankton. Nekton are strongly swimming pelagic animals such as fish, some crustaceans, cephalopods, and whales which are capable of progressing against most water currents.

Neritic, Living in coastal waters as opposed to living upon the high seas, i.e. oceanic A division of the pelagic portion of the ocean that overlies the continental shelf.

Newfoundland Basin, An ocean basin lying between Newfoundland and the Azores whose floor is transected by the Mid-Ocean Canyon joining the Labradoar Basin with the Sohm Abyssal Plain. It is separated from basins to the south by the Southeast Newfoundland Ridge.

Nivation hollow, A shallow, non-cliffed depression or hollow on a mountain side permanently or intermittently occupied by a snow bank or snow patch and produced by nivation. If the snow completely melts each summer the hollow is deepened; otherwise not; may be a cirque precursor if further enlarged and deepened by alpine glaciation.

Nivation, The process of excavation of a shallow depression or nivation hollow on a mountain side by removal of fine material around the edge of a shrinking snow patch or snow bank, chiefly through sheetwash, rivulet flow, and solution in melt water. Freeze-thaw action is apparently insignificant.

Noise, In geophysical data processing this is most simply defined as any unwanted signal, and given that one person's signal can be another person's noise, this is ultimately a relative term. For example, if a time series is created by taking the temperature at some location every hour for five years, then the daily cycle of temperature that will be seen in such a record is a signal for someone looking for the daily cycle but is noise to someone looking for monthly or seasonal temperature variations.

Nonlinearity, A process is called nonlinear when there is no simple proportional relation between cause and effect. The climate system contains many such nonlinear processes, resulting in a system with a potentially very complex behaviour. Such complexity may lead to abrupt climate change.

North American Basin, A large depression centered around the Bermuda rise at about 85° W and 30° N in the western North Atlantic Ocean. It includes the Sohm Abyssal Plain to the northeast, the Hatteras Abyssal Plain to the west, and the Nares Abyssal Plain (or Nares Deep) to the southeast. Other prominent features in this basin include the Vema

Gap, the Blake-Bahama Outer Ridge, and Blake-Bahama Basin and the Puerto Rico Trench.

North Atlantic Current (NAC), A western boundary current (WBC) that flows north along the east side of the Grand Banks in the northwestern Atlantic from 40° to 51° N, where it turns sharply to the east at a location than has come to be known as the Northwest Corner. It is part of the subtropical gyre circulation in the North Atlantic and begins where the Gulf Stream curves north around the Southeast Newfoundland Rise. The path of the NAC is delineated by a well-defined front while it flows north as a WBC, but broadens into a widening band of eastward drift without a sharp or permanent front after it makes its turn at the Grand Banks.

North Atlantic Drift, The northward limb of the anticyclonic subtropical gyre in the North Atlantic Ocean. It is a northerly extension of the Gulf Stream but, due to a different dynamical regime, is a broader, slower current that carries warm water towards Europe, serving to ameliorate the climate there.

North Atlantic Oscillation (NAO), The North Atlantic Oscillation consists of opposing variations of barometric pressure near Iceland and near the Azores. It therefore corresponds to fluctuations in the strength of the main westerly winds across the Atlantic into Europe, and thus to fluctuations in the embedded cyclones with their associated frontal systems.

North Brazil Current (NBC), A current that flows in the western South Atlantic Ocean along the Brazilian coast from about 10 to 3° S along around 35° W. Geostrophic calculations (relative to 1000 m) show a broad (300 km wide), northwestward current transporting about 37 Sv at 5° S. It is concentrated in a subsurface core at 100-200 m depth. It continues as a coherent feature until the subthermocline layers retroflect at between 3 and 5° N to feed the North Equatorial Undercurrent (NEUC) and then the upper layers retroflect at between 5 and 8° N to feed the North Equatorial Countercurrent (NECC).

North Korea Current, A current that flows along the western coast in the Japan Sea. It is the southward continuation of part of the Liman Current and ultimately turns east and then northward (at around 38-40° N) to become part of the flow in the Polar Front.

North Pacific Current, The eastward continuation of the Kuroshio and Oyashio Extensions, with which it forms the southern limb of the North Pacific subpolar gyre. This is a broad band of eastward flow around 2000 km wide that, at some not well known location east of the Emperor Seamounts, becomes well distinguished from the two aforementioned narrower and strongly frontal flows that eventually merge into its broader flow. This current eventually turns north and, along with the Alaska Current, forms the eastward limb of the North Pacific subpolar gyre.

North Sea, An epicontinental sea occupying the shelf area between the British Isles and

Norway, Denmark, Germany, Holland and Belgium. The oceanic boundaries are a line across the Straits of Dover to the south, a line running from the northern tip of Scotland to the Orkney and Shetland Islands and then directly east to the coast of Norway to the north, and the Skagerrak to the east. It covers about 575,000 km_2, has an average depth of 94 m, and a volume of 54,000 km_3.

Norwegian Sea, A marginal sea of the North Atlantic Ocean which consists of the waters between the continental shelves of Norway and Spitsbergen to the east and the Mohn Ridge and Jan Mayen Ridge to the west. It adjoins the Barents Sea to the northeast, the Greenland Sea to the northwest, the Iceland Sea to the west, and the North Sea to the southeast. It covers an area of 1,383,000 km_2, has a volume of 2,408,000 km_3, and a mean depth of 1742 m. The term Norwegian Sea has also been used to collectively refer to the sea described here along with the Greenland Sea and the Iceland Sea.

Nose slope, A geomorphic component of hills consisting of the projecting end (laterally convex area) of a hillside, resulting in predominantly divergent overland water flow (e.g., sheet wash); contour lines generally form convex curves. Nose slopes are dominated by colluvium and slope wash sediments (e.g., slope alluvium). Slope complexity (downslope shape) can range from simple to complex. Nose slopes are comparatively drier portions of hillslopes and tend to have thinner colluvial sediments and profiles.

Notch, A narrow passageway, or short defile between mountains; a deep, close pass. A gap. A breached opening in the rim of a volcanic crater.

Nunatak , An isolated hill, knob, ridge, or peak of bedrock that projects prominently above the surface of a glacier and is completely surrounded by glacier ice.

Nutrients, The nutrients used as tracers in physical oceanography are essential dissolved chemicals eaten by plants in the ocean, i.e. phytoplankton. The basic nutrients are carbon, nitrogen and phosphorous, with all three having to be present for plant material to grow. Additionally, calcium and silicon are used as skeleton building materials. Micronutrients are those nutrients used in very small quantities. These are magnesium, iron, vanadium, molybdenum and selenium. Also used in small quantities but of no known value are cadmium and barium

O

Obliquity, Also called the obliquity of the ecliptic, this term is used to denote the tilt of the earth's axis with respect to the plane of the earth's orbit.

Ocean – The continuous salt-water body that surrounds the continents and fills the Earth's great depressions; also, one of its major geographic divisions.

Ocean acidification, A decrease in the pH of sea water due to the uptake of anthropogenic carbon dioxide.

Ocean Stratosphere, The lower layer of the ocean. The stratosphere is a sluggish, cold layer which is homogeneous vertically and horizontally in its basic properties. It is a region of slow exchanges.

Ocean troposphere, The upper layer of the ocean. The troposphere is a region of relatively high temperature where there are strong vertical and horizontal variations of properties. It is a zone of perturbations and strong currents.

Ocean water cycle, The distribution of evaporation and precipitation over the ocean is the ocean component of the global water or hydrological cycle. Since the ocean covers 70% of the Earth's surface and contains 97% of its free water, it plays a dominant role in this cycle. The terrestrial component of the cycle is understandably much more well understood, although the estimated 86% of global evaporation and 78% of precipitation that occur over the ocean should be better understood given the dramatic consequences small changes in the ocean cycle could have over land.

Oceanic, Living upon the high seas as opposed to living in coastal waters, i.e. neritic.

Offshore bar, Use barrier beach.

Offshore, The comparatively flat portion of a beach profile extending seaward from beyond the breaker zone to the edge of the continental shelf.

Okhotsk Sea, A marginal sea on the northern rim of the Pacific Ocean centered near 55° N and 150° E. It is bounded by the Siberian coast to the west and north, the Kamchatka Peninsula to the east, and the Kurile Islands to the south and southeast. It covers an area of about 1,600,000 km, has an average depth of about 860 m, and a maximum depth of 3370 m in the Kurile Basin. It is connected to both the Pacific Ocean and the Japan Sea via narrow passages, the most important ones being (for the former) the Boussole Strait (2318 m) and the Kruzenshtern Strait (1920 m) and (for the latter) the Tatarskyi Strait (50 m) and the Soya (or La Perouse) Strait (200 m).

Oligocene – An epoch of the Tertiary Period of geologic time (from 23.3 to 35.4 million years ago), which follows the Eocene Epoch and precede the Miocene Epoch.

Ombai Strait, One of the main passages for waters in the Indonesian archipelago to flow into the Indian Ocean. The Ombai Strait between Alor and Timor Islands is 3250 m deep.

Open depression, A generic name for any enclosed or low area that has a surface drainage outlet whereby surface water can leave the enclosure; an area of lower ground indicated on a topographic map by contour lines forming an incomplete loop or basin indicating at least one surface exit.

Openpit mine, A relatively large depression resulting from the excavation of material and redistribution of overburden associated with surficial mining operations.

Operational oceanography, The activity of routinely making, disseminating, and interpreting measurements of the seas and oceans so as to provide continuous forecasts of the future condition of the sea for as far ahead as possible, provide the most usefully accurate description of the present state of the sea including living resources, and assemble climatic long term datasets to provide data for the description of past states as well as time series showing trends and changes.

Ordinary High Water Mark, A legal term with numerous definitions generated by court decisions, the "ordinary high water mark" on non-tidal rivers is the line on the shore established by the fluctuations of water and indicated by physical characteristics such as a clear, natural line impressed on the bank, shelving, changes in the character of soil, destruction of terrestrial vegetation, the presence of litter and debris, or other appropriate means that consider the characteristics of the surrounding areas. Though open to other interpretations, this definition implies a level similar to that of the stage of mean discharge and thus a flow duration of generally 5 to 20 percent.

Organic aerosol, Aerosol particles consisting predominantly of organic compounds, mainly carbon, hydrogen, oxygen and lesser amounts of other elements.

Organic materials, Unconsolidated sediments or deposits in which carbon is an essential, substantial component. Several types of organic materials (deposits) can be identified based on the composition of the dominant fibers (grassy organic materials, herbaceous organic materials, mossy organic materials, woody organic materials).

Outcrop – (a) That part of a geologic formation or structure that appears at the surface of the earth. (b) An actual exposure of bedrock at or above the ground surface; the miscellaneous area *rock outcrop*.

Outwash delta, A relict (inactive) delta composed of glaciofluvial sediments formed where a sediment laden outwash river emptied into an open lake, commonly a proglacial lake. Sediment attributes include very gently dipping topset beds (coarser textures) and steeply dipping foreset beds (finer textures).

Outwash fan, A fan-shaped accumulation of outwash deposited by meltwater streams in front of the end or recessional moraine of a glacier. Coalescing outwash fans form an outwash plain.

Outwash plain – An extensive lowland area of coarse textured, glaciofluvial material. An outwash plain is commonly smooth; where pitted, due to melt-out of incorporated ice masses (pitted outwash plain), it is generally low in relief and largely retains its original gradient. *(Fig. 90, 95)*

Outwash terrace, A flat-topped bank of outwash with an abrupt outer face (scarp or riser) extending along a valley downstream from an outwash plain or terminal moraine; a valley train deposit. *(Fig. 95)*

Outwash, Soil particles or sediment that moves down an upland surface with overland flow to a rill or gully and is re-deposited on areas of lesser slope; more commonly outwash is used as a geomorphic term referring to rock debris that is removed from a glacier by meltwater and is re-deposited in the stream channel as glaciofluvial sediment. Stratified and sorted sediments (chiefly sand and gravel) removed or "washed out" from a glacier by melt-water streams and deposited in front of or beyond the end moraine or the margin of a glacier. The coarser material is deposited nearer to the ice.

Overbank deposit, Fine-grained sediments (silt and clay) deposited from suspension on a flood plain by floodwaters that cannot be contained within the stream channel.

Overburden, (a) The upper part of a sedimentary deposit, compressing and consolidating the materials below. (b) The loose soil or other unconsolidated material overlying bedrock, either transported or formed in place (synonym for regolith). *(Fig. 35)*

Overflow stream channel, A watercourse that is generally dry but conducts flood waters that have overflowed the banks of a river, commonly from large storms, annual meltwater, or glacial meltwaters.

Overland flow, That part of precipitation or snowmelt that moves over the land surface, often in small rivulets owing to micro-topography, toward a rill, gully, or channel before becoming runoff as concentrated flow within the rill, gully, or channel.

Overmixing, A condition that can exist in strongly stratified estuaries with net circulation out in the upper layer and net circulation in in the lower layer. This limits the amount of salt water available for mixing inside the estuary. This condition begins as mixing proceeds within the estuary by whatever processes are dominant. The mixing causes more salt water to be added to the net circulation and volume flow out of the estuary up to a critical condition past which any more increased mixing has no further effect on the discharge flow or the exiting salinity.

Overthrust, A low angle thrust fault of large scale, with displacement generally measured in kilometers. *(Fig. 25)*

Oxbow lake, The crescent-shaped, often ephemeral body of standing water situated by the side of a stream in the abandoned channel (oxbow) of a meander after the stream formed a neck cutoff and the ends of the original bend were silted up. *(Fig. 61)*

Oxbow, (as a hydrologic feature) A horseshoe-shaped length of stream channel, a nearly closed meander loop. As a fluvial-geomorphic feature, an oxbow is an abandoned meander loop of an alluvial channel on a flood plain or alluvial terrace; evidence of an oxbow that has largely filled with sediment may remain as a meander scar on the flood plain or alluvial terrace. An oxbow lake is a horseshoe-shaped body of water, sometimes ephemeral, that occupies a geomorphic oxbow. *(Fig. 61)*

Ozone layer, The stratosphere contains a layer in which the concentration of ozone is greatest, the so-called ozone layer. The layer extends from about 12 to 40 km above the Earth's surface. The ozone concentration reaches a maximum between about 20 and 25 km. This layer is being depleted by human emissions of chlorine and bromine compounds. Every year, during the Southern Hemisphere spring, a very strong depletion of the ozone layer takes place over the antarctic region, caused by anthropogenic chlorine and bromine compounds in combination with the specific meteorological conditions of that region. This phenomenon is called the ozone hole. *(Fig. 158)*

Ozone, Ozone, the triatomic form of oxygen (O_3), is a gaseous atmospheric constituent. In the troposphere, it is created both naturally and by photochemical reactions involving gases resulting from human activities (smog). Tropospheric ozone acts as a greenhouse gas. In the stratosphere, it is created by the interaction between solar ultraviolet radiation and molecular oxygen (O_2). Stratospheric ozone plays a dominant role in the stratospheric radiative balance. Its concentration is highest in the ozone layer.

P

Pacific-Antarctic Basin, One of three major basins in the Southern Ocean. It extends from its western border with the Australian-Antarctic Basin at the longitude of Tasmania (about 145° E) to its eastern border with the Atlantic-Indian Basin at the Scotia Ridge and Drake Passage (about 70° W). It consists of the Amundsen, Bellingshausen, and Mornington Abyssal Plains and is separated from the basins further north in the Pacific by the Pacific-Antarctic Ridge and the East Pacific Rise in the east and by the Chile rise in the east.

Pack ice, Any area of sea ice, other than fast ice, no matter what form it takes or how it is disposed.

Pahoehoe lava flow, A type of basaltic lava flow with a characteristically smooth, billowy or rope-like surface. *(Fig. 33)*

Palaeoclimate, Climate during periods prior to the development of measuring instruments, including historic and geologic time, for which only proxy climate records are available.

Paleobiogeography, The study of the spatial distribution of ancient organisms, including analysis of the ecological and historical factors governing this distribution. In contrast to paleoecology, most paleo biogeographical studies have dealt with distributions of individual taxa or with questions of global or regional provincialism.

Paleobiology, The science dealing with the fields of evolution, ecology and the subsequent taphonomy of extinct animals and plants.

Paleocalibration method, A method for calculating the relationship between paleoclimates and the future climate.

Paleocene, The earliest epoch (from 56.5 to 65.0 million years ago) of the Tertiary Period of geologic time that follows the Cretaceous Period and precedes the Eocene Epoch.

Paleolimnology, The branch of limnology that studies of past fresh water, saline and brackish environments. This is done in large part by taking cores from a limnological sediment system and examining the geological, biological and chemical components preserved in the core.

Paleosol, A soil that formed on a landscape in the past with distinctive morphological features resulting from a soil-forming environment that no longer exists at the site. The former pedogenic process was either altered because of external environmental change or interrupted by burial. A paleosol (or component horizon) may be classed as relict if it has persisted in a land-surface position without major alteration of morphology by processes of the prevailing pedogenic environment. An exhumed paleosol is one that formerly was buried and has been re-exposed by erosion of the covering mantle. Most paleosols have been affected by some subsequent modification of diagnostic horizon morphologies and profile truncation.

Paleoterrace , An erosional remnant of a terrace which retains the surface form and alluvial deposits of its origin but was not emplaced by, and commonly does not grade to a present-day stream or drainage network.

Paleothermometry, The use of various paleoclimate proxy data to attempt to gauge paleotemperatures.

Palsa, An elliptical dome-like permafrost mound containing alternating layers of ice lenses and peat or mineral soil, commonly 3-10 m high and 2-25 m long, occurring in subarctic bogs of the tundra and often surrounded by water.

Panthalassa, The Early Mesozoic world ocean. It was a single ocean reaching from pole to pole, probably consisting of single southern and northern gyres, deep water formation at both poles, and slothlike deep-water circulation. *(Fig. 10)*

Parabolic dune, A sand dune with a long, scoop-shaped form, convex in the downwind direction so that its horns point upwind, whose ground plan, when perfectly developed, approximates the form of a parabola. *(Fig. 103)*

Parallel drainage pattern , A drainage pattern in which the streams and their tributaries are regularly spaced and flow parallel or subparallel to one another and tributaries characteristically join the mainstream at approximately the same angle, over a considerable area. It is indicative of a region having a pronounced, uniform slope and a homogeneous lithology and rock structure, such as young coastal plains and large basalt flows.

Parametrization, In climate models, this term refers to the technique of representing processes that cannot be explicitly resolved at the Spatial or temporal resolution of the model (sub-grid scale processes) by relationships between model-resolved larger-scale flow and the area- or time-averaged effect of such sub-grid scale processes.

Parent material, The unconsolidated and more or less chemically weathered mineral or organic matter from which a soil's solum is developed by pedogenic processes.

Park, An ecological term for a grassy or shrubby, wide, open valley lying at high elevation and confined between forested mountain slopes, as in a high meadow; sometimes marshy.

Parna dune, A dune largely composed of silt and sand-sized aggregates of clay; sometimes called a clay dune or lunette.

Partial-duration flood series, A list of all flood peaks that exceed a chosen base stage or discharge, regardless of the number of peaks occurring in a year.

Particle size, The diameter (mm), as measured along the intermediate axis of a sediment particle (thus, the maximum particle size that can pass through a screen or sieve of that mesh size); sediment types are typically specified using a phi scale, by which particle sizes of less than 0.002 mm are clay, those ranging from 0.002 to 0.062 mm are silt, those of 0.062 to 2.0 mm are sand, and particles of 2.0 to 64 mm, 64 to 256 mm, and more than 264 mm, respectively, are designated gravel, cobbles, and boulders. Sediment of wash-load size, less than 0.062 mm, is determined by hydrometer analysis.

Particle-size distribution curve, A graph, or curve, of specified particle sizes of a fluvial-sediment sample plotted against values of percent weight of incremental portions of the sediment sample finer than the total dry weight of the sediment sample. The resulting curve shows which particle sizes may be enriched or deficient, and allows comparison with other particle-size distribution curves.

Particulate matter, The suspended particle load of rivers and oceans.

Patina – A general term for a colored film or thin outer layer produced on the surface of a rock or other material by weathering after long exposure.

Patterned ground, A general term for any ground surface exhibiting a discernibly ordered, more-or-less symmetrical, morphological pattern of ground and, where present, vegetation. Patterned ground is characteristic of, but not confined to, permafrost regions or areas subjected to intense frost action; it also occurs in tropical, subtropical, and temperate areas. Patterned ground is classified by type of pattern and presence or absence of sorting and includes nonsorted and sorted circles, net, polygons, steps and stripes, garlands, and solifluction features. In permafrost regions, the most common macroform is the ice-wedge polygon and a common microform is the nonsorted circle. Stone polygons generally form on slopes of less than 8 percent, while garlands and stripes occur on slopes of 8 to 15 percent and more than 15 percent, respectively.

Pavement karst, Areas of bare limestone, usually sculpted by solution erosion into karren of various types and where soils have been stripped off, commonly by glaciation in alpine areas (e.g., Rocky Mountains, USA) and high latitudes, and by water erosion in arid karst areas.

Peak, Sharp or rugged upward extension of a ridge chain, usually at the junction of two or more ridges; the prominent highest point of a summit area. (undersea feature) A prominent elevation either pointed or of a very limited extent across the summit.

Peat plateau, A generally flat-topped expanse of peat, elevated above the general surface of a peatland, and containing segregated ice that may or may not extend downward into the underlying mineral soil. Controversy exists as to whether peat plateaus and palsen are morphological variations of the same feature.

Peat, Unconsolidated soil material consisting largely of undecomposed, or slightly decomposed, organic matter containing abundant plant fibers (e.g., "fibric soil materials" of Soil Taxonomy) and which accumulated under conditions of excessive moisture.

Pebble count, A systematic method of sampling and measuring the diameters of a sufficient number of pebbles (and possibly other rounded rock fragments of smaller and larger size) to attain a significant representation of the range of sizes and median size of a deposit of coarse sediment.

Pebble, A general term for a small rock fragment, typically from 4 to 64 mm in diameter, that has been rounded through the process of stream transport.

Pediment, A gently sloping erosional surface developed at the foot of a receding hill or mountain slope, commonly with a slightly concave-upward profile, that cross-cuts rock or sediment strata that extend beneath adjacent uplands. The erosion surface may be essentially bare bedrock (i.e., *rock pediment*), or it may be thinly mantled (e.g., 1 to 3 m) with debris (i.e., *pediment*) such as colluvium, pedisediment, or alluvium that is ultimately in transit from an upland front to basin or valley lowland. In hill-footslope terrain the debris mantle (over an erosional contact) is designated "pedisediment." The term has been used in several geomorphic contexts: Pediments may be classed with respect to (a) landscape positions (e.g., intermontane-basin piedmont = *apron pediment*, or valley-border footslope surfaces (= *terrace pediment*); (b) type of material eroded (e.g., bedrock = *rock pediment*, or regolith = *pediment*). or (c) combinations of the above. *(Fig 114)*

Pediment, A low-angle sloping surface that is typically developed on bedrock or older, partially consolidated alluvial deposits in an arid or semiarid region; pediments encroach largely by headward fluvial erosion into the bases of hills, mountains, or plateaus, forming and maintaining abrupt and slowly receding fronts or escarpments. Thus, processes of pedimentation yield low-relief surfaces of uniformly gentle slope, or ones that are slightly concave upward, on which erosion is minimal and the erosion products from the high-relief bedrock exposures move downslope with little or no permanent storage of sediment. Channel incision of a pediment may occur following renewed uplift of the bedrock area or incision of the principal stream at the downslope end of the pediment.

Pedisediment, A sediment layer, eroded from the shoulder and backslope of an erosional slope that lies on and is, or was, being transported across a pediment.

Pedogenesis, The mode of origin of a soil, with emphasis on the processes of soil-forming factors responsible for the development of the solum (true soil) from unconsolidated parent material. Among the processes that contribute to pedogenesis are additions from above of precipitation and contaminants; changes of organic matter to humus and of rock-forming minerals to hydrous oxides, clays, ions, and H_4SiO_4; downward transfer of humus compounds, clays, ions, and H_4SiO_4; upward transfer of ions and H_4SiO_4; and removal (normally by ground-water movement beneath the soil profile) of ions and H_4SiO_4.

Pedology (a synonym of soil science), The study of soil processes and treats or considers the formation, properties, classification, and mapping of soils; some soil scientists regard pedology to be one of two main sub-disciplines of soil science, the being edaphology.

Pedoturbation, The mixing of soil materials by natural processes.

Pelagic, Descriptive of organisms that inhabit open water, as opposed to benthic. This is sometimes divided into five separate ecological zones which are, proceeding from the surface to the bottom, the epipelagic, mesopelagic, bathypelagic, abyssopelagic and hadopelagic zones.

Pendant bar, A narrow, sharp-crested accumulation of relatively coarse bed sediment deposited at the downstream (lee) side of a resistant protrusion during a large flood; pendant bars, which typically are separated from the protrusion (typically bedrock) by a depression caused by heightened flow velocity and scour around the protrusion, parallel the flow direction and thus aid in the reconstruction of flood dynamics. The term pendant bar generally is applied to large-scale landforms of high-magnitude floods, whereas the term sand splay often refers to flood-plain or terrace features of smaller scale caused by similar processes during floods of high frequency.

Peneplain, A low nearly featureless, gently undulating land surface of considerable area, which presumably has been produced by the processes of long-continued subaerial erosion.

Peninsula, (a) An elongated body or stretch of land nearly surrounded by water (e.g., on three sides) and connected with a larger tract of land area, usually by a neck or an isthmus. (b) A relatively large tract of land jutting out into the water, with or without a well-defined isthmus; e.g., the Italian peninsula.

Perennial stream, A continuously flowing water in a natural stream channel; the surface of a perennial stream fluctuates at or near the upper level of the zone of saturation in the adjacent water-bearing alluvium or rocks.

Periglacial, The conditions, processes, features, and landforms of those areas at and near the margins of present or former glaciers or glacial conditions; snow and other forms of precipitation in periglacial areas generally are insufficient to result in the occurrence of glacial processes, but frost action and related types of physical weathering may be important as determinants of surface processes and landforms.

Permafrost, Ground (soil or rock and included ice and organic material) that remains at or below 0°C for at least two consecutive years.

Permanent thermocline, A relatively sharp change in temperature (and therefore density) beneath the seasonal thermocline maintained by a balance between downward diffusion of heat and the gradual upwelling of deep, cool water.

Persian Gulf, A marginal sea of the Indian Ocean centered at approximately 52° E and 27° N. It is surrounded by Iran to the north, Kuwait, Saudi Arabia, Qatar, and the United Arab Emirates to the east and south, and connects with the Gulf of Oman (and on into the Arabian Sea) through the Strait of Hormuz to the east. It has a length of 990 km, ranges in width from 56 to 338 km, covers an area of 241,000 km_2, occupies a volume of 10,000 km_3, has a mean depth of 40 m, and a maximum depth of about 170 m.

Peru Current, A component of the eastern limb of the counterclockwise-flowing southern subtropical gyre in the Pacific Ocean. *(Fig. 142)*

pH, pH is a dimensionless measure of the acidity of water (or any solution) given by its concentration of hydrogen ions H_+. pH is measured on a logarithmic scale where pH = -log]0H_+. Thus, a pH decrease of 1 unit corresponds to a 10-fold increase in the concentration of H_+, or acidity.

Phagotrophic, Descriptive of a heterotrophic phytoplankton species that feeds on phytoplankton or detritus.

Photosynthesis, The process by which plants take carbon dioxide from the air (or bicarbonate in water) to build carbohydrates, releasing oxygen in the process. There are several pathways of photosynthesis with different responses to atmospheric carbon dioxide concentrations.

Phototrophic, Descriptive of a phytoplankton species that lives primarily by photosynthesis.

Phycology, The study of algae, especially seaweeds. This is also called algology.

Physical oceanography, The study of physical conditions and physical processes within the ocean, especially the motions and physical properties of the ocean. This is usually further divided into the activities of descriptive and theoretical oceanography, the former being concerned with observing the oceans to prepare maps of the spatial and temporal variations of its properties, and the latter with constructing theoretical models to attempt to explain the observations.

Physiographic Division, A large portion of a continent of which all parts are similar in geologic structure and climate at a small scale (e.g., 1:5,000,000) and which has consequently had a unified geomorphic history and whose pattern of relief or landforms differ significantly from that of adjacent areas.

Physiographic Province , A region of which all parts are similar in geologic structure and climate and which has consequently had a unified geomorphic history; a region whose pattern of relief or landforms differ significantly from that of adjacent regions; i.e., a subset within a Physiographic Division.

Physiographic Section, An area which all parts are similar in geologic structure and climate at a relatively small scale and which has consequently had a unified geomorphic history, and whose pattern of relief or landforms differ significantly from that of adjacent areas

Phytobenthos, That part of the benthos consisting of plant life.

Phytogeomorphology, The study of interactions processes of geomorphology and plants and to how landforms and plant occurrences are mutually affected.

Phytolith, A mineral body of microscopic size that precipitates in or around cell walls of plants; the size, shape, and composition of phytoliths often are diagnostic of the plant species from which they precipitated. Most phytoliths are opaline silica but many are formed of calcium oxalate. Because phytoliths are inorganic products of plant growth, they do not decay readily after death of the plant or plant cell and if extracted from the soil in which they were deposited can be used to recognize previous vegetation patterns and climate.

Phytoplankton, One of two groups into which plankton are divided, the other being zooplankton. Phyto plankton comprise all the freely floating photosynthetic forms in the oceans i.e. they are free-floating microscopic plants which, having little mobility, are distributed by ocean currents.

Piedmont, Lying or formed at the base of a mountain or mountain range; e.g., a piedmont terrace or a piedmont pediment. (noun) An area, plain, slope, glacier, or other feature at the base of a mountain; e.g., a foothill or a bajada.

Piedmont slope, The dominant gentle slope at the foot of a mountain; generally used in terms of intermontane-basin terrain in arid to subhumid regions. Main components include: 1) An erosional surface on bedrock adjacent to the receding mountain front (pediment, rock pediment); 2) A constructional surface comprising individual alluvial fans and interfan valleys, also near the mountain front; and 3) A distal complex of coalescent fans (bajada), and alluvial slopes without fan form. Piedmont slopes grade to basin-floor depressions with alluvial and temporary lake plains or to surfaces associated with through drainage (e.g., axial streams).

Piedmont, A gently sloping surface extending from the base of a mountain or mountain range toward the valley center area.

Pillow lava flow, A lava flow or body displaying pillow structure and considered to have formed in a subaqueous environment (underwater); usually basaltic or andesitic in composition. Compare – aa lava flow, block lava flow, pahoehoe lava flow.

Pillow lava, A general term for lava displaying pillow structure (discontinuous, close-fitting, bun-shaped or ellipsoidal masses, generally < 1 m in diameter); considered to have formed in a subaqueous environment; such lava is usually basaltic or andesitic.

Pingo, A large frost mound; especially a relatively large conical mound of soil-covered ice (commonly 30 to 50 meters high and up to 400 meters in diameter) raised in part by hydrostatic pressure within and below the permafrost of Arctic regions, and of more than 1 year's duration.

Pinnacle, A tall, slender, tapering tower or spire-shaped pillar of rock, either isolated, as on steep slopes or cliffs formed in karst or other massive rocks, or at the summit of a hill or mountain.

Pinnacle, Any high tower or spire-shapred pillar of rock, or coral, alone or cresting a summit.

Pinnate drainage pattern, A variation of the dendritic drainage pattern in which the main stream receives many closely spaced, subparallel tributaries that join it at slightly acute angles upstream, resembling in plan a feather. They typically form on steep slopes with soils that have a high silt content; such as loess landscapes or fine-textured flood plains.

Piping, An erosional process, by water percolating through unsaturated soil or subsoil, that results in removal of generally fine-grained sediment particles by downward and lateral migration and the formation of small conduits, tunnels, or pipes through which the water and entrained sediment moves; the conduits created by the piping process may cause collapse of overlying sediment and surface expression as small depressions and gullies.

Pitted outwash plain, An outwash plain marked by many irregular depressions such as kettles, shallow pits, and potholes which formed by melting of incorporated ice masses; much of the gradient and internal structures of the original plain remain intact.

Pitted outwash terrace, A relict glaciofluvial terrace that retains its original attitude, composed of undistorted outwash sediments and depositional structures and whose surface is pock-marked with numerous potholes or kettle depressions.

Pitted outwash, Outwash deposits with surficial pits or kettles, produced by the partial or complete burial of glacial ice by outwash and the subsequent thaw of the ice and collapse of the surficial materials.

Plain, A general term referring to any flat, lowland area, large or small, at a low elevation. Specifically, any extensive region of comparatively smooth and level gently undulating land. A plain has few or no prominent hills or valleys but sometimes has considerable slope, and usually occurs at low elevation relative to surrounding areas. Where dissected, remnants of a plain can form the local uplands. A plain may be forested or bare of trees and may be formed by deposition or erosion.

Plankton, Micro organisms living in the upper layers of aquatic systems. A distinction is made between phytoplankton, which depend on photosynthesis for their energy supply, and zooplankton, which feed on phytoplankton. One of three major ecological groups into which marine organisms are divided, the other two being the nekton and the benthos. Plankton are small aquatic organisms (animals and plants) that, generally having no locomotive organs, drift with the currents. The animals in this category include protozoans, small crustaceans, and the larval stages of larger organisms while plant forms are mainly diatoms.

Plateau, A comparatively flat area of great extent and elevation; specifically an extensive land region considerably elevated (more than 100 meters) above adjacent lower-lying terrain, and is commonly limited on at least one side by an abrupt descent, has a flat or nearly level surface. A comparatively large part of a plateau surface is near summit level.

Plateau, (undersea feature) A flat or nearly flat elevation of considerable areal extent, dropping off abruptly on one or more sides.

Playa dune, A linear or curvilinear ridge of windblown, granular material (generally sand or parna) removed from the adjacent basin by wind erosion (deflation), and deposited on the leeward (prevailing downwind) margin of a playa, playa basin, or salina basin. The dune may be barren or vegetated.

Playa floor, The lowest extensive, flat to slightly concave surface within a playa basin, consisting of a dry lake bed or lake plain underlain by stratified clay, silt or sand, and commonly by soluble salts.

Playa lake, A shallow, intermittent lake in a arid or semiarid region, covering or occupying a playa in the wet season but drying up in summer; an ephemeral lake that upon evaporation leaves or forms a playa.

Playa rim, The convex, upper margin (shoulder) of a playa basin where the playa slope intersects the surrounding terrain.

Playa slope, The generally concave to slightly convex area within a playa basin that lies between the relatively level playa floor below (or playa step, if present) and the convex playa rim above. Overland flow is typically parallel down slope.

Playa step, The relatively level or gently inclined "terrace-like" bench or toeslope within a large playa basin flanking and topographically higher than the playa floor and below the playa slope; a bench or step-like surface within a playa basin that breaks the continuity of the playa slope and modified by erosion and/or deposition. Temporary ponding may occur in response to precipitation / runoff events.

Playa, An ephemeral lake of an arid or semiarid area, the floor of which supports sparse to seasonal vegetation and is underlain by fine-grained deposits washed to the lake bed by infrequent precipitation events. Sediment of the playa floor typically is mostly silt and clay with abundant organic material and salts that precipitate as water evaporates following runoff to the basin interior. A playa basin, or bolson, has interior drainage toward the playa and is the surface area that contributes excess precipitation, as runoff, to the playa. *(Fig. 107)*

Pleistocene, The earlier of two Quaternary epochs, extending from the end of the Pliocene, about 1.8 Ma, until the beginning of the Holocene about 11.6 ka. *(Fig. 3, 4)*

Pleuston, Marine organisms associated with the water surface or the uppermost water layer that possess special adaptions allowing them to passively float there.

Pliocene ,The last epoch (from 1.6 to 5.2 million years ago) of the Tertiary Period of geologic time that follows the Miocene and precedes the Pleistocene Epoch.

Plug dome, A volcanic dome characterized by an upheaved, consolidated conduit filling.

Plumes, Convective elements that carry fluid particles vertically over distances comparable to the depth of the ocean.

Pluton, A deep-seated igneous intrusion.

Plutonic, Pertaining to igneous rocks formed at great depth, but also including associated metamorphic rocks.

Pluvial lake, A lake formed in an extended period of exceptionally heavy rainfall.

Pluvial lake [relict], A lake formed in an extended period of exceptionally heavy rainfall, but now greatly reduced or gone; a lake formed in the Pleistocene Epoch during a time of glacial advance, and now extinct (relict) .

Pluvial, Signifies a period of abundant rainfall and runoff and the hydrologic and earth-surface processes effects of that rainfall and runoff; a principal geomorphic use of the term pluvial is to distinguish parts of Pleistocene time when rainfall rates, that were greater than present rates in much of the warmer-climate areas and runoff resulting from abundant snowfall in mountainous areas generated high water levels in pluvial lakes.

Point (or meander) bar, Bed sediment, generally sand and gravel, that is deposited on the inside part of a meander curve as part of the normal process of fluvial sorting of sediment.

Point bar [coastal] , Low, arcuate, subaerial ridges of sand developed adjacent to an inlet and formed by the lateral accretion or movement of the channel.

Point bar, One of a series of low, arcuate ridges of sand and gravel developed on the inside of a growing meander by the slow addition of individual accretions accompanying migration of the channel toward the outer bank.

Polar orbit, An orbit in which a satellite passes directly over or close to the poles. The characteristic orbital period is around 90 minutes at an altitude of between 500 and 1500 km. Such satellites are usually Sun synchronoussunsynchronous, and have a field of view such that it takes about 15 orbits to cover the globe, with a specific location being seen about twice a day.

Polder, A generally fertile tract of flat, low-lying coastal area that is at or below sea level but has been reclaimed and is constantly protected from the sea, or other body of water by an organized system of maintenance and defense that involves embankments, dikes, dams, or levees; e.g., a brackish marsh that has been drained and brought under cultivation.

Pollen analysis, A technique of both relative dating and environmental reconstruction, consisting of the identification and counting of pollen types preserved in peat, lake sediments and other deposits.

Polygon, A type of patterned ground consisting of a closed, roughly equidimensional figure bounded by more or less straight sides; some sides may be irregular. Refer to patterned ground.

Pond, (a) A natural body of standing fresh water occupying a small surface depression, usually smaller than a lake and larger than a pool. (b) A small artificial body of water, used as a source of water.

Pool , A sall, natural body of standing water, usually fresh; e.g., a stagnant body of water in a marsh, or a transient puddle in a depression following a rain.

Pool, (as applied to alluvial stream channels) A relatively deep, low velocity reach of quiescent flow between upstream and downstream riffles, or rapids, at which the flows are ordinarily more rapid and turbulent.

Pool-riffle sequence, (in alluvial stream channel) A succession of one or more combinations of pools and riffles along the channel in the downstream direction; during flood the normally low water velocities in pools and higher water velocities at riffles are reversed, causing scour and removal of accumulated sediment from pooled reaches and deposition of bed sediment on riffles.

Porcellanite, A dense, siliceous rock formed as a indurated or baked clay or shale with a dull, light-colored, cherty appearance, often found in the roof or floor of a burned-out coal seam.

Post-glacial rebound, The vertical movement of the land and sea floor following the reduction of the load of an ice mass, for example, since the Last Glacial Maximum (21 ka). The rebound is an isostatic land movement.

Potassium-argon dating, A radioisotopic dating method based on the decay of the radioisotope 40K (potassium) to a daughter isotope 40Ar (argon). This has been used to date sea-floor basalts as well as to provide the accurate dating needed to establish and correlate on a world-wide basis the geomagnetic polarity time scale.

Potential evaporation, The amount of water that would be evaporated from a land or water surface if the water supply were unlimited, as opposed to actual evaporation.

Potential evapotranspiration, The theoretical maximum amount of water vapor that can be convyed to the atmosphere by the combined processes of evaporation and transpiration by a surface covered by green vegetation with no lack of available water in the soil.

Potentiometric surface, A Thypothetical concept of ground-water hydrology representing the height or surface to which water in a well rises or maintains if pumping does not occur; for confined ground water under artesian pressure the potentiometric surface is higher than the top of the ground-water body, whereas the potentiometric surface of an unconfined ground-water body is similar to the water table.

Pothole, A type of small pit or closed depression (1 to 15 meters deep), generally circular or elliptical, occurring in river bed, an outwash plain, a recessional moraine, or a till plain. *(Fig. 55)*

Precipitable water, The total amount of atmospheric water vapour in Vertical column of unit cross-sectional area. It is commonly expressed in terms of the height of the water if completely condensed and collected in a vessel of the same unit cross section.

Precursors, Atmospheric compounds that are not greenhouse gases but that have an effect on greenhouse gas or aerosol concentrations by taking part in physical or chemical processes regulating their production or destruction rates.

Predictability, The extent to which future states of a system may be predicted based on knowledge of current and past states of the system.

Proglacial lake [relict], Remnant features of a glacial lake that is now extinct which formed just beyond the margin of an advancing or retreating glacier; generally in direct contact with the ice. Compare – proglacial lake, pluvial lake.

Proglacial lake, A type of glacial lake which formed just beyond the margin of an advancing or retreating glacier; generally in direct contact with the ice.

Promontory, A major spur-like protrusion of land or the continental slope extending to the sea or deep seafloor.

Proximal, Said of a sedimentary deposit consisting of coarse clastics and deposited nearest the source area.

Proxy, A proxy climate indicator is a local record that is interpreted, using physical and biophysical principles, to represent ome combination of climate-related variations back in time. Climate-related data derived in this way are referred to as proxy data. Examples of proxies include pollen analysis, tree ring records, characteristics of corals and various data derived from ice cores.

Psychrometrics, The study of the physical and thermodynamic properties of the atmosphere. The properties mainly of concern are dry-bulb temperature, wet-bulb temperature, dew-point temperature, absolute humidity, relative (or percent) humidity, sensible heat, latent heat, enthalpy (or total heat), density and pressure.

Psychrosphere, One of two regions into which the ocean depths are sometimes divided according to tempera-ture, the other being the thermosphere. The psychrosphere is those ocean depths where the temperature is less than 10° C, which can range anywhere from 100 to 700 m beneath the surface depending on oceanic conditions. This coincides with the ocean stratosphere.

Pteropod ooze, Ooze composed of the shells of small, planktonic swimming molluscs with a calcareous shell that live in tropical and subtropical waters. These are coarser than globigerina oozes, are found between 1500-3000 m depth and cover no more than 1% of the sea floor. *(Fig. 152)*

Pumice, Volcanic fragments e" 2 mm in diameter (i.e., retained upon a standard # 10 sieve), or coherent rock layers (pumice flow), made of light-colored, vesicular, glassy rock commonly having the composition of rhyolite. The material commonly has a specific gravity of < 1.0 and is thereby sufficiently buoyant to float on water. pumice-like fragments < 2 mm in size are called pumiceous ash.

Pycnocline, A layer where density changes most rapidly with depth. It can be associated with either a thermocline or a halocline.

Pyroclastic, Pertaining to clastic rock particles produced by explosive, aerial ejection from a volcanic vent. Such materials may accumulate on land or under water.

Pyroclastic flow, A fast density current of pyroclastic material, usually very hot, composed of a mixture of gasses and a high concentration of pyroclastic particles in a variety of sizes and composition (ash, pumice, scoria, lava fragments, etc.); produced by the explosive disintegration of viscous lava in a volcanic crater, collapse of an eruption column, or by the explosive emission of gas-charged ash from a fissure and which tends to follow topographic lows (e.g., valleys) as it moves; used in a more general sense than *ash flow*.

Q

Quarry, Excavation areas, open to the sky, usually for the extraction of stone.

Quaternary, The period of geological time following the Tertiary (65 Ma to 1.8 Ma). Following the current definition the Quaternary extends from 1.8 Ma until the present. It is formed of two epochs, the Pleistocene and the Holocene.

R

Radar altimeter, An instrument that uses radar to determine a vehicle's (e.g. a satellite) height above the surface and for measuring the height of small objects (e.g. waves, hills) on a planetary surface.

Radar, An acronym for radio detection and ranging, the use of reflected electromagnetic radiation to obtain information about distance objects. The wavelength used in normally in the radio frequency spectrum between 30 m and 3 mm.

Radial drainage pattern, A drainage pattern in which consequent streams radiate or diverge outward, like the spokes of a wheel from a high central area.; a major collector stream is usually found in a curvilinear alignment around the bottom of the elevated topographic feature. It is best developed on the slopes of a young domal structure, a volcanic cone, or isolated hills (erosional remnant). *(Fig. 69)*

Radiance, The radiation energy per unit time coming from a specific direction and passing through a unit area perpendicular to the direction.

Radioisotopic dating methods, Dating methods that take advantage of the fact that unstable atoms called radioactive isotopes undergo spontaneous radioactive decay by the loss of nuclear particles and may transmute into a new element. If the decay rate is invariable a given amount of a radioactive isotope will decay to its daughter product in a known interval of time, creating a geological clock by which large time intervals can be measured. Measuring the present isotope concentration indicates the amount of time that has passed since the sample was emplaced and the clock, i.e. the decay process, started. An important factor is the time it takes for the material to decay to half its original amount, i.e. its half-life, an indicator of the length of the time interval over which it can be used.

Radiolarian ooze, A deep-sea sediment composed of at least 30% of the remains of siliceous radiolarians. These sediments occur in the equatorial Pacific and Indian ocean regions where the depth exceeds the carbon compensation depth and therefore aren't overwhelmed by calcareous ooze. These form deep deposits covering 1-2% of the ocean floor, and are a type of siliceous ooze along with diatom ooze. *(Fig. 152)*

Rafting, Pressure process whereby one piece of ice overrides another. Most common in new ice and young ice.

Raindrop impact, or rainsplash, Terms expressing the effect that individual raindrops have on erosion processes; the energy expended, per unit area, by raindrops when they strike a soil or rock surface can be very high, resulting in the dislodging of soil particles that then are susceptible to entrapment by water moving downslope as overland flow to rills, gullies, and stream channels.

Raised beach, An ancient (relict) beach occurring above the present shoreline and separated from the present beach, having been elevated above the high-water mark either by local crustal movements (uplift) or by lowering of sea or lake level, and which may be bounded by inland cliffs. *(Fig. 84, 131)*

Raised bog, An area of acid, peaty soil especially that developed from moss, in which the center is higher than the margins.

Rating curve, A graph relating water discharge to water-surface elevation (gage height, or stage) at a specified site or cross section of a stream channel.

Ravine, A small stream channel; narrow, steep-sided, commonly V-shaped in cross section and larger than a gully, cut in unconsolidated materials.

Recessional moraine, An end or lateral moraine, built during a temporary but significant halt in the final retreat of a glacier. Also, a moraine built during a minor readvance of the ice front during a period of general recession.

Reclaimed land, (a) A land area composed of earthy fill material that has been placed and shaped to approximate natural contours, commonly part of land-reclamation efforts after mining operations. (b) A land area, commonly submerged in its native state, that has been protected by artificial structures (e.g., dikes) and drained for agricultural or other purposes (e.g., polder).

Reconstruction, The use of climate indicators to help determine (generally past) climates.

Rectangular drainage pattern, A drainage pattern in which the tributaries join the main streams at right-angles, and exhibit sections of approximately the same length which form rectangular shapes; it is indicative of streams following prominent bedrock fault, joint, or foliation systems that break the rocks into rectangular blocks. It is more irregular than the trellis drainage pattern, as the side streams are not perfectly parallel and not necessarily as conspicuously elongated, and secondary tributaries need not be present. The stronger or more harsh the pattern, the thinner the soil cover. These patterns commonly form in slate, schist, and gneiss, in resistive sandstone in arid climates, or in sandstone in humid climates if little soil has developed. *(Fig. 69)*

Recurrence interval, (of hydrologic events) The average interval of time, generally expressed in years, within which, for example, the magnitude, or discharge, of a given flood will be equaled or exceeded.

Red Sea, A long, narrow marginal sea centered a about 38° E and 22° N which separates the African and Asian continents. Its total length is 1932 km and the average width 280 km, with a maximum width of 306 km and a minimum width of 26 km. The area is about 450,000 km$_2$ and the volume around 50,000 km$_3$. The average depth is about 491 m with the greatest depths over 2500 m in the trough between 19 and 22° N. The Sinai peninsula divides the northern part into the shallow Gulf of Suez to the west and the deep Gulf of Aquaba to the east. The southern limit, which separates it from the Gulf of Aden, is a line joining Husn Murad and Ras Siyan.

Reef, A ridge-like or mound-like structure, layered or massive, built by sedentary calcareous organisms, especially corals, and consisting mostly of their remains; it is wave-resistant and stands above the surrounding contemporaneously deposited sediment. Reefs can also include a mass or ridge of rocks, especially coral and sometimes sand, gravel, or shells, rising above the surrounding estuary, sea or lake bottom to or nearly to the surface.

Reef, (undersea feature) A mass of rock or other indurated material lying at or near the sea surface that may constitute a hazard to surface navigation.

Reference level, A depth, pressure or density level at which the horizontal current field is either known from direcfr-rneasurements or indirectly estimated; This may be zero velocity surface or one with non-zero horizontal velocities. This reference level is combined with the relative velocity fields obtained via the geostrophic method to obtain fields of absolute geostrophic velocitiesa The techniques of satellite altimetry have provided another possibility for a reference level, i.e. the ocean surface. If the vertical departure of the ocfean surface from the local geoid can Be measured with sufficiently accuracy then it can be used as a referes.ee level. This is also known variously as the level of no motion, the level of known motion, the zero velocity surface, etc.

Reflectance, In radiation transfer, the fraction of incoming radiation that is reflected from a medium. The sum of this, the transmittance, and the absorptance must equal unity.

Reforestation, Planting of forests on lands that have previously contained forests but that have been converted to some other use. For a discussion of the term forest and related terms such as afforestation, reforestation and deforestation

Regime (or regime theory), The concept that alluvial stream channels are self-forming and self-adjusting; the term applies only to channels that make at least part of their boundaries from their transported load, carrying out the process at different places and times in any one stream channel in a balanced or alternating manner that prevents unlimited growth or removal of boundaries. Thus, a stream channel is said to be "in regime" when it has achieved an approximate equilibrium between matter and energy entering a stream reach and matter and energy leaving the reach.

Regime, A regime is preferred states of the climate system, often representing one phase of dominant patterns or modes of climate variability.

Region, A region is a territory characterised by specific gedgraphical and climatological features. The climate of a region is affected by regional and local scale forcings like topography, land use characteristics, lakes, etc., as well as remote influences from other regions.

Regolith, All unconsolidated earth materials above the solid bedrock. It includes material weathered in place from all kinds of bedrock and alluvial, glacial, eolian, lacustrine, and pyroclastic deposits. Soil scientists regard as soil only that part of the regolith that is modified by organisms and soil-forming processes. Most engineers describe the whole regolith, even to a great depth, as "soil."

Regulation, An imposed alteration of the discharge and discharge fluctuation of flows; most commonly regulation is caused by the construction of a dam and the control of water releases to the channel downstream from the dam. Stream regulation by a dam and reservoir has the effect of storing much of the fluvial sediment that enters the reservoir from upstream; consequently, the water released from the dam generally has a highly deficient sediment load and tends to cause downstream bed and bank erosion and related changes in fluvial landforms.

Rehabilitation, (as applied to stream corridors (bottomlands) that have been altered through human activity) The establishment or re-establishment of a condition of health and constructive activity. A goal of rehabilitation, therefore, is to minimize, not eliminate, the effects of human-induced alterations, thus promoting stable landforms, bioproductivity, and species diversity. Within industry, reclamation is often used synonymously with rehabilitation or restoration.

Relative humidity, The ratio of the observed mixing ratio in a sample of moist air to the saturation mixing ratio with respect to water at the same temperature.

Relative sea level, Sea level measured by a tide gauge with respect to thejahd upon which it is situated. Mean sea level is normally defined as the average relative sea level over a period, such as a ymonth or a year, long enough to average out transients such as waves and tides.

Relative vorticity, The vorticity imparted to a parcel or column of fluid motion.

Relict, Pertaining to surface landscape features e.g., landforms, geomorphic surfaces, and paleosols that have never been buried and yet are predominantly products of past environments.

Relief, The relative difference in elevation between the upland summits and the lowlands or valleys of a given region.

Reservoir, A component of the climate system, other than the atmosphere, which has the capacity to store, accumulate or release substance of concern, for example, carbon, a greenhouse gas or a precursor. Oceans, soils and forests are examples of reservoirs of carbon. Pool is an equivalent term (note that the definition of pool often includes the atmosphere). The absolute quantity of the substance of concern held within a reservoir at a specified time is called the stock.

Residuum, (residual soil material) Unconsolidated, weathered, or partly weathered mineral material that accumulates by disintegration of bedrock in place.

Resolution, In numerical modeling, the distance between contiguous points in the computational grid. This can refer to either temporal or spatial resolution, with the two being dependent in procedures using both.

Resonance angle, The angle at which the component of the wind speed acting in the direction of a wave field is equal to the wave speed.

Response time, The response time or adjustment time is the time needed for the climate system or its components to re-equilibrate to a new state, following a forcing resulting from external and internal processes or feedbacks. It is very different for various components of the climate system. The response time of the troposphere is relatively short, from days to weeks, whereas the stratosphere reaches equilibrium on a time scale of typically a few months. Due to their large heat capacity, the oceans have a much longer response time: typically decades, but up to centuries or millennia.

Restoration, The attempt to recreate the adjusted physical and biological conditions that were present prior to the alteration; a goal of restoration, therefore, is to minimize and eliminate the effects of human-induced alterations, thus promoting stable landforms, bioproductivity, and species diversity.

Resurgence, A general class of phenomena where, after a storm surge, the water level falls, rises, falls again, rises again, and so on for many hours after the passage of a hurricane. This has been variously explained as being due to oscillating long waves, edge waves, Kelvin waves or some combination thereof.

Reversed tide, A tide completely out of phase with the apparent motions of the principal attracting body.

Reynolds number, (as applied to hydrologic processes) A numerical quantity to describe the character of flow (typically laminar or turbulent) in a geologic or landscape setting; it is the ratio of inertial forces to viscous forces, equal to the product of velocity (often mean velocity) and a linear measure such as diameter or depth divided by the kinematic viscosity of the liquid (water/sediment mixture).

Rhythmite, An individual unit of a succession of beds developed by rhythmic sedimentation; e.g., a cyclothem. The term implies no limit as to bedding thickness or complexity and denotes no time or seasonal connotation.

Rib, A small, high angle, tertiary spur ridge or mini-interfluve that is a constituent part of rib & groove topography; (slopes generally 20 - 90 %,); common on the mid and lower hillslopes of well dissected uplands.

Ribbed fen, A nutrient-rich wetland with a surface pattern of ridges and depressions.

Ridge, A long, narrow elevation of the land surface, usually sharp crested with steep sides and forming an extended upland between valleys. The term is used in areas of both hill and mountain relief.

Riffle, (as applied to alluvial stream channels) A short, relatively shallow and coarse-bedded length over which the stream flows at ordinarily higher velocity and greater turbulence than it does through upstream and downstream pooled reaches where cross-sectional areas of the channel are greater, bed material is smaller, and velocities and turbulence are less.

Rift valley, A valley that has developed along a long, narrow continental trough that has down-dropped and is bounded by normal faults; a graben of regional size. It marks part of a zone along which the entire thickness of the lithosphere has ruptured under crustal extension. *(Fig. 27)*

Rill erosion, The development of numerous, minute to small, closely spaced incisions resulting from the uneven removal of surface soil or soft rock by flowing water that is concentrated in streamlets of sufficient volume and velocity to generate erosive power; it is an intermediate process between erosion by overland flow and gully erosion and is the most identifiable indicator of serious erosion resulting from watershed disturbance. The depth of flow that causes erosion in rills is typically less than about 30 mm. Rill erosion on lands that have been treated for rehabilitation or reclamation is considered to be accelerated erosion.

Rill, A very small incision eroded into soil or soft rock as a direct-runoff response to precipitation; it is one of the first and smallest incisions to be formed as a result of erosion by concentrated flow from upland surfaces and therefore is subject to removal by standard tillage operations of agriculture.

Rim Current, A permanent, strong current system encircling the Black Sea basin cyclonically over the continental slope zone. It is accompanied by a series of anticyclonic mesoscale eddies as well as transient waves with an embedded train of mesoscale eddies propagating cyclonically around the basin.

Rim, The border, margin, edge, or face of a landform, such as the curved brim surrounding the top part of a crater or caldera; specifically the rimrock of a plateau or canyon.

Rip current, A narrow seaward return flow caused by waves breaking in the surf zone and piling up water against the coast. This establishes a hydraulic head which, combined with bathymetric irregularities along the coast, causes the narrow seaward flow.

Rip feeder current, A current that flows parallel to the shore before converging and forming the neck of a rip current.

Riparian zone, (as applied to the study of fluvial systems) An ecological term referring to that part of the fluvial landscape inundated or saturated by flood flows; it consists of all surfaces of active fluvial landforms up through the flood plain including channel, bars, shelves, and related riverine features such as oxbow lakes, oxbow depressions, and natural levees. Particularly in arid and semiarid (water-deficient) environments, the riparian zone may support plants and other biota not present on adjacent, drier uplands.

Riparian, It pertains to the banks of a stream; within ecology the term has been broadened to refer to Biota and other characteristics of alluvial bottomlands.

Ripple mark, An undulating surface of alternating, subparallel, small-scale ridges and depressions, commonly composed of loose sand. It is produced on land by wind and under water by the agitation of water by currents or wave action, and generally tends at right angles or obliquely to the direction of flow of the moving fluid.

Rise, A general term for a slight increase in slope (e.g., d" 3%) and elevation of the land surface, usually with a broad, low summit and gently sloping sides. The term is restricted to landforms and microfeatures in areas of very low relief such as lake plains or coastal plains.

Rise, (undersea feature) a broad elevation that rises gently and generally smoothly from the sea floor; and the linked major mid-oceanic mountain systems of global extent; also called mid-oceanic ridge.

Rise, A geomorphic component of flat plains (e.g., lake plain, low coastal plain, low-gradient till plain) consisting of a slightly elevated but low, broad area with low slope gradients (e.g., 1-3 % slopes); typically a microfeature but can be fairly extensive. Commonly soils on a rise are better drained than those on the surrounding talf.

Riser, A geomorphic component of terraces, flood-plain steps, and other stepped landforms consisting of the vertical or steep side slope (e.g., escarpment) typically of minimal aerial extent. Commonly a recurring part of a series of natural, step-like landforms such as successive stream terraces. Its characteristic shape and alluvial sediment composition are derived from the cut and fill processes of a fluvial system.

River continuum, A biotic gradient, resulting from variations in physical characteristics along an adjusted stream (in dynamic equilibrium and thus time-independent), that is defined by a series of biological responses and consistent patterns of loading, transport, use, and storage of organic matter along the stream length. Because the river-continuum concept addresses biology, it is more specific than that of the biophysical continuum, which considers habitat gradients.

River valley, An elongate depression of the Earth's surface carved by a river during the course of its development. *(Fig. 64, 65, 66)*

River, A general term for a natural, freshwater surface stream of considerable volume and generally with a permanent base flow, moving in a defined channel toward a larger river, lake, or sea. *(Fig. 68)*

Riverine, The characteristic by which a feature or process pertains to or is formed by a river.

Roaring forties, The region between 40 and 50° S latitude where the prevailing westerly winds blow largely unobstructed by land over the open oceans, and also the winds themselves. They are constant and of great velocity, whence comes the term " roaring". The weather is stormy, rainy, and comparatively mild in the wake of constantly appearing depressions. The land areas that do obstruct them, the western mountainous coasts of southern Chile, Tasmania and New Zealand, experience tremendous rainfall through the year on the western sides (up to 100 in.) and much less on the eastern sides (around 20 in.). These are also known as brave west winds.

Roche moutonnée, A small elongate protruding knob or hillock of bedrock, so sculptured by a large glacier as to have its long axis oriented in the direction of ice movement, an upstream (stoss or scour) side that is gently inclined, smoothly rounded, and striated, and a downstream (lee or pluck) side that is steep and rough. It is usually a few meters in height, length, and breadth. *(Fig. 93)*

Rock anhydrite, A sedimentary rock (evaporite) composed chiefly of mineral anhydrite (anhydrous $CaSO_4$); The rock is generally massive, cryptocrystalline, and may exhibit rhythmic sedimentation (rhymites).

Rock glacier, A mass of poorly sorted, coarse rock debris that typically occurs in periglacial, high-relief areas of mountains and that contains interstitial ice subject to deformational processes of glaciers and therefore downslope movement of the ice and rock as a plastic mass; a landform that previously was deposited as a rock glacier, but, owing to subsequent melting or insufficient additions of snow, ice, and water to maintain a matrix of interstitial ice subject to glacial deformation, is an inactive rock glacier.

Rock gypsum, A sedimentary rock (evaporite) composed primarily of mineral gypsum ($CaSO_4'''2H_2O$). The rock is generally massive, ranges from coarse crystalline to fine granular, may show disturbed bedding due to hydration expansion of parent anhydrite (anhydrous $CaSO_4$), and may exhibit rhythmic sedimentation (rhymites).

Rock halite, A sedimentary rock (evaporite) composed primarily of halite (NaCl).

Rock pediment, An erosion surface of low relief, cut directly into and across bedrock and composed of either bare rock or thinly veneered pedisediment or residuum (e.g., < 1.5 m) over bedrock; it occurs along the flanks of mountain fronts, or at the base of mountains or high hills. Its surface grades to the backwearing mountain slopes or hillslopes above, and generally grades down to and merges with a lower-lying alluvial plain, piedmont slope or valley floor below.

Rock spread , The mass movement process, associated sediments (rock spread deposit), or resultant landform characterized by a very rapid type of *spread* dominated by lateral movement in a rock mass resulting from liquefaction or plastic flow of underlying materials that may be extruded out between intact units; rock bodies predominate.

Rock topple, The mass movement process, associated sediments (rock topple deposit), or resultant landform characterized by a localized, very rapid type of fall in which large blocks of rock material literally fall over, rotating outward over a low pivot point; rock bodies predominate (little fine earth). Portions of the original material may remain intact, although reoriented, within the resulting deposit.

Rock varnish, A thin, dark, shiny film or coating, composed of iron oxide accompanied by traces of manganese oxide and silica, formed on the surfaces of pebbles, boulders, and other rock fragments, commonly on rock outcrops in arid regions. It is believed to be caused by exudation of mineralized solutions from within and deposition by evaporation on the surface.

Rock veneer, A thin accumulation of rock clasts that partially or fully cover a surface or hillslope. The concentrations of generally gravel- or cobble-sized rock fragments develop by a variety of processes, all of which increase slope stability by protecting underlying fine sediment from erosion. Rock veneers typically extend no deeper than one or two clast thicknesses, thereby distinguishing them from thicker rock accumulations such as talus, or coarse channel sediment.

Rockfall avalanche, The mass movement process, associated sediments (rockfall avalanche deposit), or resultant landform characterized by an extremely rapid, large type of *flow* (a type of landslide) that starts as a rockfall but turns into a flow and characteristically deposits rock-dominated debris long distances from the failure face (such as 10 – 20 times the fall height); occurs only when huge rockfalls and rockslides involving millions of metric tons of material attain extremely rapid speeds; most common in a rugged mountainous area; ex. the 1903 Franks, Alberta, Canada avalanche. Sometimes loosely referred to as a long run-out landslide.

Rockfall, The mass movement process, associated sediments (rockfall deposit), or resultant landform characterized by a very rapid type of *fall* dominated by downslope movement of detached rock bodies which fall freely through the air or by leaps and bounds (lacks an underlying slip face); also spelled *rock fall. (Fig. 47, 48)*

Rossby number, A non-dimensional number expressing the ratio of intertial to Coriolis forces in the atmosphere or oceans.

Rotational debris slide, The mass movement process, associated sediments (rotational debris slide deposit), or resultant landform characterized by an extremely slow to moderately rapid type of slide, composed of comparatively dry and largely unconsolidated earthy material, portions of which remain largely intact and in which movement occurs along a well-defined, concave shear surface and resulting in a backward rotation of the displaced mass; sediments have substantial proportions of both fine earth and rock fragments. The landform may be single, successive (repeated up and down slope), or multiple (as the number of slide components increase).

Rotational earth slide, The mass movement process, associated sediments (rotational earth slide deposit), or resultant landform characterized by an extremely slow to moderately rapid type of slide, composed of comparatively dry and largely unconsolidated earthy material, portions of which remain largely intact and in which movement occurs along a well-defined, concave shear surface and resulting in a backward rotation of the displaced mass; sediments predominantly fine earth (< 2 mm). The landform may be single, successive (repeated up and down slope), or multiple (as the number of slide components increase).

Rotational rock slide, The mass movement process, associated sediments (rotational rock slide deposit), or resultant landform characterized by an extremely slow to moderately rapid type of slide, composed of comparatively dry and largely consolidated rock bodies, portions of which remain largely intact but reoriented, and in which movement occurs along a well-defined, concave shear surface and resulting in a backward rotation of the displaced mass. The landform may be single, successive (repeated up and down slope), or multiple (as the number of slide components increase).

Rotational slide, The mass movement process, associated sediments (rotational slide deposit), or resultant landform characterized by an extremely slow to moderately rapid type of slide, composed of comparatively dry and largely soil-rock materials, portions of which remain largely intact and in which movement occurs along a well-defined, concave shear surface and resulting in a backward rotation of the displaced mass. The landform may be single, successive (repeated up and down slope), or multiple (as the number of slide components increase).

Roughness coefficient, A factor in formulas for computing the average velocity of flow of water in a conduit or channel that represents the effect of roughness of the confining material on the energy losses in the flowing water. The most widely used roughness coefficient is "n" of the Manning equation; other roughness coefficients are the Chezy resistance factor and the Darcy-Weisbach friction factor.

Rubble, An accumulation of loose angular rock fragments, commonly overlying outcropping rock; the unconsolidated equivalent of a breccia.

Runoff (or rainfall excess), Part of precipitation that appears in surface streams (m_3S_{-1}), is the amount of rainfall input minus hydrologic abstractions, or losses, of interception, depression storage, infiltration, and evaportranspiration; it is more restricted than streamflow as it does not include stream channels affected by artificial diversions, storage, or other works of man.

Runon, Water on the land surface that moves from upslope sites as overland flow or within small rills into a specified area of observation; where appropriate, runon should be included in the I (inflow) factor of a water-balance computation, but frequently it is ignored.

S

Sabkha , A flat area of eolian sedimentation and erosion formed under semiarid or arid conditions in: 1) interior areas (e.g. on basin floors slightly above playa lake beds (e.g., playa step), or: 2) along coastal areas (e.g., just above intertidal zones), where, through deflation and evaporation, gypsum, halite, or other soluble minerals crystallize at or near the surface to form a thin, irregular mineral crust that is intermittently deflated away. Microbiotic crusts are not extensive and vegetation is very sparse and consists primarily of small, halophytic shrubs (e.g., iodine bush).

Saddle, A low point on a ridge or interfluve, generally a divide (pass, col) between the heads of streams flowing in opposite directions.

Sag, A small, partially or completely closed depression formed by movement along a strike-slip fault, or by mass movement (i.e., landslide) that may or may not temporarily pond water from impounded drainage or surface runoff. For example, a closed depression formed between a scarp or headwall and an adjacent rotated slump block of a landslide.

Sag pond, A small, permanent body of water in a semi-closed or closed depression formed by movement along a strike-slip fault or by mass movement (i.e., landslide) that ponds water from impounded drainage or surface runoff.

Salinity, A quantitative expression of the concentration of dissolved solids in water or soil and is generally measured and represented by the electrical conductivity of a sample of the water or soil; salinity is an important measure of the tolerance of a plant species to subsist with the available water.

Salt marsh, Flat, poorly drained area that is subject to periodic or occasional overflow by salt water, containing water that is brackish to strongly saline, and usually covered with a thick mat of grassy halophytic plants; e.g., a coastal marsh periodically flooded by the sea, or an inland marsh, (or salina) in an arid region and subject to intermittent overflow by salty water.

Salt pond, A large or small body of salt water in a marsh or swamp along the seacoast.

Salt water, Water on or beneath a land (or water) surface that accumulates as a result of natural processes of precipitation and which contains concentrations of dissolved solids (mostly salts) typical of normal sea water or of other small water bodies such as the Dead Sea or the Great Salt Lake; the concentration of dissolved solids in salt water is sufficient to cause deleterious effects by ingestion of living organisms adapted to a dependency on fresh water or brackish water.

Saltation, The process by which sediment, generally of sand size and coarser, bounces along the stream bed by the impact of the flow of water or of other moving particles;

saltation can also occur by the movement of wind .

Sample, A small part or quantity that is randomly obtained to represent the whole of a larger mass, volume, group, or population; it is limited in size to be easily analyzed, studied, characterized, and stored, large enough to be typical of the larger feature, element, or landscape process, and has a degree of permanence. In general, a sample (such as a small volume of sand from a selected part of a dune field) has properties that allow it or a derivative (such as a known volume of water, snow, or ice that is evaporated but all solid residue is retained) to be preserved without employing measures that are destructive to the properties that characterize the sample as representative. Relative to *statistical measures of hydrology,* a sample is a value or element within a larger population of values; as an example, an annual flood discharge from a gage site is a sample of the entire list of floods for an annual series.

Sand flow, (a) A flow of wet sand, as along banks of noncohesive clean sand that is subject to scour and to repeated fluctuations in pore-water pressure due to rise and fall of the tide. (b) A flow of loose, dry sand, as along the slip face of a sand dune; typically a microfeature.

Sand pit, A depression, ditch or pit excavated to furnish sand for roads or other construction purposes off-site; a type of borrow pit.

Sand plain, A sand-covered plain, which may originate by deflation of sand dunes, and whose lower limit of erosion is governed by the water table.

Sand ramp, A sand sheet blown up onto the lower slopes of a bedrock hill or mountain and forming an inclined plane, sometimes filling small mountain-side valleys and even crossing low passes.

Sand ridge, An imprecise, generic name for any low ridge of sand, formed at some distance from shore, e.g., submerged (longshore bar) or emergent (barrier beach). One of a series of long, wide, extremely low, parallel ridges believed to represent the eroded stumps of former longitudinal sand dunes.

Sand sheet, A large, irregularly shaped, commonly thin, surficial mantle of eolian sand, lacking the discernible slip faces that are common on dunes.

Sand splay, A low ridge or rounded length of deposits of sand to fine gravel on a flood plain or low terrace; sand splays typically are flood sediment extending from the lee, or downstream, side of an obstacle (most typically large trees) to the flood flow.

Sand, (as fluvial sediment) Sediment defined to be of particle diameter between 0.062 and 2.0 mm in diameter.

Sandhills, A region of semi-stabilized sand dunes or sandy hills, either covered with vegetation or bare.

Sandstone, Sedimentary rock containing dominantly sand-size clastic particles. *(Fig. 39, 41)*

Sanitary landfill, A land area where municipal solid waste is buried in a manner engineered to minimize environmental degradation. Commonly the waste is compacted and ultimately covered with soil or other earthy material.

Sapping, or ground-water sapping, A process of steady sediment removal by the laminar flow to and release of ground water as seepage at the saturated base of an escarpment, arroyo, or similar erosional feature, above which the soil, subsoil, alluvium, or bedrock is unsaturated. Sapping results in the separation at the seepage site of sand and silt particles from the rock or sediment through which the ground-water movement occurs; coupled with sediment-particle separation due to evaporation and precipitation of salts, the process causes erosion, undercutting, over-steepening of slope at the base of the landform, and eventually slope failure and cliff retreat.

Saprolite, Soft, friable, isovolumetrically weathered bedrock that retains the fabric and structure of the parent rock and exhibiting extensive inter-crystal and intra-crystal weathering. In pedology, saprolite was formerly applied to any unconsolidated residual material underlying the soil and grading to hard bedrock below.

Sargasso Sea, A clockwise-circulating region in the North Atlantic Ocean bound by the Gulf Stream on the west and north and less definitely to the east at 40° W near the Canary Current and to the south at 20° N near the North Equatorial Drift Current. It is so named because of the indigenous, yellow-brown seaweed called Sargassum that is found there in great abundance. The Sargasso is part of the subtropical gyre circulation system in the North Atlantic and comprises a large part of its interior circulation, covering an area of around 5.2 million square kilometers. *(Fig. 144)*

Sargassum, The name given to about eight species of seaweed that float in clumps and long windrows in the Sargasso Sea.

Saturated adiabatic lapse rate, The temperature lapse rate of air which is undergoing a reversible natural adiabatic process.

Scabland, An elevated, flat-lying, basalt-floored area, with little if any soil cover, sparse vegetation, and usually deep, dry channels scoured into the surface, especially by glacial meltwaters.

Scalped area , A modified slope, feature, or land area where much or all of the natural soil has been mechanically removed (e.g., scraped off) due to construction or other management practices.

Scarp slope, The relatively steeper face of a cuesta, facing in a direction opposite to the dip of the strata.

Scarp, An escarpment, cliff, or steep slope of some extent along the margin of a plateau, mesa, terrace, or structural bench. A scarp may be of any height. *(Fig. 115)*

Scattering, The process by which some of a stream of radiation is dispersed to travel in directions other than that which from it was incident by particles suspended in the medium through which it is travelling. *(Fig. 165)*

Scoria, Vesicular rock fragments e" 2 mm in at least one dimension and a specific gravity > 2.0, or a cindery crust of such material on the surface of andesitic or basaltic lava; the vesicular nature is due to the escape of volcanic gases before solidification; it is usually heavier, darker, and more crystalline than pumice.

Scour and fill, A *process* of alternate excavation and refilling of a channel, as by a stream or the tides; especially such a process occurring in time of flood, when the discharge and velocity of an aggrading stream are suddenly increased, causing the digging of new channels that become filled with sediment when the flood subsides.

Scour channel, A large, groove-like erosional feature in a stream bed swept (scoured) by running water, generally leaving a gravel bottom.

Scour, The powerful and concentrated clearing and digging action of flowing air, water, or ice, especially the downward erosion by stream water in sweeping away mud and silt on the outside curve of a bend, or during the time of a flood.

Scree slope, A portion of a hillside or mountainslope mantled by scree and lacking an up-slope rockfall source (i.e., cliff).

Scree, A collective term for an accumulation of coarse rock debris or a sheet of coarse debris mantling a slope. Scree is not a synonym of talus, as scree includes loose rock fragments on slopes without cliffs.

Sea breeze, A wind blowing from the ocean towards land caused by the effects of differential heating. In the summer when the land surface is warmer than the ocean, the air over the land heats up more than over the ocean, expands and becomes less dense, and rises. This rising air is replaced, due to the constraints of continuity, with moisture-rich air from over the oceans.

Sea cliff, A cliff or slope produced by wave erosion, situated at the seaward edge of the coast or the landward side of the wave-cut platform. It may vary from an inconspicuous slope to a high, steep escarpment. *(Fig. 78)*

Sea ice, Any form of ice found at sea that has originated from the freezing of seawater. Sea ice may be discontinuous pieces (ice floes) moved on the ocean surface by wind and currents (pack ice), or a motionless sheet attached to the coast (land-fast ice). Sea ice less than one year old is called first-year ice. Multi-year ice is sea ice that has survived at least one summer melt season.

Sea ice, Any form of ice found at sea which has originated from the freezing of sea water.

Sea level change, Sea level can change, both globally and locally, due to (i) changes in the shape of the ocean basins, (ii) changes in the total mass of water and (iii) changes in water density. Sea level changes induced by changes in water density are called steric. Density changes induced by temperature changes only are called thermosteric, while density changes induced by salinity changes are called halosteric.

Sea level equivalent (SLE), The change in global average sea level thiat would occur if a given amount of water or ice were added to or removed from the oceans.

Sea surface temperature (SST), The sea surface temperature is the temperature of the subsurface bulk temperature in the top few metres of the ocean, measured by ships, buoys and drifters. From ships, measurements of water samples in buckets were mostly switched in the 1940s to samples from engine intake water. Satellite measurements of skin temperature (uppermost layer; a fraction of a millimetre thick) in the infrared or the top centimetre or so in the microwave are also used, but must be adjusted to be compatible with the bulk temperature.

Sea, (a) A large inland body of salt water (e.g., the Salton Sea, CA). (b) A geographic subdivision of an ocean (e.g., the South China Sea).

Seachannel, (undersea feature) A continuously sloping elongated discrete depression found in fans or abyssarplains and customarily bordered by levees on one or both sides.

Seamount chain, (undersea feature) A linear or arcuate alignment of disccrete seamounts, with their bases their bases clearly separtated.

Seamount, (undersea feature) A discrete (or group of) large isolated elevation(s), greater than 1000 m in relief above the sea floor, characteristically of conical form; see also guyot.

Sediment budget, An accounting, or inventory, of sediment-transport rate, generally as components based on particle-size ranges entering and leaving a specified area or stream reach; when the fluxes of sediment that enter and leave are unequal, the assumption follows that the differences signify the net amounts of sediment that are stored or taken from storage within the area or reach.

Sediment concentration, (of streamflow) The amount of sediment, generally as a dry weight, that is entrained in a specified volume of water; sediment concentration is typically expressed in milligrams of sediment per liter of the water/sediment mixture.

Sediment delivery, The sum of hydrologic and geomorphic processes resulting in the availability of sediment for transport in a stream network; sediment-delivery processes range from entrainment in overland flow to rapid mobilization by bank failure to much slower movement as soil creep.

Sediment duration, The percentage of time that a specified concentration of fluvial sediment is equaled or exceeded; a range of sediment durations from the same stream permits the construction of a sediment-duration curve.

Sediment station, An installation with a sampling device, generally for collecting samples of suspended sediment, at a stream site at or near a gaging station; the purpose of a sediment station is the collection of sediment-concentration values for the prevailing water discharge, thereby permitting the computation of an instantaneous value for sediment discharge.

Sediment yield, The sediment-transport rate per unit area, generally from watersheds or drainage basins larger than the field scale; erosion studies, however, may consider sediment yield from smaller areas of the hillslope or plot scale..

Sediment, Material, both mineral and organic, that is in suspension, is being transported, or has been moved from its site of origin by water, wind, ice or mass-wasting and has come to rest on the earth's surface either above or below sea level. Sediment in a broad sense also includes materials precipitated from solution or emplaced by explosive volcanism, as well as organic remains; e.g., peat that has not been subject to appreciable transport.

Sediment, The detached fragmental material that originates from either chemical or physical weathering of rocks and minerals and is transported by, suspended in, or deposited by water or air or is accumulated in beds by other natural agencies.

Sedimentary peat, An accumulation of organic material that is predominantly the remains of floating aquatic plants (e.g., algae) and the remains and fecal material of aquatic animals, including coprogenous earth.

Sedimentary rock, A consolidated deposit of clastic particles, chemical precipitates, or organic remains accumulated at or near the surface of the earth under "normal" low temperature and pressure conditions. Sedimentary rocks include consolidated equivalents of alluvium, colluvium, drift, and eolian, lacustrine, marine deposits; e.g., sandstone, siltstone, mudstone, claystone, shale, conglomerate, limestone, dolomite, and coal. *(Fig. 39)*

Sedimentation, The process by which sediment is mechanically deposited from suspension within a fluid, generally water, or ice, thereby accumulating as layers of sediment that are segregated owing to differences in size, shape, and composition of the sediment particles.

Sediment-delivery ratio, The ratio, expressed as a percent, of sediment yield of a drainage basin to the total amount of sediment moved downslope by denudational processes during a specified period of time; over long time periods, mass balance must be maintained and the mean sediment-delivery ratio must approach 1.0.

Sediment-duration curve, A cumulative-frequency curve, derived from a flow-duration curve and sediment concentrations in water samples collected at known discharge rates (a sediment-rating curve), that shows the percentage of time that specified discharges of suspended sediment are equaled or exceeded.

Sedimentology, The study of the characteristics of sediment forming sedimentary rocks, unconsbfidated fluvial, mass-movement, and eolian deposits, and soils; as part of the disciplines of geomorphology and hydrology, sedimentology is the study of (1) mineral composition, particle size or particle-size distributions and sorting, physical metrics such as orientation and angularity, chemistry, porosity and permeability, organic and fossil content, age, and history or evolution of sediment particles or of a sediment body, and (2) the rates of movement of sediment on hillslopes, with water as fluvial sediment, and in glacial ice.

Sediment-rating curve, A line (curve) averaging concentrations of fluvial sediment in transport, generally as measured from suspended-sediment samples, collected through the range of discharges typical of a stream; it shows mean variation in sediment concentration with variation in discharge for the period of data collection.

Sediment-transport rate, (commonly termed sediment discharged) The rate at which a dry weight of sediment passesasection of a stream in a given time; total sediment-transport rate, or total sediment load, is the sum of the suspended-sediment and the bed-load transport rates or loads. It is the total quantity of sediment, as measured by dry weight, or by volume, that is transported during a given time and is reported in watts per meter (W m$_{-1}$) or in mass per unit time.

Seep, An area, generally small, where water outflows slowly at the land surface. Flow rates for seeps are too small to be considered as springs, but reflow and / or lateral subsurface flow keeps the surface or near soil saturated during dry periods.

Seif dune, A large, sharp-crested, elongated, longitudinal (linear) dune or chain of sand dunes, oriented parallel, rather than transverse (perpendicular), to the prevailing wind. If unmodified, the crest, in profile, commonly consists of a succession of curved slip faces produced by strong, but infrequent cross winds. A seif dune may be as much as 200 m high and from 400 m to more than 100 km long.

Semiarid, A climatic zone that receives an average 250 to 500 mm of precipitation annually; in semiarid areas potential evapotranspiration typically exceeds precipitation.

Semi-bolson, A wide desert basin or valley that is drained by an intermittent stream, an externally drained (open) intermontane basin.

Semidiurnal, Descriptive of a tide that has a cycle of approximately one-half a tidal day, as opposed to diurnal.

Semi-open depression, A topographically enclosed basin that generally functions as a closed depression and lacks a defined exit channel. Surface water loss may occur via overland flow through a topographic low area or gap in response to large storm events. Semi-open depressions commonly contain small lakes, ponds, or wet meadows dominated by hydric soils (e.g., in karst valleys, or in low areas on marine terraces with < 1 % slopes).

Sensible heat flux, The flux of heat from the Earth's surface to the atmosphere that is not associated with phase changes of water; a component of the surface energy budget.

Sewage lagoon ,Any artificial pond or other water-filled excavation for the natural oxidation of sewage or disposal of animal manure.

Shale, Sedimentary rock formed by induration of a clay, silty clay, or silty clay loam deposit and having the tendency to split into thin layers, i.e., fissility.

Shear stress, That portion of stress acting tangentially as a tearing action (as opposed to that portion that acts as a normal stress) to a plane or surface; thus, a sediment particle resting on a channel bed is affected by the shear stress created by water moving on the bed.

Shear, A strain, or change in shape or volume of a body resulting from stress; as applied to fluvial'processes and sediment transport, it typically refers to the stress that is exerted on sediment particles by a moving fluid - air, water, and ice.

Sheet erosion, The process by which thin layers of surface material are gradually removed more or less evenly from an extensive area of gently sloping land by broad, continuous sheets of running water rather than by streams flowing in well-defined rills, gullies, or channels. Because overland flow typically occurs in small rivulets owing to micro-topography, sheet erosion is more of a theoretical concept that an actual process.

Sheet flow, An overland flow or downslope movement of water taking the form of a relatively thin, continuous film or veneer moving over relatively smooth soil or rock surfaces and not concentrated into rills or channels. Like sheet erosion, sheet flow is a theoretical concept that can be observed under controlled laboratory conditions but may never occur as a natural process.

Shelf edge, (undersea feature) The line along-which there is marked increase of slope at the seaward margin of a continental (or island) shelf; also called a shelf break.

Shelf sea, A shallow sea that occupies a portion of a wide continental shelf. This is one type of epicontinental sea.

Shelf, (undersea feature) A zone adjacent to a continent (or around an island) and extending from the low water line to a depth at which there is usually a marked increase of slope towards oceanic depths. *(Fig. 119)*

Shield volcano, A volcano having the shape of a very broad, gently sloping dome, built by flows of very fluid basaltic lava or rhyolitic ash flows. *(Fig. 37)*

Shoal [relict] – A surficial ridge, bank, or bar consisting of sand or other subaqueous deposit that has become permanently exposed by the retreat or lowering of a proglacial lake or other body of water.

Shoal, (undersea feature) An offshore hazard to surface navigation with substantially less clearance than the surrounding area and composed of unconsolidated material.

Shoal, A relatively shallow area of a stream channel or other water body that is caused by the deposition of sediment, generally sand or gravel, or by bedrock that is more resistant to erosion than are adjacent areas of the stream or water body.

Shore, The narrow strip of land immediately bordering any body of water, esp. the sea or a large lake; specifically the zone over which the ground is alternately exposed and covered by tides or waves, or the zone between high water and low water. *(Fig. 79)*

Shore complex, Generally a narrow, elongate area that parallels a coastline, commonly cutting across diverse inland landforms, and dominated by landforms derived from active coastal processes which give rise to beach ridges, washover fans, beaches, dunes, wave-cut platforms, barrier islands, cliffs, etc.

Shoreline, The intersection of a specified plane of water with the beach; it migrates with changes of the tide or of the water level. *(Fig. 79)*

Short-crested waves, A propagating surface gravity wave with a free surface which is doubly periodic in two perpendicular directions, along and normal to the direction of propagation. These can be produced either by the interaction of two progressive waves angles to each other or by oblique reflection from a maritime structure.

Shoulder, The hillslope profile position that forms the convex, erosional surface near the top of a hillslope. If present, it comprises the transition zone from summit to backslope.

Shrub-coppice dune, A small, streamlined dune that forms around brush and clump vegetation.

Side slope, A geomorphic component of hills consisting of a laterally planar area of a hillside, resulting in predominantly parallel overland water flow (e.g., sheet wash); contour lines generally form straight lines. Side slopes are dominated by colluvium and slope wash sediments. Slope complexity (downslope shape) can range from simple to complex. It is generally linear along the slope width.

Significant wave height, A quantity defined as the average height of the one-third highest waves.

Significant wave height, The average height of the highest one-third of the wave heights (sea and swell) occurring in a particular time period.

Silica, One of the major nutrients in marine ecosystems, which is also used as a tracer in physical oceanog-raphy.

Siliceous ooze, A fine-grained sediment of pelagic origin found on the deep-ocean floor. It contains more than 30% siliceous material of organic origin and is usually found below the carbon compensation depth at depths greater than 4500 m. Two types of this are radiolarian oozes and diatom oozes. *(Fig. 153)*

Sill, A tabular, igneous intrusion that parallels the bedding or foliation of the surrounding sedimentary or metamorphic rock. *(Fig. 34, 38)*

Sill, The (undersea feature) A sea floor barrier of relatively shallow depth restricting water movement between basins.

Silt, (as fluvial sediment) Sediment defined to be of particle diameter between 0.002 and 0.062mm; some systems define the lower size limit to be 0.004 mm.

Siltite, A compact, weakly metamorphosed rock formed by alteration of siltstone, mudstone, or silty shale. Siltite is more indurated than mudstone or shale and lacks either shale fissility or slate-like cleavage. Siltite differs from argillite in that silt-size grains (0.002 to 0.062 mm) dominate the matrix rather than clay-size particles (<0.002 mm). Siltite differs from siltstone, mudstone, or shale in that it exhibits very low to low grade metamorphic or diagenetic layer silicate and feldspar alteration to sericite, chlorite, and albite.

Siltstone, An indurated silt having the texture and composition of shale but lacking its fine lamination or fissility; a massive mudstone in which silt predominates over clay.

Since fjords are associated with glacial carving, they occur at higher latitudes where there are mountainous coasts.

Sink, Any process, activity or mechanism that removes a greenhouse gas, an aerosol or a precursor of a greenhouse gas or aerosol from the atmosphere.

Sinkhole karst, A landscape dominated by subsurface drainage and sinkholes (dolines) that range widely in sizes and density; the most common type of karst in upland areas of temperate regions. also called doline karst. *(Fig. 193)*

Sinkhole, A shallow circular- to oval-shaped depression of a karst landscape; sinkholes typically form by surface collapse following solution and often cave formation in underlying carbonate rocks. *(Fig. 86, 204)*

Sinuosity, (as applied to stream-channel) patterns a non-dimensional ratio, generally expressed in meters per meter or kilometers per kilometer, of the length of the channel thalweg to the length of the stream valley, measured between the same points

Six thermometer, A self-registering maximum and minimum thermometer invented by James Six of England in 1782. It consisted of a U-shaped tube with mercury in the bend, one side filled with alcohol, and the other partially filled. Indices marked the highest and lowest temper-atures. This was the most widely used thermometer for taking deep sea temperatures up until the 1870s.

Slack water, (as applied to fluvial systems) Runoff or streamflow that is prevented in some manner from maintaining a normal velocity and thereby becomes ponded or nearly so.

Slack-water deposit, A fine-textured sediment that falls from suspension in a body of slack water owing to little or no stream velocity; slack-water deposits resemble and in many cases are nearly the same as deposits of lacustrine sediment.

Slickensides, Shrink-swell produced slip faces on pedo-structure faces (e.g., wedges, bowls); grooves, striations, glossy sheen. Most evident in (but not limited to) Vertisols. Vertical or oblique, roughly planar slip face produced by external forces such as tectonics (e.g., fault), or mass movement (e.g., large slump blocks; grooves, striations on slip face).

Slide, A category of mass movement processes, associated sediments (slide deposit), or resultant landform (e.g., rotational slide, translational slide, and snowslide) characterized by a failure of earth, snow, or rock under shear stress along one or several surfaces that are either visible or may reasonably be inferred. The moving mass may or may not be greatly deformed, and movement may be rotational (rotational slide) or planar (translational slide). A slide can result from lateral erosion, lateral pressure, weight of overlying material, accumulation of moisture, earthquakes, expansion owing to freeze-thaw of water in cracks, regional tilting, undermining, fire, and human agencies. The track of bare rock or furrowed earth left by a slide. The mass of material moved in or deposited by a slide.

Slip face, The steeply sloping surface on the lee side of a dune, standing at or near the angle of repose of loose sand, and advancing downwind by a succession of slides wherever that angle is exceeded.

Slip surface, A landslide displacement surface, often slickensided and striated, or brecciated, and subplanar. It is best exhibited in argillaceous materials and in those materials which are highly susceptible to clay alteration when granulated.

Slippery sea, A phenomenon occurring in the wind-driven layer at the surface of the sea. In conditions of strong surface heating, a well-mixed warmer (and lighter) layer if formed, which is of limited depth because the stabilizing density distribution inhibits vertical mixing with the deeper, colder water. At the bottom of this surface layer is a strong density gradient where the turbulence is suppressed.

Slope alluvium, Sediment gradually transported down mountain or hill slopes primarily by non-channel alluvial processes (i.e., slope wash processes) and characterized by particle sorting. Lateral particle sorting is evident on long slopes. In a profile sequence, sediments may be distinguished by differences in size and/or specific gravity of rock fragments and may be separated by stone lines. Sorting of rounded or subrounded pebbles or cobbles and burnished peds distinguish these materials from unsorted colluvial deposits.

Slope wash – A collective term for non-fluvial, incipient alluvial *processes* (e.g., overland flow, minor rills) that detach, transport, and deposit sediments down hill and mountain slopes. Related sediments (*slope alluvium*) exhibit nominal sorting or rounding of particles, peds, etc., and lateral sorting downslope on long slopes; stratification is crude and intermittent and readily destroyed by pedoturbation and frost action.

Slope, (undersea feature) The deepening sea floor out from the shelf edge to the upper limit of the continental rise, or the point where there is a general decrease in steepness.

Slope, Any inclined surface of the earth. As a geomorphic measurement, slope is the inclination, generally measured in degrees departure from horizontal or expressed as a non-dimensional number (meters per meter), of any surface of the earth's landscape (including sub-aqueous surfaces); for application to models of hillslope soil loss, steepness is often used synonymously with slope. *(Fig. 114, 115)*

Slot canyon – A long, narrow, deep and tortuous channel or drainageway with sheer rock walls eroded into sandstone or other sedimentary rocks, especially in the semiarid western USA (e.g., Colorado Plateau); subject to flash flood events; depth to width ratios exceed 10:1 over most of its length and can approach 100:1; commonly containing unique ecological communities distinct from the adjacent, drier uplands.

Slough, (a) A small marsh, especially a marshy area lying in a local, shallow, closed depression on a piece of dry land. (b) A term used, especially in the Mississippi Valley, for a creek or sluggish body of water in a tidal flat, flood plain, or coastal marshland. (c) A sluggish channel of water, such as a side channel of a river, in which water flows slowly through low, swampy ground, as along the Columbia River, or a section of an abandoned river channel which may contain stagnant water and occurs in a flood plain or delta.

Slump block, A mass of material torn away as a coherent unit during a landslide; a largely intact but displaced and commonly reoriented body of rock or soil.

Slush, Snow which is saturated and mixed with water on land or ice surfaces, or as a viscous floating mass in water after heavy snowfall.

Snow line, The lower limit of permanent snow cover, below which snow does not accumulate.

Snowfield, (a) A broad expanse of terrain covered with snow, relatively smooth and uniform in appearance, occurring usually at high latitudes or in mountainous regions above the snowline and persisting throughout year. (b) A region of permanent snow cover, as at the head of a glacier; the accumulation area of a glacier.

Soil association, (or soil complex) Two or more soils that are closely related, and are mapped as contiguous features, owing to similar conditions of climate, topography, and vegetation; if the soils have similar characteristics owing to common parent material from which they have developed, they represent a catena.

Soil fall, The mass movement process, associated sediments (soil fall deposit), or resultant landform characterized by a rapid type of *fall* involving the relatively free, downslope movement or collapse of detached, unconsolidated soil material which falls freely through the air (lacks an underlying slip face); sediments predominantly fine earth (< 2 mm); common along undercut stream banks. Also called earth fall.

Soil horizon, A thickness of soil that differs from adjacent strata in terms of physical properties such as structure, color, or particle size distribution, or by chemical composition, especially the amount and alteration of organic matter or the content of clays and related weathering products; standard designations of the three mostly commonly recognized mineral horizons of soils are the uppermost, dark-colored A horizon, which is a zone of humic-material accumulation, reducing conditions, and leaching, the underlying B horizon, which is generally lighter or reddish in color owing to oxidizing conditions and is the zone or horizon at which humus, silicates, and clays typically accumulate, and the lowest C horizon, which contains little organic material and is formed of partially weathered, unconsolidated rock material and fragments that are transitional between the developing soil above and bedrock below. *(Fig. 116)*

Soil loss, That portion of eroded sediment that moves from agricultural fields, small catchments, or other sites of disturbance or interest; the remainder of eroded sediment is stored at various sites of microtopography, behind vegetation, or in other small depressions on the hillslope surface. More precisely, soil loss is the rate of soil eroded from that portion of the land surface experiencing a net loss of soil mass or volume.

Soil moisture, The water held by capillary forces, including adhesion, between soil particles and organic material and as a film on soil particles in an aerated (unsaturated) soil zone; soil moisture is lost to the atmosphere by processes of evapotranspiration and is replenished by precipitation.

Soil moisture, Water stored in or at the land surface and available for evaporation.

Soil profile, An assemblage of all soil horizons at a site that in vertical section extends from the surface to the parent material from which the soil was derived.

Soil science, The study of soil processes and treats or considers the formation, properties, classification, and mapping of soils; a synonymous term is pedology although some soil scientists regard soil science to have two principal sub-disciplines, pedology and edaphology.

Soil, A layered mass of minerals and, generally, organic matter and rock fragments that differs from the parent material (rocks) from which it is derived in terms of morphology, physical and chemical characteristics, and organisms and organic content; the layers, or horizons, that comprise a soil are of variable thickness (as also are soil bodies), are typically but not always unconsolidated, and differ from each other in terms of degree of alteration that has occurred during the weathering process of the underlying parent material. A fundamental classification of soil types includes clay, silt, sand, gravel, peat, chalk, and loam (having significant amounts of clay, silt, sand, and possibly gravel) soils.

Solar ('11 year') cycle, A quasi-regular modulation of solar activity with varying amplitude and a period of between 9 and 13 years.

Solar activity, The Sun exhibits periods of high activity observed in numbers of sunspots, as well as radiative output, magnetic activity and emission of high-energy particles. These variations take place on a range of time scales from millions of years to minutes.

Solar radiation, Electromagnetic radiation emitted by the Sun. It is also referred to as shortwave radiation. Solar radiation has a listinctive range of wavelengths (spectrum) determined by the temperature of the Sun, peaking in visible wavelengths. *(Fig. 161, 162, 163, 164)*

Solifluction deposit, A deposit of nonsorted, water-saturated, earthy material locally derived that is moving or has moved down slope en masse, caused by the melting of seasonal frost or permafrost, resulting in an over-thickened leading edge of linear, lobate, or irregular forms that loosely parallel or obliquely follow the slope contour; may be surficially armored by rock fragments on the leading edge.

Solifluction lobe, An isolated tongue-shaped feature up to 25 m wide and 150 m or more long, formed by rapid solifluction on certain sections of a slope showing variations in gradient. This feature commonly has a steep (e.g., 15°- 60°) front and a relatively smooth upper surface.

Solifluction sheet – A broad deposit of nonsorted, water-saturated, locally derived material that is moving or has moved downslope, en masse. Stripes are commonly associated with solifluction sheets.

Solifluction terrace , A low step with a straight or lobate front, the latter reflecting local differences in rate of flow. A solifluction terrace may have bare mineral soil on the upslope part and 'folded under' organic matter in both the seasonally thawed and the frozen soil.

Solifluction, A slow (normally at a velocity less than $5 \times 10_{-2}$ m yr_{-1}) type of mass movement by viscous processes of a non-Newtonian, generally saturated, mixture of poorly sorted sediment and related soil material; the term applies in particular to the plastic flow of surficial material, in areas of high relief and high elevation, that is underlain by frozen ground, thereby preventing the downward movement of meltwater during episodes of near-surface thawing.

Solute, Any dissolved substance; in natural environments it is generally rock, mineral, soil, or organic matter dissolved in water.

Solution chimney, Small diameter (e.g., 1-5 m), irregular, hollow, vertical shaft 5-10+ m deep on karst landscapes, typically covered with a thin layer of soil or plant debris that can collapse and expose the shaft to the surface; represents a significant safety hazard.

Solution corridor, A straight, open trench about 3 to 10 m wide in a karst area, formed by vertical and lateral solution zones developed along bedrock fractures.

Solution fissure, One of a series of vertical open cracks commonly < 0.5 m wide dissolved along joints or fractures, separating limestone pavement (pavement karst) into blocks (clints).

Solution pipe, A subsurface, vertical, cylindrical or cone-shaped hole, formed by dissolution in soluble bedrock (e.g., limestone) and often without surface expression, that is filled with detrital material (e.g., soil) and which serves as a bypass route for internal water flow.

Solution platform, A broad, nearly horizontal intertidal surface (modern or relict) formed across carbonate rocks, produced primarily by solution with contributions by intertidal weathering and biological erosion and deposition, not by abrasion.

Solution sinkhole , The most common type of sinkhole, caused by dissolution that forms fissures or a chimney and a depression in the bedrock surface which grows when closely spaced fissures underneath it enlarge and coalesce.

Somali Current, A current near the western boundary of the Indian Ocean that flows southward during the boreal winter and northward during the summer. The southward flow during the northeast monsoon is limited to south of 10°N. It occurs first in early December near the equator and expands rapidly north in January with velocities from 0.7-1.0 m/s. The surface flow reverses in April during the inter-monsoon period, and develops into an intense jet during the southwest monsoon with velocities reaching 3.5 m/s in June. During the southwest monsoon a two gyre system develops in the region -the Great Whirl between 5-10°N with clockwise rotation and a secondary eddy towards its south. This two gyre system is stable until August or September, when the southern gyre propagates northward and merges with the Great Whirl. This has also been called the East Africa Coast Current.

Soot, Particles formed during the quenching of gases at the outer edge of flames of organic vapours, consisting predominantly of carbon, with lesser amounts of oxygen and hydrogen present as carboxyl and phenolic groups and exhibiting an imperfect graphitic structure.

Sorting, The process by which sediment particles of similar characteristics or size but shape and specific gravity as well, are selectively separated from other particles, concentrated, and deposited as a sedimentary mass by an entraining fluid, generally water and wind but to a lesser degree by ice and slurries (mass movement).

Sound, (a) A relatively long, narrow waterway connecting two larger bodies of water (as a sea or lake with the ocean or another sea) or two parts of the same water body, or an arm of the sea forming a channel between the mainland and an island (e.g., Puget Sound, WA); it is generally wider and more extensive than a strait [coast]. (b) A long, large, rather broad inlet of the ocean, generally extending parallel to the coast (e.g., Long Island Sound, NY). (c) A lagoon along the southeast coast of the USA (e.g., Pamlico Sound, NC). (d) A long bay or arm of a lake; a stretch of water between the mainland and a long island in a lake.

Source area, The area of a watershed supplying water and sediment to the area of stored sediment above the highest point of an identifiable channel; thus, a source area supplies sediment to a drainage network, and some or most of that sediment may be temporarily stored before entrainment as fluvial sediment.

South China Sea, A regional sea in the western Pacific Ocean centered at about 115° E and 12° N that includes the Gulf of Thailand and the Gulf of Tonkin. It is bordered to the west by Vietnam, Thailand and the Malay Peninsula, to the south by a line joining the southern tip of the Malay Peninsula to Borneo, to the east by Borneo, the Phillipines and Taiwan, and to the north by the Taiwan Strait and China. It covers an area of 3,685,000 km$_2$, has a volume of 3,907,000 km$_3$, a mean depth of 1060 m, and a maximum depth of 5016 m.

Southern Ocean, An unofficial term used to describe the oceans surrounding the continent of Antarctica, which cover approximately 30,000,000 km$_2$, or about 20% of the total world ocean area. The northern limit is generally considered to be the broad zone of transition where the permanent thermocline reaches the surface at the Subtropical Convergence/Front and the southern limit the continent of Antarctica. It is distinguished from the other oceans by the relative uniformity of its characteristics of hydrography and circulation and that it influences more than it is influenced by the others.

Southern Oscillation, The name given to the atmospheric component of the El Nino/Southern Oscillation (or ENSO) phenomenon. The SO is a large-scale shift in atmospheric mass between the western and eastern Pacific.

Spatial and temporal scales, Climate may vary on a large range of spatial and temporal scales. Spatial scales may range from local (less than 100,000 km$_2$), through regional (100,000 to 10 million km2) to continental (10 to 100 million km$_2$). Temporal scales may range from seasonal to geological (up to hundreds of millions of years).

Spatter cone, A small, steep-sided cone (e.g., 3 to 15 m high, or more) built up on a lava flow, usually pahoehoe, composed of clots of lava ejected with escaping gases from a vent or fissure which spatters and congeals as it hits the ground to form a small cone; rougher lava clots than a spiracle.

Specific gravity, The ratio of a material's density to that of water [material weight in air, (weight in air - weight in water)]. Used to differentiate different kinds of volcaniclastics and other materials.

Specific mass balance, net mass loss or gain over a hydrological cycle at a point on the surface of a glacier.

Spit, (a) A small point or low tongue or narrow embankment of land, commonly consisting of sand or gravel deposited by longshore transport and having one end attached to the mainland and the other terminating in open water, usually the sea; a finger-like extension of the beach. (b) A relatively long, narrow shoal or reef extending from the shore into a body of water.

spoil bank – A bank, mound, or other artificial accumulation of rock debris and earthy dump deposits removed from ditches, strip mines, or other excavations. Compare – dredge spoil bank. SW

Sporadic permafrost, The area near the southern boundary of discontinuous permafrost where permafrost occurs in isolated patches or islands.

Spring tide, The high tides of greatest amplitude caused by the Earth, Sun and Moon being almost co-linear. This causes the gravitational pulls of both the Sun and Moon to reinforce each other. The high tide is higher and low tide is lower than the average, and spring tides occur twice a month at the times of both new moon and full moon.

Spur, A subordinate elevation or ridge protruding from a larger feature, such as a plateau or island foundation.

Squall, A violent wind that begins suddenly, lasts for a short time, and dies suddenly. It is sometimes associated with a temporary change of direction.

Stability, (as a descriptor of geomorphic processes and landforms) A condition of approximate balance between inflows and outflows of matter through or over a landscape feature. As a geomorphic concept, stability generally is regarded as being an integration of processes affecting a system and thus has time-independence; the term often is used synonymously with (dynamic or quasi) equilibrium.

Stack, An isolated pillar-like rocky island or mass near a cliffy shore, detached from a headland by wave erosion assisted by weathering; especially one showing columnar structure with horizontal stratification. *(Fig. 76)*
A steep-sided mass of rock rising above its surroundings on all sides from a slope or hill.

Stage, or gage height, The height of a water surface above an established datum plane, generally at a gaging station.

Stage-discharge curve, or rating curve A graph showing the relation between the gage height, usually plotted as the ordinate, and the amount of water flowing in a channel, expressed as volume per unit time, plotted as abscissa.

Stage-discharge relation, The relation between stage and discharge expressed by the stage-discharge curve.

Stagnant ice, (a) Glacial ice that is not flowing forward and is not receiving material from an accumulation area. (b) Detached blocks of ice left behind by a retreating glacier, usually buried in a moraine and melting very slowly.

Star dune, A large, isolated sand dune whose base, in plan view, resembles a star, with sharp-crested ridges converging from basal points to a central peak that may be as high as 100 m above the surrounding plain. It tends to remain fixed for centuries in an area where the wind blows from all directions. *(Fig. 103)*

Stemflow, An effect of interception that results in the gravitational movement of water down the limbs, stems, or trunk of plants, especially trees. Particularly for trees, stemflow concentrates intercepted rainfall by the crown of the tree at the surfaces of stems or trunks, causing enhanced wetting and soil moisture in the ground areas beside the trunks. This process set minimizes the erosive impact of raindrop impact beneath the tree, but especially during intense storms may cause overland flow and rill erosion at the base of the plant owing to the concentration of water.

Stock – A relatively small, concordant and / or discordant plutonic rock body exposed at the land surface, with an aerial extent < 40 sq. mi. (100 km2) and no known bottom.

Stone line, In vertical cross-section, a line formed by scattered fragments or a discrete layer of angular and subangular rock fragments, commonly a gravel- or cobble-sized lag concentration that drape across a former topographic surface and later buried by additional sediments. A stone line generally caps material that was subject to weathering, soil formation, and erosion before burial. Many stone lines seem to be buried erosion pavements, originally formed by sheet and rill erosion across the land surface. It can best be observed as outcrops in natural and artificial cuts.

Storm surge, The temporary increase, at a particular locality, in the height of the sea due to extreme meteorological conditions (low atmospheric pressure and/or strong winds). The storm surge is defined as being the excess above the level expected from the tidal variation alnne at that time and place

Storm tracks, Originally, a term referring to the tracks of individual cyclonic weather systems, but now often generalised to refer to the regions where the main tracks of extratropical disturbances occur as sequences of low (cyclonic) and high (anticyclonic) pressure systems.

Stoss, Said of the side of the hill or knob that faces the direction from which an advancing glacier or ice-sheet moved; facing the upstream ("up-ice") side of a glacier, and most exposed to its abrasive action.

Stoss and lee, An arrangement of small hills or prominent rocks, in a strongly glaciated area, having gentle slopes on the stoss ("up-ice") side and somewhat steeper, plucked slopes on the lee ("down-ice") side. This arrangement is the opposite of crag and tail.

Strait of Gibraltar, A shallow strait that separates the eastern Atlantic Ocean from the Mediterranean sea. *(Fig. 143)*

Strait, A relatively narrow waterway connecting two larger bodies of water.

Strand plain, A prograded shore built seaward by waves and currents, and continuous for some distance along the coast. It is characterized by subparallel beach ridges and swales, in places with associated dunes.

Strandline, (a) The shoreline, especially a former (relict) shoreline now elevated above the present water level, that commonly appears as a bench or line wrapping around the landscape at a common elevation. (b) A beach, especially one raised above the present sea or lake level.

Strath terrace, A type of stream terrace, formed as an erosional surface cut on bedrock and thinly mantled (e.g., < 3 m) with stream deposits (alluvium), commonly with a gravel lag deposit immediately above the bedrock.

Stratification, In oceanography, the vertical density structure resulting from a balance among atmospheric heating, surface water exchange, freezing, stirring and diffusion of heat, and the horizontal and vertical motion (advection) of waters with different temperature and salinity characteristics.

Stratified , Formed, arranged, or laid down in layers. The term refers to geologic deposits. Layers in soils that result from the processes of soil formation are called horizons; those inherited from the parent material are called strata.

Stratified estuary, One of four principal types of estuaries as distinguished by prevailing flow conditions. This type is stratified with a halocline between the upper and lower portions of the water column of nearly constant salinity.

Stratigraphy, The branch of geology that deals with the definition and interpretation of layered earth materials; the conditions of their formation; their character, arrangement, sequence, age, and distribution; and especially their correlation by the use of fossils and other means. The term is applied both to the sum of the characteristics listed and a study of these characteristics.

Stratosphere, The highly stratified region of the atmosphere above the troposphere extending from about 10 km (ranging from 9 km at high latitudes to 16 km in the tropics on average) to about 50 km altitude. *(Fig. 158, 159)*

Stratovolcano, A volcano that is constructed of alternating layers of lava and pyroclastic deposits, along with abundant dikes and sills. Viscous, acidic lava may flow from fissures radiating from a central vent, from which pyroclastics are ejected.

Stream, (a) Any body of running water that moves under gravity to progressively lower levels, in a relatively narrow but clearly defined channel on the ground surface, in a subterranean cavern, or beneath or in a glacier. It is a mixture of water and dissolved, suspended, or entrained matter. (b) A term used in quantitative geomorphology interchangeably with channel.

Stream order, A designation indicating the position that a stream-channel segment has within the hierarchy of channels of a drainage network; the uppermost, headwater channels of a drainage network are typically assigned a stream order of 1 and the most downstream channel segment has the highest stream-order designation, perhaps 6 or 8. Owing to subjectivity in how a channel hierarchy is interpreted (where, for example, a 1st-order headwater channel begins), and confusion caused by a variety of stream-ordering systems, the use of stream order, which was extensive in the 1950s and 1960s, is now limited.

Stream order, An integer system applied to tributaries (stream segments) that documents their relative position within a drainage basin network as determined by the pattern of its confluences. The order of the drainage basin is determined by the highest integer. Several systems exist. In the Strahler system, the smallest unbranched tributaries are designated order 1; the confluence of two first-order streams produces a stream segment of order 2; the junction of two second-order streams produces a stream segment of order 3, etc. *(Fig. 53)*

Stream power, The ability of flowing water to accomplish work (sediment transport, erosion), is the product of discharge and water-surface slope; stream power, per unit length of channel, is typically expressed in watts per meter (W m$_{-1}$).

Stream terrace, One, or a series of flat-topped landforms in a stream valley that flank and are parallel to the stream channel, originally formed by a previous stream level, and representing remnants of an abandoned flood plain, stream bed, or valley floor produced during a past state of fluvial erosion or deposition (i.e., currently very rarely or never flooded; inactive cut and fill and/or scour and fill processes). Erosional surfaces cut into bedrock and thinly mantled with stream deposits (alluvium) are called "strath terraces." Remnants of constructional valley floors thickly mantled with alluvium are called alluvial terraces.

Stream, A general term for a body of flowing water; in hydrology the term is generally applied to the water flowing in a natural channel as opposed to a canal or a drainage ditch.

Streamflow, The discharge (m$_3$s$_{-1}$) that occurs in (and, during floods, adjacent to) a natural channel. The term streamflow is more general than runoff and can be applied to discharge regardless of whether it is affected by diversion or regulation; streamflow is the water remaining after losses of precipitation or snowmelt to evaporation or sublimation and after available water has satisfied the needs of vegetation and replenishment of soil moisture. Ground water, as inputs from springs and seeps, may be a significant component of streamflow in some channels.

Strength of ebb, In the description of tides, the magnitude of the ebb current at the time of maximum speed. This is usually associated with lunar tide phases at spring at spring tides near perigee or with maximum river discharge. This is also known as ebb strength.

Strike valley, A subsequent valley eroded in, and developed parallel to the strike of, underlying weak strata, such as a cuesta; a valley that commonly, but not necessarily contains a stream valley.

Strike, The compass direction or trend taken by a structural surface (e.g., a bed or fault plane) as it intersects the horizontal; used in combination with "dip" to describe the orientation of bedrock strata.

String bog, A peatland with roughly parallel, narrow ridges of peat dominated by peat vegetation interspersed with slight depressions, many of which contain shallow pools. The ridges are at right angles to low (< 2°) slopes. They are typically 1 to 3 m wide, up to 1 m high and may be over 1 km long. The ridges are slightly elevated and are better drained allowing shrubs and trees to grow. They are best developed in areas of discontinuous permafrost.

Stripe – A type of patterned ground; one of the alternating bands of fine and coarse surface material, or of rock or soil and vegetation-covered ground, commonly found on steeper slopes. It is usually straight, but may be sinuous or branching.

Strom surge, A phenomena wherein sea level rises above the normal tide level when hurricanes or tropical storms move from the ocean along or across a coastal region. Technically, this is defined as the difference between the actual sea (tide) level under the influence of a meteorological disturbance (storm tide) and the level which would have been reached in the absence of the meteorological disturbance.

Structural bench, A shelf or step-like landform produced or controlled by erosion resistant, horizontally-bedded rock. Erosion removes overlying weaker rock or sediment forming a nearly level to gently inclined surface that rests on a relatively resistant strata or rock that ascends to a higher slope or platform. Structural benches may occur as a single feature or as a series of stepped-surfaces where alternating weak and resistant strata exist. Due to erosion resistance, structural benches may have little or no geomorphic implication regarding fluvial deposition, past erosion cycles or former stream, basin, or base levels.

Subaerial, Said of conditions and processes, such as erosion, that exist or operate in the open air on or immediately adjacent to the land surface; or of features and materials, such as eolian deposits, that are formed or situated on the land surface.

Subantarctic Zone, The name given to the region in the Southern Ocean between the Subantarctic Front to the south and the Subtropical Front to the north.

Subaqueous landscapes, Permanently submerged areas that are fundamentally the same as subaerial (terrestrial) systems in that they have a discernable topography composed of mappable, subaqueous landforms.

Subaqueous soil, Soil that forms in sediment found in shallow, permanently flooded environments. Excluded from the definition of these soils are any areas "permanently covered by water too deep (typically greater than 2.5 m) for the growth of rooted plants."

Subaqueous, Said of conditions and processes, features or deposits, that exist or operate in or under water.

Subcritical flow, (or tranquil flow) The flow which occurs when the water velocity is lower than that of critical flow and the Froude number is less than 1.0; in subcritical flow, ripples caused by a water-surface disturbance move both upstream and downstream.

Subduction, Ocean process in which surface waters enter the ocean interior from the surface mixed layer through Ekman pumping and lateral advection. The latter occurs when surface waters are advected to a region where the local surface layer is less dense and therefore must slide below the surface layer, usually with no change in density.

Subglacial – (a) Formed or accumulated in or by the bottom parts of a glacier or ice sheet; said of meltwater streams, till, moraine, etc. (b) Pertaining to the area immediately beneath a glacier, as subglacial eruption or subglacial drainage.

Subglacial till, Till deposited beneath, in, or by the bottom part of a glacier or ice sheet; subglacial till types include lodgment till, subglacial flow till, and subglacial melt-out till.

Sublimation, The direct conversion of ice or snow to a gaseous or vapor state.

Submerged back-barrier beach, A permanently submerged extension of the back-barrier beach that generally parallels the boundary between estuary and the barrier island.

Submerged mainland beach, A permanently submerged extension of the mainland beach that generally parallels the boundary between an estuary or lagoon and the mainland.

Submerged point bar, The submerged extension of an exposed (subaerial) point bar.

Submerged wave-built terrace, A subaqueous, relict depositional landform originally constructed by river or longshore sediment deposits along the outer edge of a wave-cut platform and later submerged by rising sea level or subsiding land surface.

Submerged wave-cut platform – A subaqueous, relict erosional landform that originally formed as a wave-cut bench and abrasion platform from coastal wave erosion and later submerged by rising sea level or subsiding land surface.

Submerged-upland soil – Mineral or organic soil that primarily formed in a subaerial setting but is now under water, commonly in intertidal or subaqueous settings. Inundation could occur for various reasons (e.g., sea-level rise in a marine or estuarine system or ponding from a dam). In intertidal settings, tidal marsh soils may occur above former subaerial soils (see *submerged-upland tidal marsh*). In subaqueous settings (permanently submerged), submerged-upland soils typically occur below a cap of subaqueous soil forming in the subaqueous environment.

Submerged-upland tidal marsh, An extensive nearly level, intertidal landform composed of unconsolidated sediments (clays, silts, and/or sand and organic materials), a resistant root mat, vegetated dominantly by hydrophytic (water loving) plants. The mineral sediments largely retain pedogenic horizonation and morphology (e.g., argillic horizons) developed under subaerial conditions prior to submergence due to sea level rise; a type of tidal marsh.

Subsidence, (as an earth-surface process) The gradual lowering or sinking of a land area, with little or no horizontal component, owing to steady compaction of subsurface rock or sediment. Natural subsidence can result from a variety of causes including solution of carbonate or evaporate rocks, erosion and weathering processes of soil and subsoil materials, and processes related to tectonism, volcanic activity, and freeze-thaw cycles. Induced subsidence may occur beneath areas underlain by soft, easily sheared rocks, especially poorly consolidated alluvium of the Basin and Range Province, where water (or gas or oil) have been extracted, thereby reducing the buoyancy effect provided by the subsurface fluid; similarly, if a large volume of water is introduced to porous, unsaturated alluvial beds, the added weight and reduction of shear strength may cause steady compaction of the underlying alluvial beds.

Subtidal wetlands, Permanently inundated areas within estuaries dominated by subaqueous soils and submerged aquatic vegetation.

Subtidal, Continuous submergence of substrate in an estuarine or marine ecosystem; these areas are below the mean low tide.

Subtropics, The part of the Earth's surface between the tropics and the temperate regions, or between about 40° N and S.

Sulu Sea, A regional sea contained within the Australasian Mediterranean Sea at the southwestern edge of the Pacific Ocean. It is centered at about 120° E and 8° N and connected to the Sulawesi Sea to the southeast via many passages through the Sulu Archipelago, the Bohol Sea to the east, and the South China Sea to the west and northwest chiefly via the Mindoro, Linapacan, North Balabac, and Balabac Straits. It borders the Philippine islands of Mindanao, Negros, and Panay to the east, Mindoro and the Calamin Group to the north, Palawan to the west, and the aforementioned Sulu Archipelago to the southeast. The Malaysian portion of the island of Borneo lies to the southwest.

Summit, (a) The topographically highest position of a hillslope profile with a nearly level (planar or only slightly convex) surface. Compare – shoulder, backslope, footslope, and toeslope, crest. (b) A general term for the top, or highest area of a landform such as a hill, mountain, or tableland. It usually refers to a high interfluve area of relatively gentle slope that is flanked by steeper slopes, e.g., mountain fronts or tableland escarpments.

Sunda Sea, A marginal sea in the southwest Pacific Ocean. This is a name sometimes given to the combined areas of the Java Sea and the shelf sector of the South China Sea.

Sunda Shelf, One of the largest continental shelves in the world. It covers around 1,800,000 km2, is centered around 108° E and 2° N, and occupies the regions of the Java Sea, the southern parts of the South China Sea, and the Gulf of Thailand.

Sunspots, Small dark areas on the Sun. The number of sunspots is higher during periods of high solar activity, and varies in particular with the solar cycle.

Supercritical flow, (or rapid flow, in open channels) That flow which occurs when the water velocity is greater than that of critical flow and the Froude number is more than 1.0; in supercritical flow, ripples caused by a water-surface disturbance all move downstream.

Supraglacial till, Till deposited on top of or within the upper part of a glacier or ice sheet. Melting of glacial ice deposits supraglacial till atop subjacent material, which forms topographic highs on a resultant landscape. Supraglacial till types include supraglacial flow till and supraglacial melt-out till.

Supraglacial, Carried upon, deposited from, or pertaining to the top surface of a glacier or ice sheet; said of meltwater streams, till, drift, etc.

Surf beat, The rising and falling of the water level in the surf zone at intervals in the vicinity of 2 to 5 minutes, especially noticeable on a flat beach. This is caused by the pattern of incoming waves being such that groups of high waves and low waves follow each other at the same intervals.

Surf zone, The portion of the nearshore zone in which borelike translation waves occur following wave breaking. It extends from the inner breakers shoreward to the swash zone.

Surface mine, A depression, open to the sky, resulting from the surface extraction of earthy material (e.g., soil / fill) or bedrock material (e.g., coal).

Surface water, Water evident above the land surface either flowing in a **channel** or collected in a lake, pond, or reservoir.

Suspended sediment, (or suspended load) Sediment moved in suspension in water and is maintained in suspension by the upward component of turbulent currents or by colloidal suspension. The regulatory acronym for suspended load is Total Suspended Solids (TSS).

Swale – (a) A shallow, open depression in unconsolidated materials which lacks a defined channel but can funnel overland or subsurface flow into a drainageway. Soils in swales tend to be moister and thicker (cumulic) compared to surrounding soils. (b) A small, shallow, typically closed depression in an undulating ground moraine formed by uneven glacial deposition. (c) A long, narrow, generally shallow, trough-like depression between two beach ridges, and aligned roughly parallel to the coastline.

Swallow hole, A closed depression or doline into which all or part of a stream disappears underground. *(Fig. 204)*

Swamp, An area of low, saturated ground, intermittently or permanently covered with water, and predominantly vegetated by shrubs and trees, with or without the accumulation of peat.

Swash zone, The portion of nearshore zone in which the beach face is alternately covered by the uprush of wave swash and exposed by the backwash.

Swash zone, The sloping part of the beach that is alternately covered and uncovered by the uprush of waves, and where longshore movement of water occurs in a zigzag (upslope-downslope) manner.

Swell and swale topography – A local scale topography composed of small, well-rounded hillocks and shallow, closed depressions irregularly spaced across low-relief ground moraine (slopes generally 2 – 6%); the effect is a subdued, irregularly undulating surface that is common on ground moraines. Micro-elevational differences generally range from < 1 to < 5 m.

Syncline – (a) A unit of folded strata that is concave upward whose core contains the stratigraphically younger rocks, and occurs at the earth's surface. In a single syncline, beds forming the opposing limbs of the fold dip toward its axial plane. (b) A fold, at any depth, generally concave upward whose core contains the stratigraphically younger rocks. *(Fig. 26)*

Synoptic, Descriptive of data simultaneously obtained over a large area.

Tableland, A general term for a broad upland mass with nearly level or undulating summit area of large extent and steep side slopes descending to surrounding lowlands (e.g., a large plateau). .

Talf, A geomorphic component of flat plains (e.g., lake plain, low coastal plain, low-gradient till plain) consisting of an essentially flat (e.g., 0-1 % slopes) and broad area dominated by closed depressions and a non-integrated or poorly integrated drainage system. Precipitation tends to pond locally and lateral transport is slow both above and below ground, which favors the accumulation of soil organic matter and a retention of fine earth sediments; better drained soils are commonly adjacent to drainageways.

Talus cone, A steep (e.g., 30 - 40°), cone-shaped landform at the base of a cliff or escarpment that heads in a relatively small declivity or ravine, and composed of poorly sorted rock and soil debris that has accumulated primarily by episodic rockfall or, to a lesser degree, by slope wash. Finest material tends to be concentrated at the apex of the cone. Not to be confused with an *alluvial cone*; a similar feature but of fluvial origin, composed of better stratified and more sorted material, and that tapers up into a more extensive drainageway.

Talus slope, a portion of a hillslope or mountainslope mantled by talus and lying below a rockfall source (e.g., cliff).

Talus, Rock fragments of any size or shape (usually coarse and angular) derived from and lying at the base of a cliff or very steep rock slope. The accumulated mass of such loose broken rock formed chiefly by falling, rolling, or sliding.

Tank, A natural depression or cavity in impervious rocks in which water collects and remains for the greater part of the year.

Tarn, A relatively deep, steep-banked lake or pool occupying an ice-gouged rock basin amid glaciated mountains. A cirque lake. *(Fig. 91)*

Tasman Sea, A marginal sea located in the southwest Pacific centered at about 160° E and 37° S off the southwest coast of Australia. It is also surrounded by New Zealand to the east, Tasmania to the southwest, and the Coral Sea to the north. The maximum depth is 5943 m. The bathymetry is essentially composed of the east Australian Basin in the westerly part and the depression of New Caledonia to the east, with the two separated by the Lord Howe Sill.

Teleconnection, A connection between climate variations over widely separated parts of the world. In physical terms, teleconnections are often a consequence of large-scale wave / motions, whereby energy is transferred from source regions along preferred paths in the atmosphere.

Temperature inversion, A region of negative lapse rate. *(Fig. 177)*

Temperature lapse rate, The rate of decrease of temperature with height.

Tephra, A collective, general term for any and all clastic materials, regardless of size or composition, ejected from a vent during a volcanic eruption and transported through the air; including ash [volcanic; < 2 mm], blocks [volcanic; > 64 mm], cinders [2 - 64 mm], lapilli [2 - 76 mm & specific gravity > 2.0], pumice [> 2 mm & specific gravity < 1.0], and scoria [> 2 mm & specific gravity < 2.0]. Tephra, unlike many volcaniclastic terms, does not denote properties of composition, vesicularity, or grain size.

Terminal moraine, An end moraine that marks the farthest advance of a glacier and usually has the form of a massive arcuate or concentric ridge, or complex of ridges, underlain by till and other drift types.

Terrace remnant, A stream terrace eroded and dissected to such an extent that it occurs as a scattered and isolated geomorphic surface generally on interfluve noses above a younger, more continuous stream terrace. A continuous tread surface no longer exists, but alluvium is present in or below the soil profile. In contrast to a paleoterrace, a terrace remnant corresponds to the present-day drainage system.

Terrace, A relatively flat horizontal or gently linclined surface, sometimes long and narrow, which is bounded by a steeper ascending slope on one side and by a steeper descending slope on the opposite side.

Terrace, A valley-contained surface that typically is expressed as a long, narrow, nearly level or gently inclined landform bounded along the lower edge by a steeper descending slope and along the higher edge by a steeper ascending slope; a terrace is always topographically higher than the flood plain, and is inundated by floods of greater magnitude than the mean annual flood. An alluvial terrace is an aggradational feature, is composed of unconsolidated to poorly consolidated alluvium and its weathering products, and generally reflects an abandoned flood-plain surface; a strath terrace is an erosional feature formed by stream incision into a bedrock surface, and may have little or no relation to a former flood plain.

Terracettes, Small, irregular step-like forms on steep hillslopes, especially in pasture, formed by creep or erosion of surficial materials that may be induced or enhanced by trampling of livestock such as sheep or cattle.

Terrain, A generic name for a tract or region of the Earth's surface considered as a physical feature, an ecological environment, or a site of some planned human activity.

Tertiary – A period of the Cenozoic Era of geologic time (from 65 to 1.6 million years ago). The Tertiary epoch/series subdivisions comprise, by increasing age, the Pliocene, Miocene, Oligocene, Eocene, and Paleocene.

Tethys Sea, A paleogeographic term for a sea that partly intersected Pangaea in the Permian and later separated the two Mesozoic supercontinents of Laurasia and Gondwana. (Fig. 10)

Thalweg, The line of continuous, maximum descent from any point on a land surface; e.g., the line connecting the lowest points along the bed of a stream, or the line crossing all contour lines at right angles.

Thalweg, The line within a stream channel connecting the lowest points at all sites of the channel.

Thaw-sensitive permafrost, Perennially frozen ground which, upon thawing, will experience significant thaw settlement and suffer loss of strength to a value significantly lower than that for similar material in an unfrozen condition.

Thermal equator, An imaginary line connecting those points around the globe with the highest mean temperature for the given period. As such, the position of the thermal equator varies with the season. Due to the thermal inertia of the ocean, the position of this moves north and south with the Sun but is always between the Sun and the geographic equator. The mean position is north of the geographic equator due mainly to the majority of land masses being in the northern hemisphere.

Thermal expansion, In connection with sea level, this refers to the increase in volume (and decrease in density) that results from \vafming water. A warming of the ocean leads to an expansion of ocean volume and hence an increase in sea level.

Thermal infrared radiation, Radiation emitted by the Earth's surface, the atmosphere and the clouds. It is also known as terrestrial or longwave radiation, and is to be distinguished from the near-infrared radiation that is part of the solar spectrum. Infrared radiation, in general, has a distinctive range of wavelengths (spectrum) longer than the wavelength of the red colour in the visible part of the spectrum. The spectrum of thermal infrared radiation is practically distinct from that of shortwave or solar radiation because of the difference in temperature between the Sun and the Earth-atmosphere system.

Thermocline, Specially the depth at which the temperature gradient is as maximum. Generally a layer of water with a more intensive vertical gradient in temperature than in the layers either above or below it.

Thermocline, The layer of maximum vertical temperature gradient in the ocean, lying between the surface ocean and the abyssal ocean. In subtropical regions, its source waters are typically surface waters at higher latitudes that have subducted and moved equatorward. At high latitudes, it is sometimes absent, replaced by a halocline, which is a layer of maximum vertical salinity gradient.

Thermograph, A recording thermometer which measures a continuous trace of temperature called a ther mogram. The classical version of this featured a bi-metallic strip attached to a lever holding a pen. As the strip expanded and contracted in response to temperature changes, the pen moved across a piece of paper on a drum rotating via some clockwork mechanim. Such things are done using solid state devices sending binary data to other solid state devices in these modern times.

Thermohaline circulation (THC), Large-scale circulation in the ocean that transforms low-density upper ocean waters to higher-density intermediate and deep waters and returns those waters back to the upper ocean. The circulation is asymmetric, with conversion to dense waters in restricted regions at high latitudes and the return to the surface involving slow upwelling and diffusive processes over much larger geographic regions. The THC is driven by high densities at or near the surface, caused by cold temperatures and/or high salinities, but despite its suggestive though common name, is also driven by mechanical forces such as wind and tides. Frequently, the name THC has been used synonymously with Meridional Overturning Circulation.

Thermohaline, In oceanography, descriptive of a combination of temperature and salinity effects.

Thermokarst depression, A hollow in the ground resulting from subsidence following the local melting of ground ice in a permafrost region.

Thermokarst drainage pattern, Drainage patterns that form polygonal and hexagonal shapes with streams that may connect rounded depressions, exhibiting a beaded appearance; developed in poorly drained, fine-grained sediments and in organic materials in regions of permafrost. Freezing causes many cracks to develop; thawing causes slumping, settlement, and depressions. This type of drainage pattern with its associated hexagons and beaded ponds indicates the existence or previous presence of permafrost conditions.

Thermokarst lake, Lake or pond produced in a permafrost region by melting of ground ice.

Thermokarst, Karst-like topographic features produced in a permafrost region by local melting of ground ice and subsequent settling of the ground.

Thermokarst, The process by which characteristic landforms result from the thawing of ice-rich permafrost or the melting of massive ground ice.

Tidal epoch, The phase lag of the maximum of a given constituent of an observed tide behind the corresponding maximum of the theoretical equilibrium tide.

Tidal evolution, The changing of the Earth-Moon tidal characteristics over time.

Tidal flat, An extensive, nearly horizontal, barren or sparsely vegetated tract of land that is alternately covered and uncovered by the tide, and consists of unconsolidated sediment (mostly clays, silts and/or sands and organic materials).

Tidal inlet [relict], A channel remnant of a former tidal inlet. The channel was cutoff or abandoned by infilling from migrating shore sediments.

Tidal inlet, Any inlet through which water alternately floods landward with the rising tide and ebbs seaward with the falling tide.

Tidal marsh , An extensive, nearly level marsh bordering a coast (as in a shallow lagoon, sheltered bay or estuary) and regularly inundated by high tides; formed mostly of unconsolidated sediments (e.g., clays, silts, and/or sands and organic materials), and the resistant root mat of salt tolerant plants; a marshy tidal flat.

Tidal wave, An egregious misnomer for a type of wave that has nothing to do with tides or tide-producing forces. *(Fig. 132)*

Tide Chart, A map showing the water levels throughout a bay or estuary at a particular point in time. Tide Charts normally show the water levels on an hourly basis after high tide.

Tide gauge, A device at a coastal location (and some deep-sea locations) that continuously measures the level of the sea with respect to the adjacent land. Time averaging of the sea level so recorded gives the observed secular changes of the relative sea level.

Tide Table, A tidal prediction table showing the daily high and low tide predictions for a particular location.

Tide, The periodic rising and falling of the water that results from the gravitational attraction of the moon and sun acting on the rotating earth. There are related phenomena that occur in the solid earth and the atmosphere called, strangely enough, earth tides and atmospheric tides. The forces that significantly effect the tides of the oceans are the gravitational forces of the sun and moon, the centrifugal force due to the movement of the earth in its orbit, the Coriolis force, and the frictional force due to the movement of the water with respect to its boundaries. *(Fig. 136, 137, 138, 139)*

Till plain, An extensive, flat to gently undulating area underlain predominantly by till and bounded on the distal end by subordinate recessional or end moraines.

Till, That portion of drift deposited directly by glacial ice; till generally lacks stratification, is poorly sorted or unsorted, and is formed of all sediment sizes, the largest of which may be poorly rounded.

Till-floored lake plain, A glaciated land area that has characteristics of a till plain, but that was also inundated by a glacial lake. The area possesses a gently undulating till-topography, rather than a distinctive, low-relief lake plain surface, and has thin (e.g. **H"** 1-3 m), continuous or discontinuous lacustrine sediment atop the till. Topography that once existed as islands may exhibit shore features (e.g., wave-cut scarps, strandlines, beach deposits).

Tilted fault block, A fault block that has become tilted, perhaps by rotation on a hinge line (fault).

Time series, Any series of observations of a physical variable that is sampled at changing time intervals. A regular sampling interval is usually presumed although not required.

Timor Sea, A regional sea located in the Australasian Mediterranean Sea and centered at about 12° S and 127° E. It consists of Timor Strait to the north and the Sahul Shelf to the south, with the former having a width of 80 km and a maximum depth of 3 km in the Timor Trench. Sills to the west (1860 m) and east (1400 m) control the allowable flow at depth. Overall, the flow is strongest in the strait and extends with decreasing velocities onto the shelf.

Toe, The lowest, usually curved margin of displaced material of a landslide, most distant from the main scarp. Commonly it has an irregular surface that has ripples and may be breached by radial cracks or gaps.

Toeslope, The hillslope position that forms the gently inclined surface at the base of a hillslope. Toeslopes in profile are commonly gentle and linear, and are constructional surfaces forming the lower part of a hill-slope continuum that grades to valley or closed-depression floors.

Tombolo, A sand or gravel bar or barrier that connects an island with the mainland or with another island. (Fig. 83, 127)

Topography, The relative position and elevations of the natural or manmade features of an area that describe the configuration of its surface.

Topple – A category of mass movement processes, associated sediments (topple deposit), or resultant landform characterized by a localized, very rapid type of fall in which large blocks of soil or rock literally fall over, rotating outward over a low pivot point. Portions of the original material may remain intact, although reoriented, within the resulting debris pile. Types of topples can be specified based on the dominant particle size of sediments (i.e., debris topple, soil topple, rock topple.

Tor, A high, isolated pinnacle, or rocky peak; or a pile of rocks, much-jointed and usually granitic, exposed to intense weathering, and often assuming peculiar or fantastic shapes.

Total load, The total amount of any physical or chemical constituent or contaminant that is transported by a moving fluid, generally water as streamflow. The term most typically is used to characterize sediment discharge in streams, for which it is the combined fluxes of suspended sediment and bed load, expressed often in (metric) tons per day.

Total mass balance (of the glacier): The specific mass balance spatially integrated over the entire glacier area; the total mass a glacier gains or loses over a hydrological cycle.

Total sediment-transport rate, or total sediment load, The sum of the suspended-sediment and bed-load transport rates; it is the total quantity of sediment, as measured by dry weight or volume, that moves past a site during a given time. Often the suspended-sediment transport rate is measured, but the bed-load transport rate must be estimated.

Total solar irradiance (TSI), The amount of solar radiation received Outside the Earth's atmosphere on a surface normal to the incident radiation, and at the Earth's mean distance from the Sun.

Total suspended solids (TSS), A measure of the suspended-solids, or solid-phase, content of a water sample. According to Standard Methods for the Analysis of Water and Wastewater (1995), TSS is determined from a sub-sample of an original water sample

Tower karst, (a) A type of tropical karst topography characterized by isolated, steep-sided, residual limestone hills or ridges with vertical or near-vertical walls, and may be relatively flat-topped; commonly surrounded by a flat alluvial plain or lagoons. (b) A cluster of peaks or ridges with vertical or near-vertical walls, and convex upper side slopes where towers rise from a common base and are separated by deep, rugged ravines or large sinkholes.

Trade winds, The trade winds, or tropical easterlies, are the winds which diverge from the subtropical high-pressure belts, centered at 3-40° N and S, towards to equator, from north to east in the northern hemisphere and south to east in the southern hemisphere.

Transect, A line or path along which measurements or observations are taken, generally at equal intervals, as a means of compiling data for an investigation. As applied to geomorphology or sedimentology, for example, it could be the measurement of the diameter of each sediment particle or rock fragment occurring at 1-m intervals along a 100-m length of channel bed or hillslope; as applied to plant ecology, a transect is a line along which observations of vegetation are made, often within quadrats, that might include presence or absence of species, height or truck diameter of trees, or surface area covered by individual plants, as a means to study characteristics of a particular assemblage of species. The use of transects in geomorphic or ecological investigations is a means to minimize the potential for introducing bias into the study.

Translational debris slide, The mass movement process, associated sediments (translational debris slide deposit), or resultant landform characterized by an extremely slow to moderately rapid type of slide, composed of comparatively dry and largely unconsolidated earthy material, portions or blocks of which remain largely intact and in which movement occurs along a well-defined, planar slip face roughly parallel to the ground surface and resulting in lateral displacement but no rotation of the displaced mass; sediments have substantial proportions of both fine earth and rock fragments. The landform may be single, successive (repeated up and down slope), or multiple (as the number of slide components increase).

Translational earth slide, The mass movement process, associated sediments (translational earth slide deposit), or resultant landform characterized by an extremely slow to moderately rapid type of slide, composed of comparatively dry and largely unconsolidated earthy material, portions or blocks of which remain largely intact and in which movement occurs along a well-defined, planar slip face roughly parallel to the ground surface and resulting in lateral displacement but no rotation of the displaced mass; sediments predominantly fine earth (< 2 mm). The landform may be single, successive (repeated up and down slope), or multiple (as the number of slide components increase).

Translational rock slide, The mass movement process, associated sediments (translational rock slide deposit), or resultant landform characterized by an extremely slow to moderately rapid type of slide, composed of comparatively dry and largely consolidated rock bodies, portions or blocks of which remain largely intact and in which movement occurs along a well-defined, planar slip face roughly parallel to the ground surface and resulting in lateral displacement but no rotation of the displaced mass; sediments predominantly fine earth (< 2 mm). The landform may be single, successive (repeated up and down slope), or multiple (as the number of slide components increase).

Translational slide, A category of mass movement processes, associated sediments (translational slide deposit), or resultant landform characterized by the extremely slow to moderately rapid downslope displacement of comparatively dry soil-rock material on a surface (slip face) that is roughly parallel to the general ground surface, in contrast to falls, topples, and rotational slides. The term includes such diverse *slide* types as translational debris slides, translational earth slide, translational rock slide, block glides, and slab or flake slides.

Transmission loss, The abstraction, or reduction, of flow in ephemeral or intermittent stream channels as discharge migrates downstream; the loss occurs by infiltration of streamflow into normally dry (unsaturated) sediment forming the channel bed and banks and therefore much of the flow abstraction becomes recharge to the ground-water reservoir.

Transport, The movement, shifting, or carrying away by natural agents of sediment (and dissolved load) from one place to another on or near the earth's surface.

Transverse dune, A very asymmetric sand dune elongated perpendicular to the prevailing wind direction, having a gentle windward slope and a steep leeward slope standing at or near the angle of repose of sand; it generally forms in areas of sparse vegetation. *(Fig. 103)*

Tread, A geomorphic component of terraces, flood-plain steps, and other stepped landforms consisting of the flat to gently sloping, topmost and laterally extensive slope. Commonly a recurring part of a series of natural, step-like landforms such as successive stream terraces. Its characteristic shape and alluvial sediment composition is derived from the cut and fill processes of a fluvial system.

Tree rings, Concentric rings of secondary wood evident in a Crossection of the stem of a woody plant. The difference between the dense, small-celled late wood of one season and the wide-celled early wood of the following spring enables the age of a tree to be estimated, and the ring widths or density can be related to climate parameters such as temperature and precipitation.

Trellis drainage pattern , A drainage pattern characterized by parallel main streams intersected at, or nearly at, right angles by their tributaries, which in turn are fed by elongated secondary tributaries and short gullies parallel to the main streams, resembling, in plan view, the stems of a vine on a trellis. This pattern indicates marked bedrock structural control rather than a type of bedrock and usually indicates in which the main parallel channels follow the strike of the beds. It is commonly developed where the beveled edges of alternating hard and soft rocks outcrop in parallel belts, as in titled, interbedded sedimentary rocks in a rejuvenated folded-mountain region or in a maturely dissected belted coastal plain of tilted strata.

Trend, In this report, the word trend designates a change, generally monotonic in time, in the value of a variable.

Tripoli, A light-colored, porous, friable, siliceous (largely chalcedonic) sedimentary rock, which occurs in powdery or earthy masses that result from the weathering of siliceous limestone. It has a harsh, rough feel and is used to polish metals and stones.

Tropical cyclone, A non-frontal, synoptic scale, low pressure system originating over tropical or sub-tropical waters with organized convection and definite cyclonic wind circulation.

Tropical depression, A tropical cyclone with maximum sustained winds of 33 knots or less near the center.

Tropical storm, A tropical cyclone with maximum sustained winds of 34 to 47 knots near the center.

Tropopause, The boundary between the troposphere and the stratosphere. *(Fig. 158)*

Troposphere, The narrowest of the atmospheric layers, extending from the surface of the Earth to about 10 km at the Equator and 6 km at the poles near the 200 mbar level. This layer contains about 80-85% of the atmosphere's total mass and almost all of the water vapor and clouds. Temperatures fall with height at the rate of about 0.5° F per 100 feet. It is bounded above by the tropopause which varies with latitude and season. This layer is characterized by strong vertical mixing associated with latent heat effects and clouds. *(Fig. 158, 159)*

Trough , (a) Any long, narrow depression in the earth's surface, such as one between hills or with no surface outlet for drainage. (b) A broad, elongate U-shaped valley, such as a glacial trough.

Trough end, The steep, semicircular rock wall forming the abrupt head or end of a U-shaped valley.

Trough, (undersea feature) A long depression of the sea floor characteristically flat bottomed and steep sided and normally shallower than a trench.

Truncated soil , Soil that has had part or all of the upper soil horizon(s) removed by erosion, excavation, etc., but retains some portion of the original subsoil horizons intact.

Truncation error, That which occurs when a function, theoretically represented exactly as the summation of an infinite (or otherwise bloody huge) number of terms, is represented by a smaller subset of these terms. The difference between the exact function and the function represented by the finite number of terms is called the truncation error. This is one of several kinds of errors inherent in representing a continuous world discretely on computers.

T-S diagram, A graph showing the relationship between temperature and salinity as observed together at, for example, various depths in a water column.

Tsunami, A Japanese word meaning "harbor wave". This is often used (along with the even more incorrect "tidal wave") as a name for what is more correctly called a seismic sea wave. A true harbor wave is a type of seiche and can be excited by, among other things, seismic sea waves. Tsunami originally applied to all large waves including storm surges but is now more or less restricted to seismic sea waves, and has mostly supplanted both seismic sea wave and tidal wave in the literature.

Tsunamis are primarily created by vertical movements of the sea floor caused by tectonic activity. This causes rapid vertical movements in the sea surface over a large area which leads to the formation of a train of very long period waves, with periods exceeding one hour not unusual. Secondary mechanisms for tsunami formation are landslides and volanic activity, with the effects of the resultant waves more localized than those of the tectonic variety which may travel across ocean basins.

Tuff, A generic term for any consolidated or cemented deposit that is ^{3} 50 percent volcanic ash (< 2 mm); various types of tuff can be recognized based on composition: acidic tuff is predominantly composed of acidic particles; basic tuff is predominantly composed of basic particles.

Tunnel valley, A relatively shallow trench or depression cut into drift and other loose material, or in bedrock, by a subglacial stream not loaded with coarse sediment that may or may not be part of the present day drainage pattern.

Turbidity, The optical property (state, condition, or quality) of opaqueness or reduced clarity of a fluid, due to suspended, colloidal, and organic matter and dissolved solids that provide color, that causes light to be scattered, absorbed, and diffracted rather than being transmitted directly through the water.

Turbulent flow, (as hydrologic term) The water movement (flow) in which the lines of flow are erratic and mixed and in which flow direction at all sites changes frequently and nearly instantaneously; turbulent flow is typical of stream and other surface-water bodies whereas laminar flow is typical of slowly moving ground water.

Turf hummock, A hummock consisting of vegetation and organic matter with or without a core of mineral soil or stones (typically 10-50 cm height; 20-90 cm diameter). Groups of hummocks can form a type of patterned ground common to tundra or wet areas (e.g., marsh).

Typhoon, A tropical cyclone with maximum sustained winds of 64 knots or more near the center.

Tyrrhenian Sea, One of the seas that comprise the western basin of the Maditerranean Sea. It is separated from the Balearic Sea to the west by Sardinia and Corsica and from the eastern basin by the Straits of Sicily. It has a central abyssal plain along with some smaller plains located within slope basins. The central plain is pierced by a large seamount that rises 2850m above the sea floor to within 743 m of the surface.

Ultraplankton, Phytoplankton whose lengths range from 0.5 to $10°$m. Compare to nanoplankton and microplankton.

Unconformity, A substantial break or gap in the geologic record where a unit is overlain by another that is not in stratigraphic succession.

Underfit stream, A stream that appears to be too small to have eroded the valley in which it flows; a stream whose volume is greatly reduced or whose meanders show a pronounced shrinkage in radius. It is a common result of drainage changes effected by capture, glaciers, or climatic variations.

Underflow, The down-valley movement of water in a near-surface alluvial aquifer that is hydraulically connected and directly related to the stream channel; underflow is most descriptive of near-surface ground-water movement beneath stream channels of arid and semiarid areas where it typically provides water adequate to sustain phreatophytic trees such as cottonwoods despite unreliable amounts of streamflow.

Upland, An informal, general term for (a) the higher ground of a region, in contrast with a low-lying, adjacent land such as a valley or plain. (b) Land at a higher elevation than the flood plain or low stream terrace; land above the footslope zone of the hillslope continuum.

Uplift, A structurally high area in the earth's crust, produced by positive movements that raise or upthrust the rocks, as in a dome or arch.

Upthrust, (a) An upheaval of rock; said preferably of a violent upheaval. (b) A high angle gravity or thrust fault in which the relatively upthrown side was the active (moving) element.

Urban heat island (UHI), The relative warmth of a city compared with surrounding rural areas, associated with changes in runoff, the concrete jungle effects on heat retention, changes in surface albedo, changes in pollution and aerosols etc.

U-shaped valley – A valley having a pronounced parabolic cross profile suggesting the form of a broad letter "U", with steep walls and a broad, nearly flat floor; specifically a valley carved by glacial erosion. *(Fig. 91)*

V

Valley fill, The unconsolidated sediment deposited by any agent (water, wind, ice, mass wasting) so as to fill or partly fill a valley.

Valley flat, A generic term for the low or relatively level ground lying between valley walls and bordering a stream channel; especially the small plain at the bottom of a narrow, steep-sided valley. The term can be generally applied noncommittally to a flat surface that cannot be identified with certainty as a floodplain or terrace.

Valley floor, A general term for the nearly level to gently sloping, lowest surface of a valley. Landforms include axial stream channels, the flood plain, flood-plain steps, and, in some areas, low terrace surfaces.

Valley side – The sloping to very steep surfaces between the valley floor and summits of adjacent uplands. Well-defined, steep valley sides have been termed valley walls.

Valley train , A long narrow body of outwash confined within a valley beyond a glacier; it may, or may not, emerge from the valley and join an outwash plain.

Valley, A relatively shallow, wide depression, the bottom of which usually has a continuous gradient; this term is generally not used for features that have canyon-like characteristics for a significant portion of their extent.

Valley-border surfaces, A general grouping of valley-side geomorphic surfaces of relatively large extent that occur in a stepped sequence graded to successively lower stream base levels, produced by episodic valley entrenchment; for example, multiple stream terrace levels, each with assemblages of constituent landforms (e.g., interfluves, hillslopes, fans, etc.) that dominate the margins of large river valleys.

Valley-floor remnant, Hills that are now erosion remnants of a former valley or basin floor, composed mostly of unconsolidated valley / basin fill sediments (e.g., alluvium) and typically lie well above the modern valley floor and flood plain. Former basin floor surfaces have become dissected and irregular and consist of hillslope positions (shoulder, backslope, etc.) and hill components (interfluve, headslope, etc.).

Valley-side alluvium ,A concave "slope wash" deposit at the base of a hill slope, mountain slope, terrace escarpment, etc., that may or may not include the alluvial toe slope.

Variable source area, A geomorphic concept acknowledging that within a drainage basin the amounts of water, sediment, and organic matter entering the drainage network from sub-basins (or source areas) vary depending on local characteristics such as climate, geology and soils, topography, and history (especially floods, fires, and land use).

Varve, A sedimentary layer, lamina, or sequence of laminae, deposited in a body of still water within 1 year; specifically, a thin pair of graded glaciolacustrine layers seasonally deposited, usually by meltwater streams, in a glacial lake or other body of still water in front of a glacier.

Ventifact, A stone or pebble that has been shaped, worn, faceted, cut, or polished by the abrasive action of windblown sand, usually under arid conditions. When the pebble is at the ground surface, as in a desert pavement, the upper part is polished while the lower or below ground part is angular or subangular. *(Fig. 101)*

Ventilation, The exchange of ocean properties with the atmospheric Surface layer such that property concentrations are brought closer to equilibrium values with the atmosphere.

Vernal pool – A natural, seasonal pond in a small closed depression (micro-low) which supports a semi-aquatic or aquatic ecosystem adapted to annual cycles of standing water in the springtime followed by drying in the summer / autumn.

Viscosity, (or internal friction) The property of a substance, a water/sediment mixture when applied to fluvial systems, to resist flow; viscosity is measured as the coefficient of viscosity, the ratio of shear-stress rate to the shear-strain rate.

Vitric, Pyroclastic material that is more than 75% glass.

Volcanic block, A pyroclast that was ejected in a solid state; it has a diameter greater than 64 mm.

Volcanic bomb, A pyroclast > 64 mm in at least one dimension that was ejected while still viscous and solidified into its rounded form in flight.

Volcanic breccias, A volcaniclastic rock composed mostly of angular rock fragments greater than 2 mm in size. The name volcanic breccia is not synonymous with pyroclastic breccia (volcanic breccia forms in different ways).

Volcanic cone, A conical hill of lava and/or pyroclastics that is built up around a volcanic vent. *(Fig. 36)*

Volcanic crater, A basin-like, rimmed structure, usually at the summit of a volcanic cone. It may be formed by collapse, by an explosive eruption or by the gradual accumulation of pyroclastic material into a surrounding rim.

Volcanic dome, A steep-sided, rounded extrusion of highly viscous lava squeezed out from a volcano, and forming a dome-shaped or bulbous mass of congealed lava above and around the volcanic vent. *(Fig. 37)*

Volcanic field – A more or less well defined area that is covered with volcanic rocks of much more diverse lithology and distribution than a lava field, or that is so modified by age and erosion that its original topographic configuration, composition and extent is uncertain. Compare – lava field, lava plain. SW

Volcanic neck, A vertical, pipe-like tower of solidified lava or consolidated fragmental igneous rock that represents a former volcanic vent whose surrounding material (e.g., tuff and tephra) has been largely removed by erosion. *(Fig. 36)*

Volcanic pressure ridge, An elongate uplift of the congealing crust of a lava flow, probably due to the pressure of the underlying, still-flowing lava; commonly < 5 m in height (but range up to 15 m) and < 100 m length (but can exceed 500 m).

Volcanic, Pertaining to 1) the deep seated (igneous) processes by which magma and associated gases rise through the crust and are extruded onto the earth's surface and into the atmosphere, and 2) The structures, rocks, and landforms produced.

Volcaniclastic, Pertaining to the entire spectrum of fragmental materials with a preponderance of clasts of volcanic origin. The term includes not only pyroclastic materials but also epiclastic deposits derived from volcanic source areas by normal processes of mass movement and stream erosion.

Volcano, (a) A vent in the surface of the Earth through which magma and associated gases and ash erupt; also, the form or structure, usually conical, that is produced by the ejected material. (b) Any eruption of material, e.g., mud, sand, etc. that resembles a magmatic volcano. *(Fig. 36)*

V-shaped valley – A valley having a pronounced cross profile suggesting the form of the letter "V", characterized by steep sides and short tributaries; specifically a narrow valley resulting from downcutting by a stream. The "V" becomes broader as the downcutting progresses.

W

Wadi, A channel, generally in arid or semiarid areas of southwestern Asia, the Arabian Peninsula, and northern Africa, in which streamflow occurs inconsistently or infrequently and, except during periods of streamflow, is directly underlain by unsaturated alluvium; wadis typically have a rectangular to steeply sided trapezoidal cross section, banks a meter or more in height formed of fine-grained, poorly consolidated over-bank sediment, and a nearly flat, sandy bed. Synonyms are ephemeral-stream channel, dry wash, and arroyo. *(Fig. 104, 106)*

Walker circulation, A name coined by Bjerknes for two circulation cells in the equatorial atmosphere, one over the Pacific and one over the Indian Ocean. Direct thermally driven zonal overturning circulation in the atmosphere over the tropical Pacific Ocean, with rising air in the western and sinking air in the eastern Pacific.

Wash load, The part of the total sediment load of a stream that is usually supplied from bank erosion or from upland sources by overland flow. It is the finest part of the load (that part which typically can be held in suspension at even very low stream velocity) that can be easily carried in large quantities it is generally determined by assuming that suspended sediment in transport that is finer than 0.062 mm is the wash load.

Wash, The broad, flat-floored channel of an ephemeral stream, commonly with very steep to vertical banks cut in alluvium. When channels reach intersect zones of ground-water discharge they are more properly classed as "intermittent stream" channels.

Washover fan, A fan-like deposit of sand washed over a barrier island or spit during a storm and deposited on the landward side. Washover fans can be small to medium sized and completely subaerial, or they can be quite large and include subaqueous margins extending into adjacent lagoons or estuaries. Large fans can be subdivided into sequential parts: ephemeral washover channel (microfeature) cut through dunes or beach ridges, back-barrier flats, (subaqueous) washover-fan flat, (subaqueous) washover-fan slope. Subaerial portions can range from barren to completely vegetated.

Washover-fan flat – A gently sloping, fan-like, subaqueous landform created by overwash from storm surges that transports sediment from the seaward side to the landward side of a barrier island . Sediment is carried through temporary overwash channels that cut through the dune complex on the barrier spit and spill out onto the lagoon-side platform where they coalesce to form a broad belt. Also called storm-surge platform flat and washover fan apron.

Washover-fan slope – A subaqueous extension of a washover-fan flat that slopes toward deeper water of a lagoon or estuary and away from the washover-fan flat.

Water balance, An accounting of the volumes of water entering, leaving, and stored in a hydrologic area or unit, typically a drainage basin or aquifer, during a specified time period in which the amount of water entering the area or unit equals the amount leaving

Water mass, A volume of ocean water with identifiable properties (temperature, salinity, density, chemical tracers) resulting from its unique formation process. Water masses are often identified through a vertical or horizontal extremum of a property such as salinity.

Water table, Term to describe the surface defined by the top of the zone of saturation in a non-confined, often alluvial, aquifer.

Water-lain moraine, A terminal, end, or recessional moraine formed subaqueously by a glacier that terminated in a water body (e.g., glacial lake, sea, or ocean). A water-lain moraine may occur at the present land surface as a result of isostatic rebound or lake drainage. Compared to a land-based moraine of similar origin, a water-lain moraine displays sediment (till) modification by wave and/or current action and has a somewhat subdued topography.

Watershed management, The administration and regulation of water and related natural resources of land, soil, and biota of the watershed for the beneficial use and conservation of those resources; included are the management of water and plant resources and the control of fluvial processes (especially erosion and sediment deposition).

Watershed, A drainage divide or a "water parting", but commonly usage of the term has been altered to signify a drainage-basin area contributing water to a network of stream channels, a lake, or other topographic lows where water can collect. *(Fig. 53)*

Waterway, (a) A general term for a way or channel, either natural (as a river) or artificial (as a canal), for conducting the flow of water. (b) A navigable body or stretch of water available for passage; a watercourse.

Wave climate, The general condition of sea state at a particular location, the principal elements of which are the wave height, period parameters, and the wave direction.

Wave forecasting, Predicting the development and characteristics of ocean surface gravity waves via semiempirical methods.

Wave set-up, A phenomenon local to the surf zone wherein wave breaking causes a stress or a landward push of the water which causes it to pile up against the shore until the seaward slope of this set-up is sufficient to oppose the wave stresses.

Wave-built terrace, A gently sloping coastal feature at the seaward or lakeward edge of a wave-cut platform, constructed by sediment brought by rivers or drifted along the shore or across the platform and deposited in the deeper water beyond.

Wave-cut platform, A gently sloping surface produced by wave erosion, extending into the sea or lake from the base of the wave-cut cliff. This feature represents both the wave-cut bench and the abrasion platform. *(Fig. 78)*

Wave-worked till plain, A glaciated land area that has the characteristics of a till plain, but that was also inundated by a glacial lake. The area possesses a gently undulating till-topography rather than a distinctive, low-relief lake plain surface. Lacustrine sediments, however, are absent or occur only sparsely, but a wave/current-modified, surficial mantle may commonly exist atop the till. Topographic highs, which were once islands, may possess shore features (e.g., wave-cut scarps, strandlines, beach deposits).

Weathering, All physical disintegration, chemical decomposition, and biologically induced changes in rocks or other deposits at or near the earth's surface by atmospheric or biologic agents or circulating surface waters with essentially no transport of the altered material. These changes result in disintegration and decomposition of the material.

Weathering, The destruction or alteration, through chemical and biochemical processes, of near-surface rock and sediment; weathering leads to the removal of waste products as dissolved loads in water but results in little or no transport of solids (erosion) that are released or modified by the weathering process. *(Fig. 42)*

Welded tuff, A glass-rich, pyroclastic rock composed of volcanic ash indurated at the time of deposition by the welding together of its glass shards under the combined action of the heat retained by particles, the weight of overlying material, and hot gasses. It is generally composed of silica pyroclasts and appears banded or streaked.

Well mixed estuary, One of four principal types of estuaries as distinguished by prevailing flow conditions. In this type the water column is well mixed with essentially no variation in salinity in a vertical column.

Wet-bulb temperature, The temperature obtained by convering the bulb of a dry-bulb thermometer with a silk or cotton wick saturated with distilled water and drawing air over it at a velocity not less than 1000 ft/min. This is often accomplished by swinging the covered thermometer on the end of a string or rope.

Wetland, A bottomland or low-lying area, including ephemeral-lake floors, at which water either is shallowly ponded on the surface or has a persistent (weeks or longer) near-surface condition of ground-water saturation adequate to support hydrophytic vegetation.

Wetted perimeter, (of a channel section) The length of which water is in contact with the channel bed and banks; wetted perimeter is a hydraulic parameter in the computation of streamflow from physical properties of the channel.

Wind gap, A former water gap now abandoned by the stream that formed it, suggesting river capture, stream piracy or stream diversion. *(Fig. 73)*

Wind-tidal flat, A broad, low-lying, nearly-level sand flat that is alternately inundated by ponded rainwater or by wind-driven bay or estuarine water from storm surges or seiche. Frequent salinity fluctuations and prolonged periods of subaerial exposure preclude establishment of most types of vegetation except for mats of filamentous blue-green algae.

Winnowing, The preferential entrainment and transport of fine particles from those of the coarse fraction of a sediment deposit by fluid motion; the term is applied especially to the transport of fine sediment sizes from a poorly sorted reservoir of sediment by wind, but the winnowing process occurs also by the action of water moving on hillslopes, in rills and gullies, in stream channels, and along beaches and other parts of lakes or oceanic tidal zones.

Woody peat, An accumulation of organic material that is predominantly composed of trees, shrubs, and other woody plants.

Yardang trough, A long, shallow, round-bottomed groove, furrow, trough, or corridor excavated in the desert floor by wind abrasion, and separating two yardangs. *(Fig. 99)*

Yardang, A sharp-crested landform, of relatively soft, generally fine-grained sedimentary or volcanic rocks, that is typically oriented parallel to the dominant wind direction an arid region or desert and has surfaces sculpted by processes of abrasion by wind-entrained sediment (mostly sand and silt). *(Fig. 99)*

Yellow Sea, A marginal sea centered at around 124° E and 37° N in the western Pacific Ocean that is distinguished traditionally although not hydrographically from the adjoining East China Sea to the south. It is also called the Huanghai Sea. The name comes from huge quantities of sediment discharged into the Bohai Gulf by the Yellow River in China. The traditional demarcation line between the Yellow and East China Seas varies but usually lies somewhere around 33° N. The Yellow Sea can be separated into a northern part, the aforementioned Bohai Bay, and the Yellow Sea proper to the south and east of Bohai Bay. The average depth of the Yellow Sea is 44 m. A shallow trough runs through it and can be traced south to the northern end of the Okinawa Trough in the East China Sea.

Younger Dryas, A period 12.9 to 11.6 kya, during the deglaciation, characterised by a temporary return to colder conditions in many locations, especially around the North Atlantic.

Zero velocity surface, A reference level at which the horizontal velocities are thought to be practically zero.

Zibar – A small, low-relief sand dune that lacks discernible slip faces and commonly occurs on sand sheets, in interdune areas, or in corridors between larger dunes. Zibar spacing can range from 50 to 400 m with local relief of less than 10 m. Unlike coppice dunes, zibars are not related to deposition around vegetation. Generally dominated by coarser sands.

Zone of aeration, or **zone of vadose water,** The typically moist but unsaturated subsurface zone between the land surface and the top of the zone of saturation (water table).

Zone of saturation, That part of the subsurface in which the interstices of porous and permeable rocks are saturated with water under pressure equal to or greater than atmospheric pressure.

Zooplankton, One of two groups into which plankton are divided, the other being phytoplankton. Zooplankton are a large group of micro- and macroscopic animals ranging in size from a fraction of a millimeter to 30-50 millimeters, with a few, such a certain jellyfish, being up to a meter in diameter. Some plankton, called permanent plankton or holoplankton, are adapted to a pelagic mode of existence and remain floating or feebly swimming throughout their entire life cycle. Others, called temporary plankton, are the transitory floating stages such as eggs, larvae, and juveniles of the benthos and nekton. This latter category is usually seasonal in occurrence and the abundance is primarily neritic since it derives from the benthos and nekton of shallow areas.

Essential Diagrams
and Illustrations

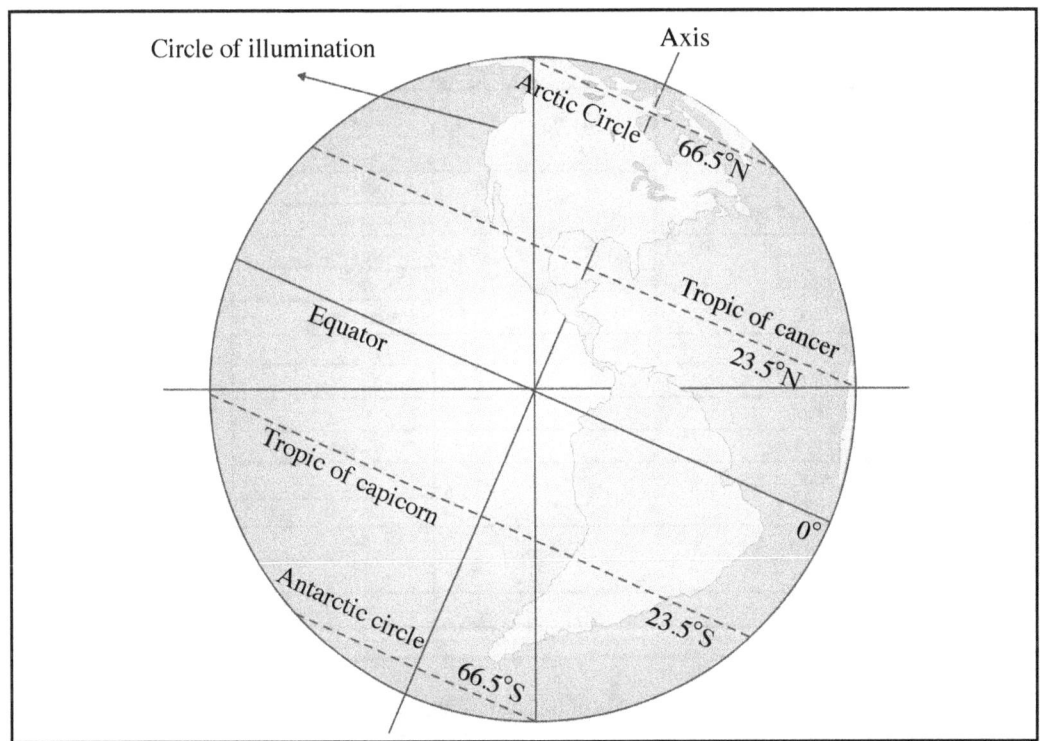

FIg. 1 : The Earth

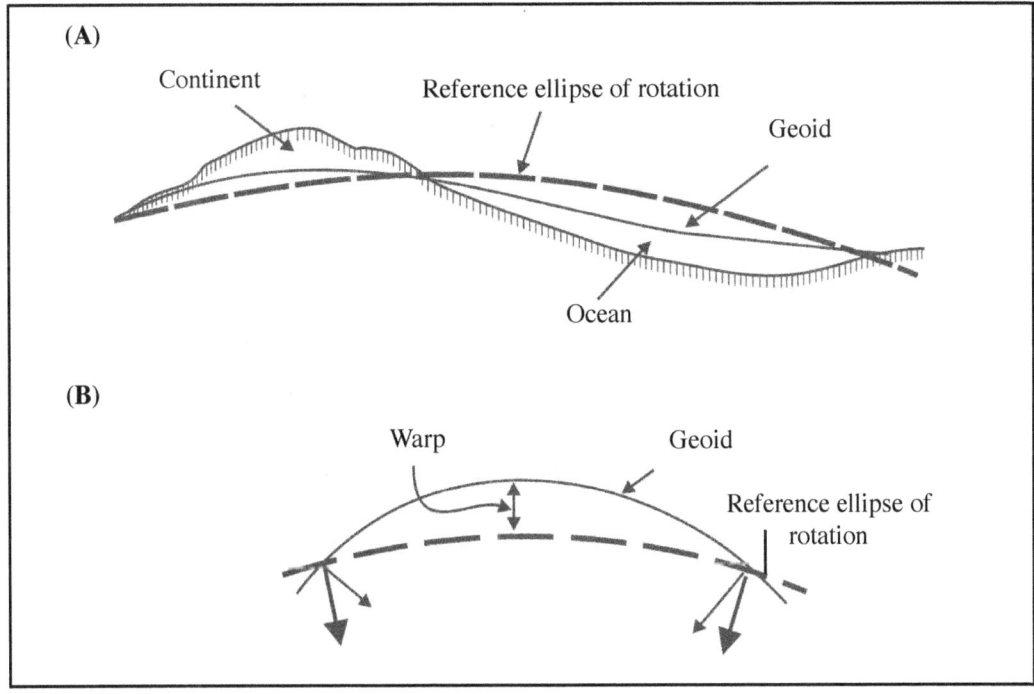

Fig. 2 : Geoid

Era	Period		Epoch	Estimated Millions of Years Ago
Cenozoic	Neogene	Quaternary	Holocene	.01
			Pleistocene	2
		Tertiary	Pliocene	5
			Miocene	24
	Paleogene		Oligocene	38
			Eocene	55
			Paleocene	63
Mesozoic	Cretaceous			138
	Jurassic			205
	Triassic			240
Paleozoic	Permian			290
	Carboniferous			330
				360
	Devonian			410
	Silurian			435
	Ordovician			500
	Cambrian			570
Precambrian The Precambrian is the time between the origin of the Earth and the beginning of the Cambrian period.				4,550

Fig. 3 : Geological Time Scale

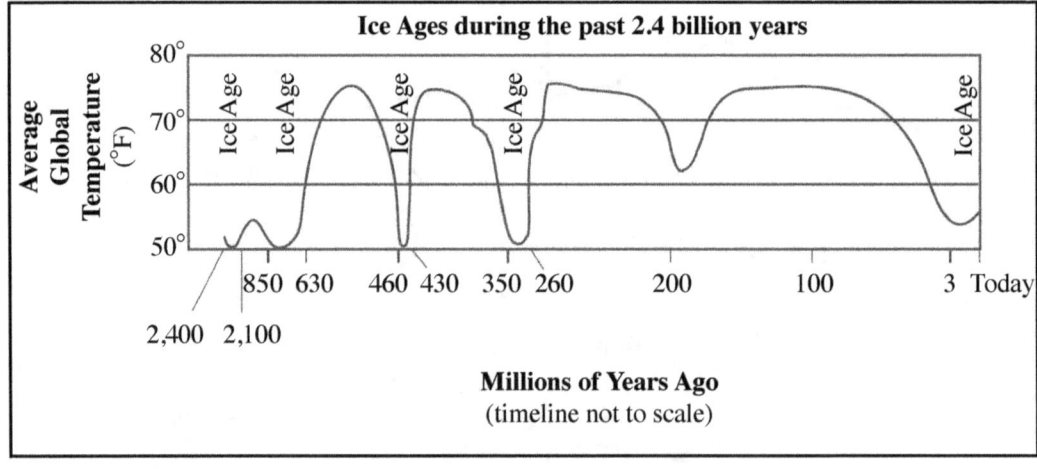

Fig. 4 : Ice Ages

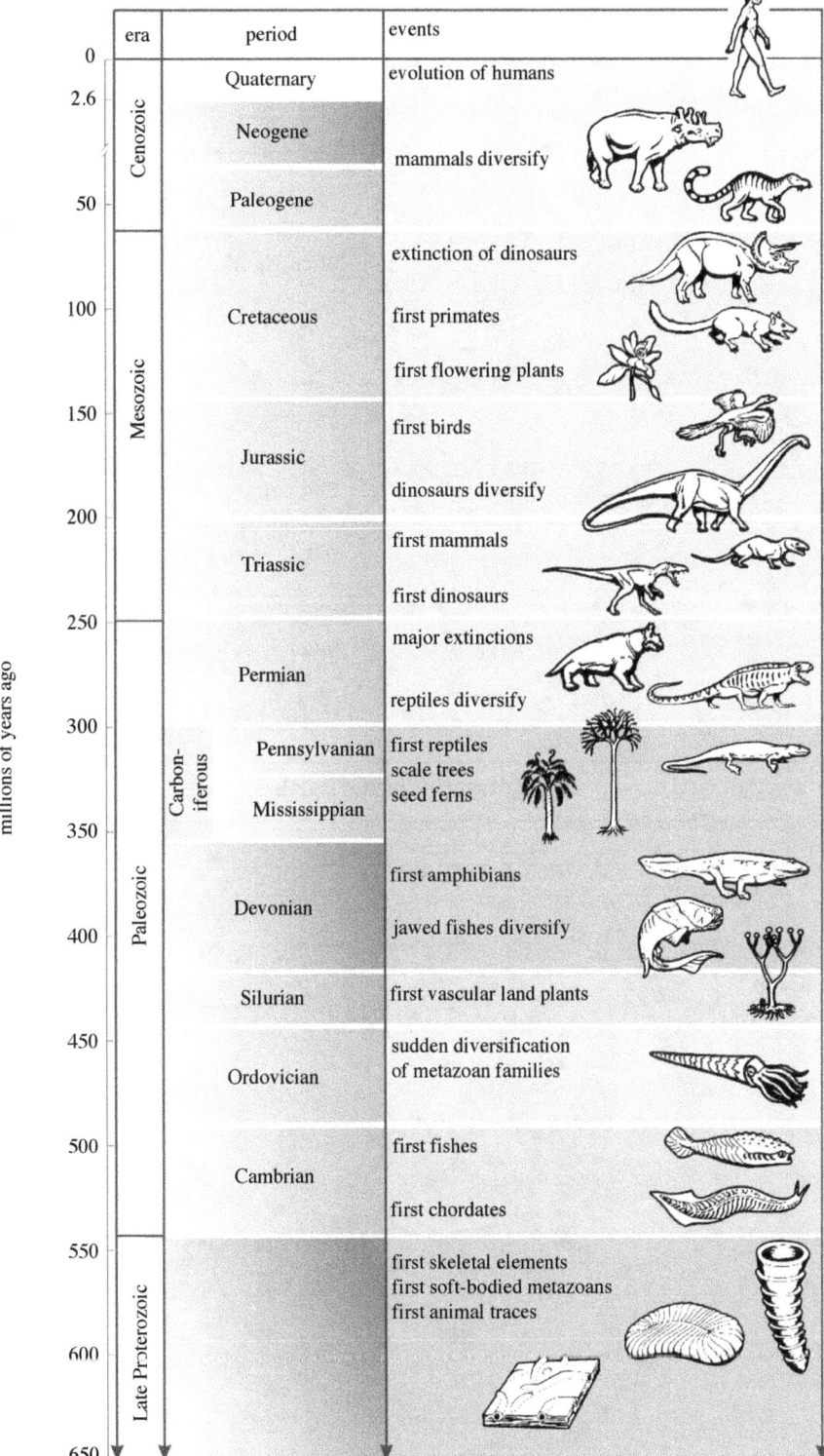

era	period	events

millions of years ago

0		Quaternary	evolution of humans
2.6		Neogene	mammals diversify
50	Cenozoic	Paleogene	
		Cretaceous	extinction of dinosaurs
100			first primates
			first flowering plants
150	Mesozoic	Jurassic	first birds
			dinosaurs diversify
200		Triassic	first mammals
			first dinosaurs
250		Permian	major extinctions
			reptiles diversify
300		Pennsylvanian	first reptiles / scale trees / seed ferns
	Carbon-iferous	Mississippian	
350		Devonian	first amphibians
400	Paleozoic		jawed fishes diversify
		Silurian	first vascular land plants
450		Ordovician	sudden diversification of metazoan families
500		Cambrian	first fishes
			first chordates
550			first skeletal elements / first soft-bodied metazoans / first animal traces
600	Late Proterozoic		
650			

Fig. 5 : Geochronological Time Scale

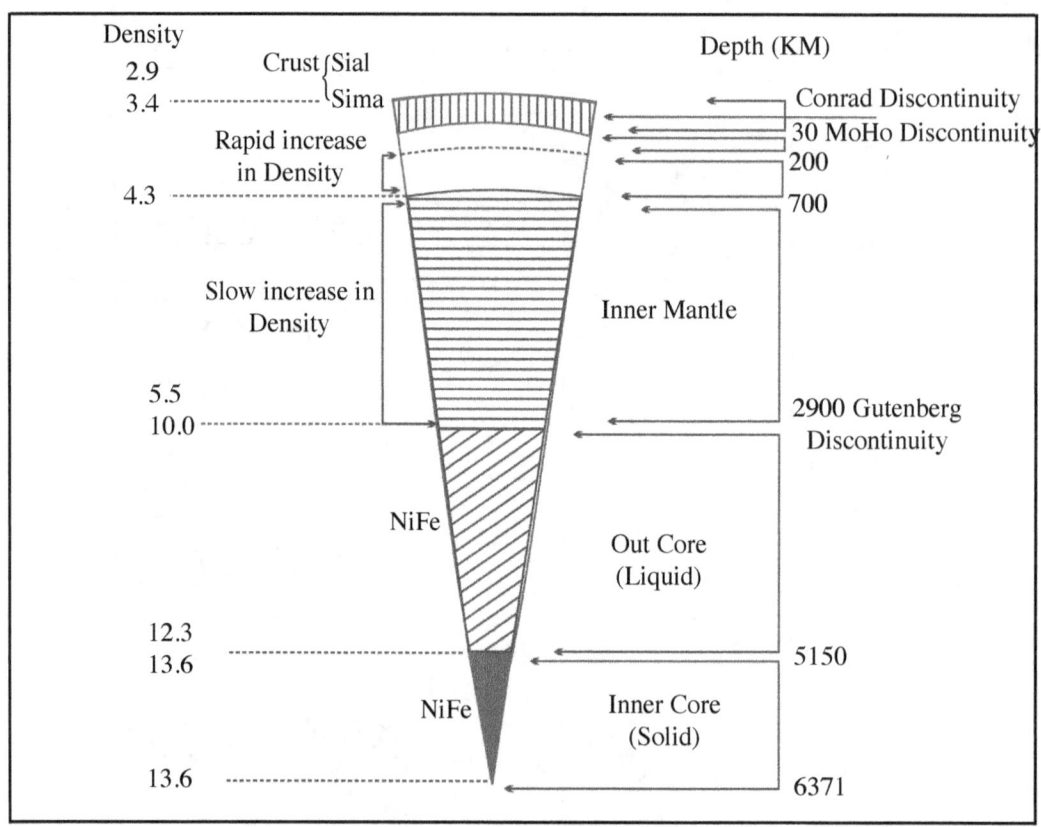

Fig. 6 : Interior of the Earth

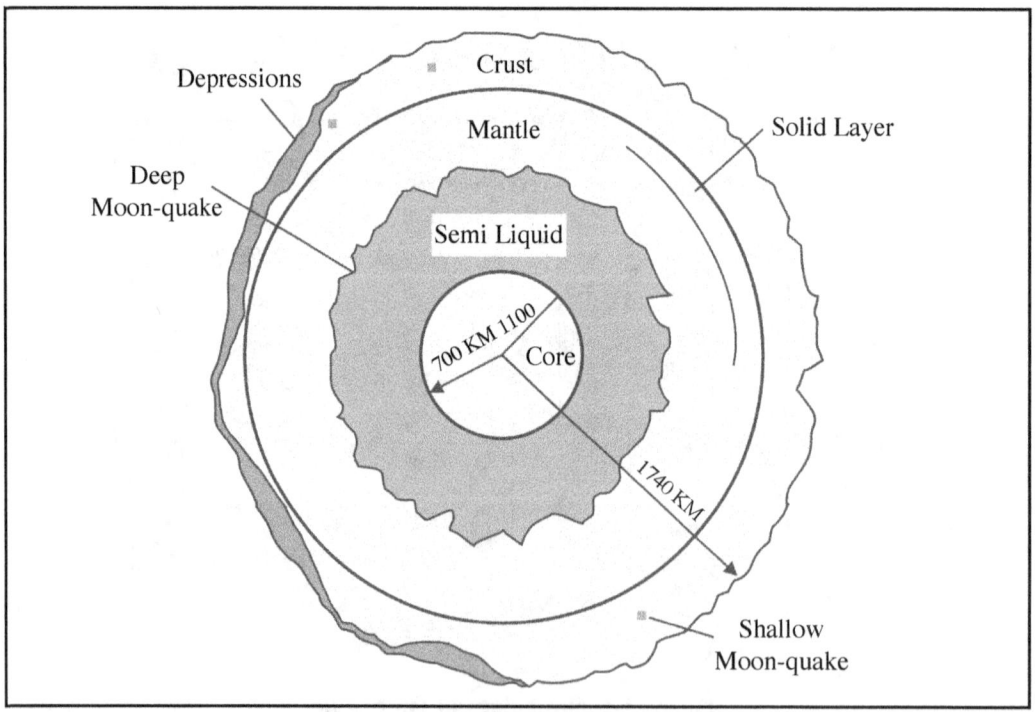

Fig. 7 : Interior of the Moon

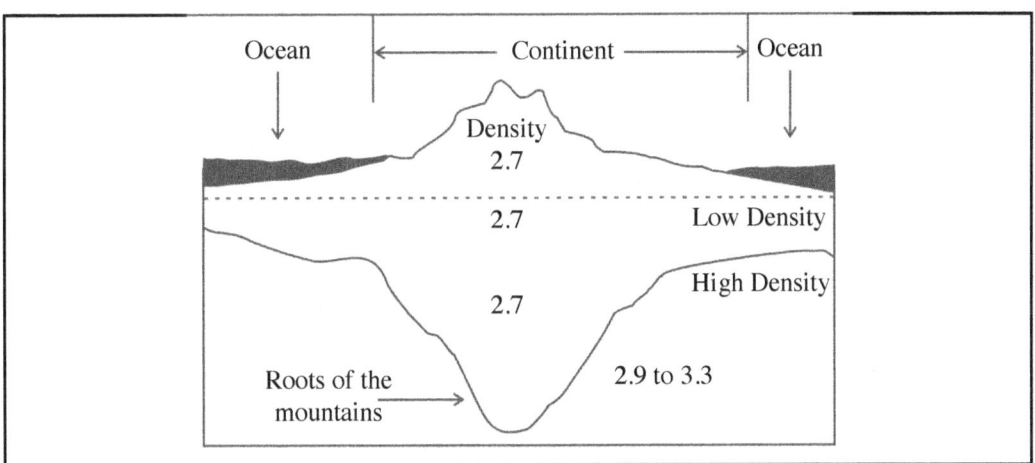

Fig. 8 : Airy's Concept of Isostasy

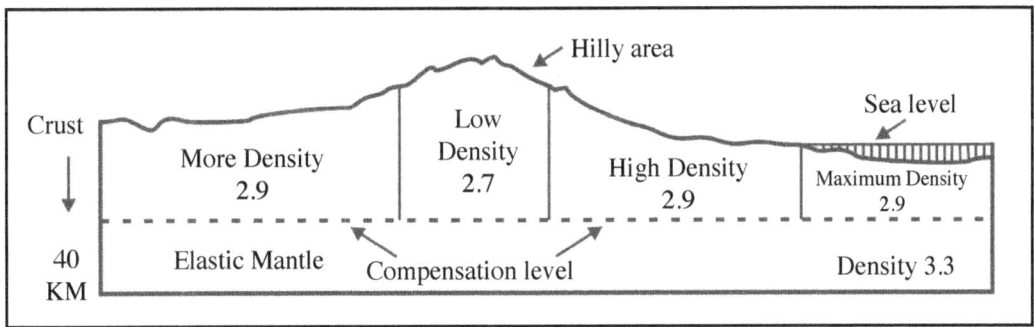

Fig. 9 : Pratt's Concept of Isostasy

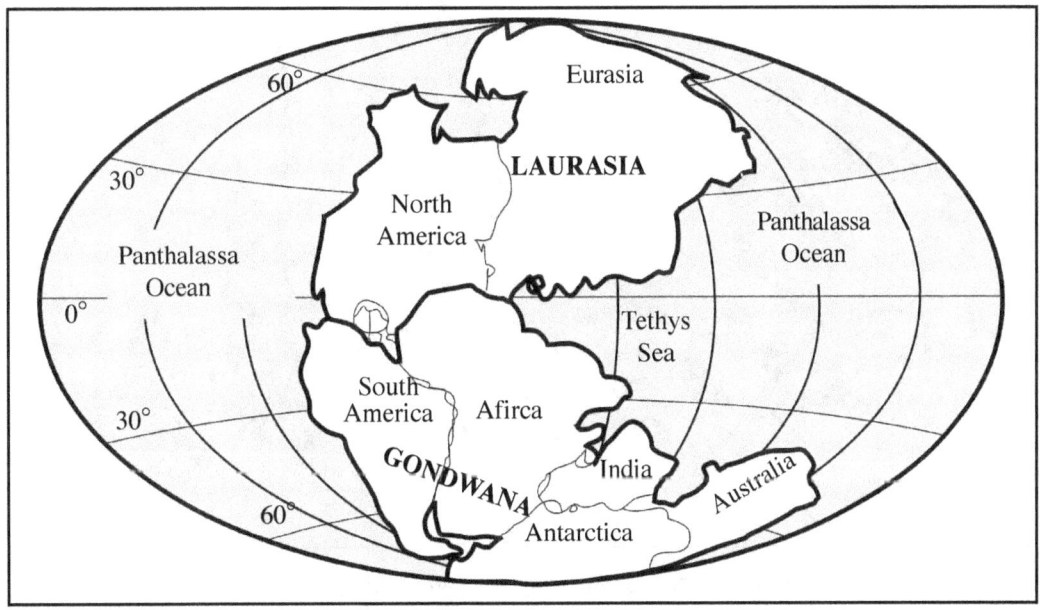

Fig. 10 : Panthalassa and Pangea

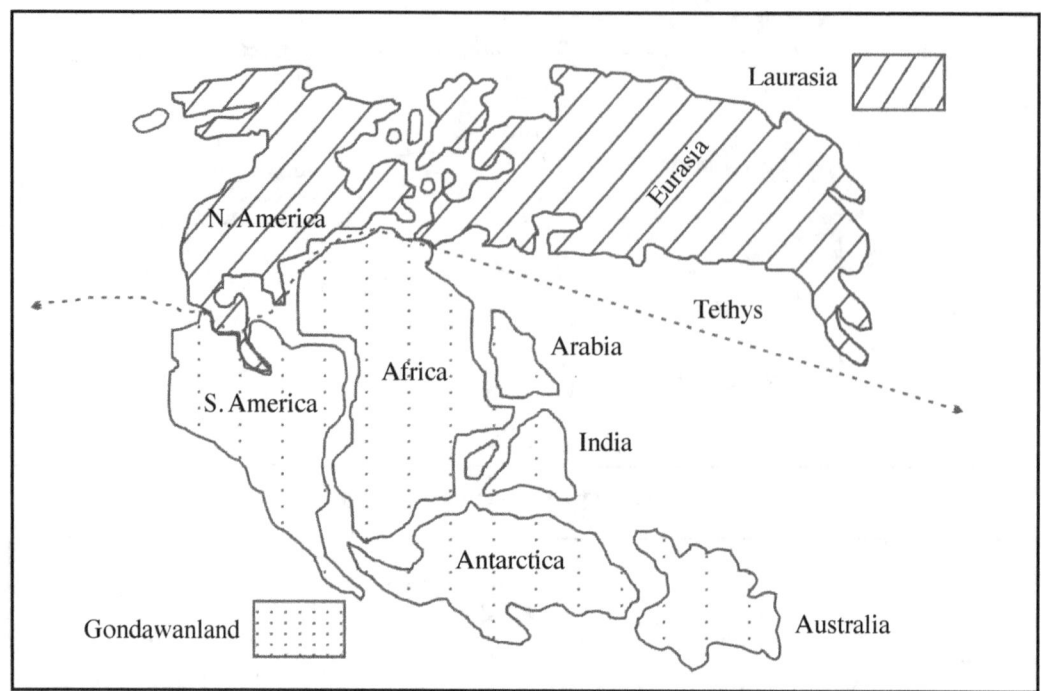

Fig. 11 : Tethys, Laurasia and Gondwanland

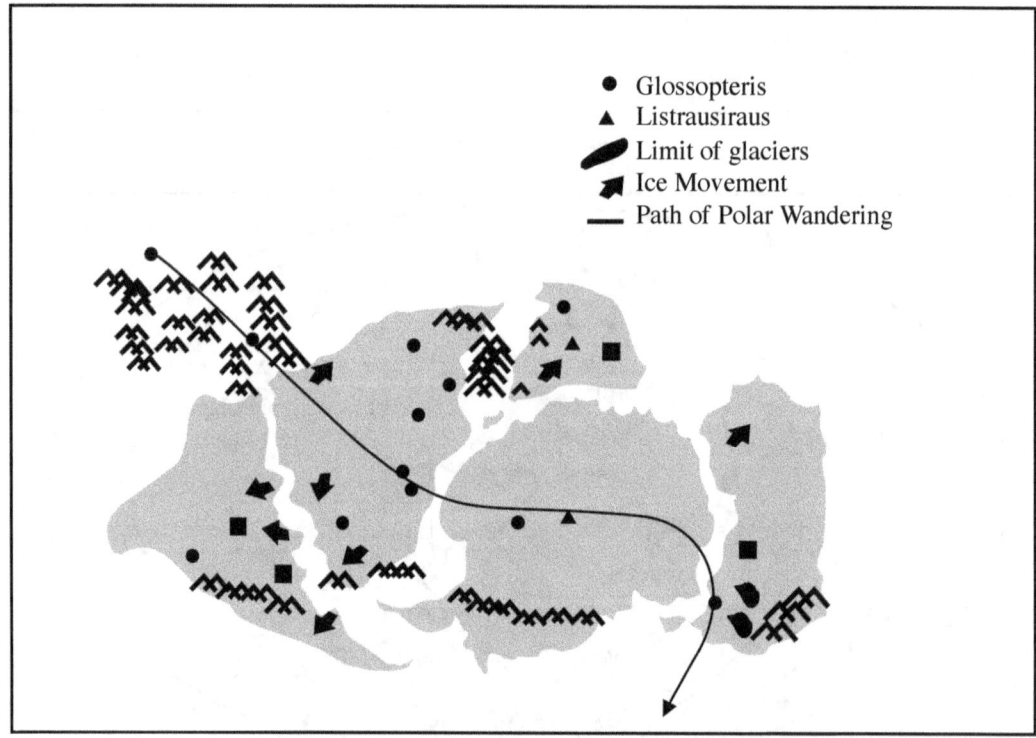

Fig. 12 : Continental drift and Polar Wandering

Fig. 13 : Static and Shifting deserts

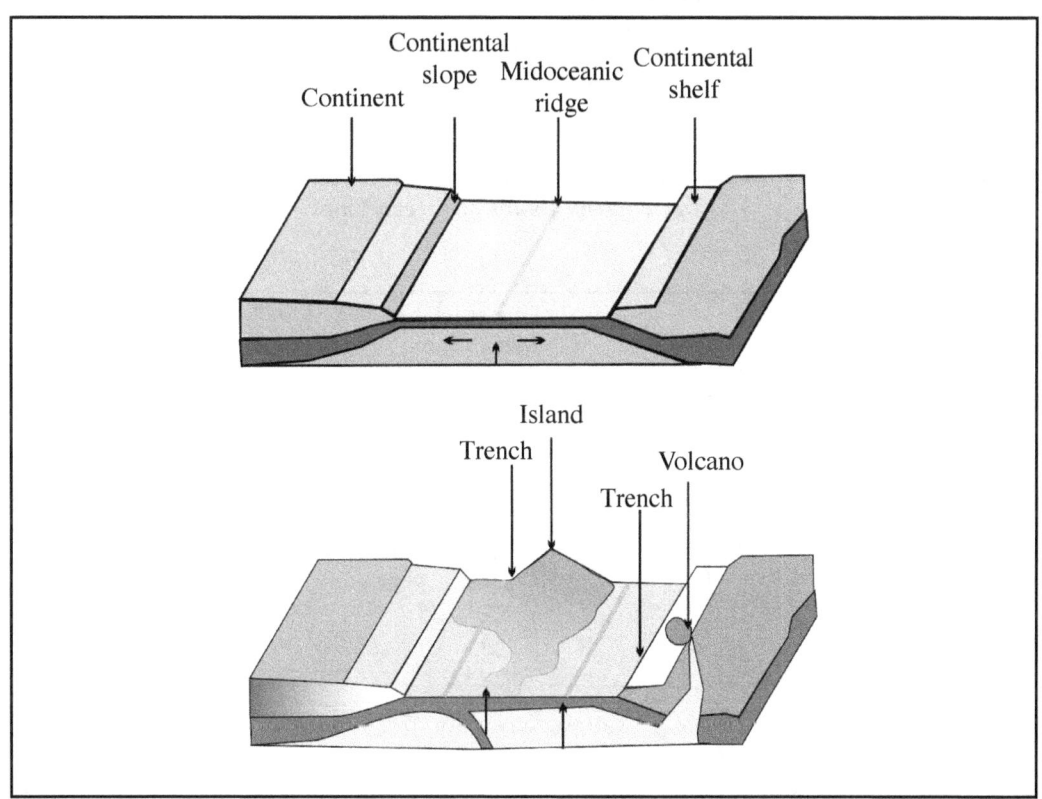

Fig. 14 (A) : Sea Floor Spreading   (B) : Origin of Islands

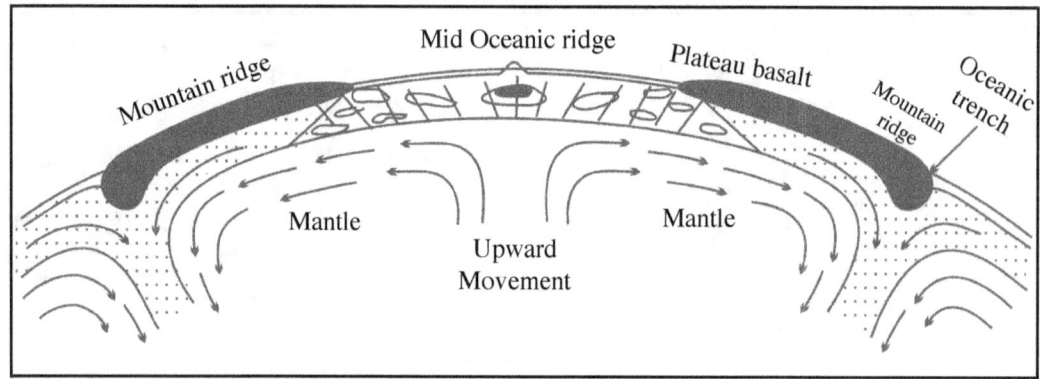

Fig. 15 : Sea Floor Spreading

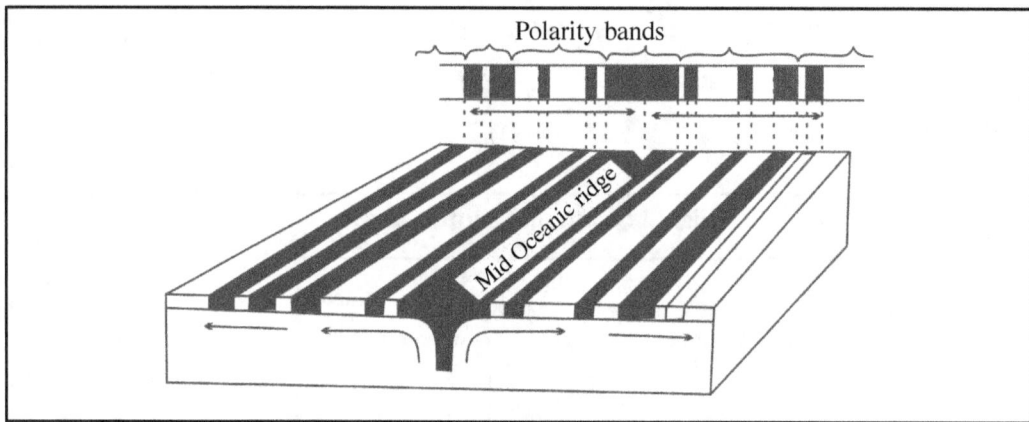

Fig. 16 : Polarity Bands on Ocean Floor

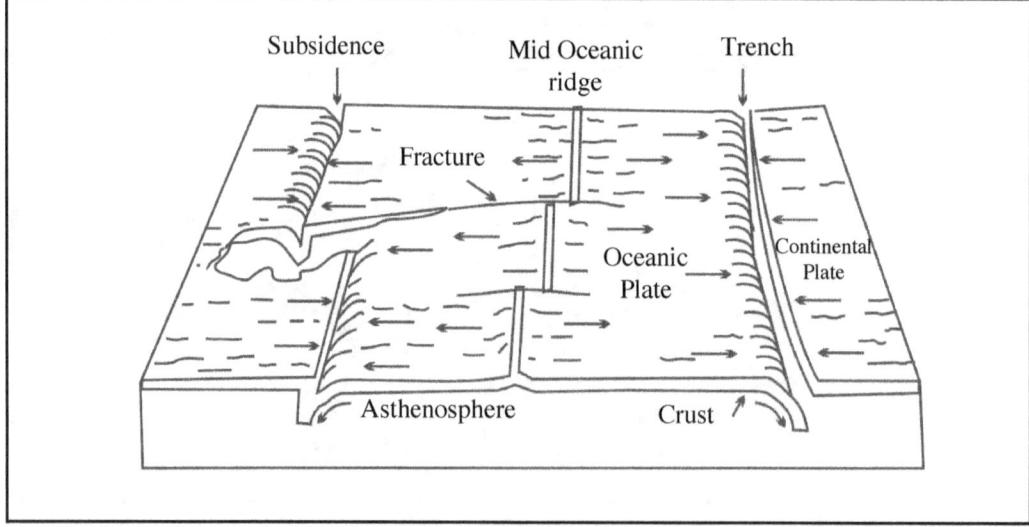

Fig. 17 : Structure of a tectonic plate

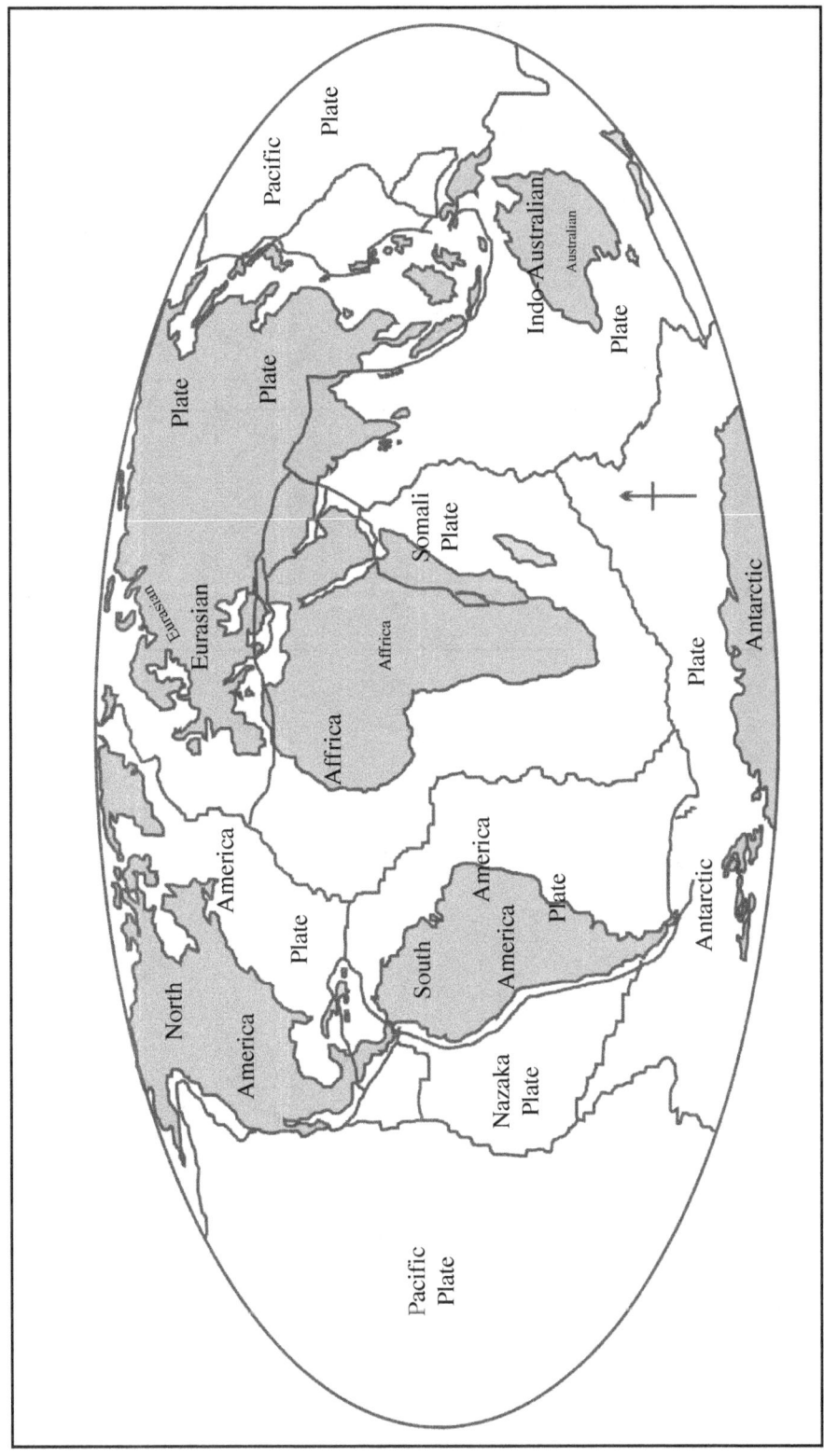

Fig. 18 : Major Plates on Earth

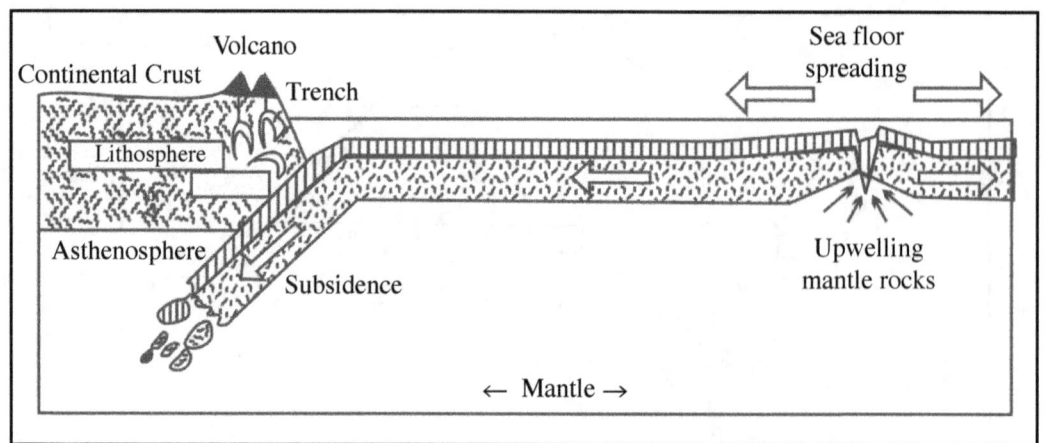

Fig. 19 : Plate boundaries

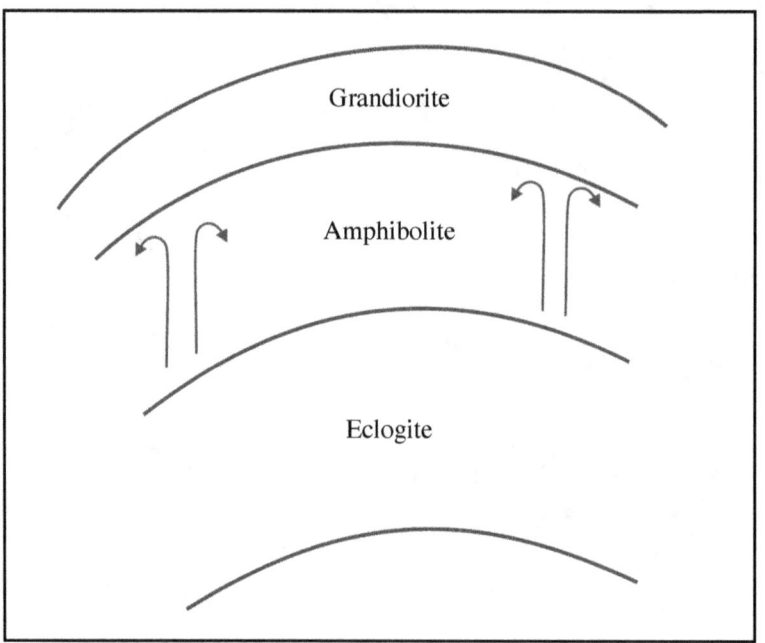

Fig. 20 : Convectional Currents in Mantle

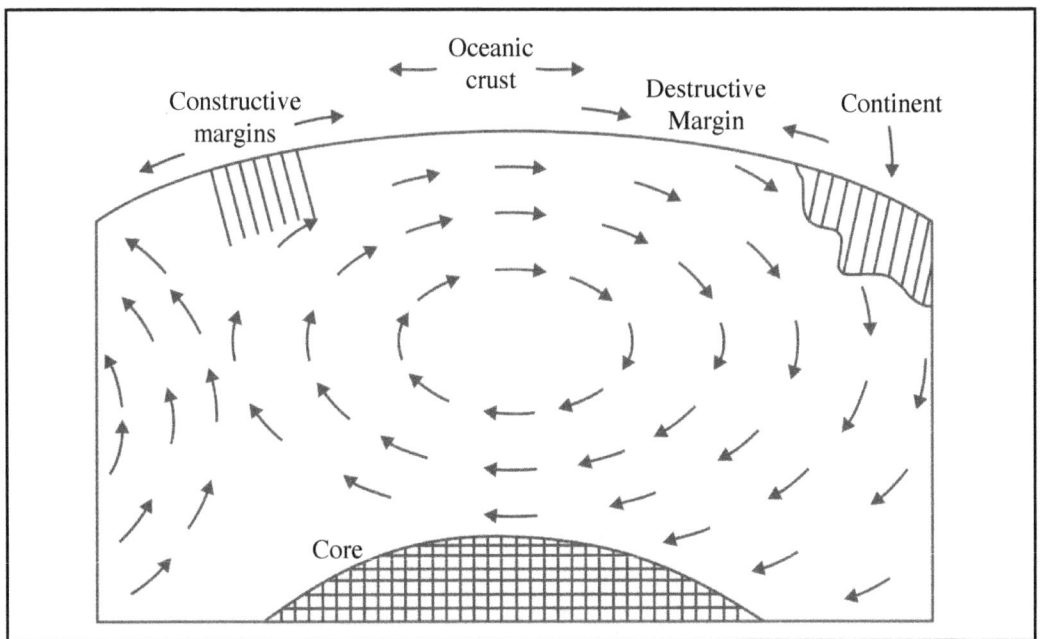

Fig. 21 : Holme's Convection Currents Theroy

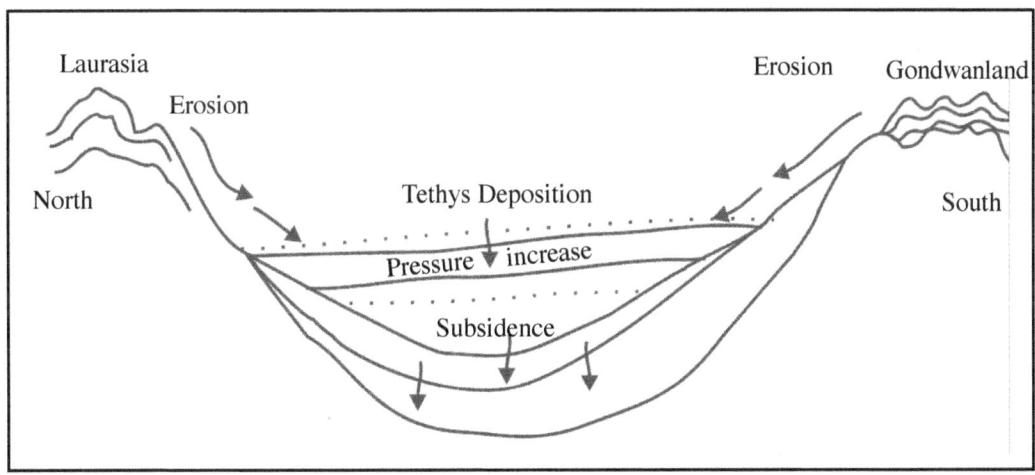

Fig. 22 : Deposition in Tethys

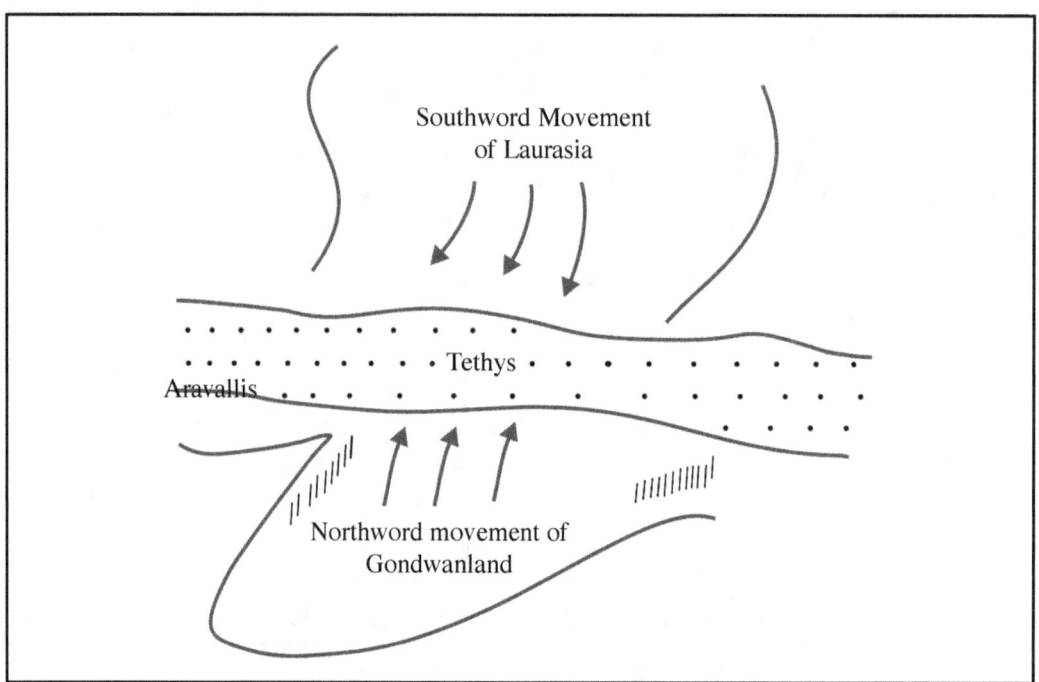

Fig. 23 : Unstable Laurasia and Gondwanland

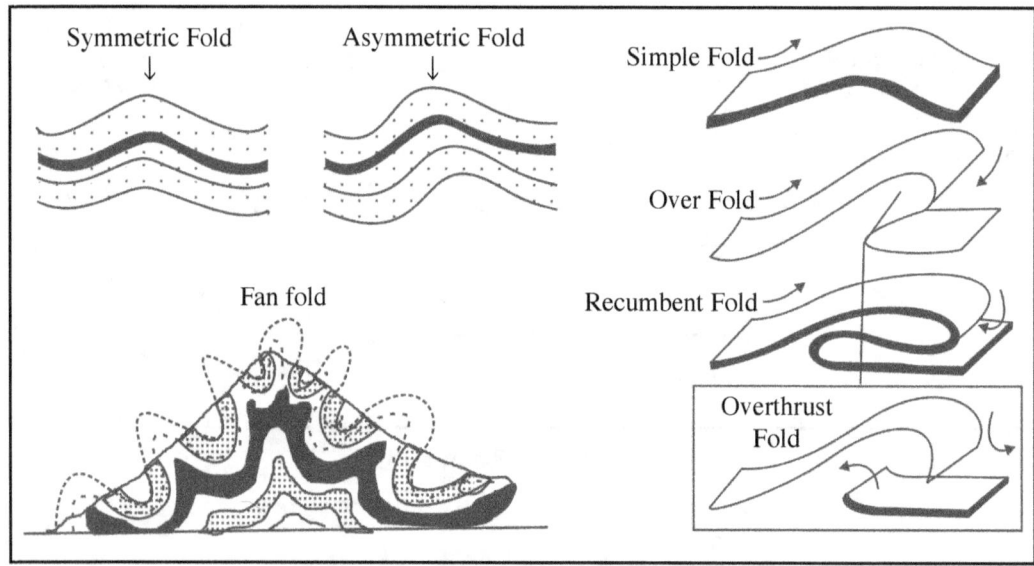

Fig. 24 : Types of Folds

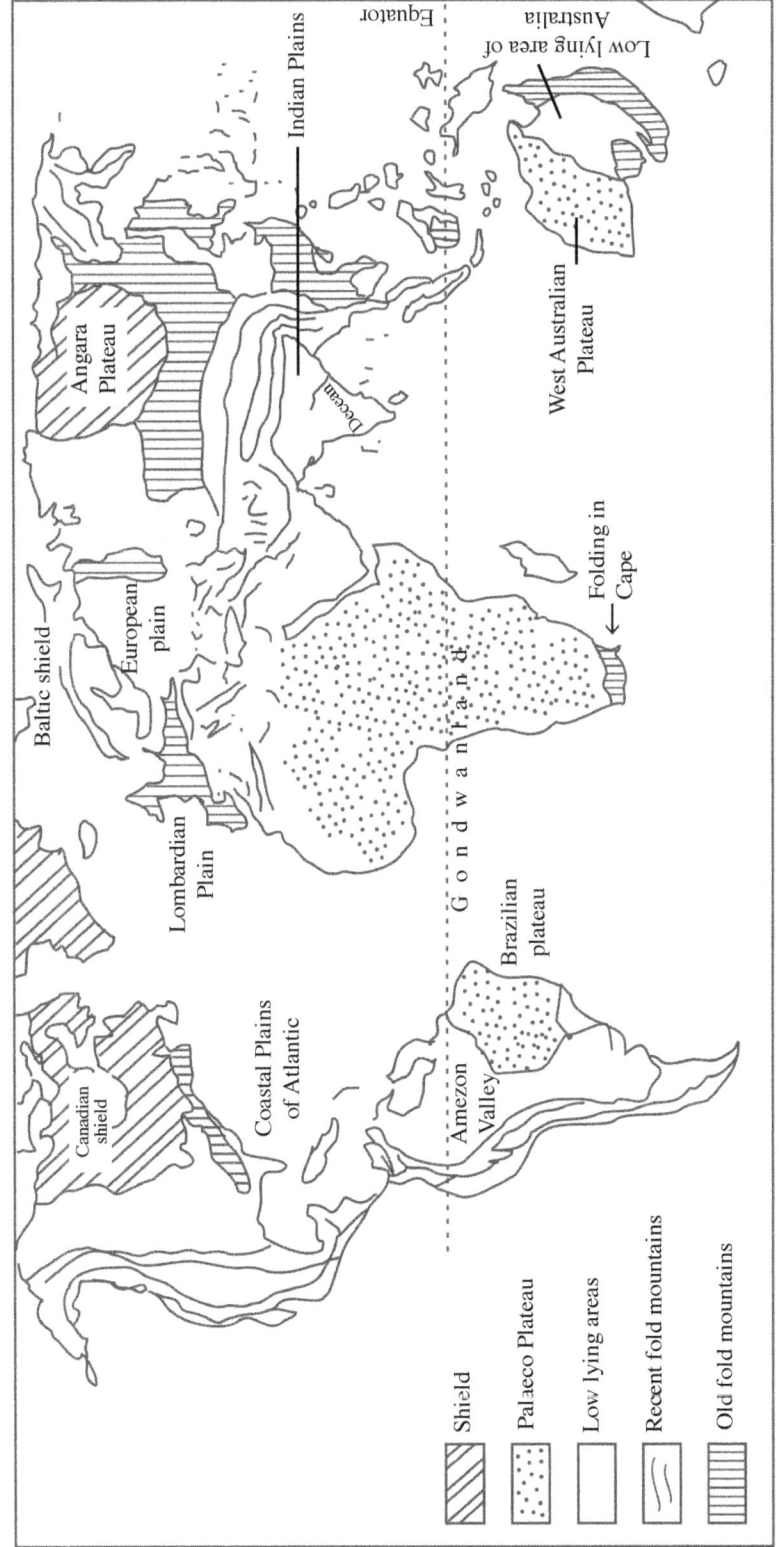

Fig. 25 : Structural Divisions of the Earth

Legend:

Shield

Palaeco Plateau

Low lying areas

Recent fold mountains

Old fold mountains

Map labels:

Canadian shield

Coastal Plains of Atlantic

Amezon Valley

Brazilian plateau

Baltic shield

European plain

Lombardian Plain

Angara Plateau

Deccan

Indian Plains

Equator

Gondwanaland

Folding in Cape

West Australian Plateau

Low lying area of Ausralia

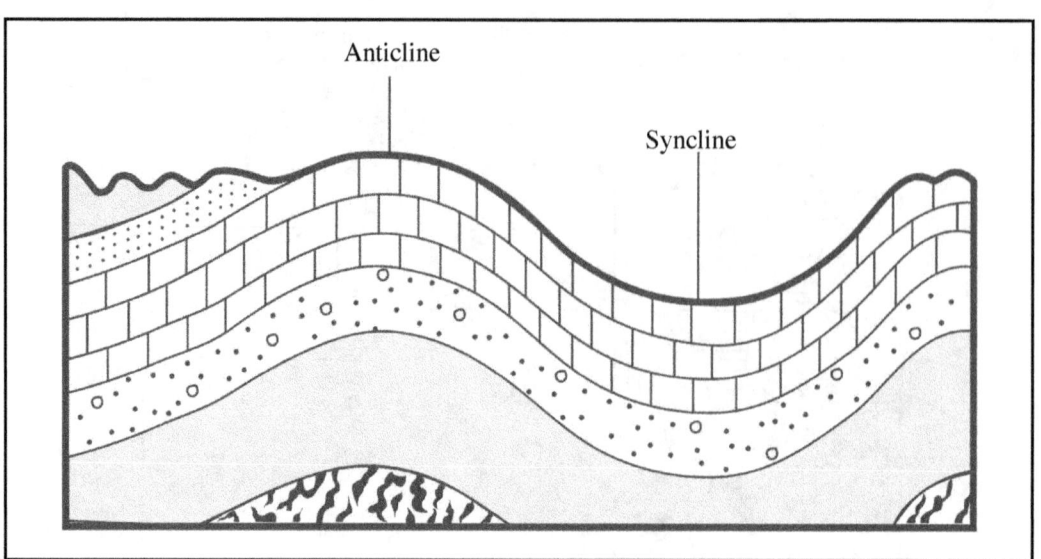

Fig. 26 : Anticline and Syncline

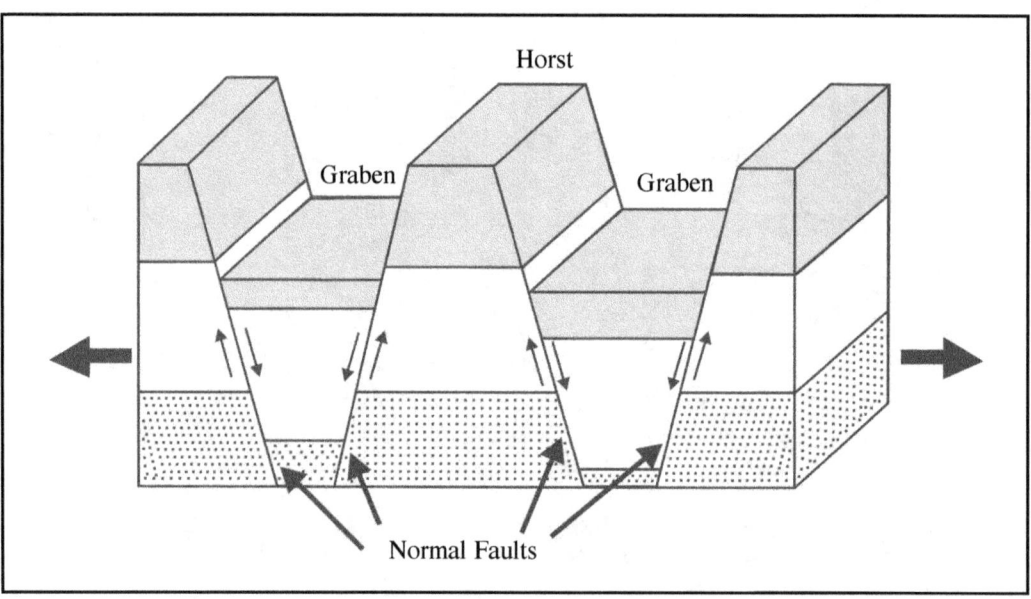

Fig. 27 : Horst and Graben

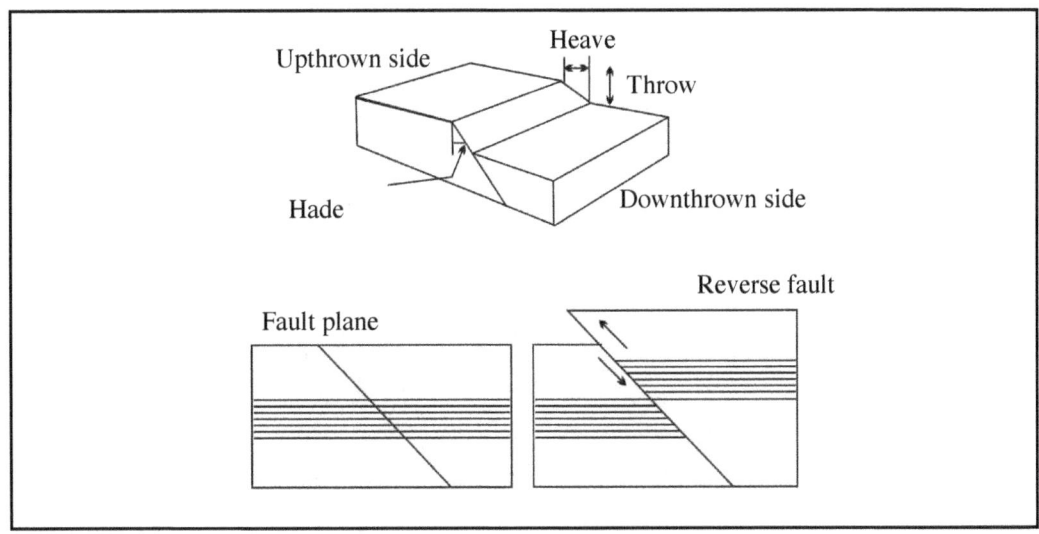

Fig. 28 : Simple and Reverse Fault

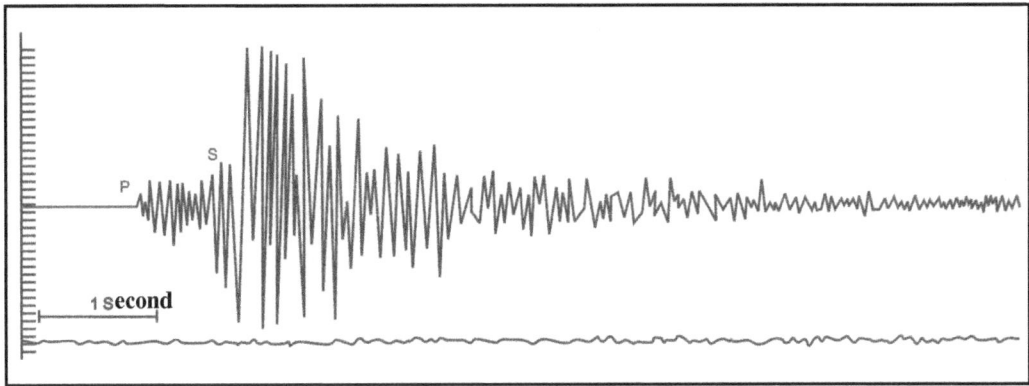

Fig. 29 : Earthaquake Waves

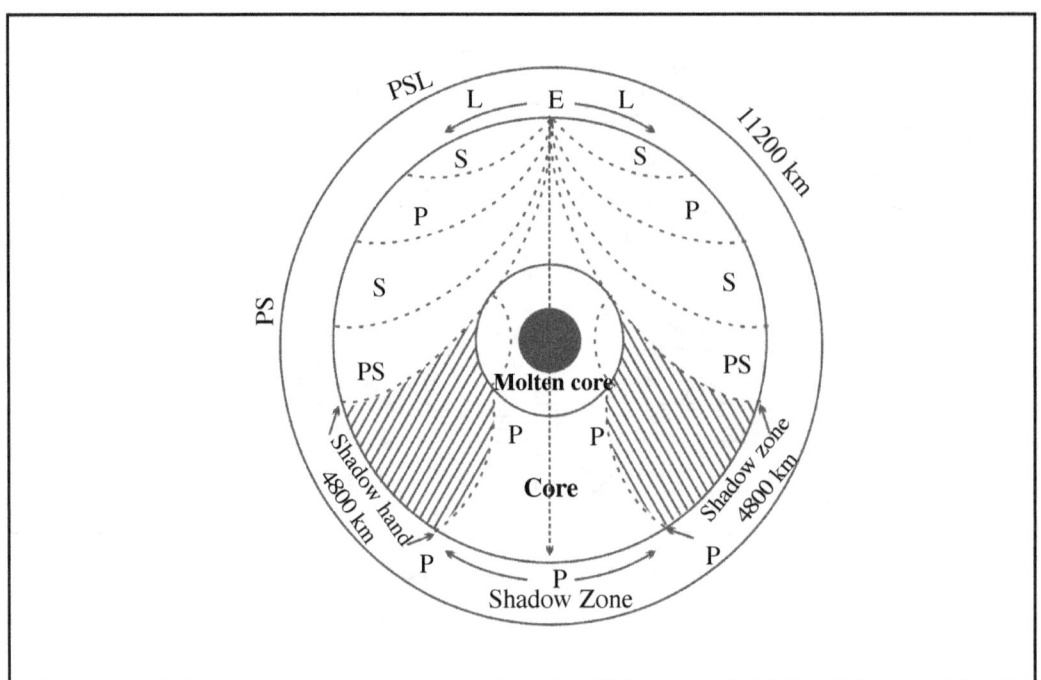

Fig. 30 : Earthquake Waves

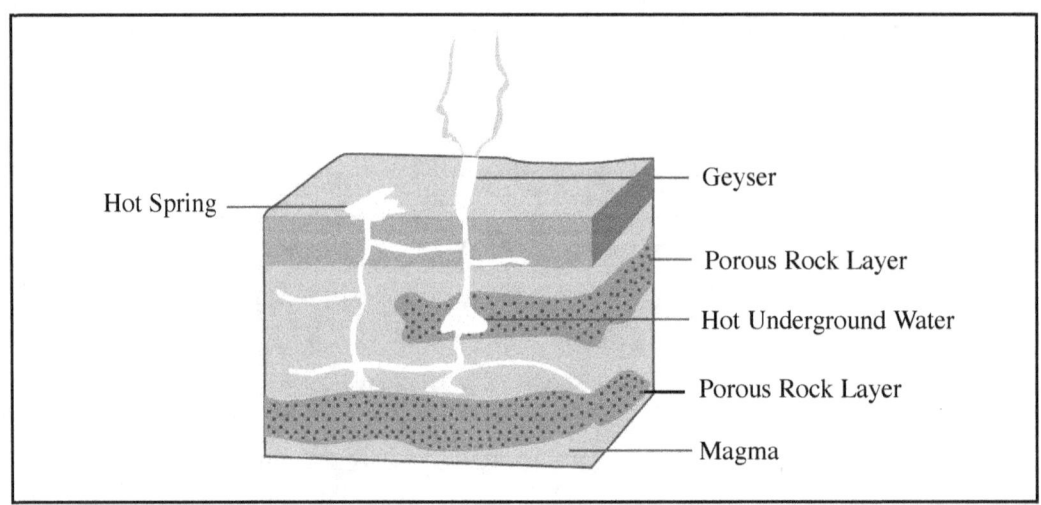

Fig. 31 : Geysers and Hot Springs

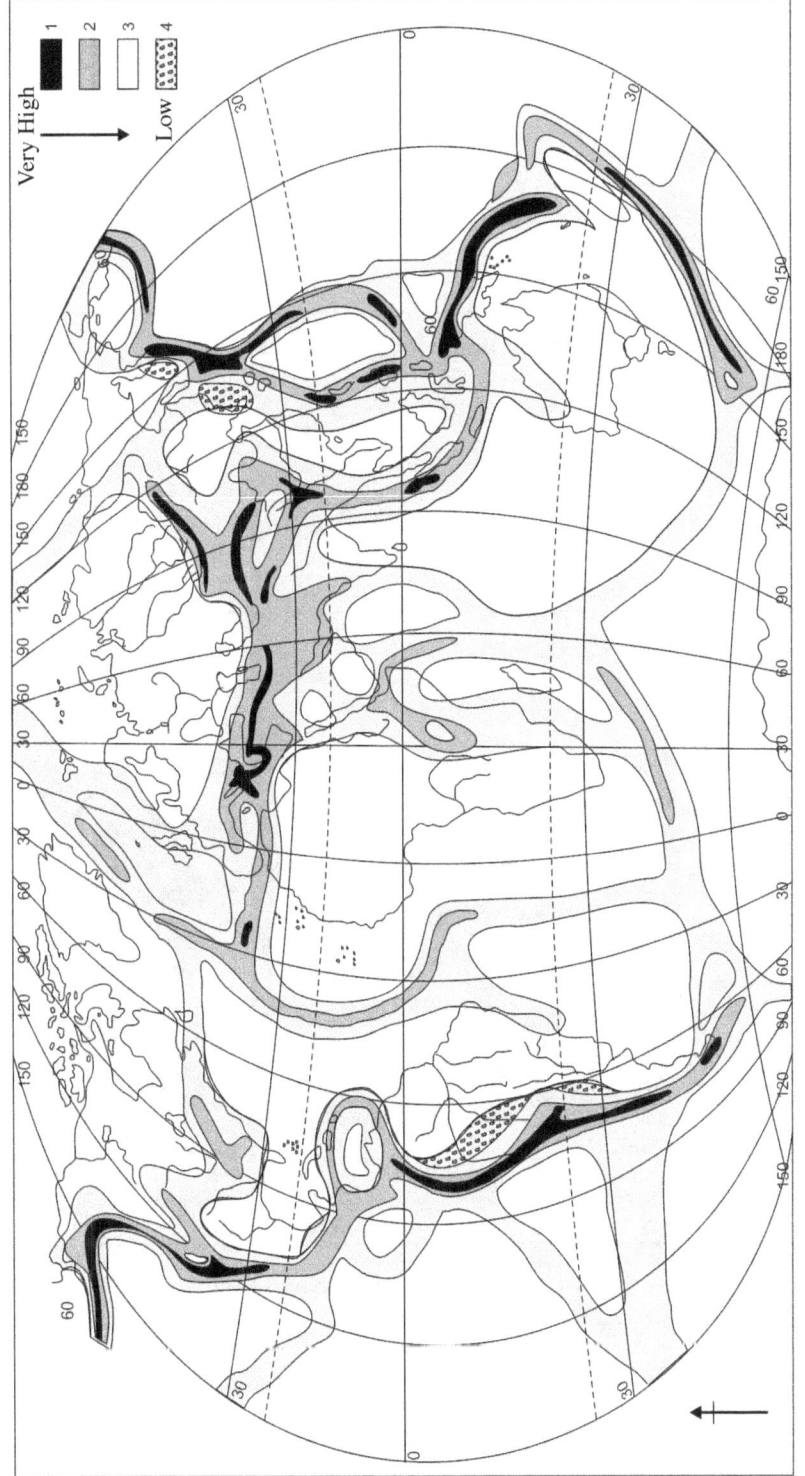

Fig. 32 : Global to Distribution of Earthquakes according intensity

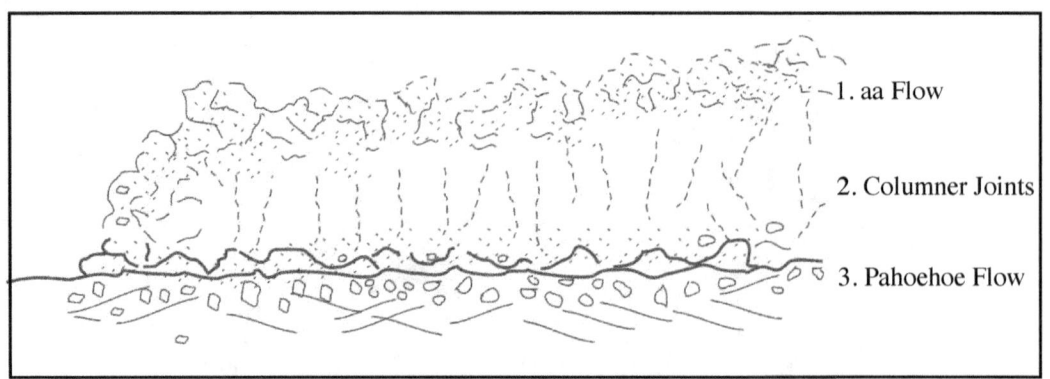

Fig. 33 : aa and Pahoehoe Lava Flows

1. aa Flow
2. Columner Joints
3. Pahoehoe Flow

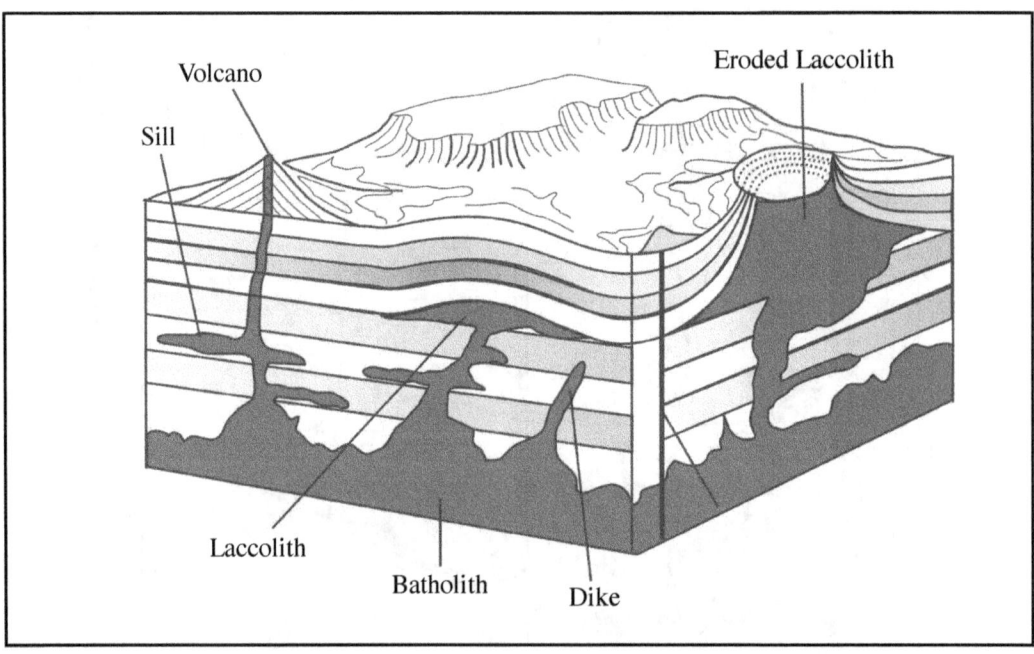

Volcano

Eroded Laccolith

Sill

Laccolith

Batholith

Dike

Fig. 34 : Batholith, Laccolith and Dike

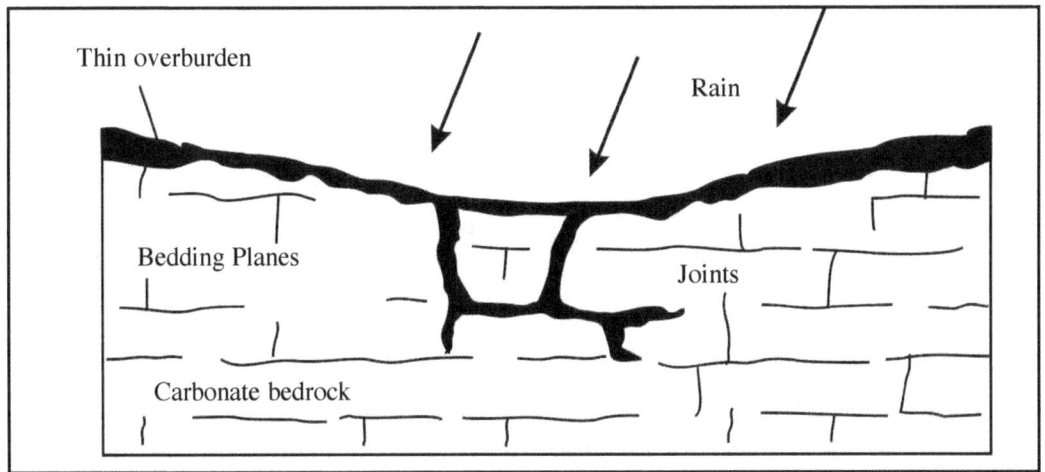

Fig. 35 : Bedding Plane

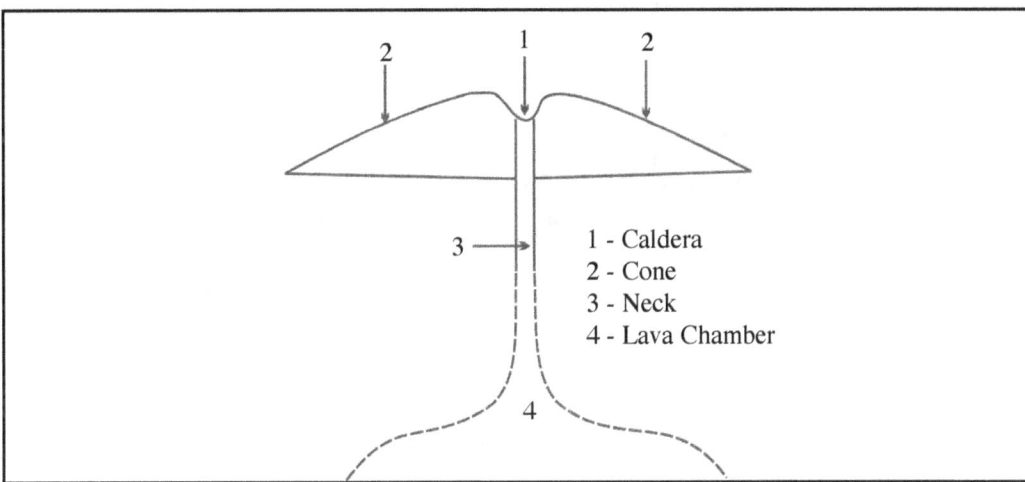

1 - Caldera
2 - Cone
3 - Neck
4 - Lava Chamber

Fig. 36 : Structure of a Volcano

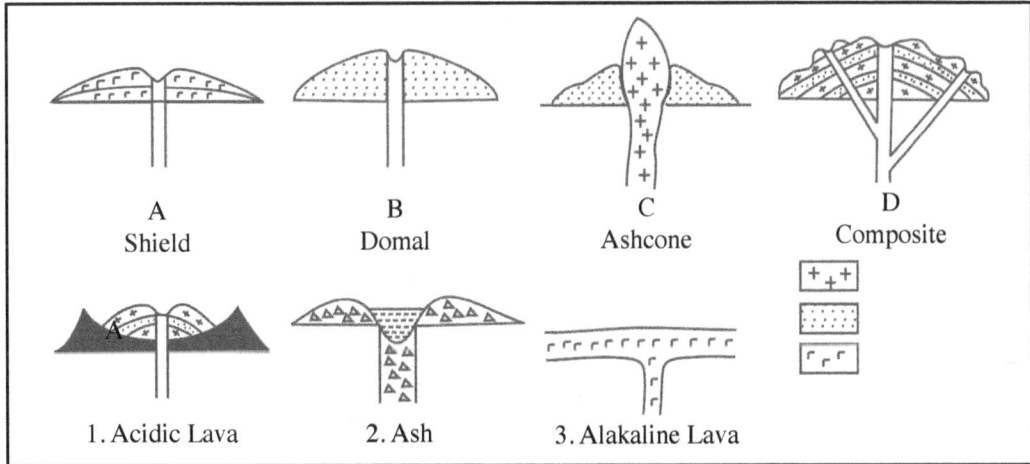

Fig. 37 : Types of Volcanoes and Lava

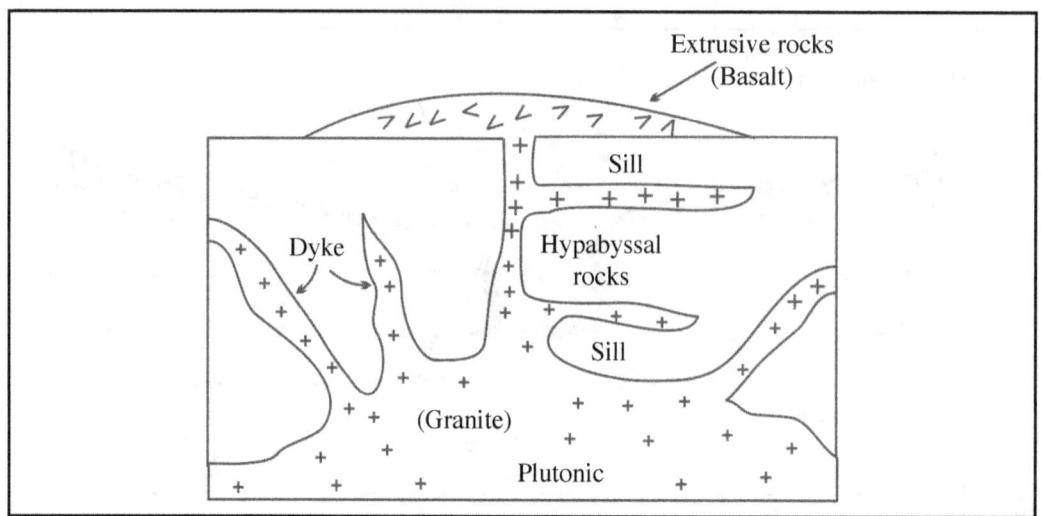

Fig. 38 : Types of Igneous rocks

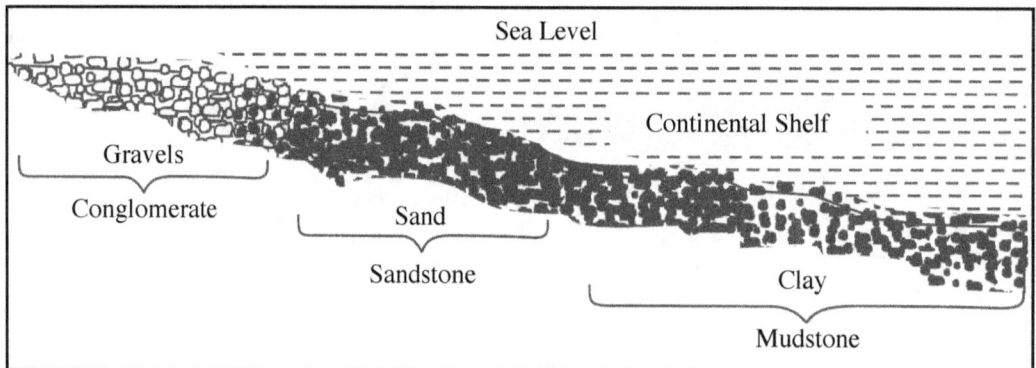

Fig. 39 : Types of Sedimentary Rocks

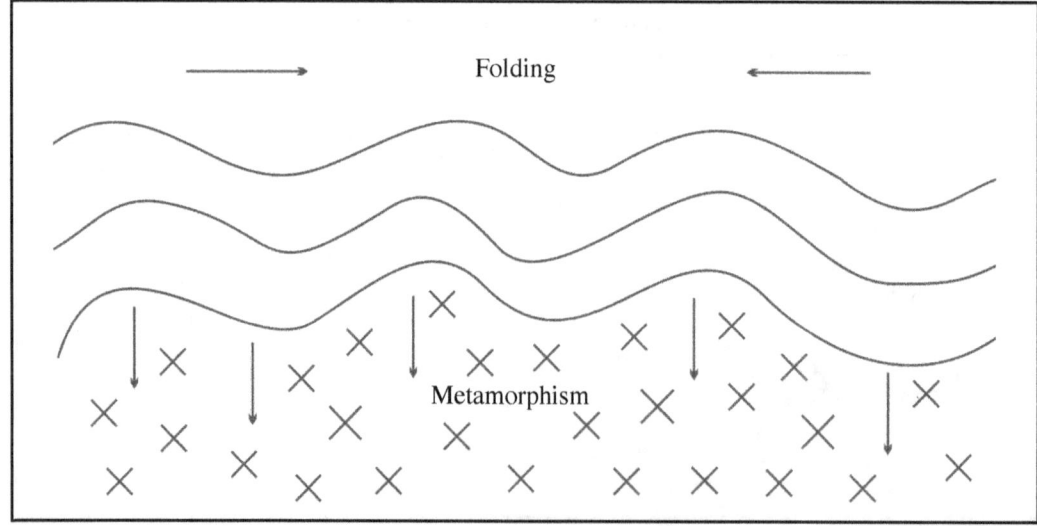

Fig. 40 : Process of Metamorphism

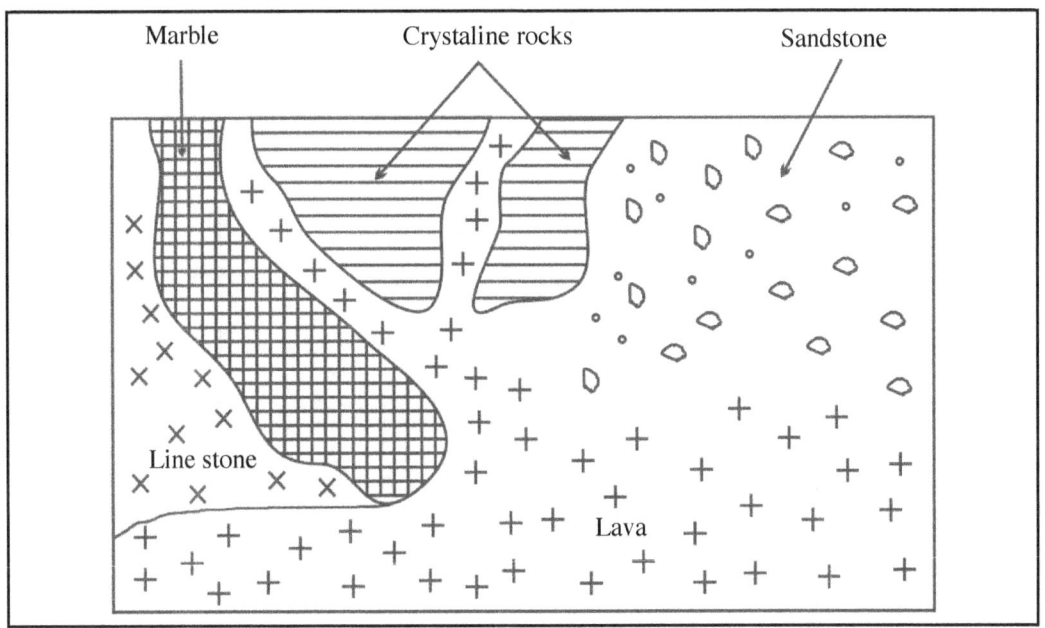

Fig. 41 : Formation of Marble

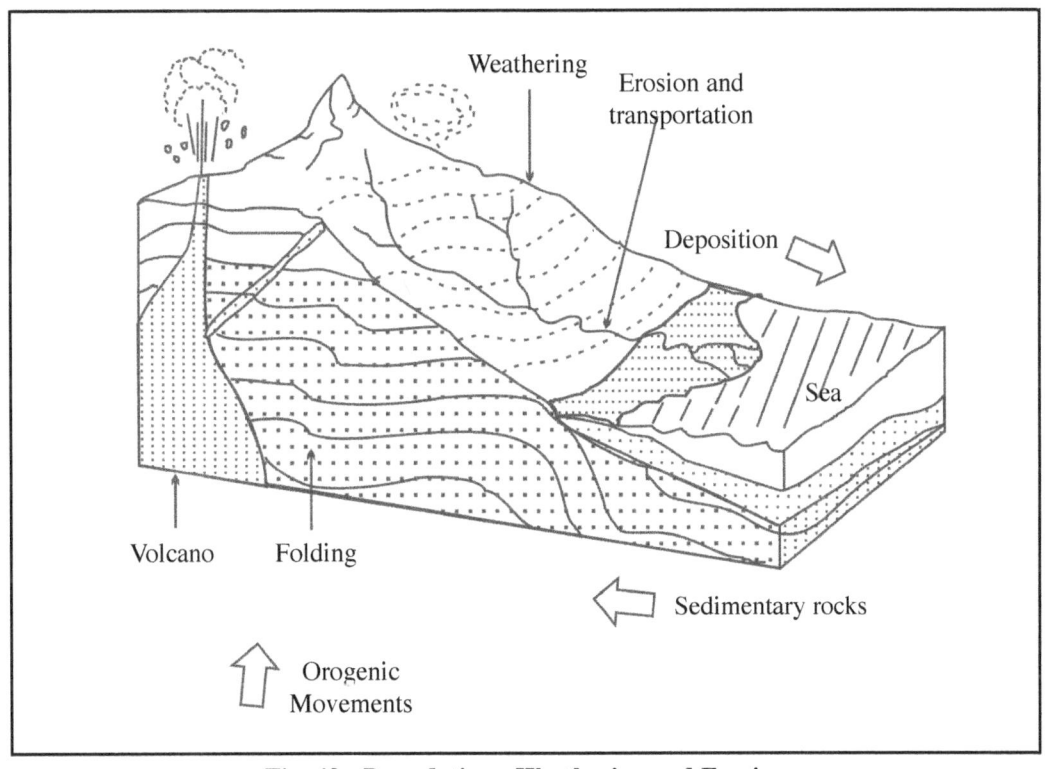

Fig. 42 : Denudation : Weathering and Erosion

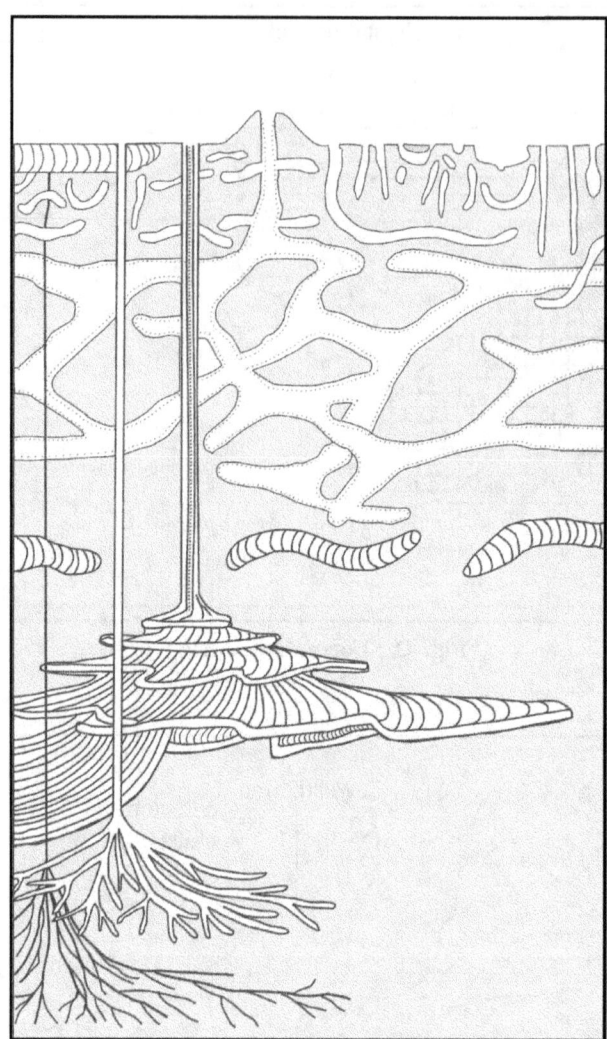

Fig. 43 : Bioturbation

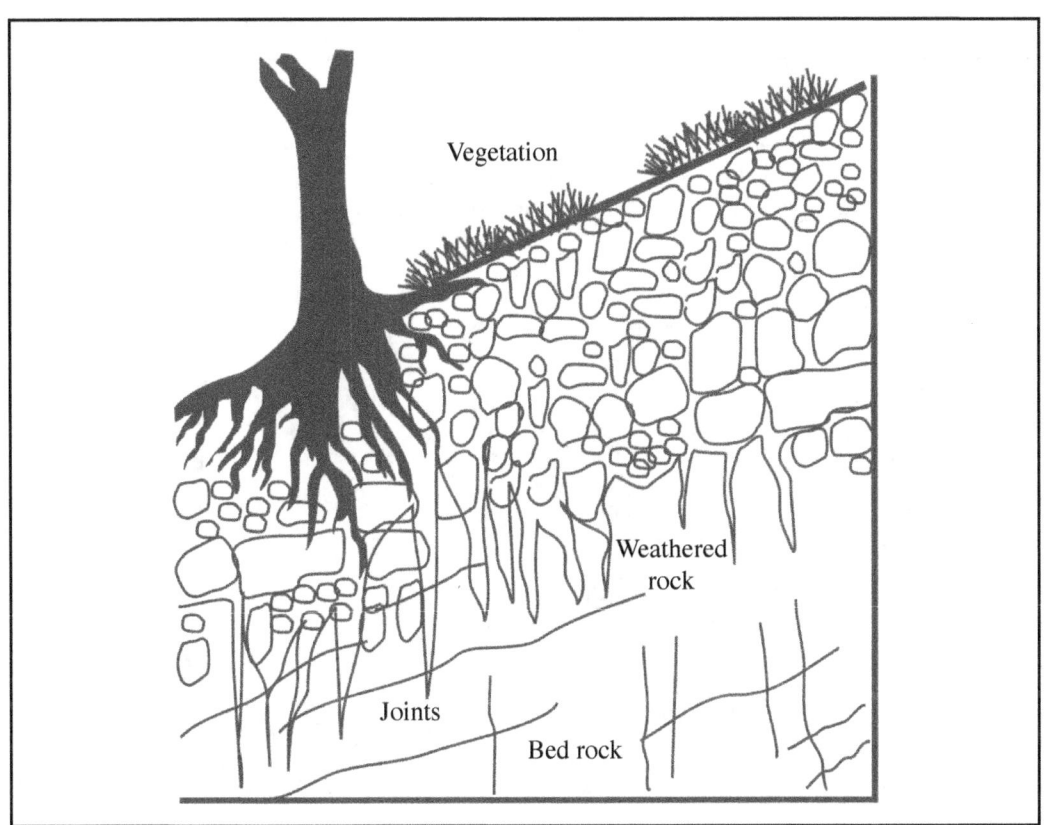

Fig. 44 : Weathered rock

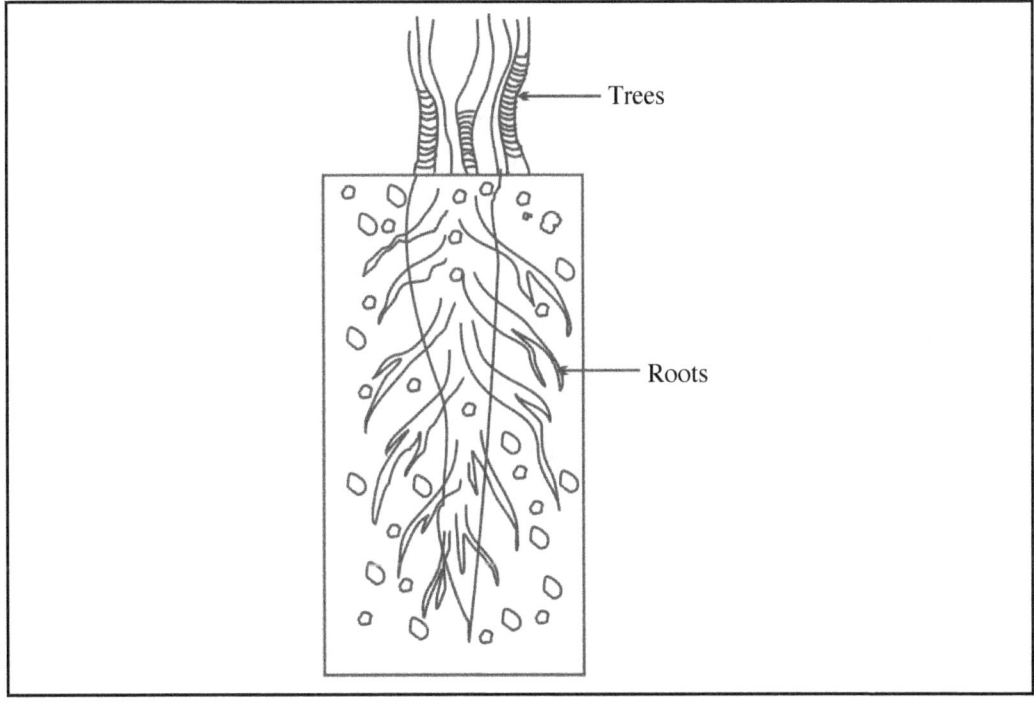

Fig. 45 : Biological Weathering

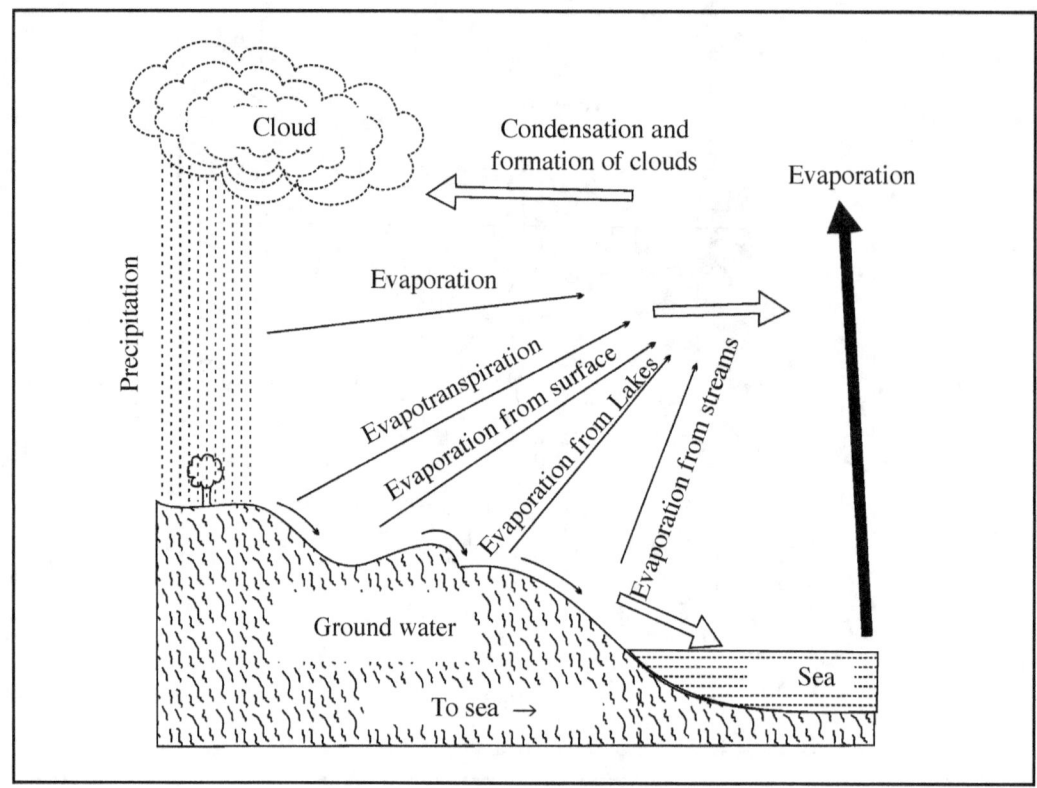

Fig. 46 : Global Hydrological Cycle

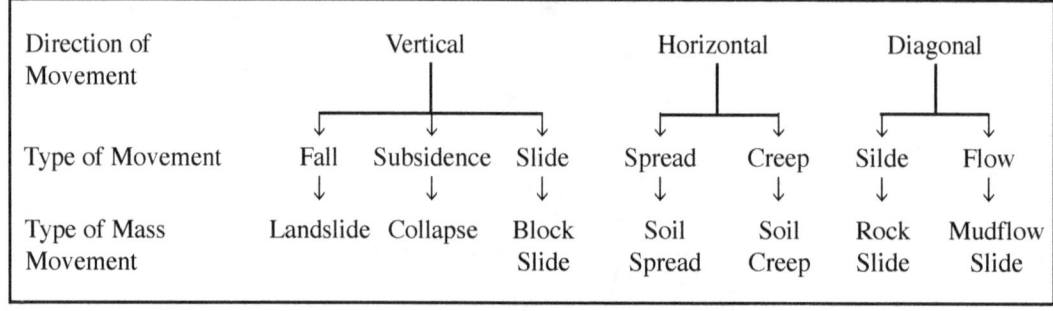

Fig. 47 : Classification of Mass Movements

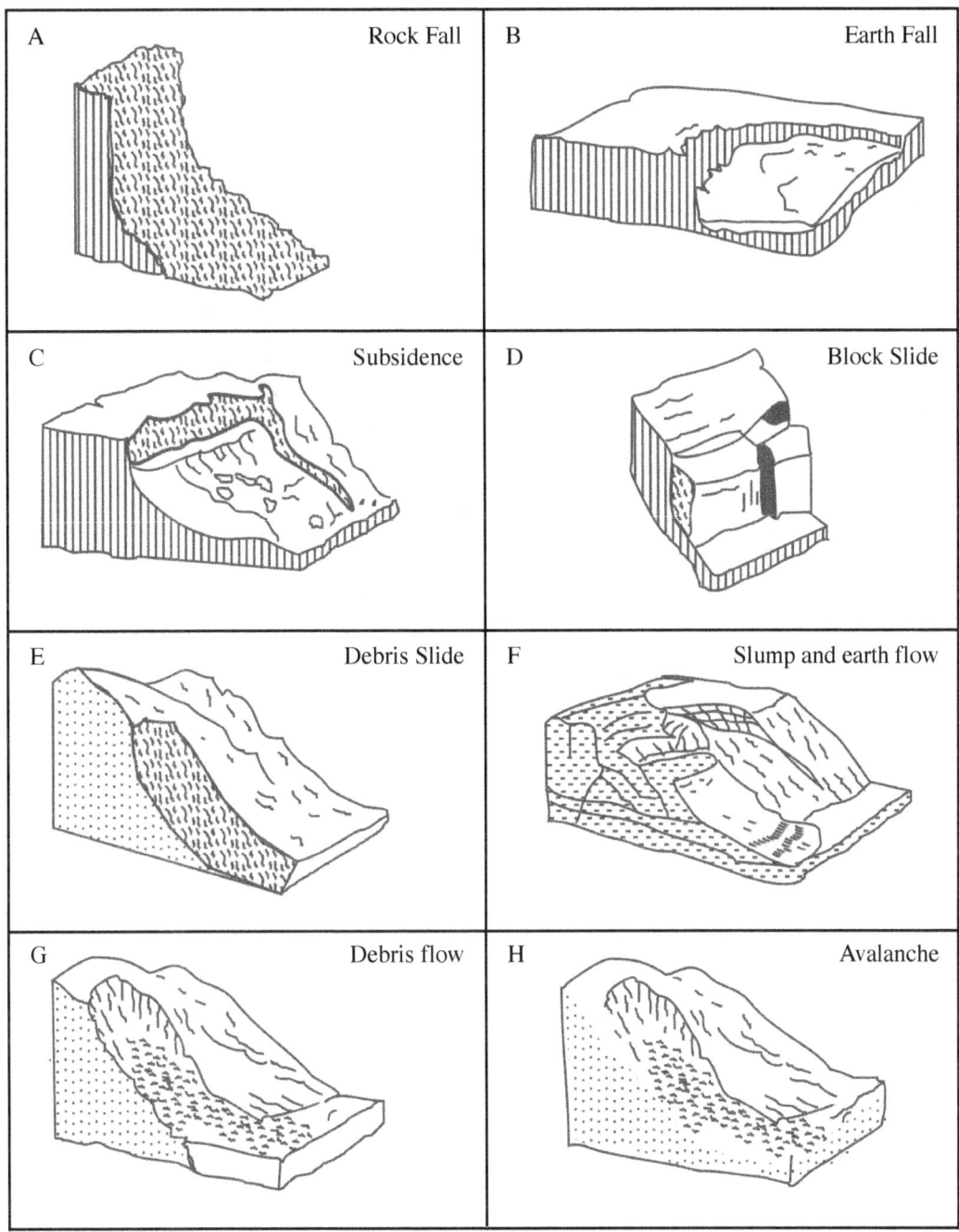

Fig. 48 : Types of Mass Movement

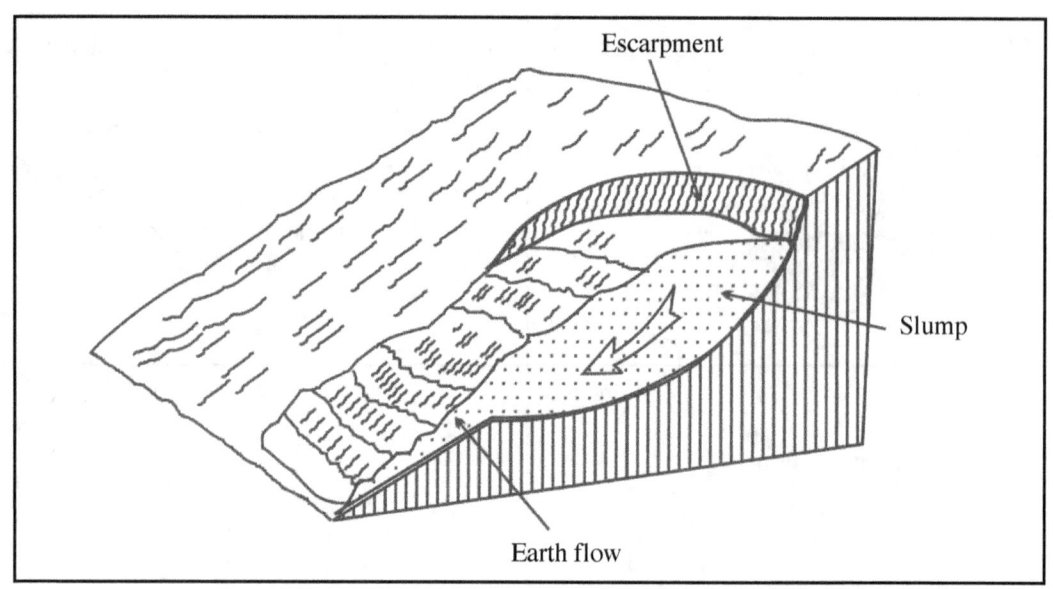

Fig. 49 : Sliding and Slumping

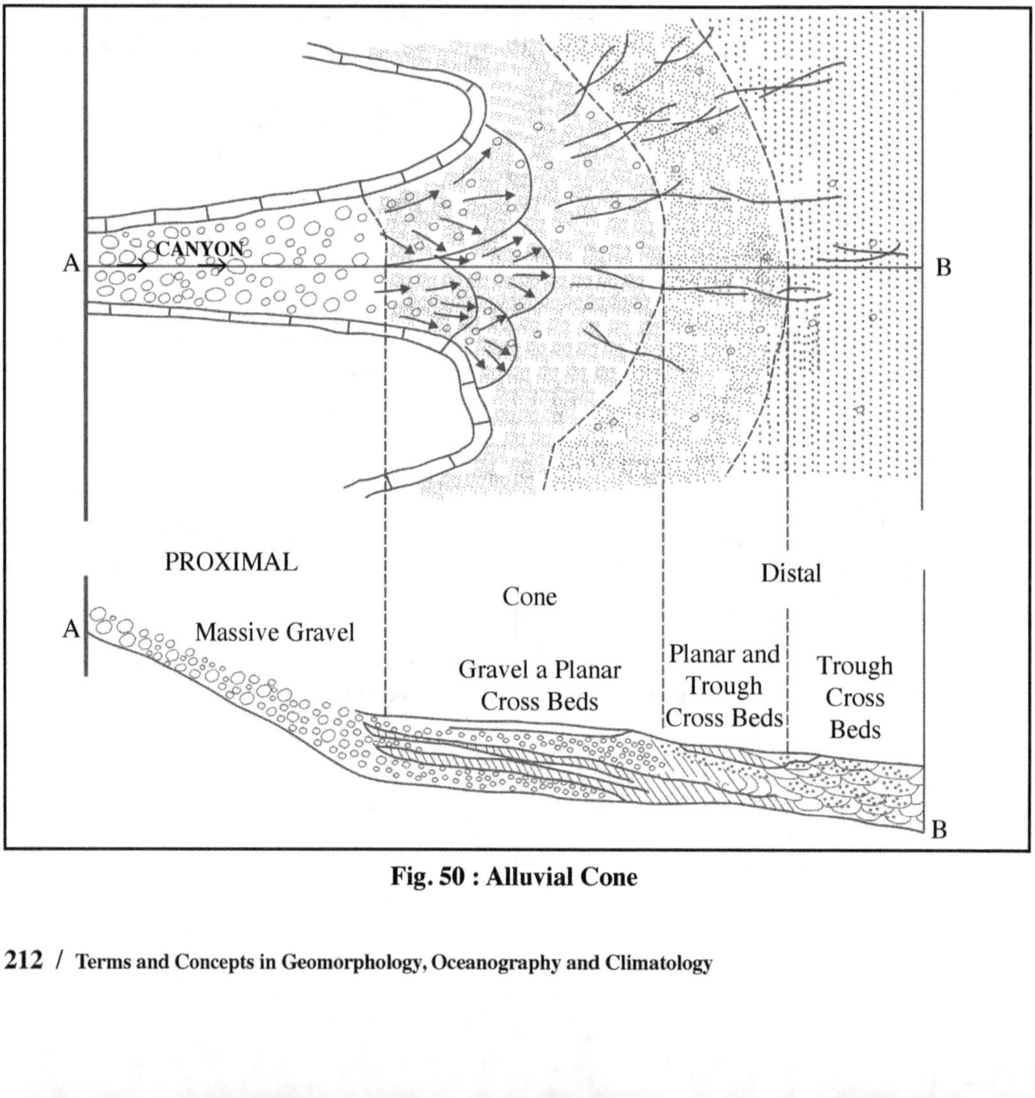

Escarpment

Slump

Earth flow

A → **CANYON** → B

PROXIMAL

Cone

Distal

A

Massive Gravel

Gravel a Planar
Cross Beds

Planar and
Trough
Cross Beds

Trough
Cross
Beds

B

Fig. 50 : Alluvial Cone

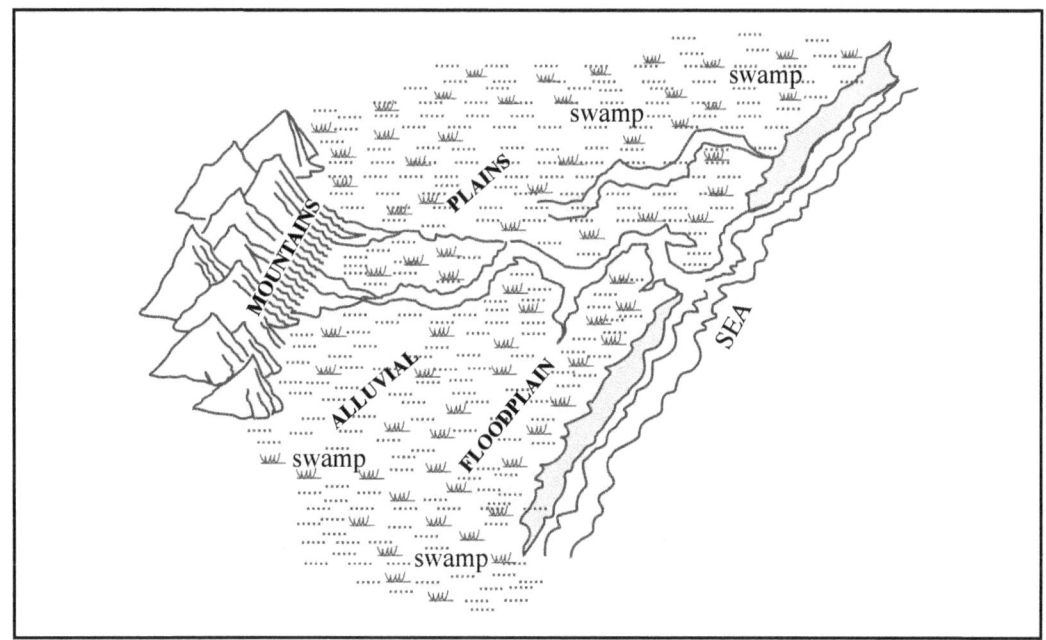

Fig. 51 : Alluvial Plain

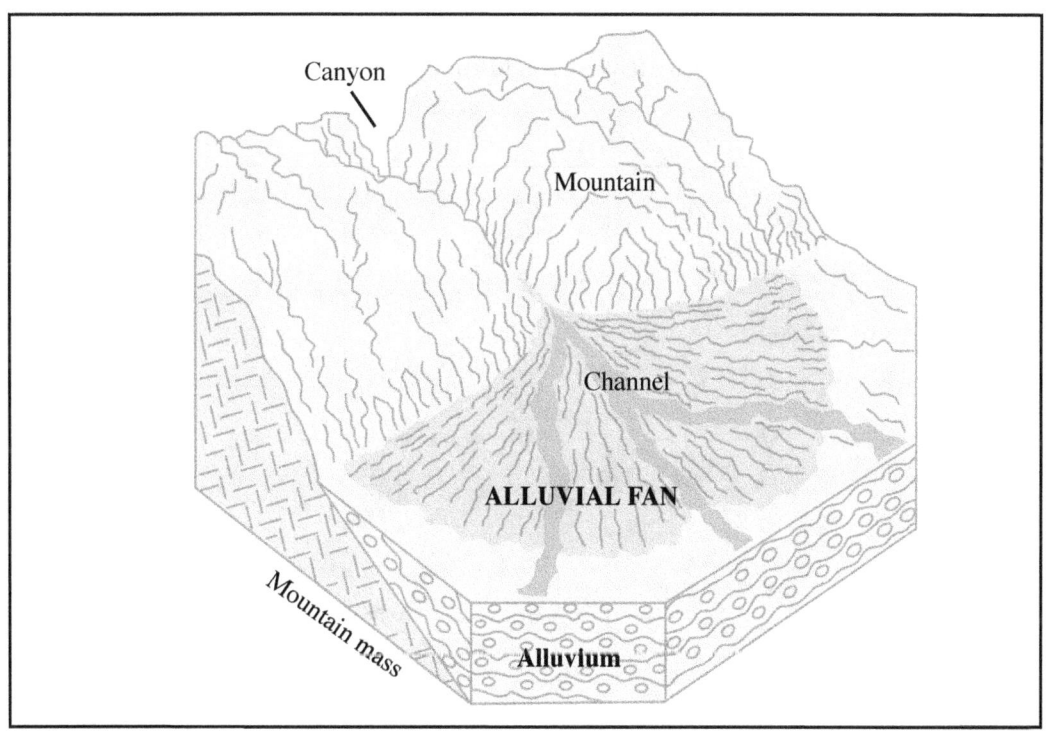

Fig. 52 : Alluvial Fan

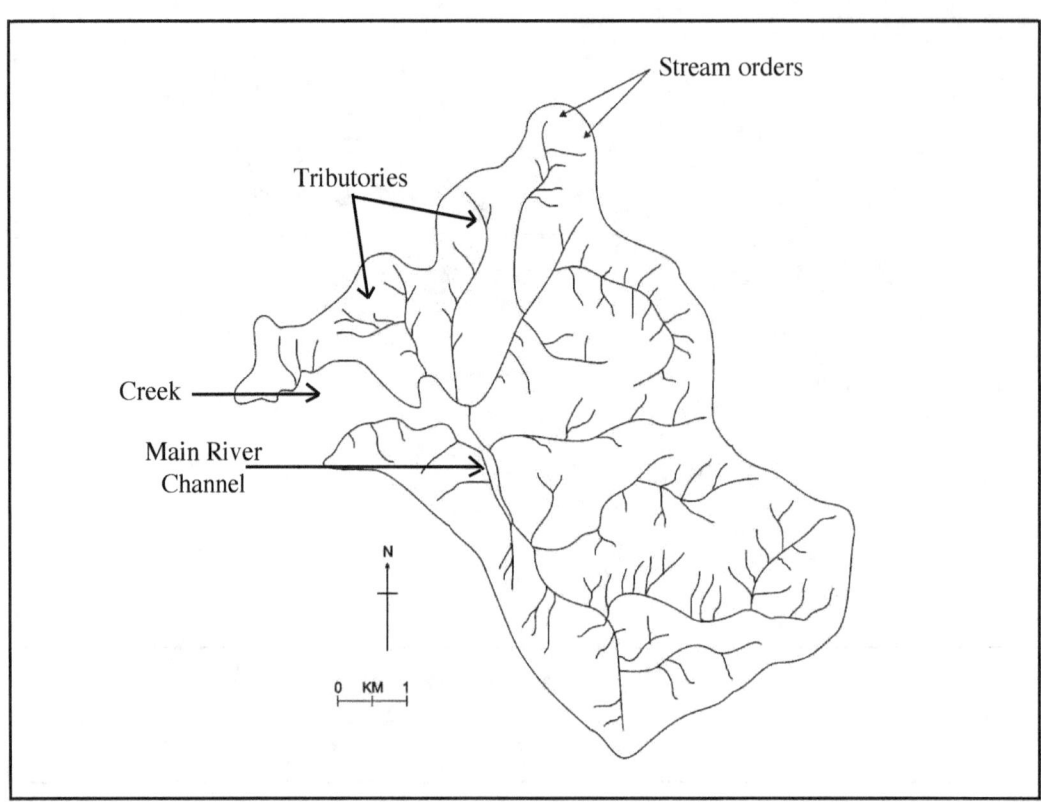

Fig. 53 : Watershed / River basin / Drainage basin / Catchment

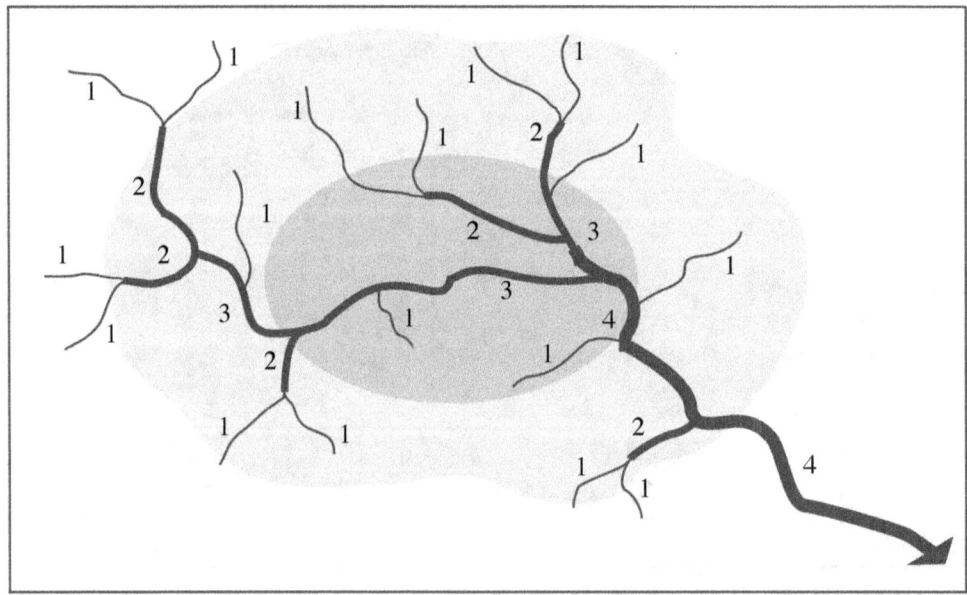

Fig. 54 : A Reach of a Stream

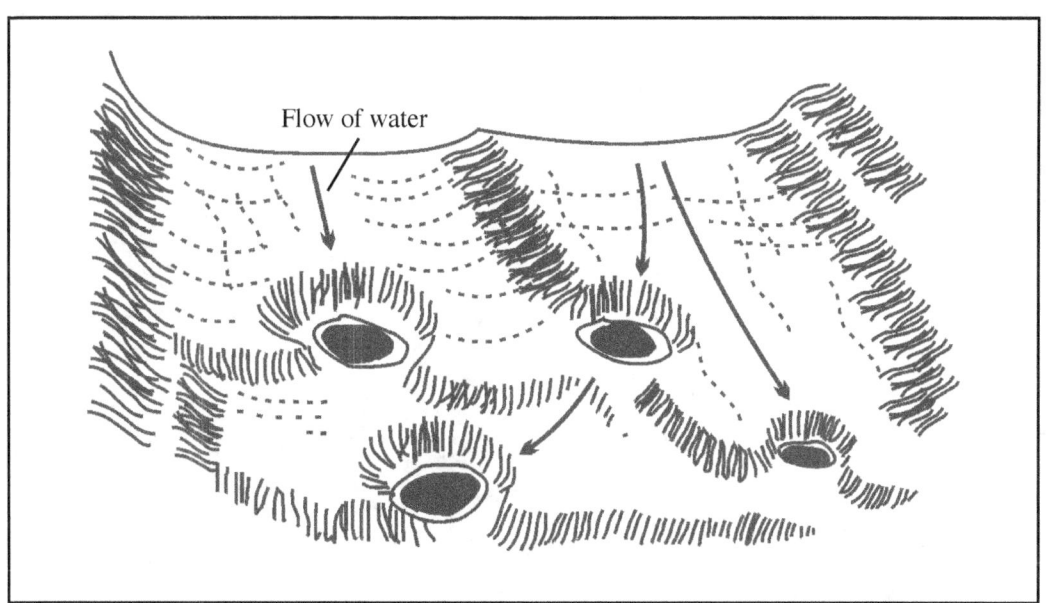

Flow of water

Fig. 55 : Potholes

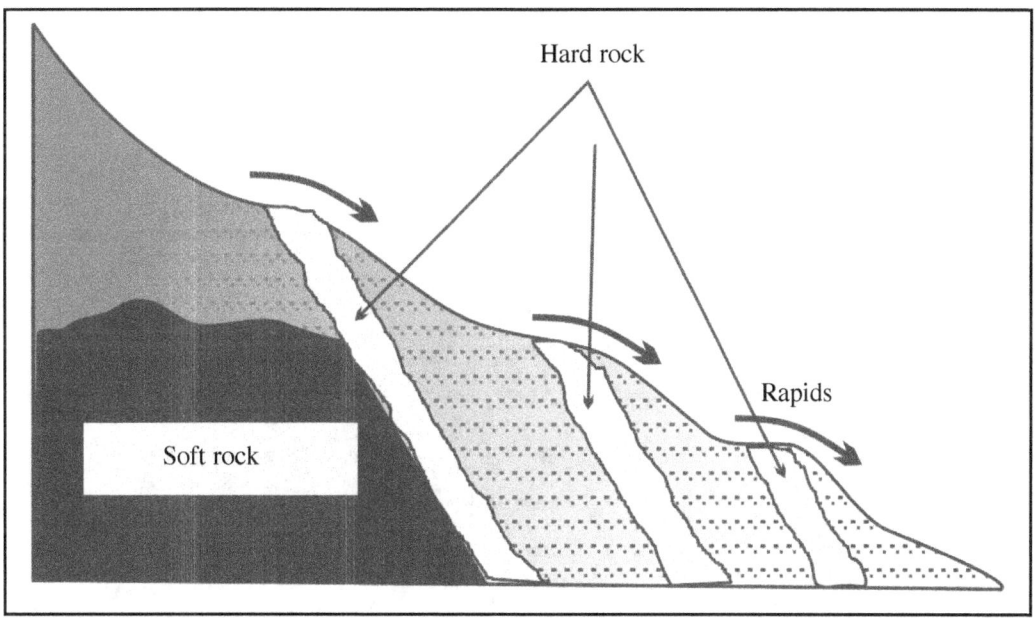

Hard rock

Soft rock

Rapids

Fig. 56 : Rapids

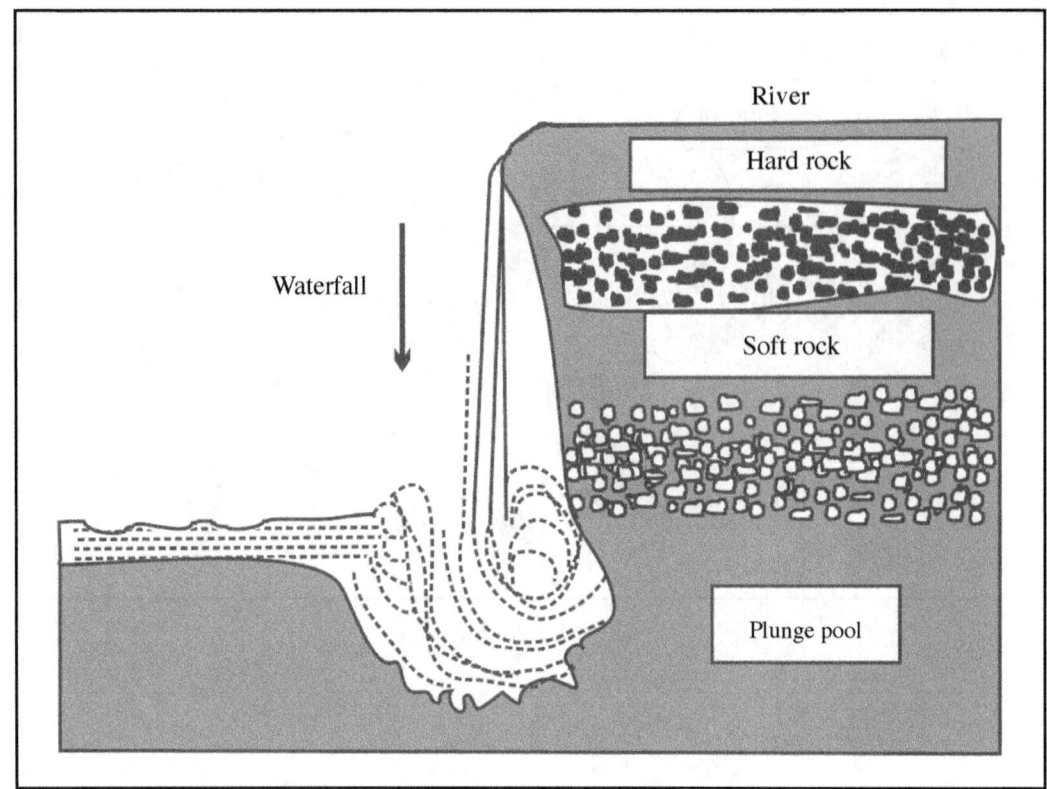

Fig. 57 : Waterfall

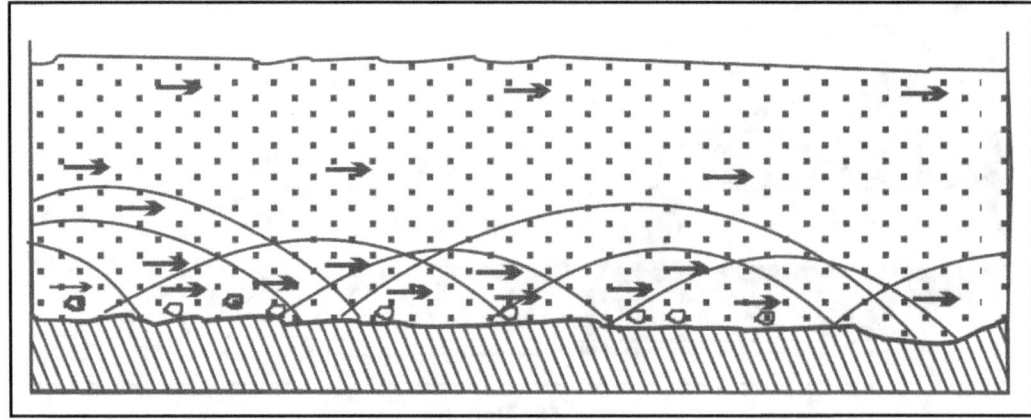

Fig. 58 : Transporation in river

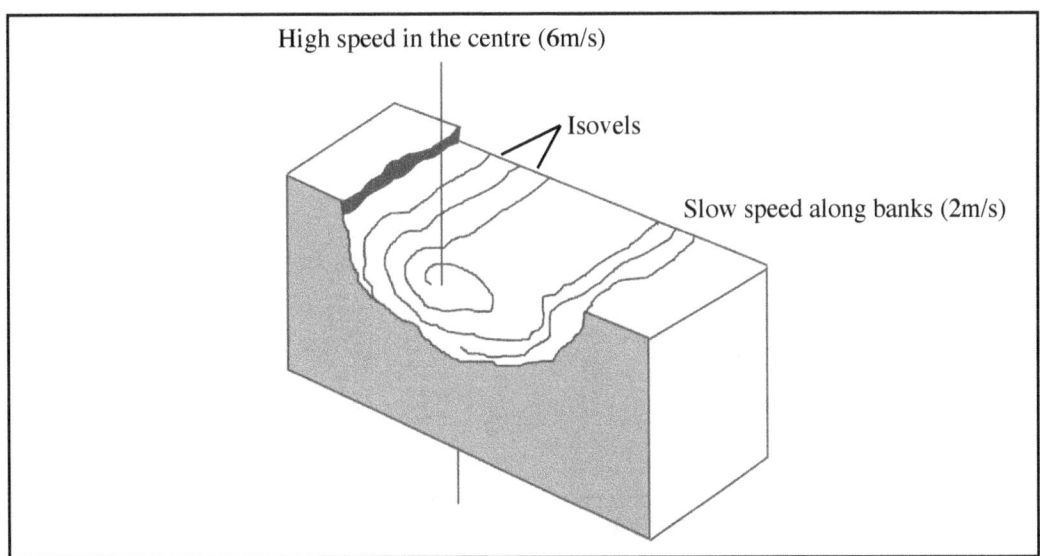

Fig. 59 : Velocity distribution in rivers

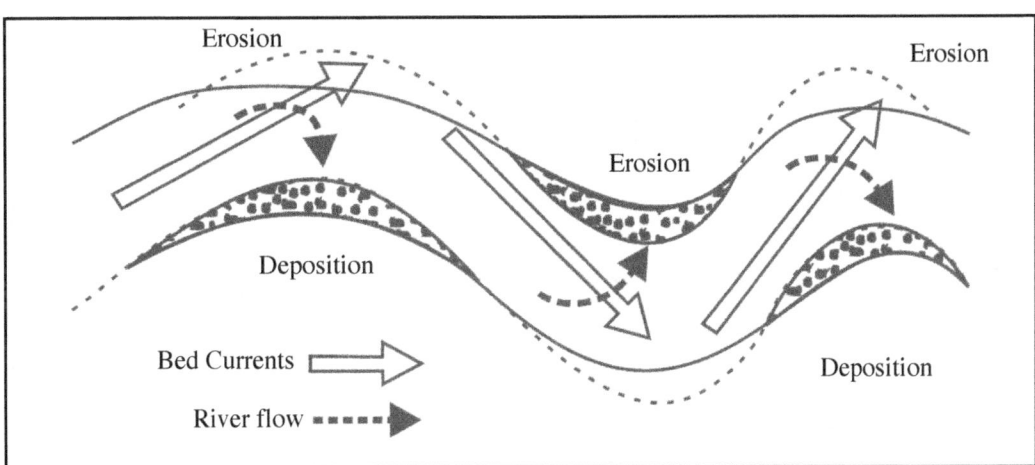

Fig. 60 : Meanders

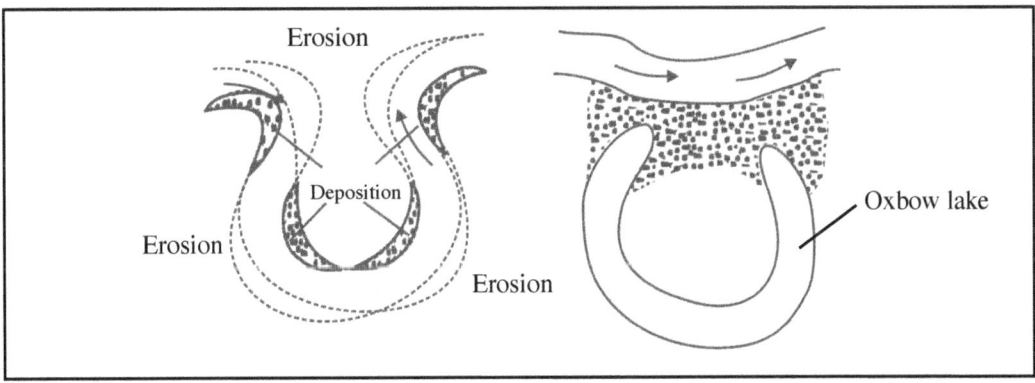

Fig. 61 : Oxbow lake

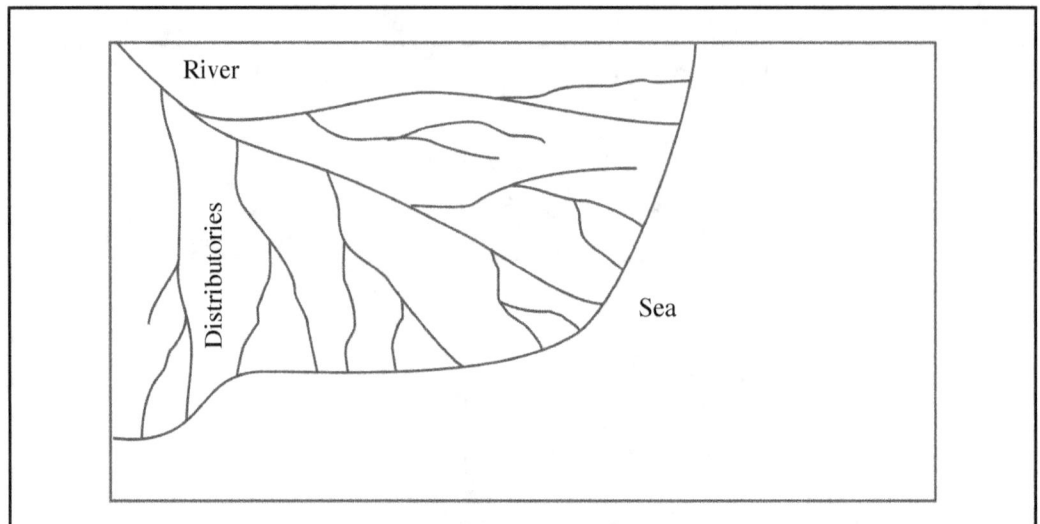

Fig. 62 : River Delta

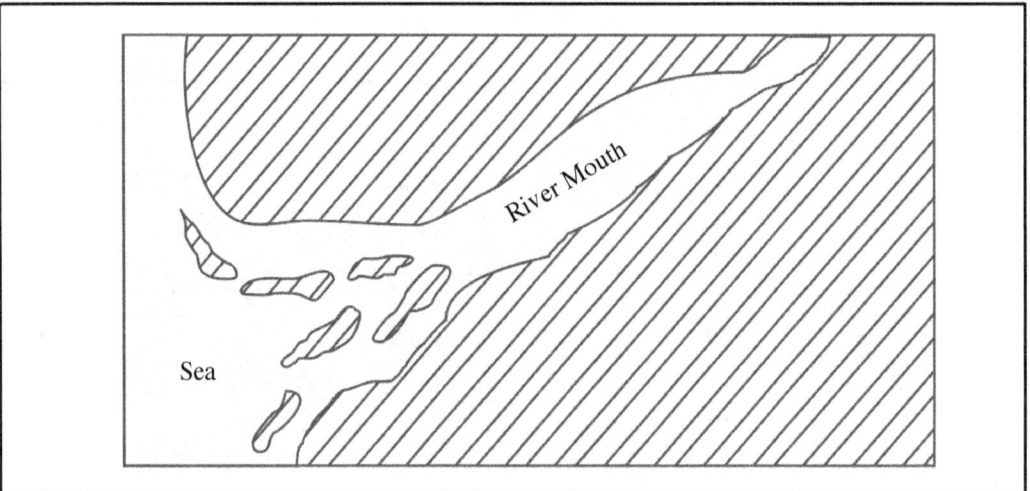

Fig. 63 : Estuarine Delta

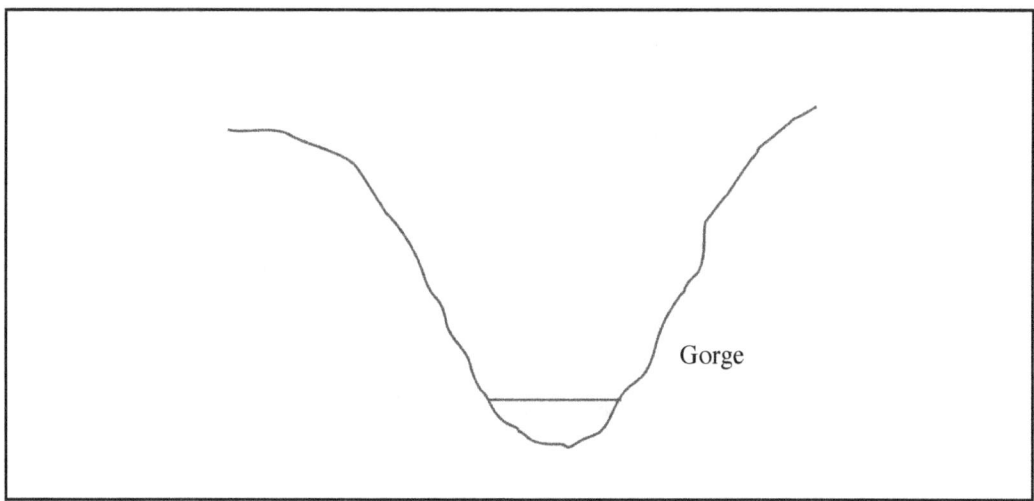

Fig. 64 : Youthful stage of river

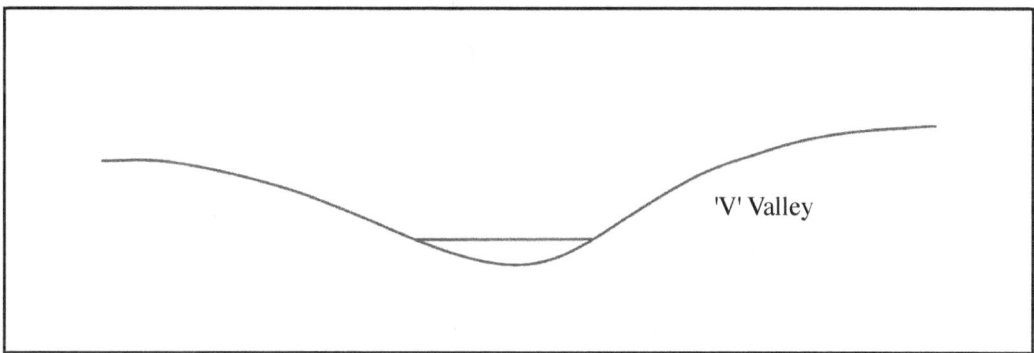

Fig. 65 : Maturity stage of river

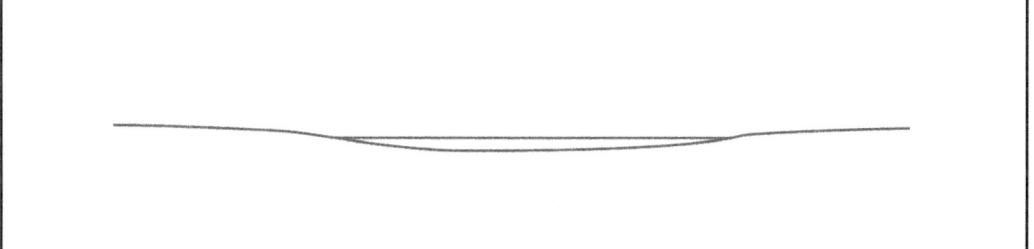

Fig. 66 : Old Stage of river

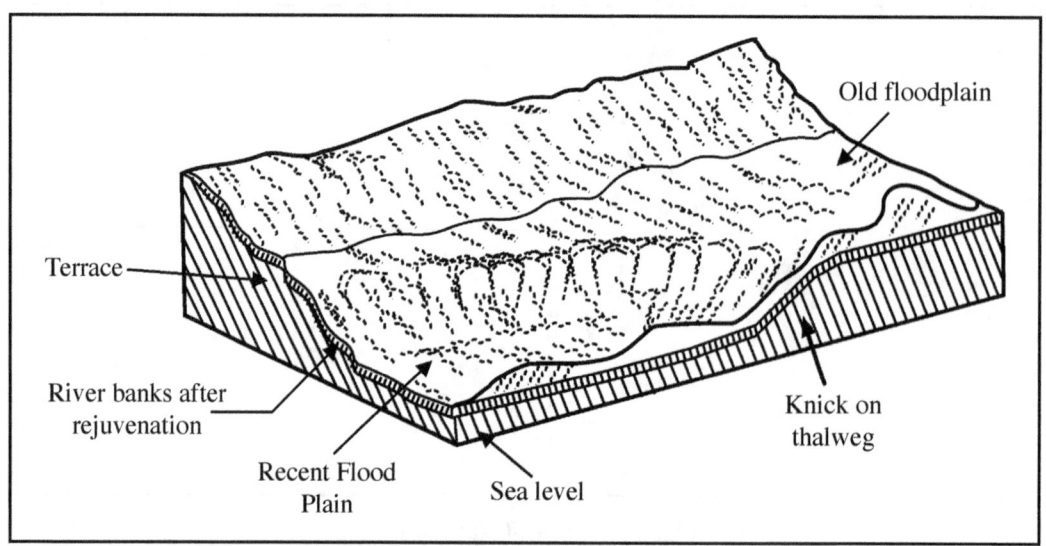

Fig. 67 : Knick point and Flood plain

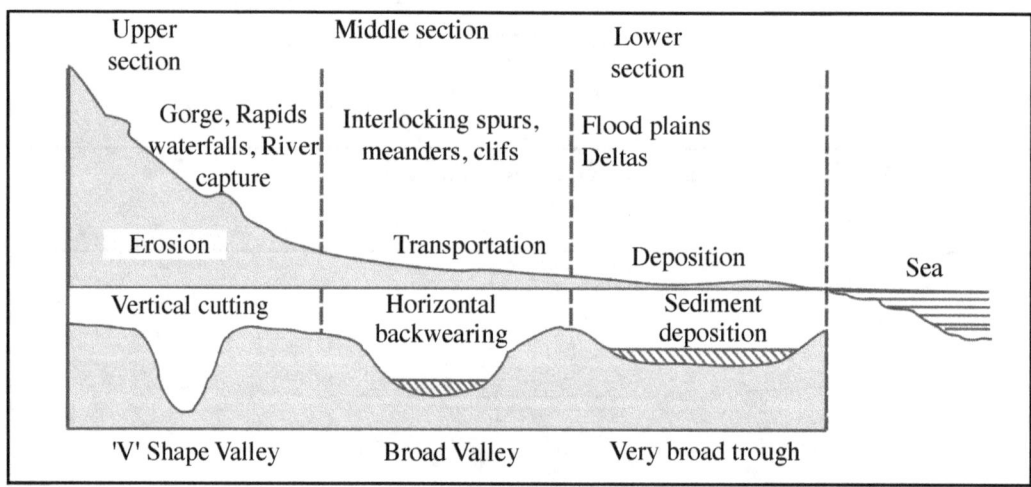

Fig. 68 : River thalweg

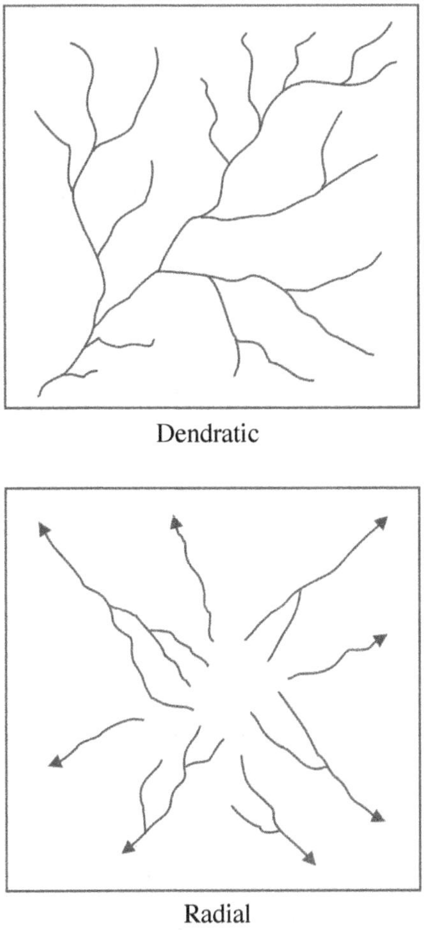

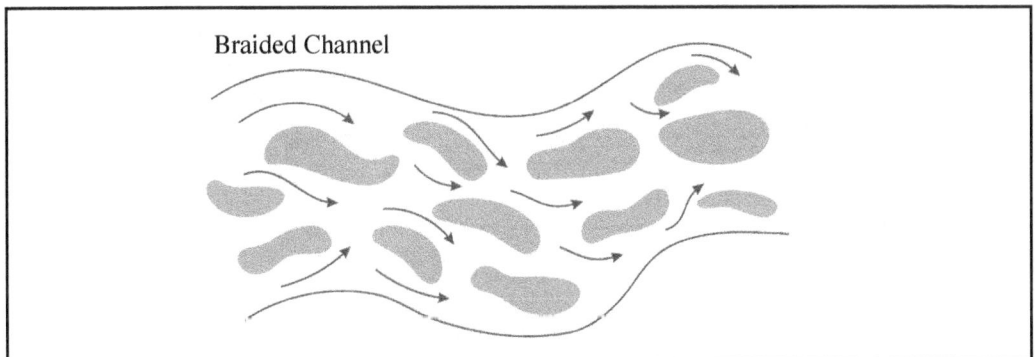

Dendratic

Trellis

Radial

Rectangular

Fig. 69 : Drainage Patterns

Braided Channel

Fig. 70 : Braided Channel

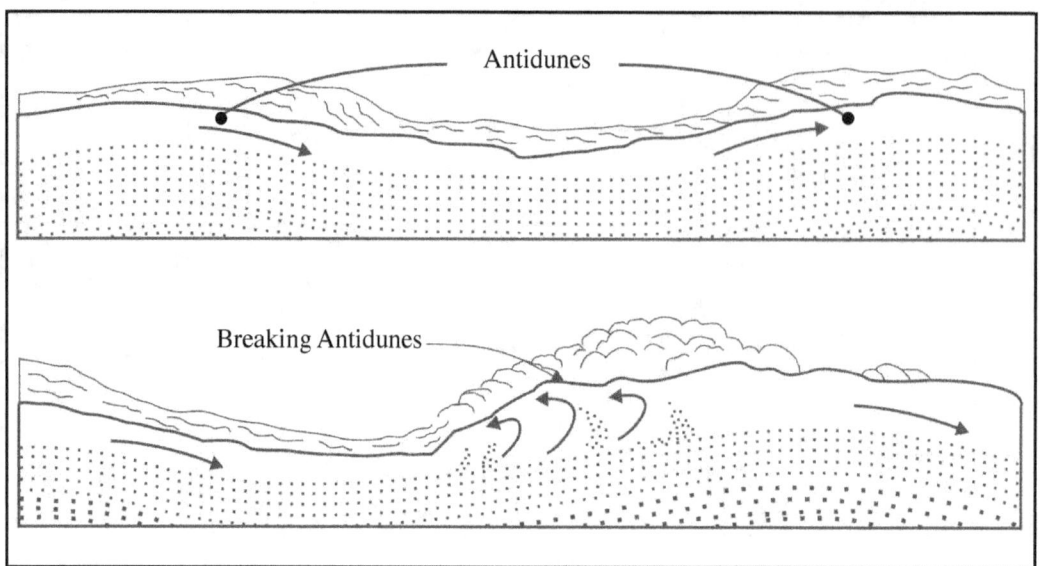

Fig. 71 : Antidunes

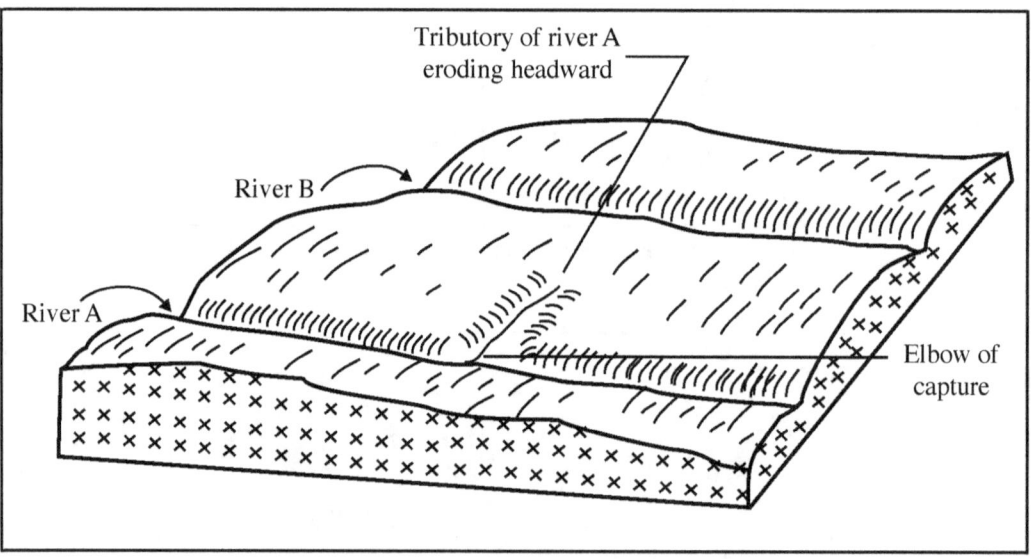

Fig. 72 : Headward erosion of a river

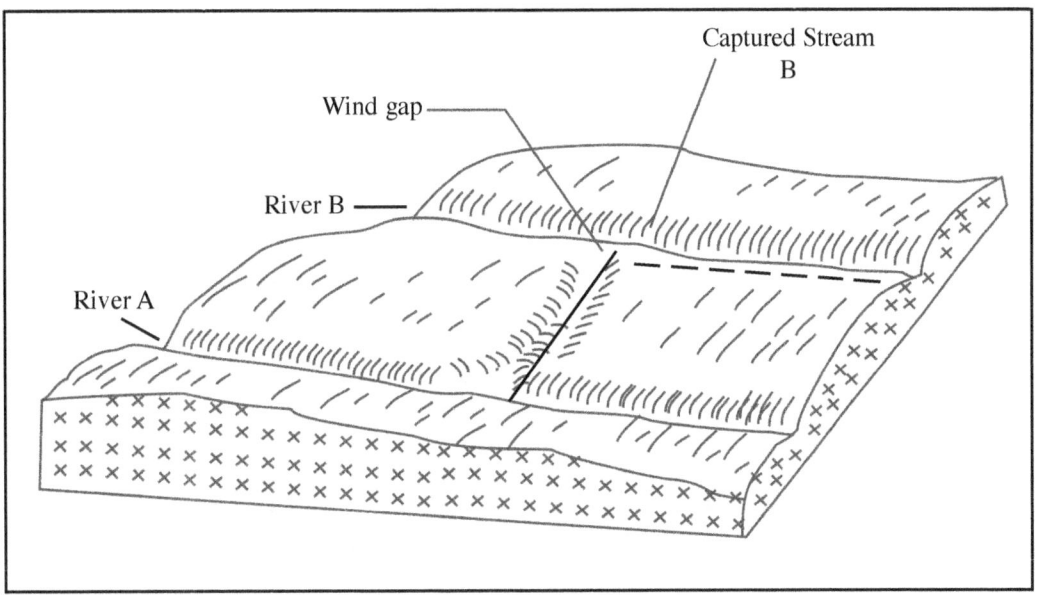

Fig. 73 : River Capture and wind gap

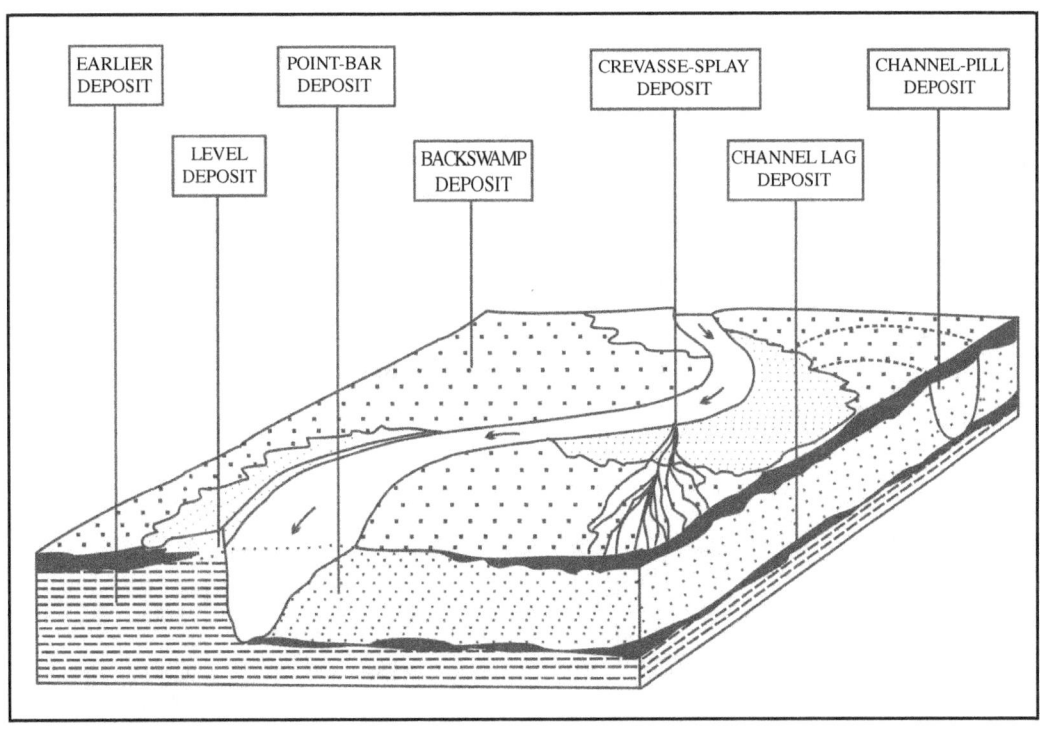

Fig. 74 : Backswamp Deposit

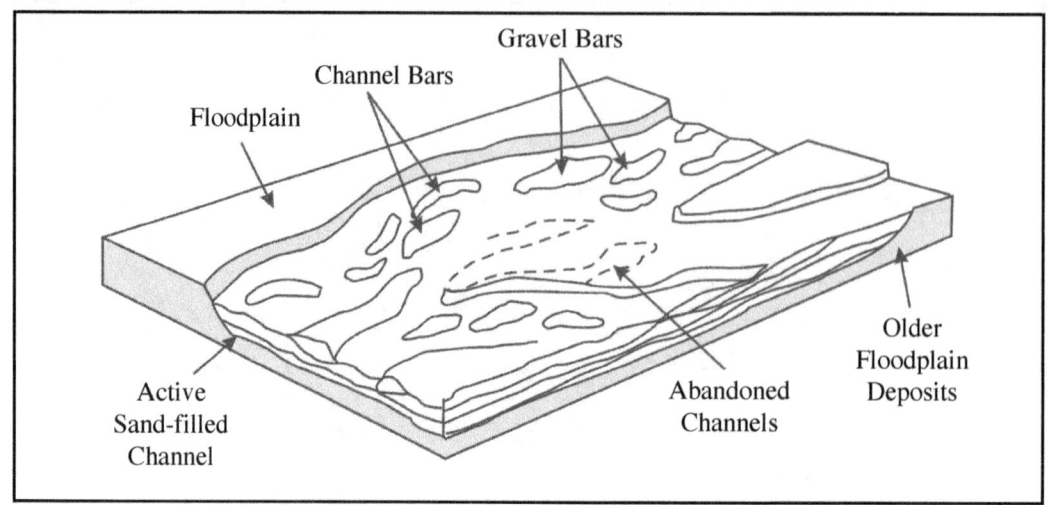

Fig. 75 : Bar and Channel Topography

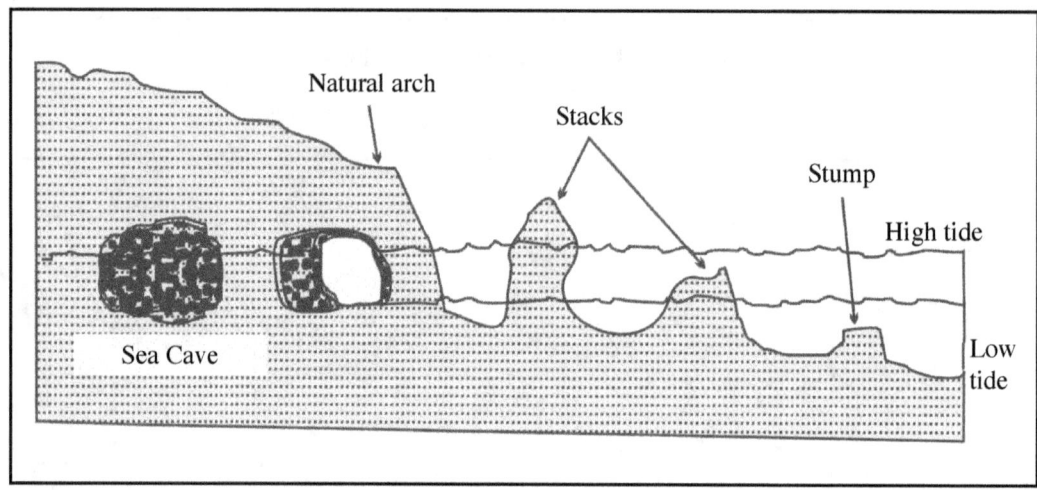

Fig 76 : Sea caves, Arch, Stumps and Stacks

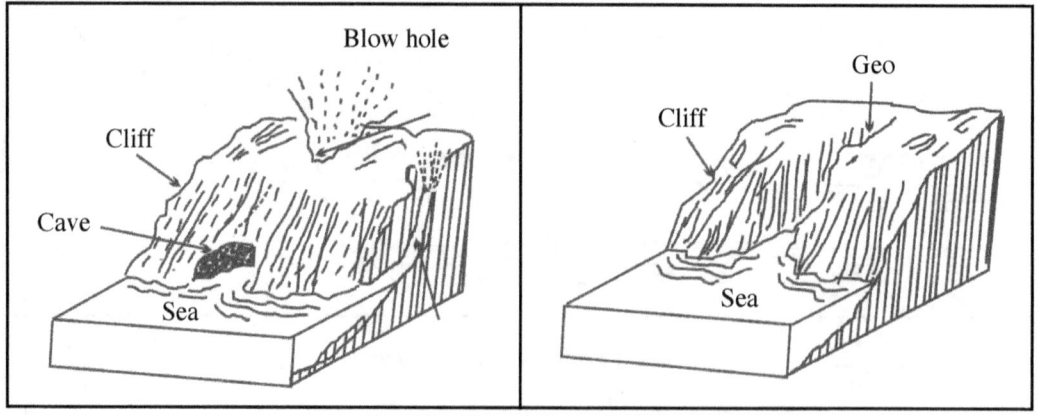

Fig. 77 : Blow hole and Geo

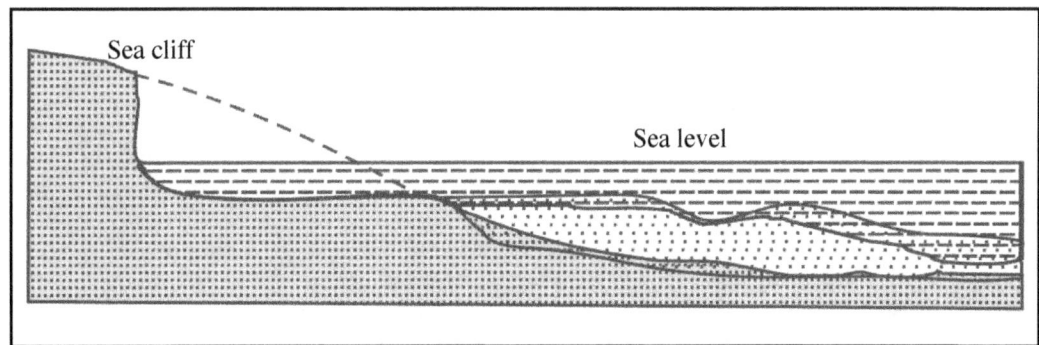

Fig. 78 : Sea Cliff and Wave built platfrom

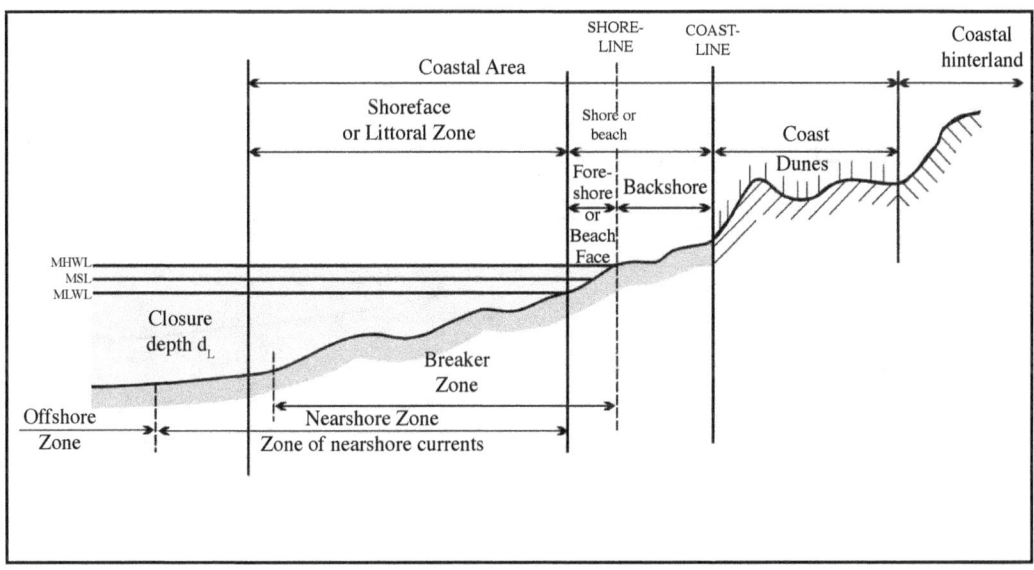

Fig. 79 : Beach profile

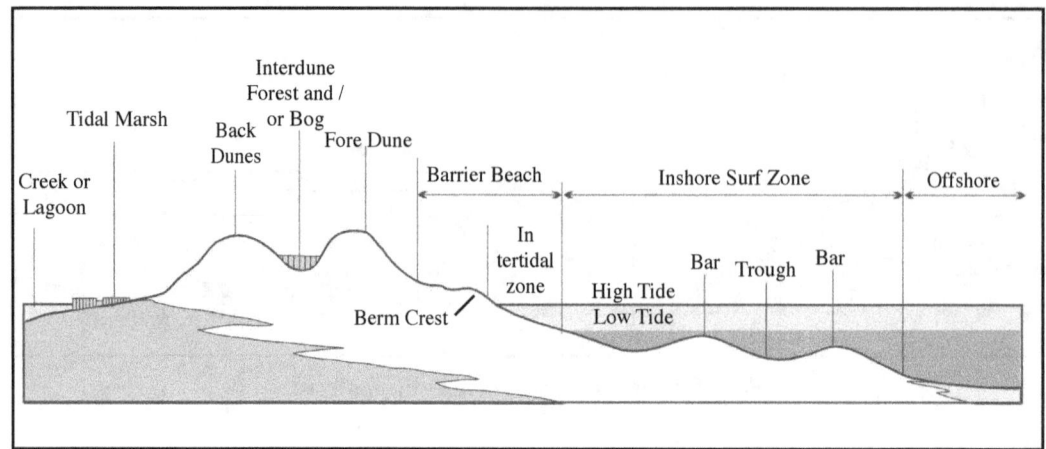

Fig. 80 : Barrier Beach on Barrier Island

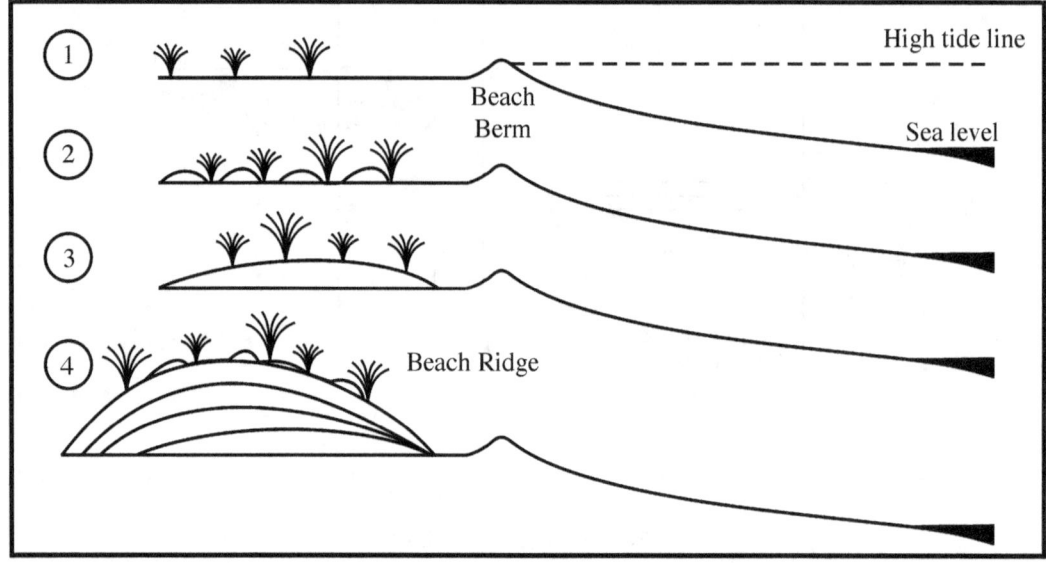

Fig. 81 : Beach Ridge and Berm

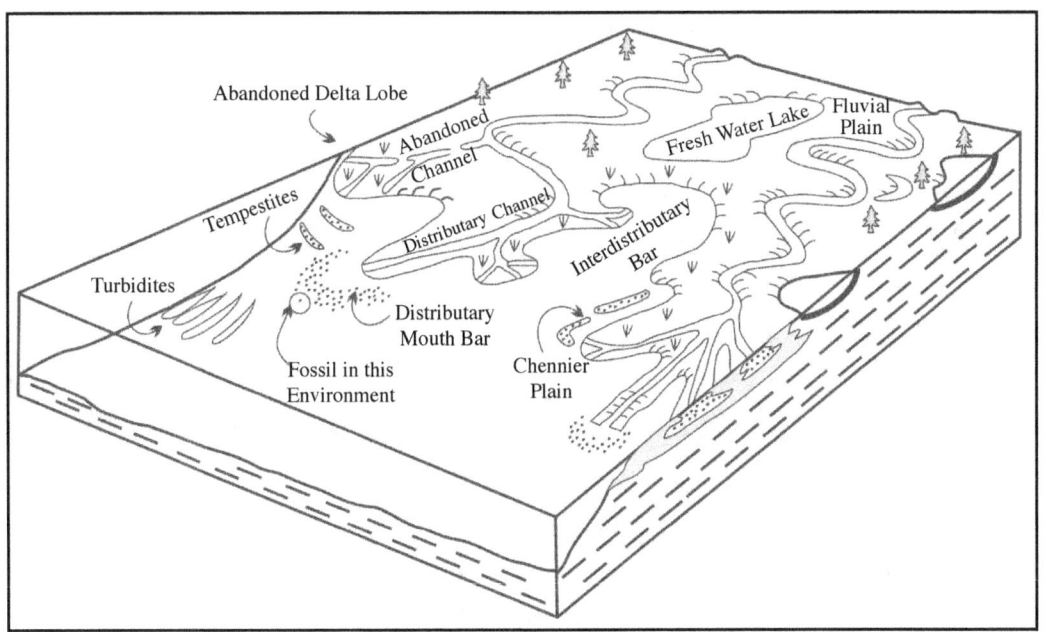

Fig. 82 : Chennier Plain

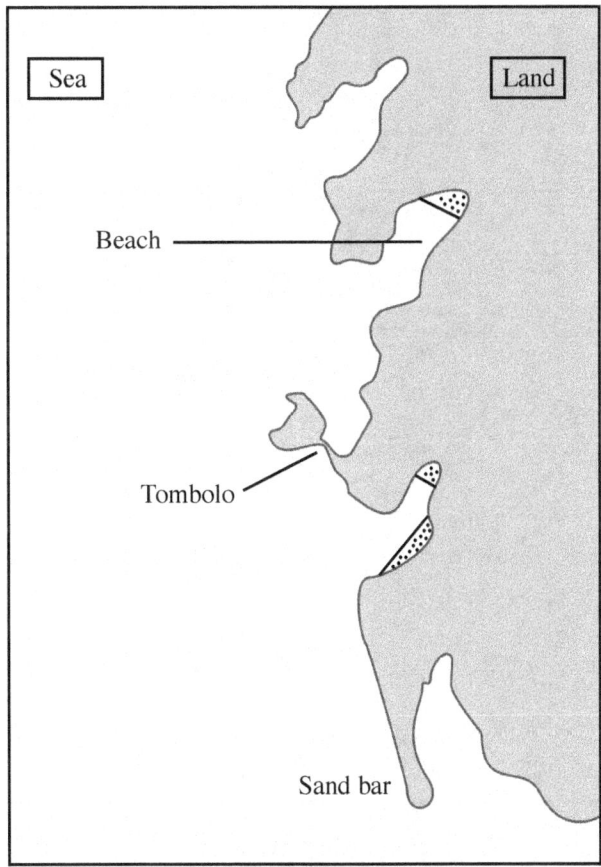

Fig. 83 : Sand bar, Beach and Tombolo

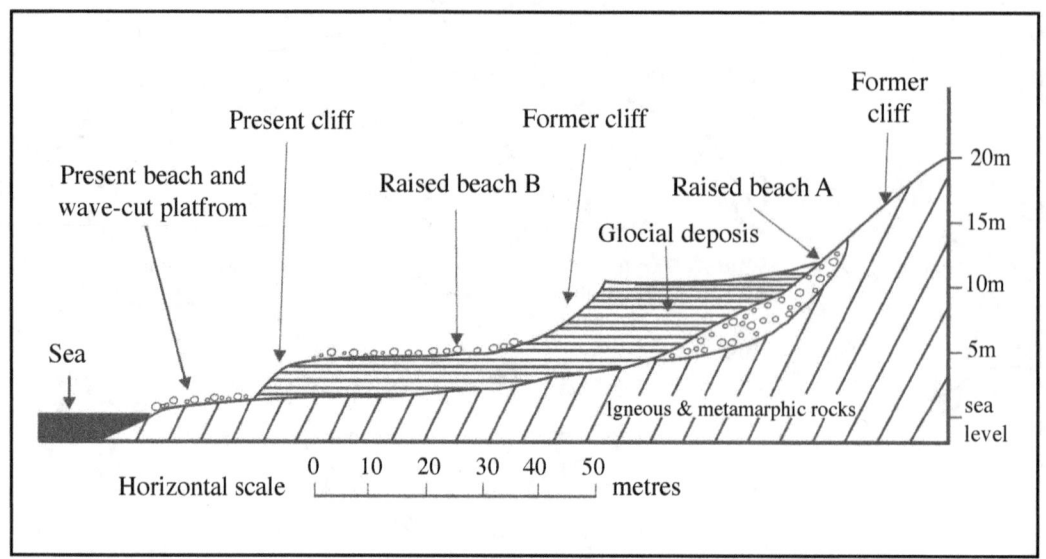

Fig. 84 : Raised beach

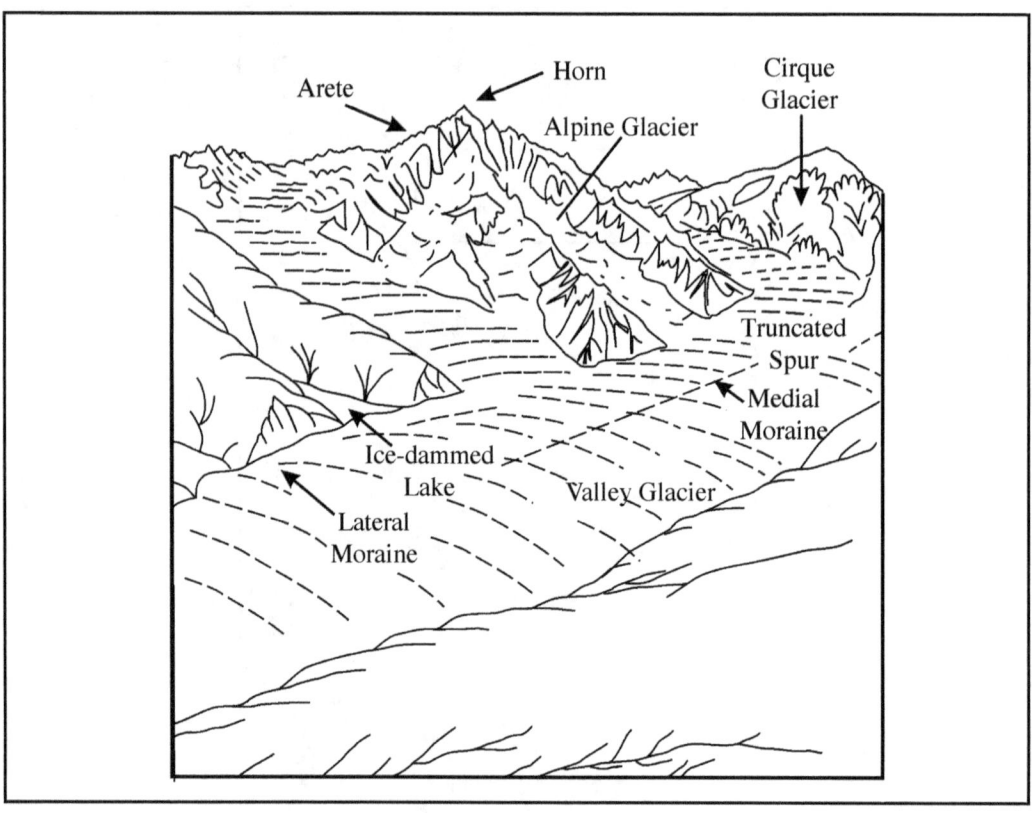

Fig. 85 : Alpine Glacier

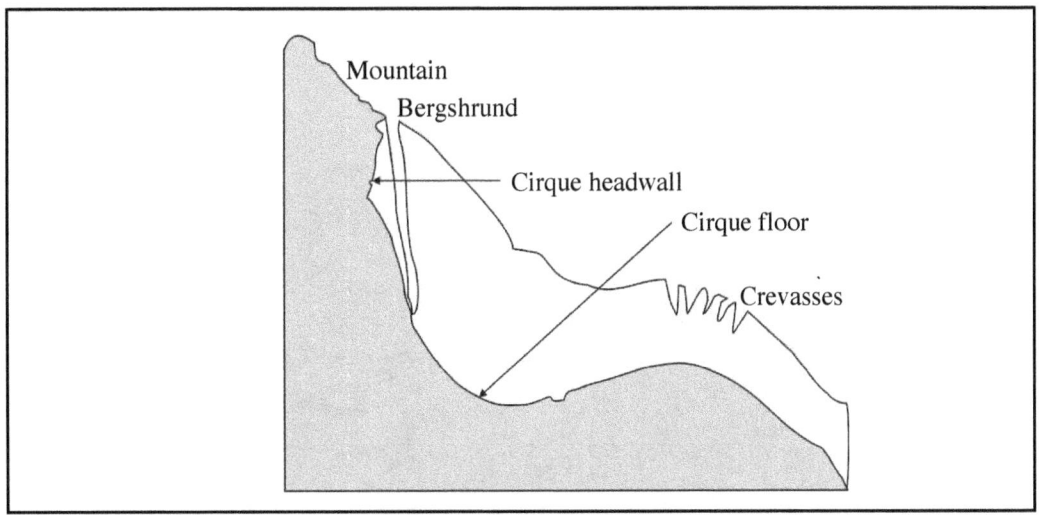

Fig. 86 : Section of Cirque

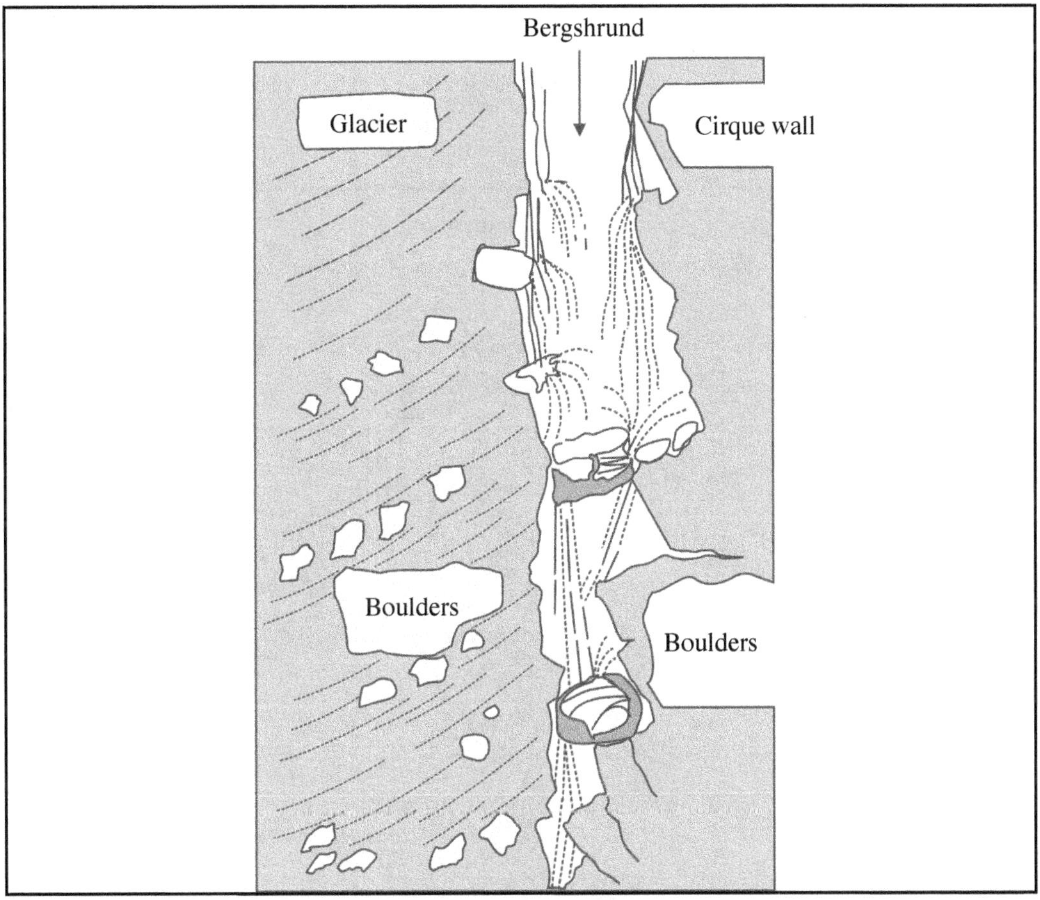

Bergshrund

Glacier

Cirque wall

Boulders

Boulders

Fig. 87 : Bergshrund

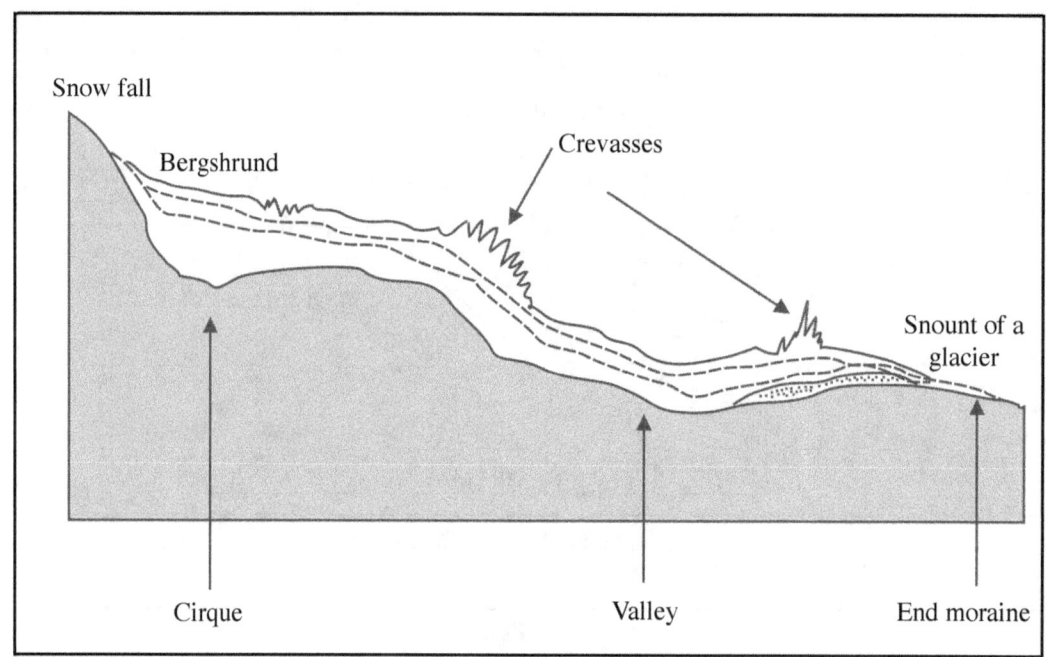

Fig. 88 : Crevasses

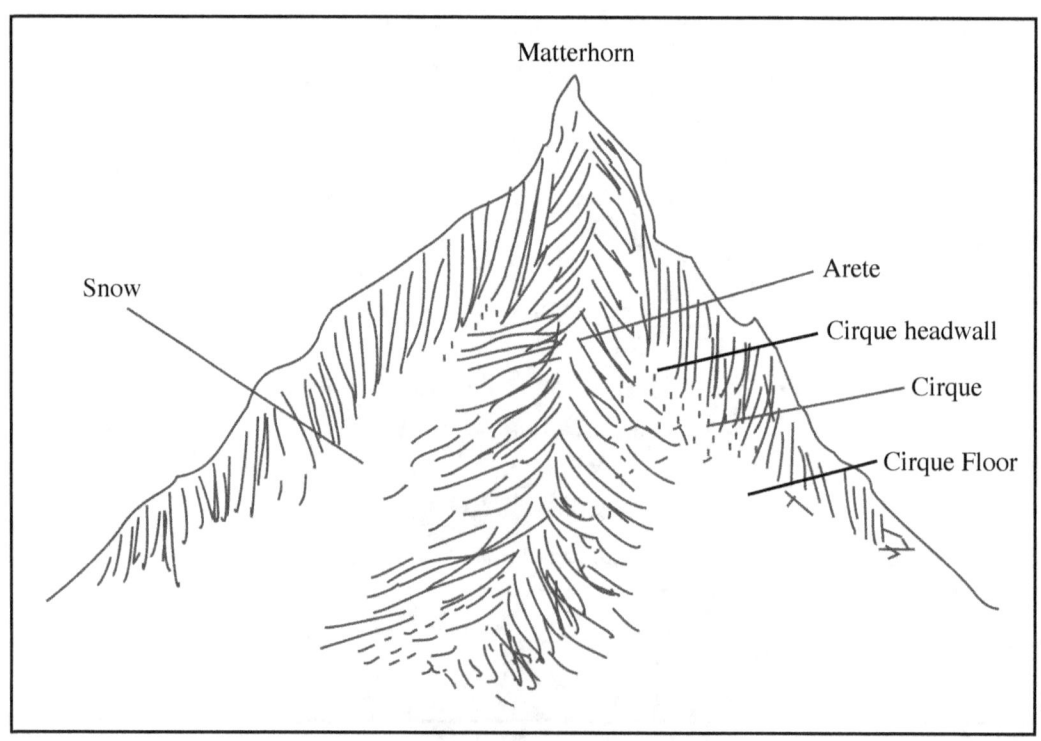

Fig. 89 : Matterhorn, Arete, Cirque

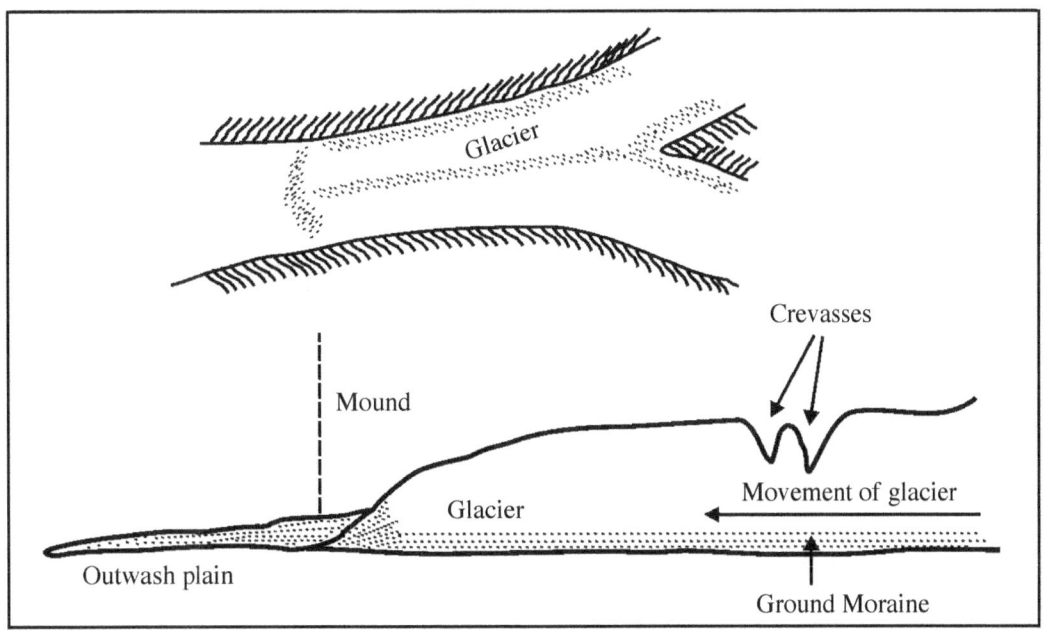

Fig 90 : Glacier and Outwash plain

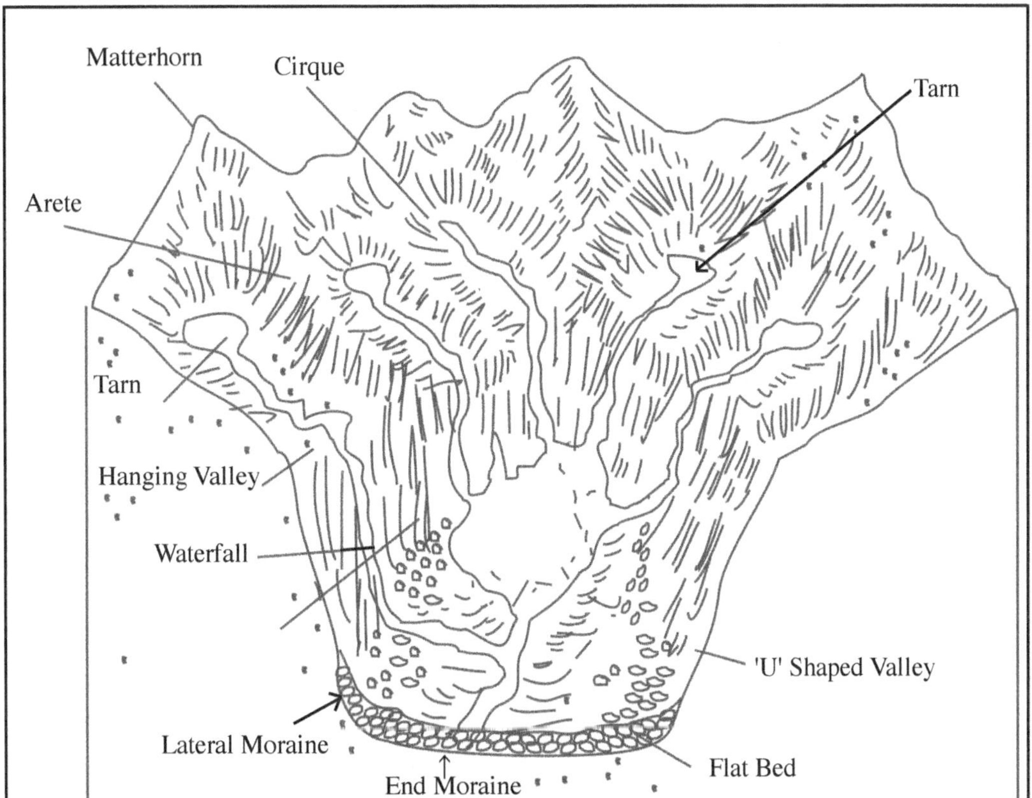

Matterhorn

Cirque

Tarn

Arete

Tarn

Hanging Valley

Waterfall

'U' Shaped Valley

Lateral Moraine

End Moraine

Flat Bed

Fig. 91 : 'U' Shaped and Hanging Valley, Moraines

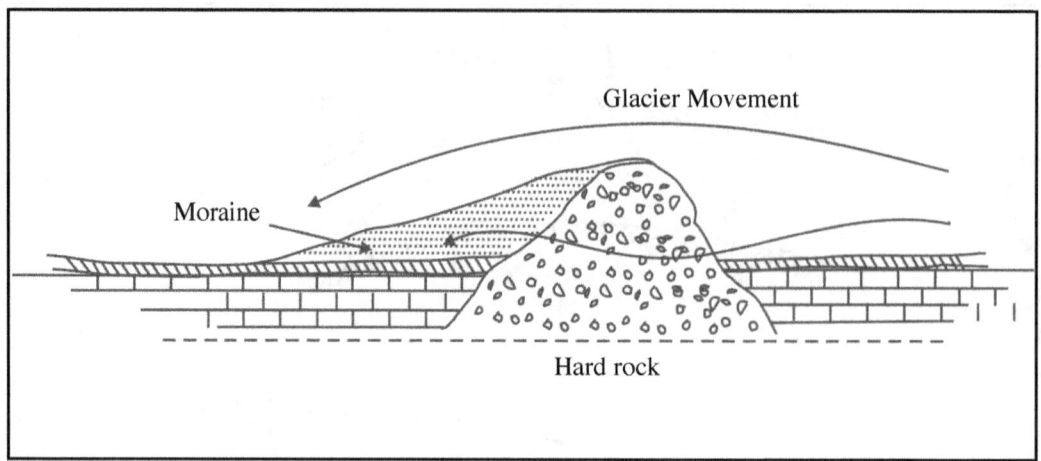

Fig. 92 : Crag and Tail

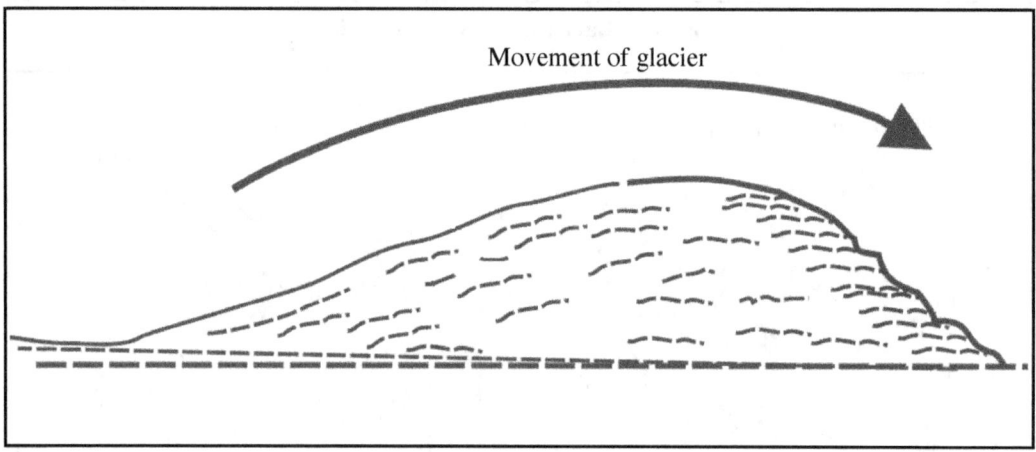

Fig. 93 : Roche Moutonnee

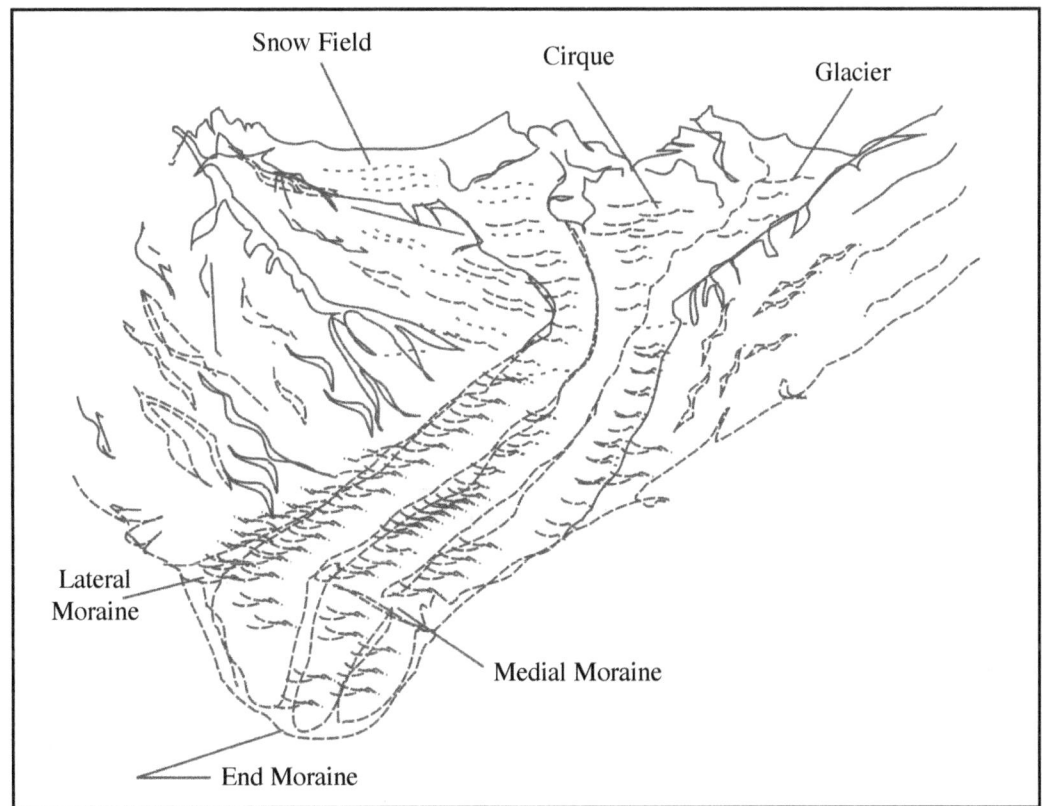

Fig. 94 : Moraines

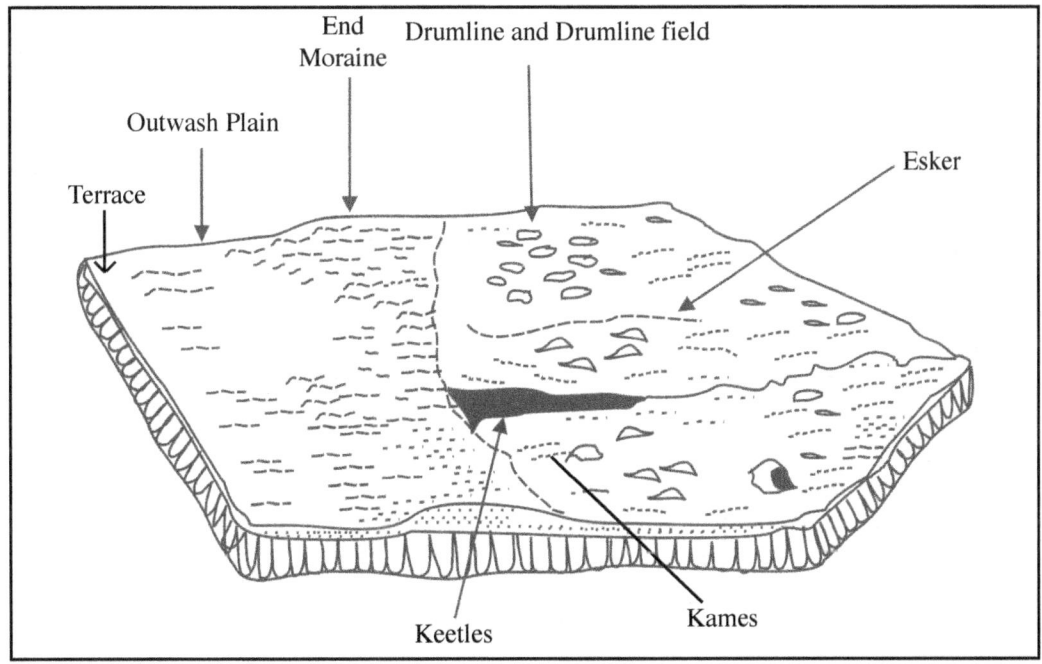

Fig. 95 : Drumlines and Eskers

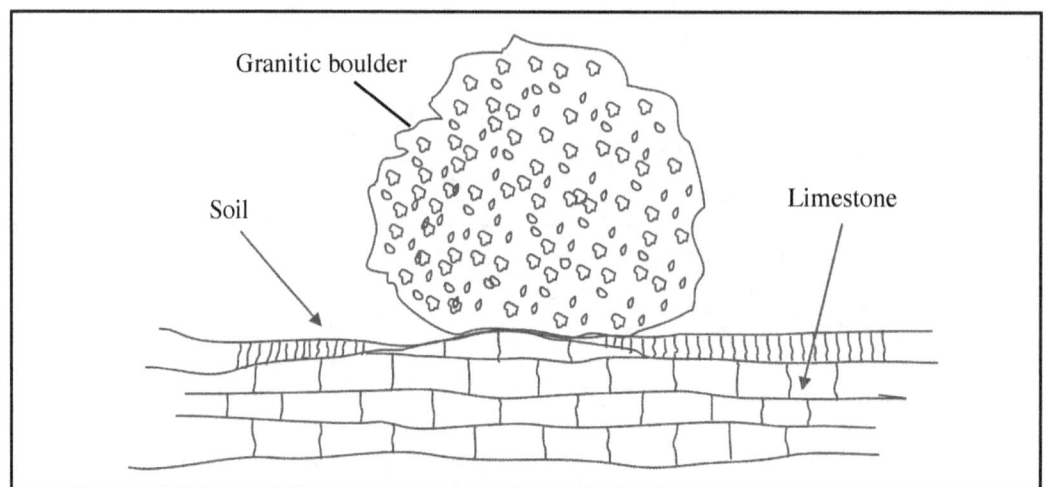

Granitic boulder

Soil

Limestone

Fig. 96 : Erratic boulder

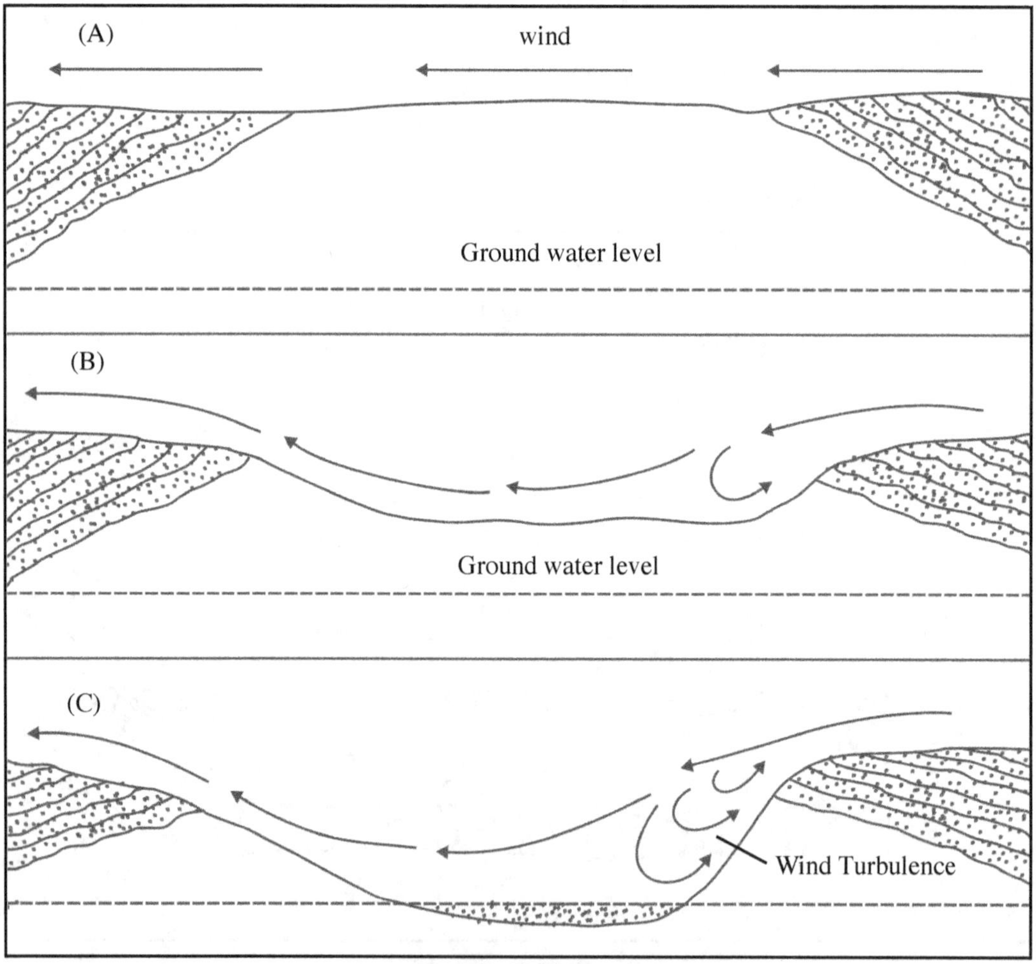

(A)　　　　　　　　　　wind

Ground water level

(B)

Ground water level

(C)

Wind Turbulence

Fig. 97 : Defletion

Fig. 98 : Mushroom rock

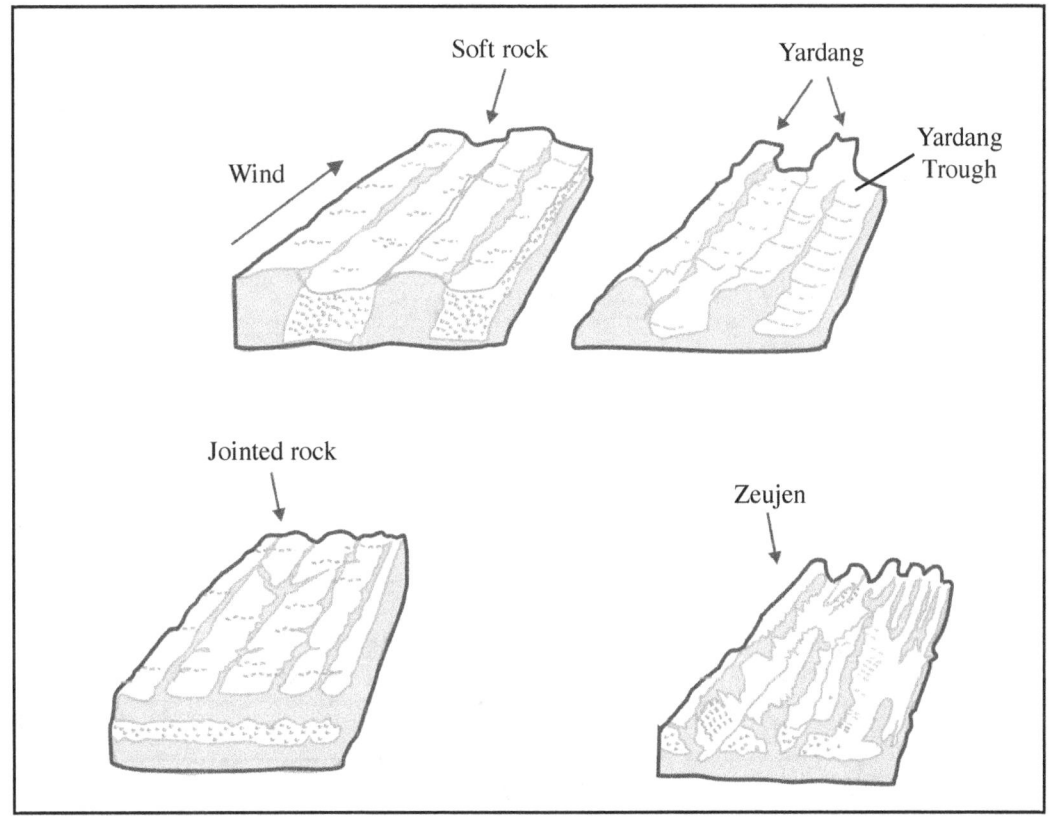

Fig. 99 : Yardang and Zeujen

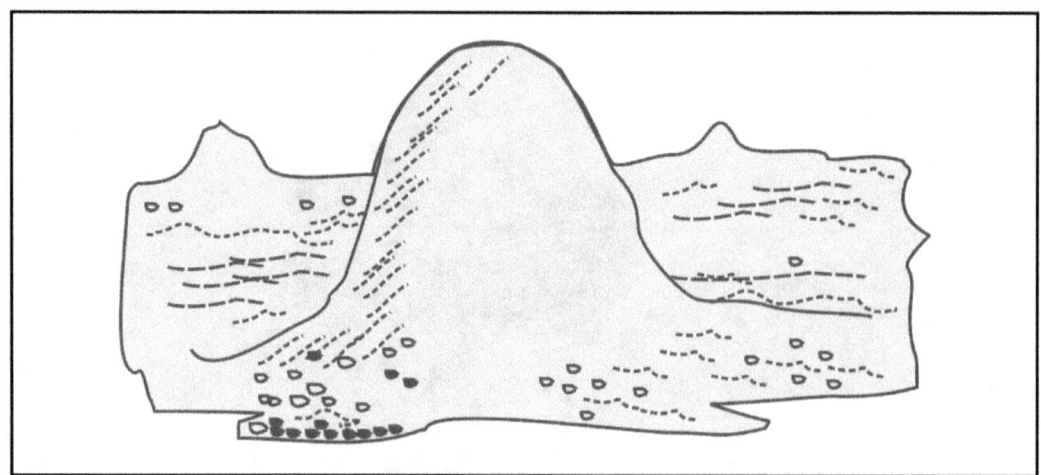

Fig. 100 : Inselberg

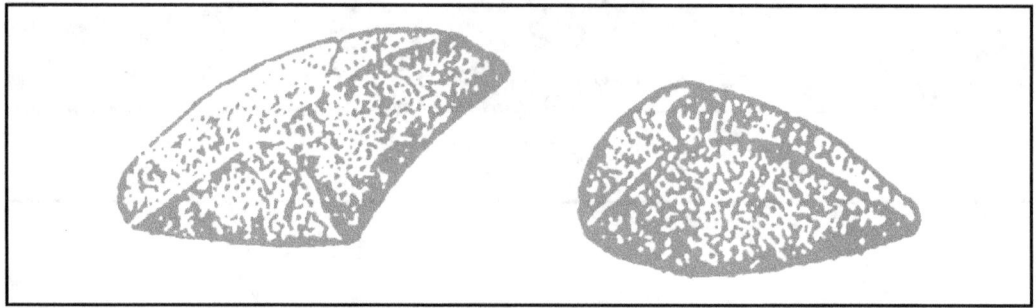

Fig. 101 : Ventifacts and Dreikanters

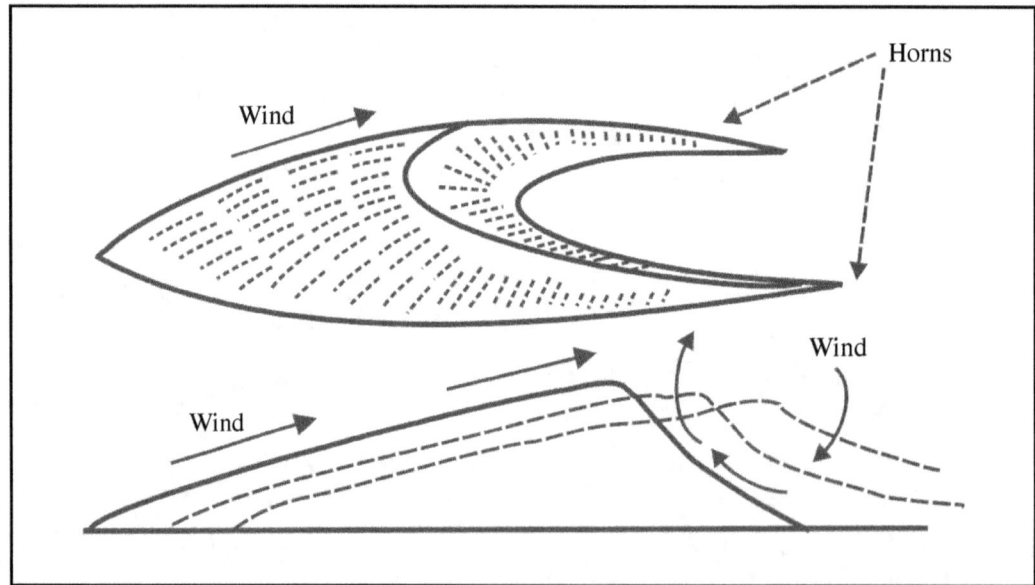

Fig. 102 : Barchan dune

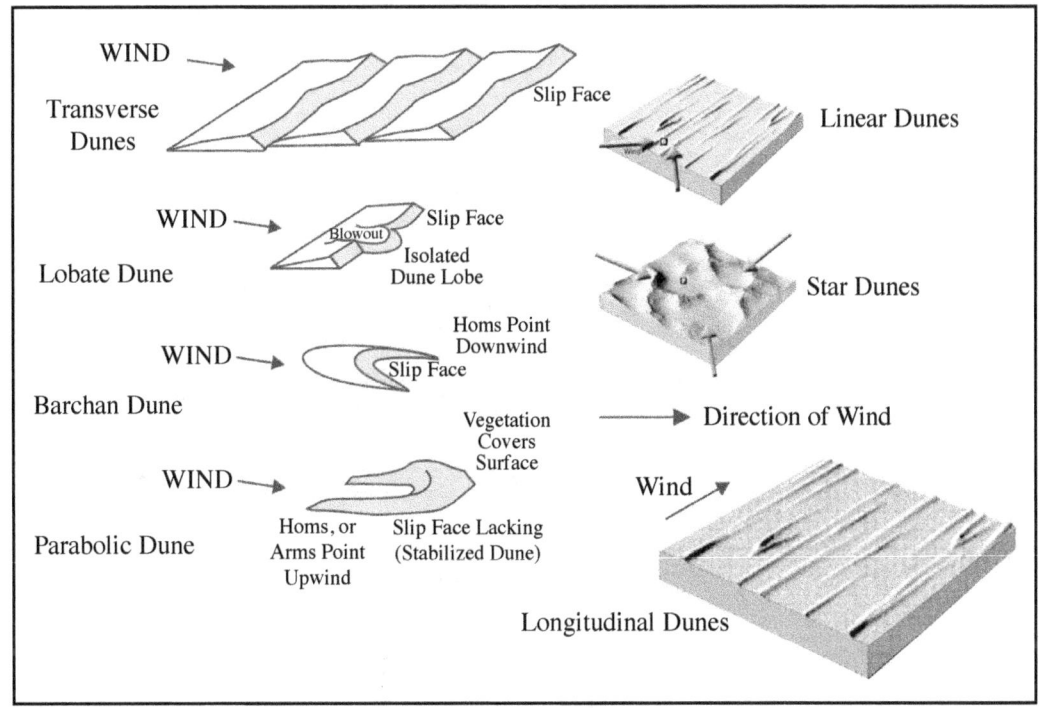

Fig. 103 : Desert Dunes

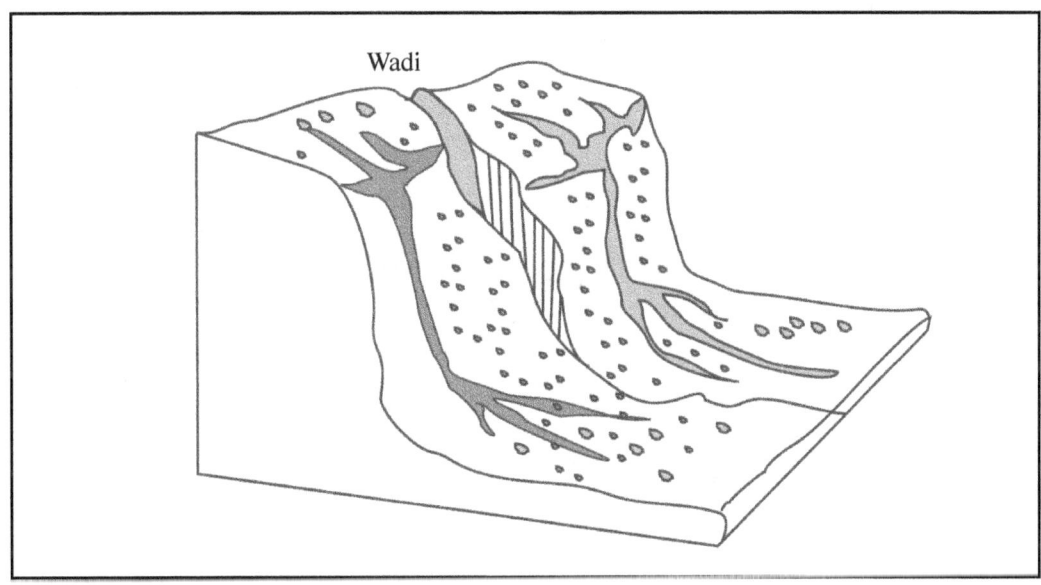

Fig. 104 : Wadi

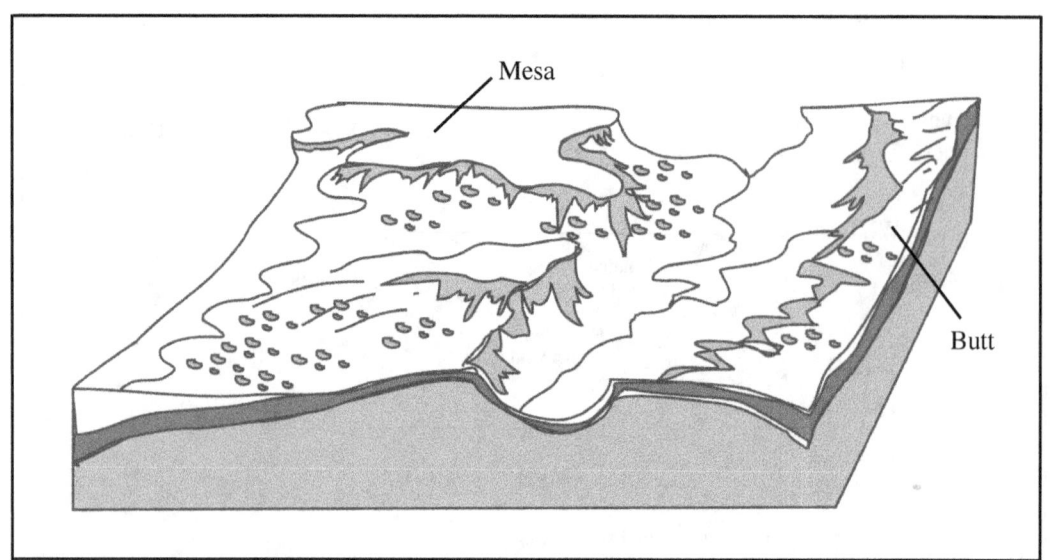

Fig. 105 : Mesa and Butt

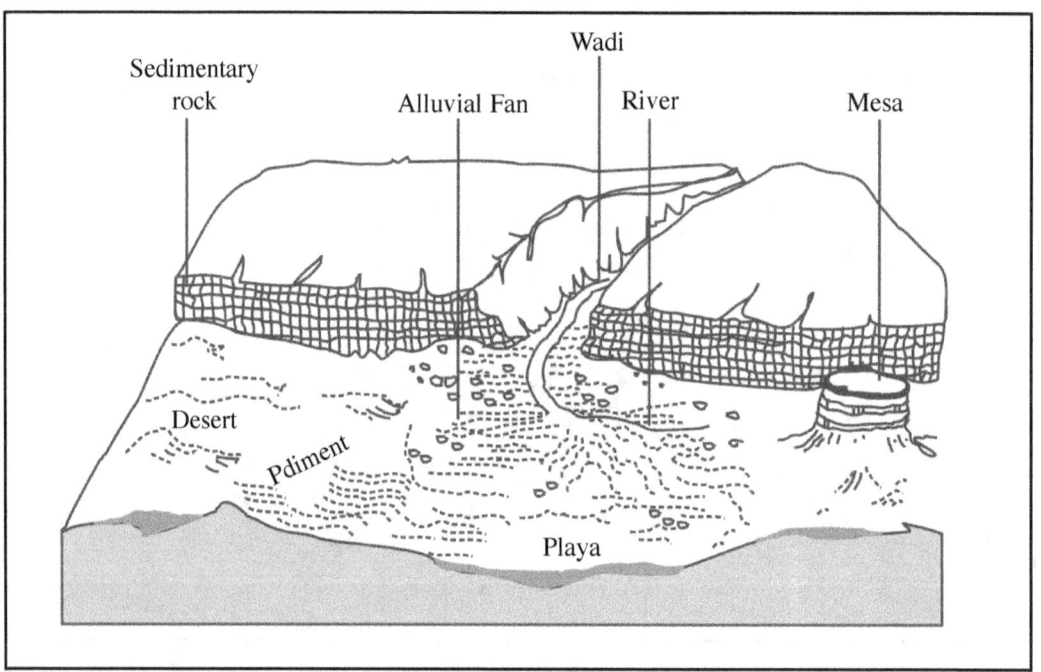

Fig. 106 : Mesa

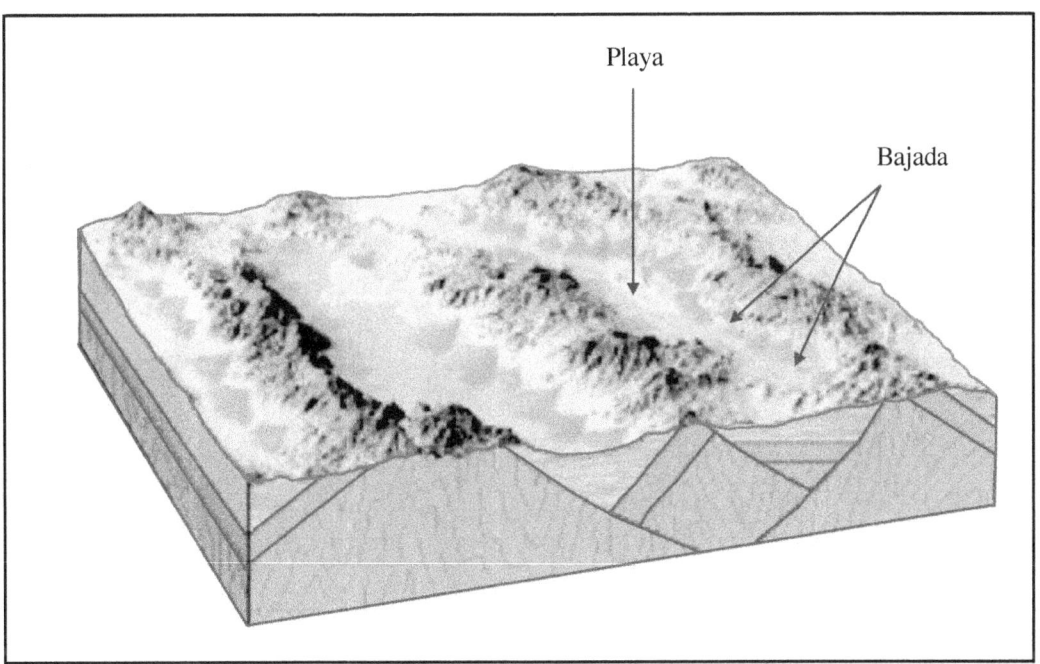

Fig. 107 : Bajada and Playa

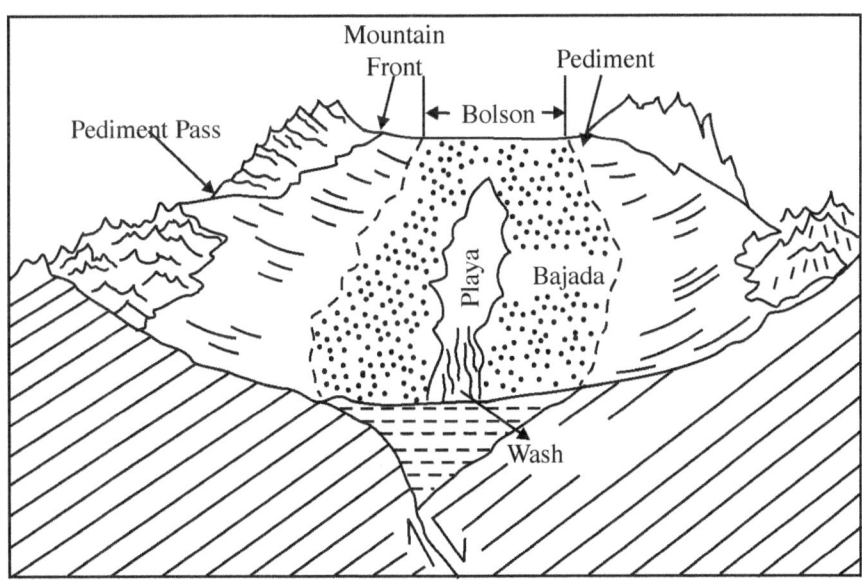

Fig. 108 : Bolson and Playa

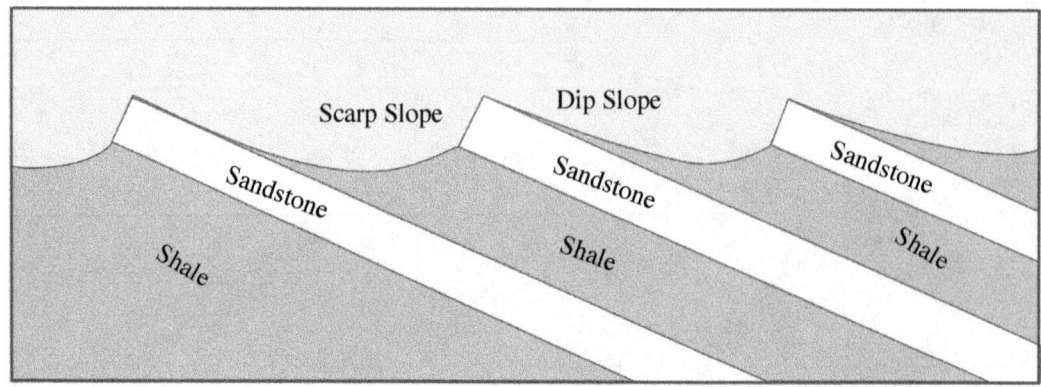

Fig. 109 : Hogback

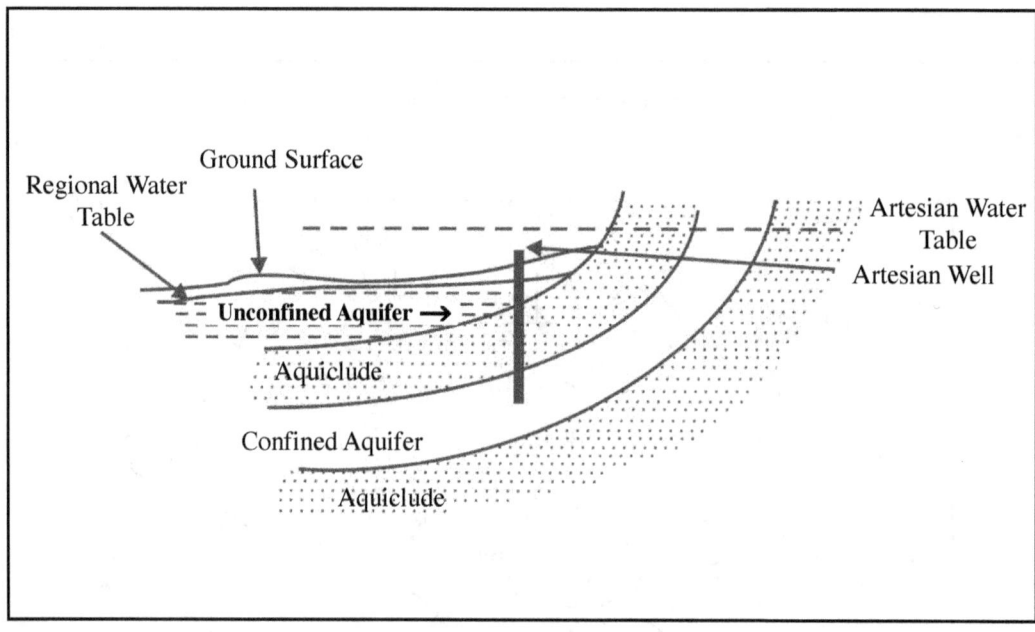

Fig. 110 : Aquiclude and Aquifer

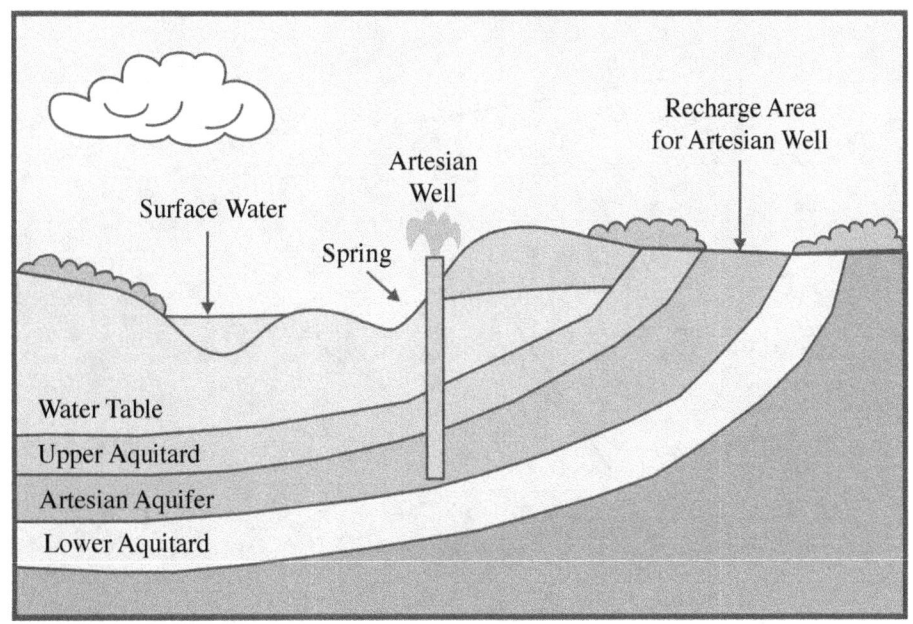

Fig. 111 : Aquitard

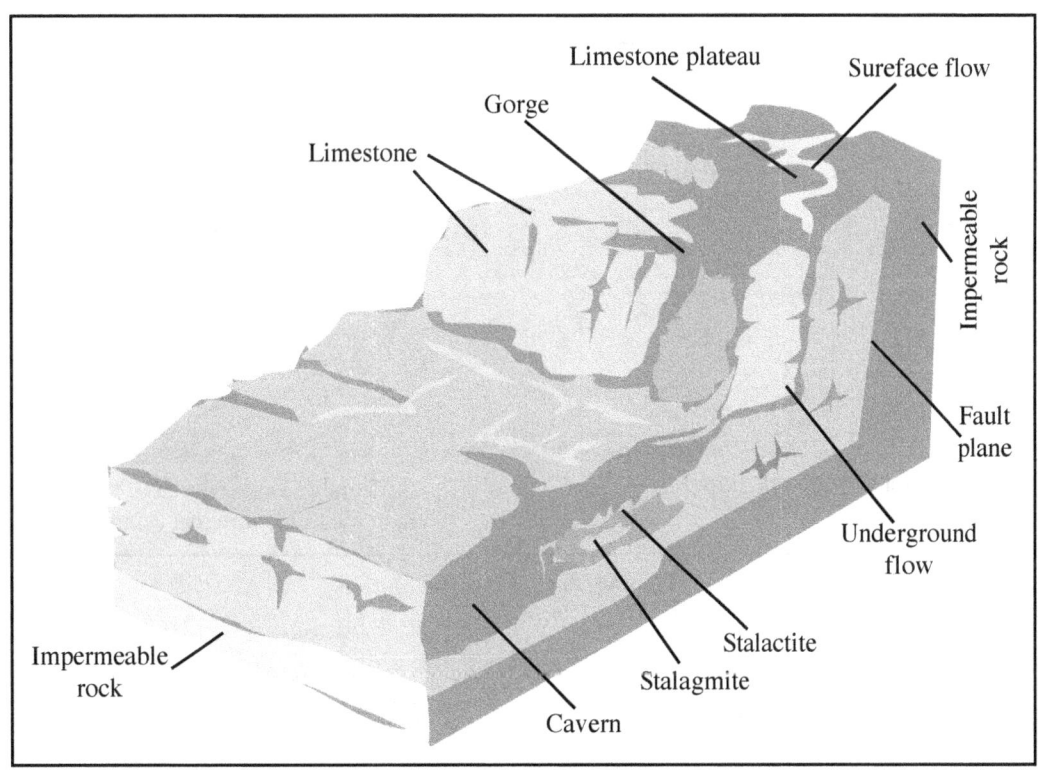

Fig. 112 : Landforms due to Ground water in Limestone

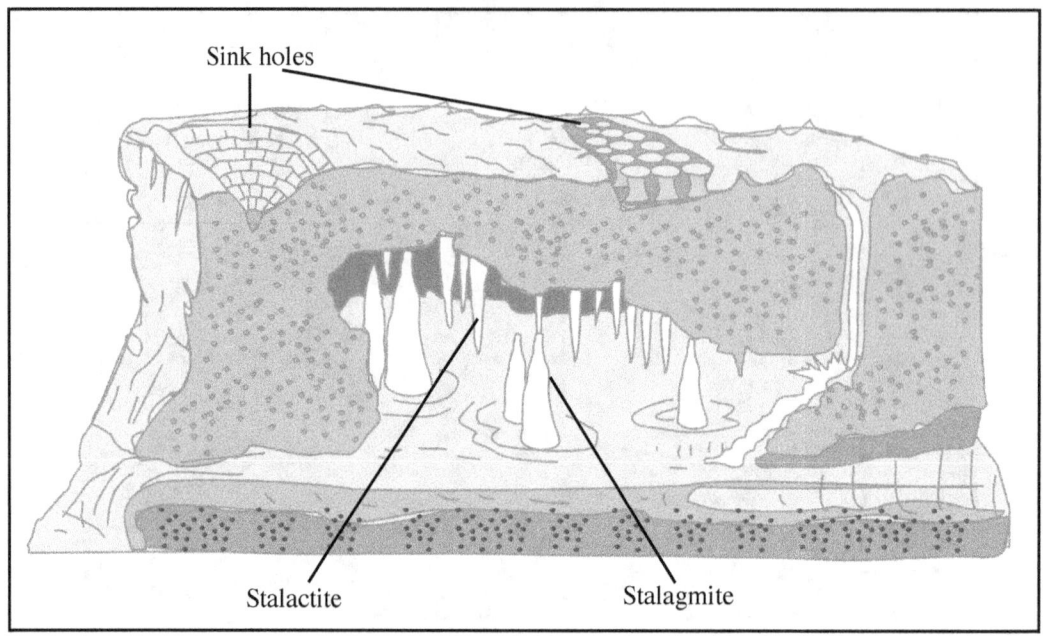

Fig. 113 : Structure of a limestone cavern

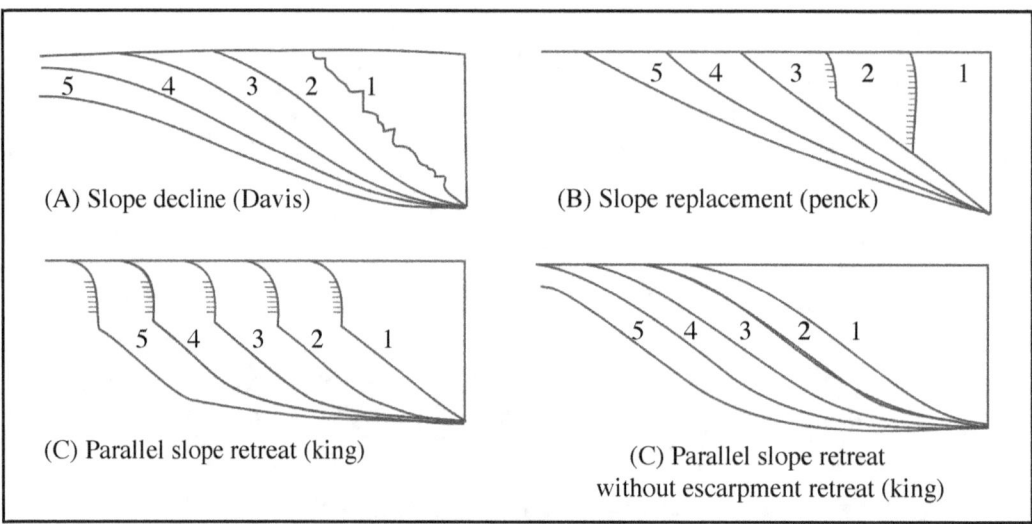

(A) Slope decline (Davis)

(B) Slope replacement (penck)

(C) Parallel slope retreat (king)

(C) Parallel slope retreat
without escarpment retreat (king)

Fig. 114 : Models of slope evolution

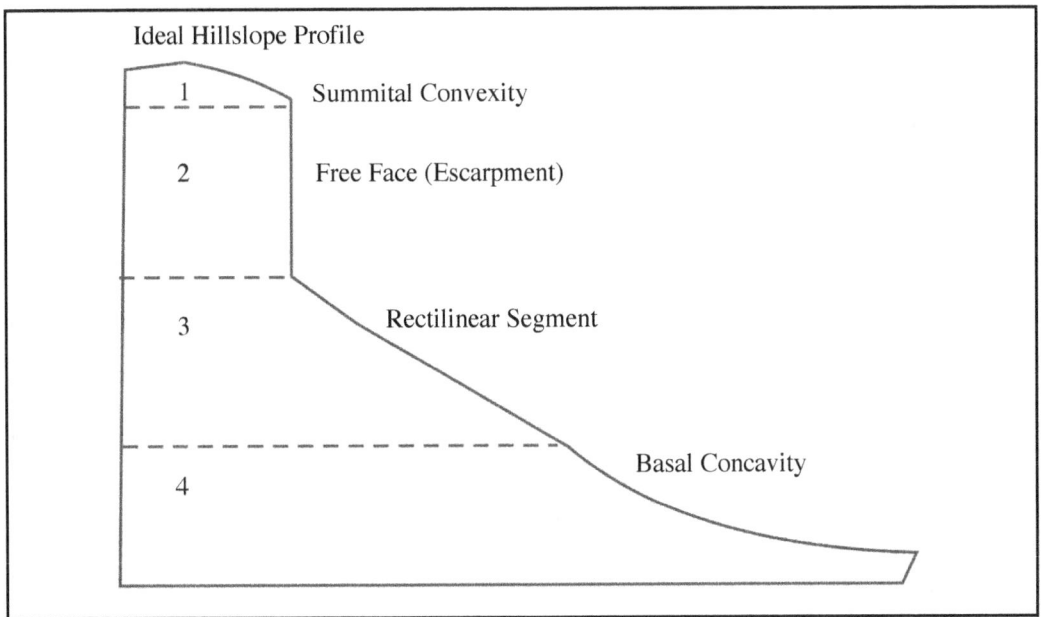

Fig. 115 : Major slope Segments

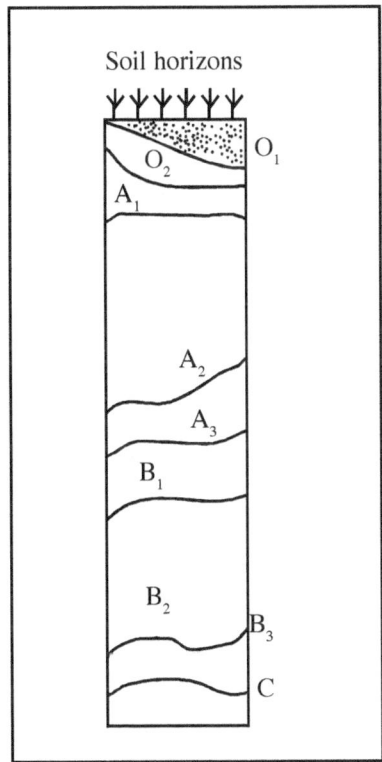

Fig. 116 : Soil section

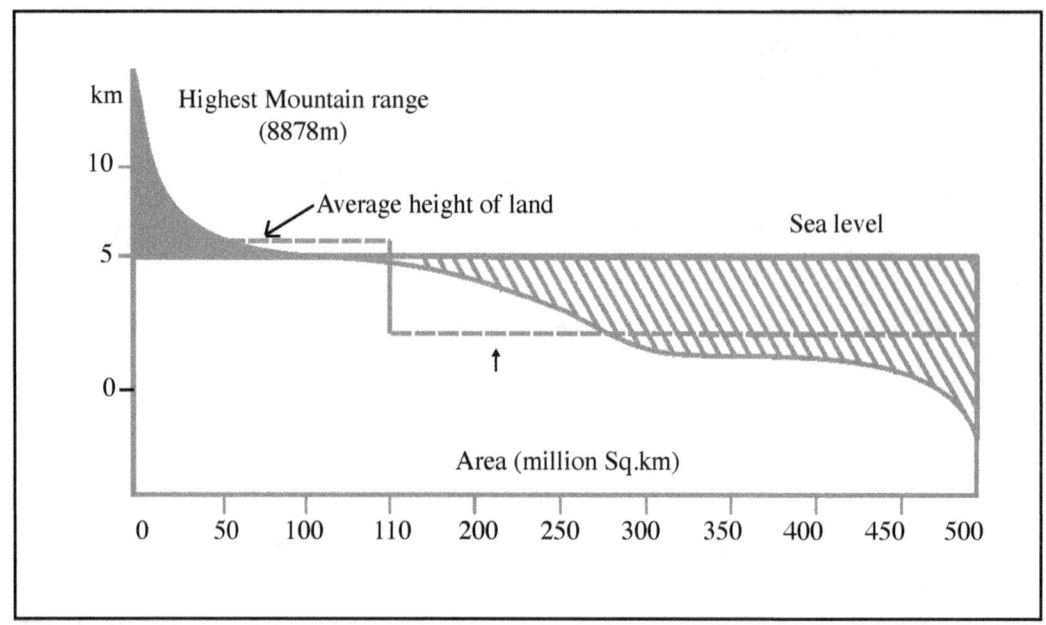

Fig. 117 : Hypsometric Curve

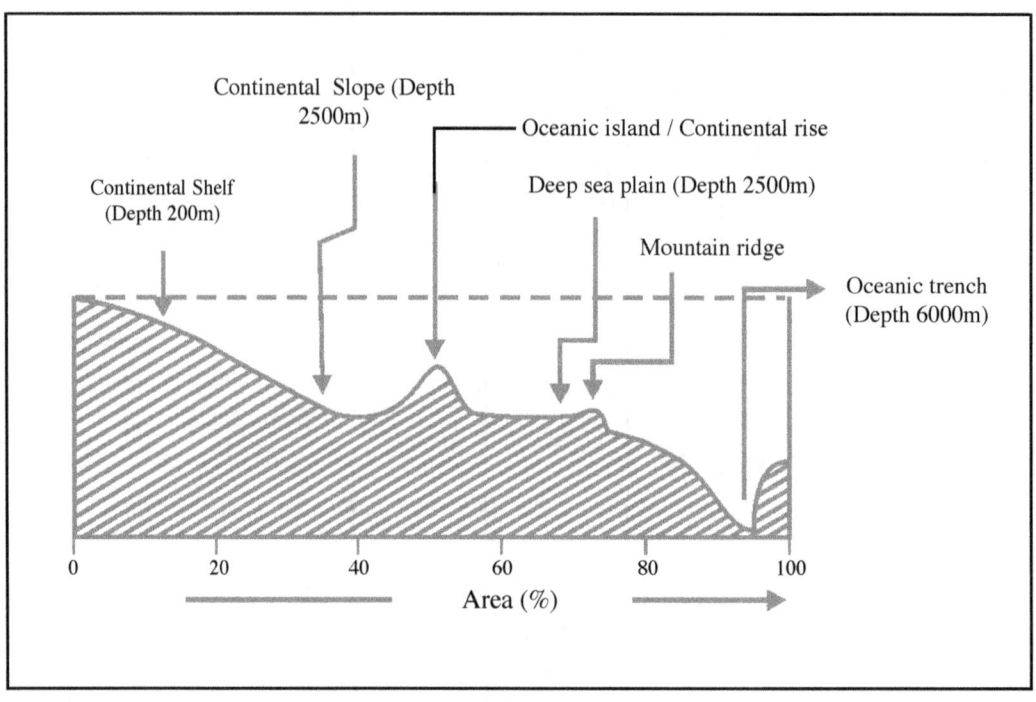

Fig. 118 : Ocean Floor

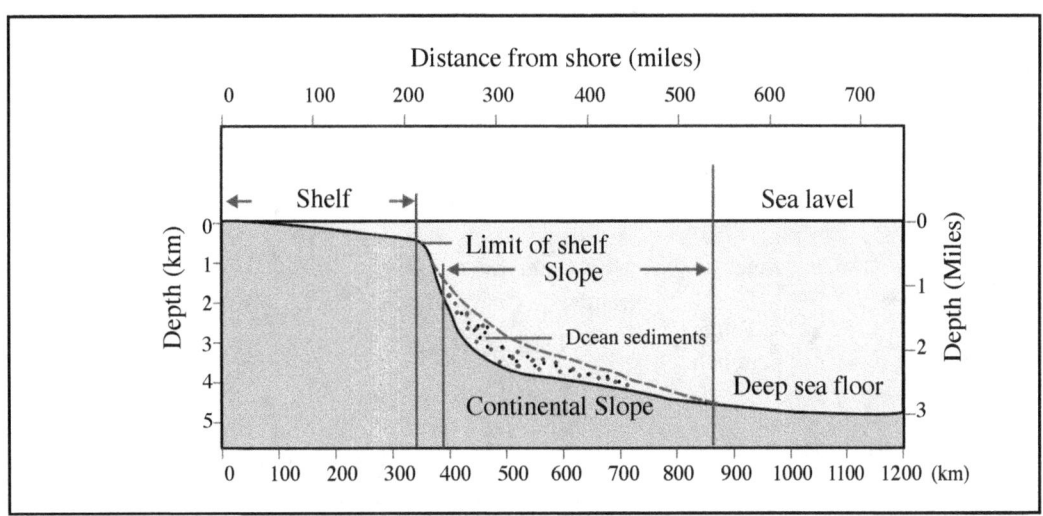

Fig. 119 : Continental Shelf and slope

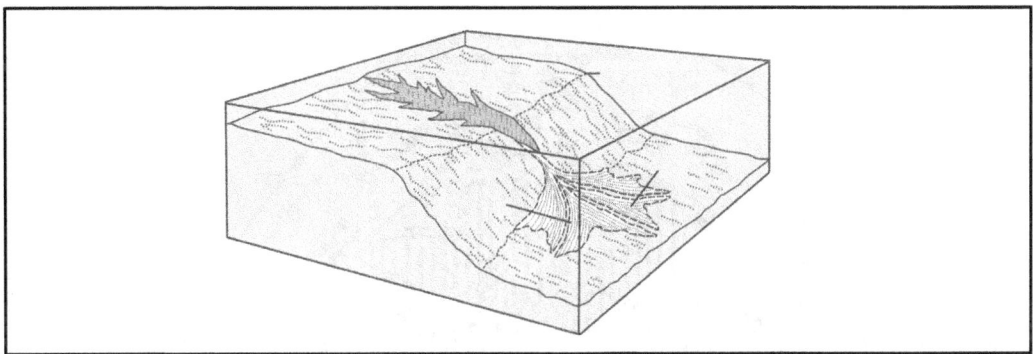

Fig. 120 : Valleys on Continental Slope

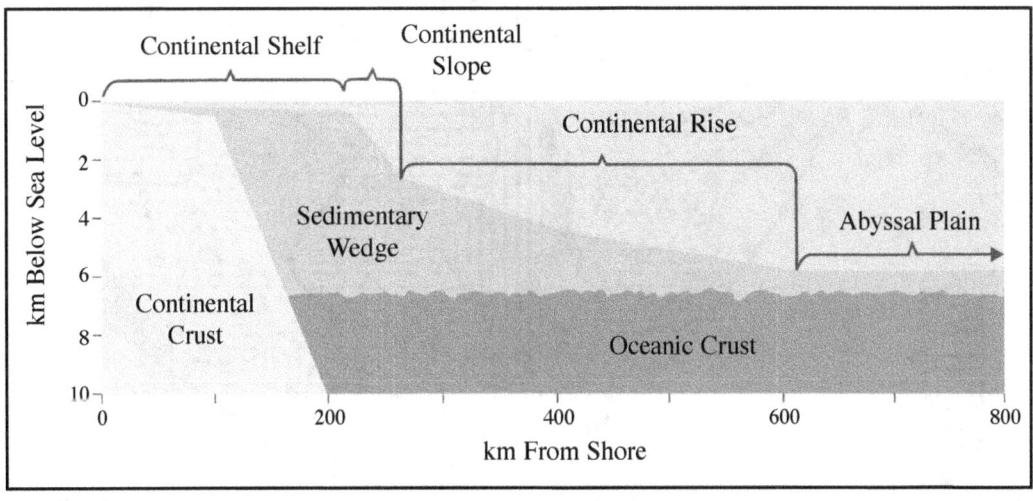

Fig. 121 : Abyssal Plain

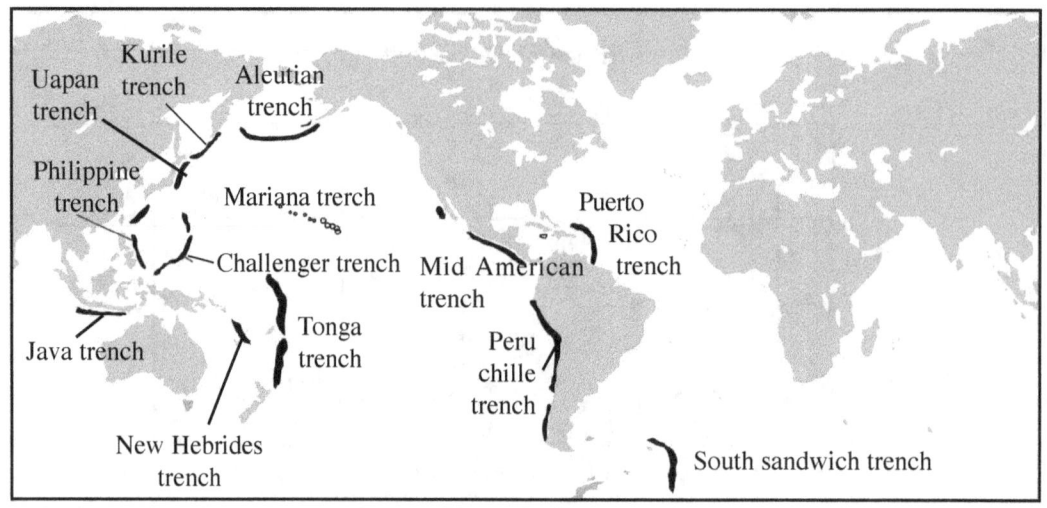

Fig. 122 : Oceanic trenches

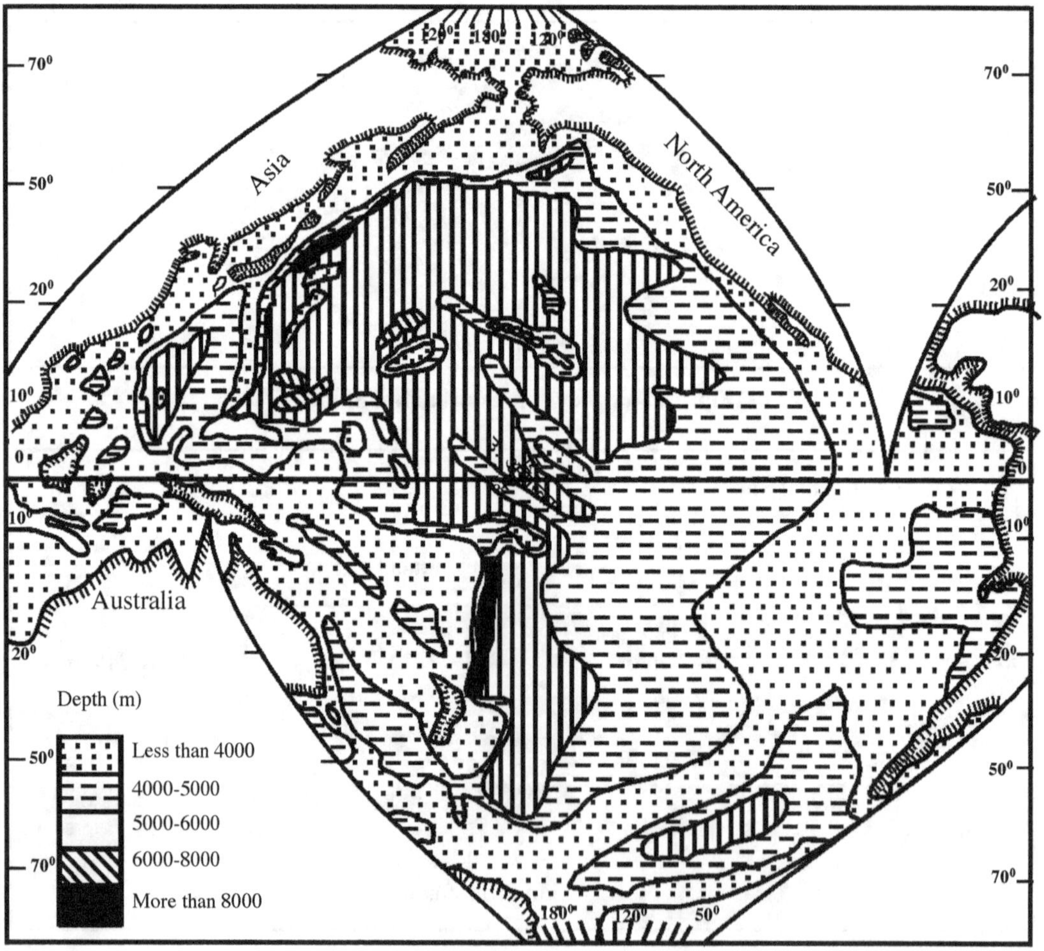

Depth (m)

	Less than 4000
	4000-5000
	5000-6000
	6000-8000
	More than 8000

Fig. 123 : Relief of Pacific Ocean bed

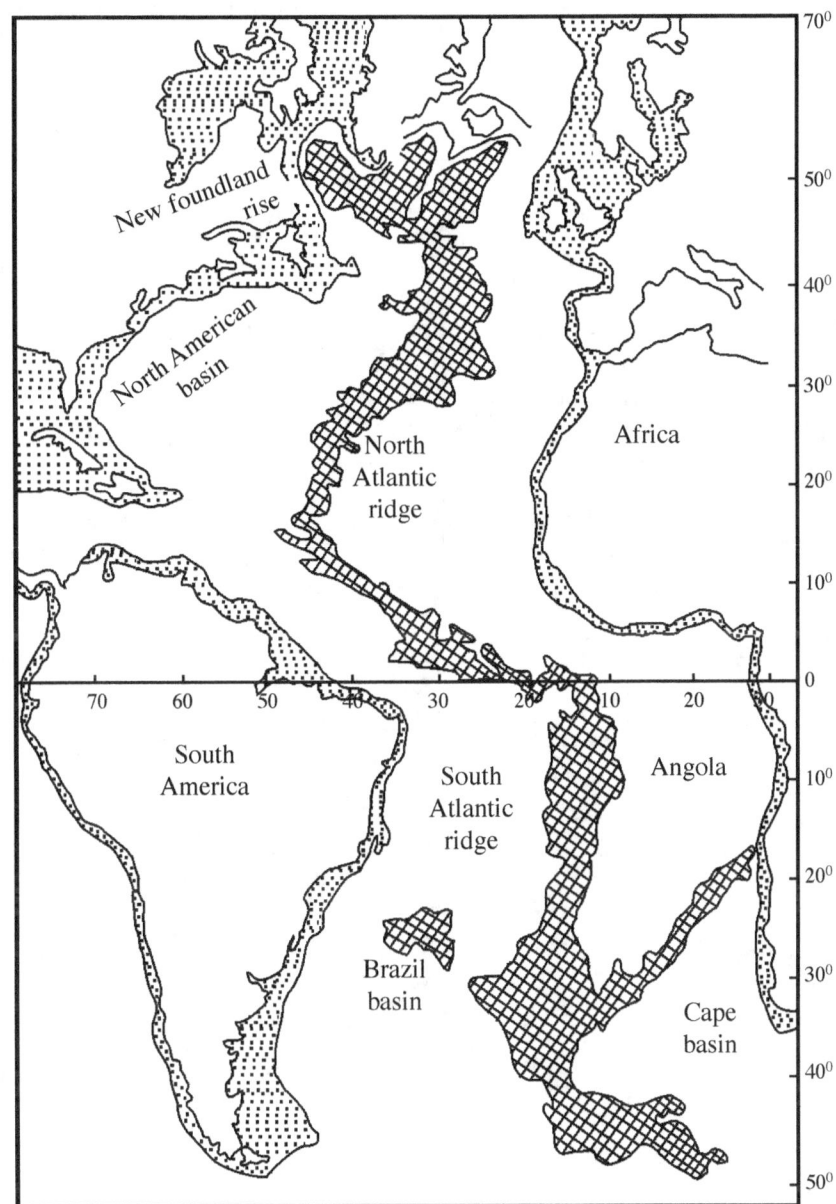

Fig. 124 : Relief of Atlantic Ocean bed

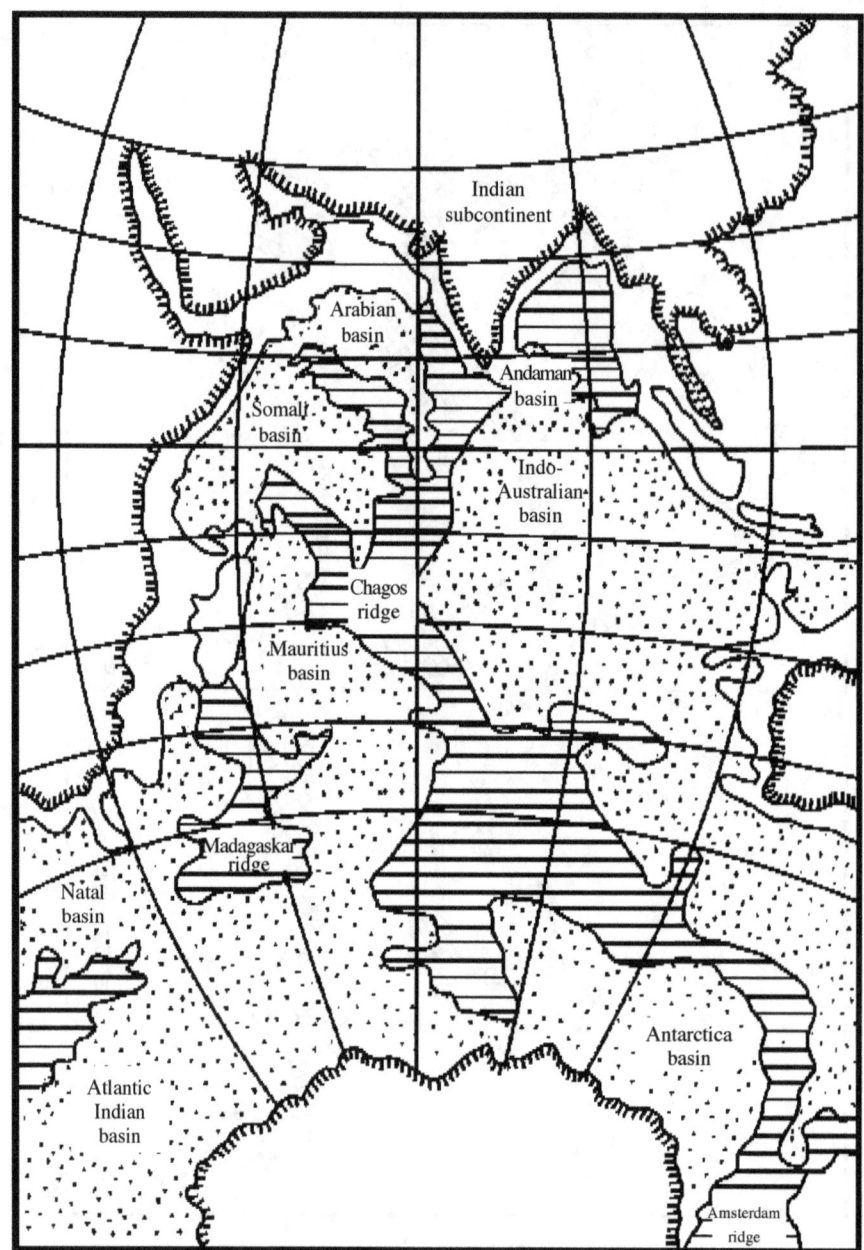

Fig. 125 : Relief of Indian Ocean bed

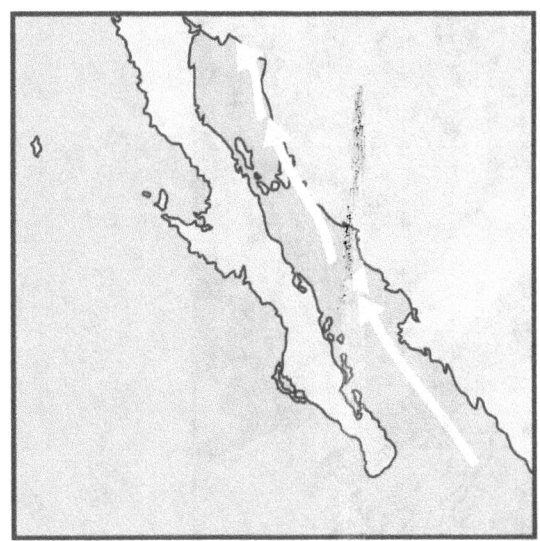

Fig. 126 : Gulf

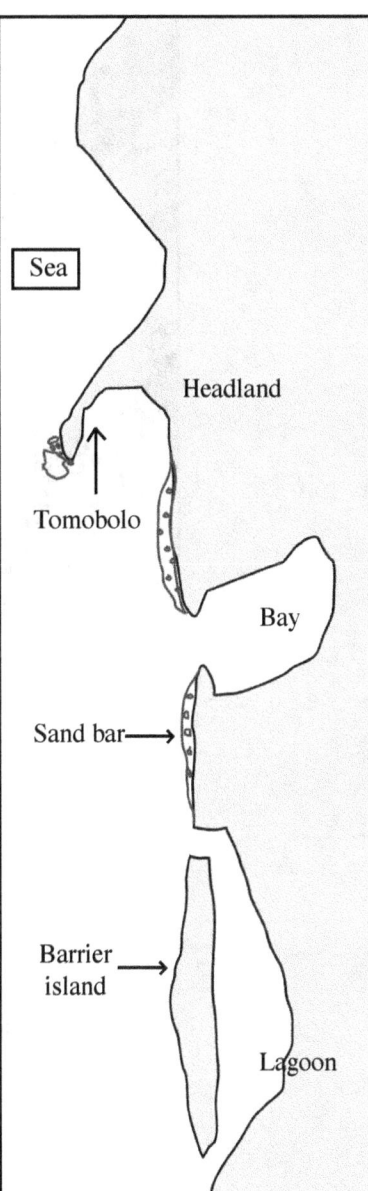

Fig. 127 : Ria Coast

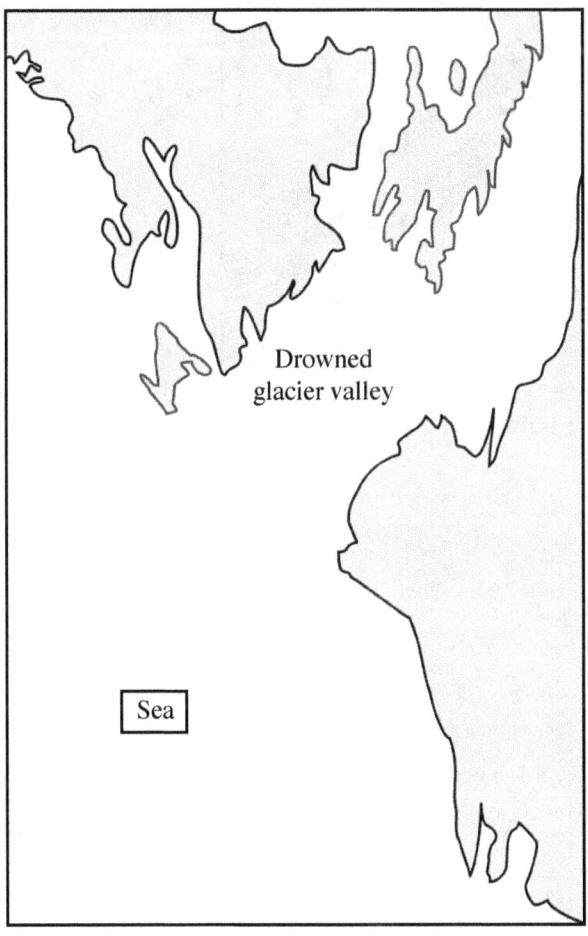

Fig. 128 : Fjord Coast

Fig. 129 : Dalmatian Coast

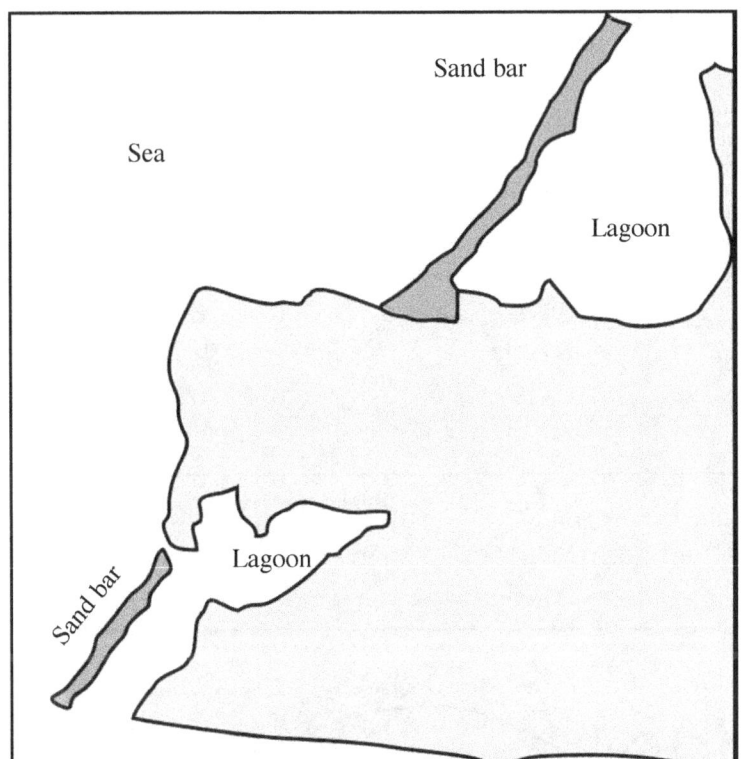

Fig. 130 : Haff Nehrung Coast

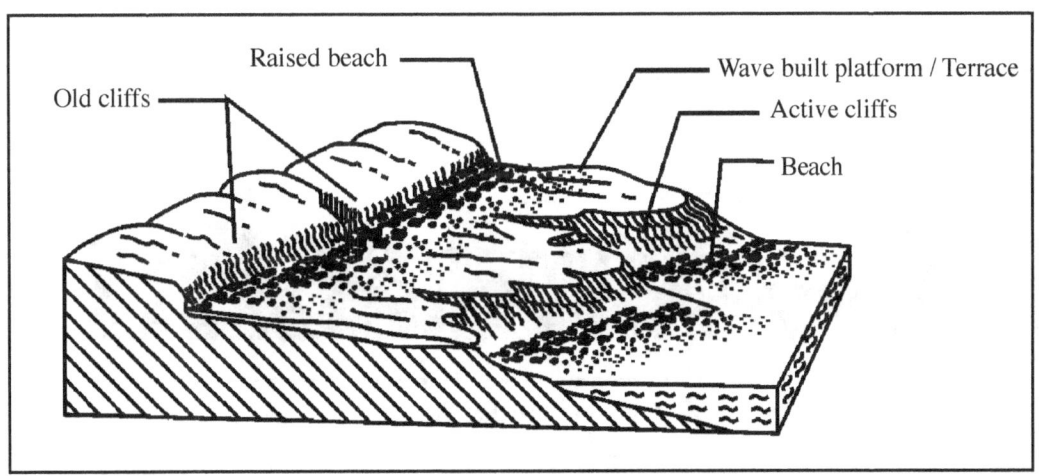

Fig. 131 : Emergent upland Coast

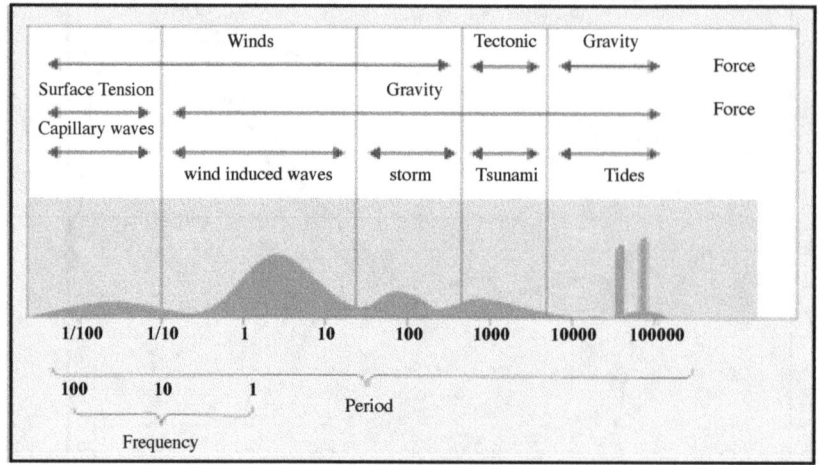

Fig. 132 : An Ideal sea wave

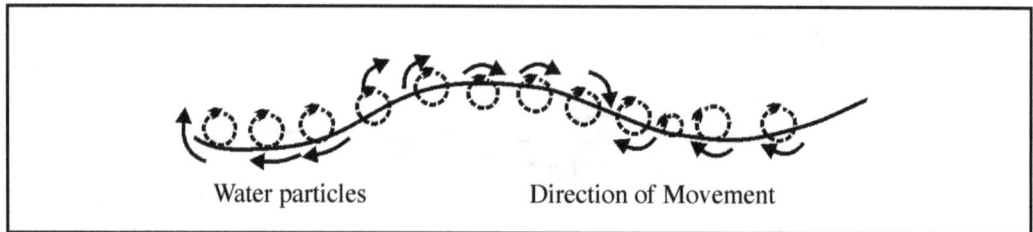

Fig. 133 : Movement of water droplets in a sea wave

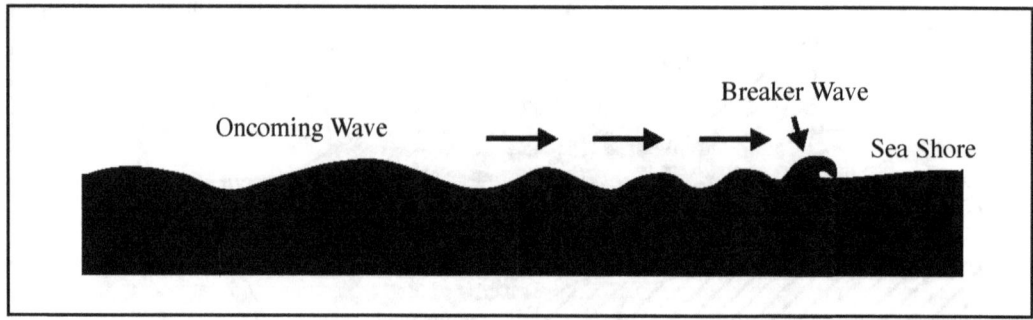

Fig. 134 : Breaker Wave

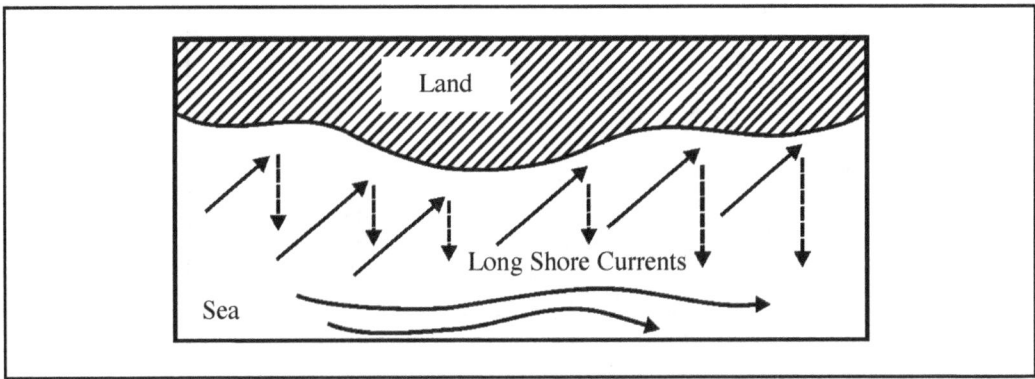

Fig. 135 : Long Shore Current

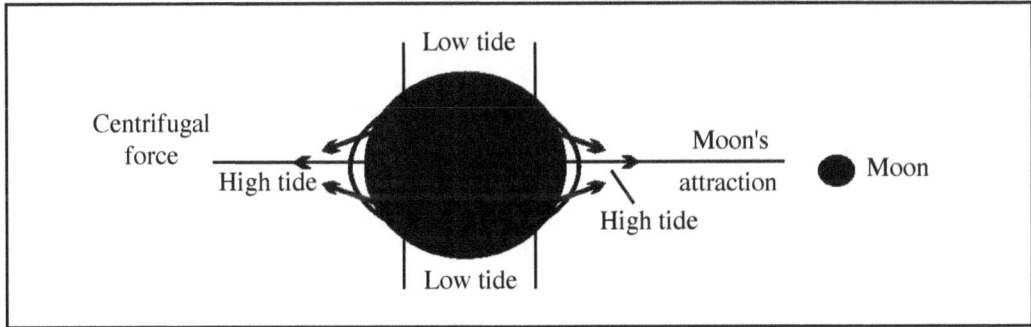

Fig. 136 : Formation of Tides (Equillibrium Theory)

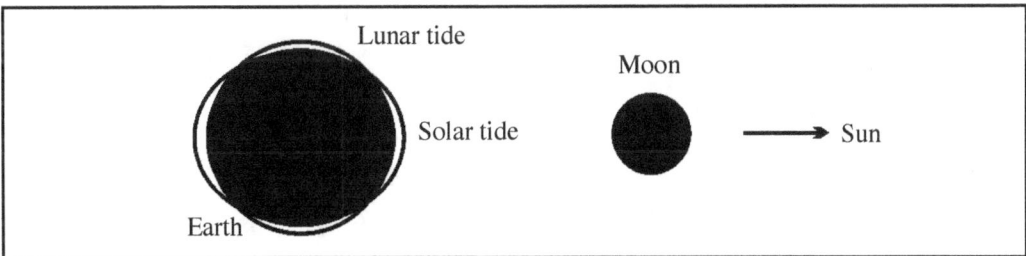

Fig. 137 : Spring tide

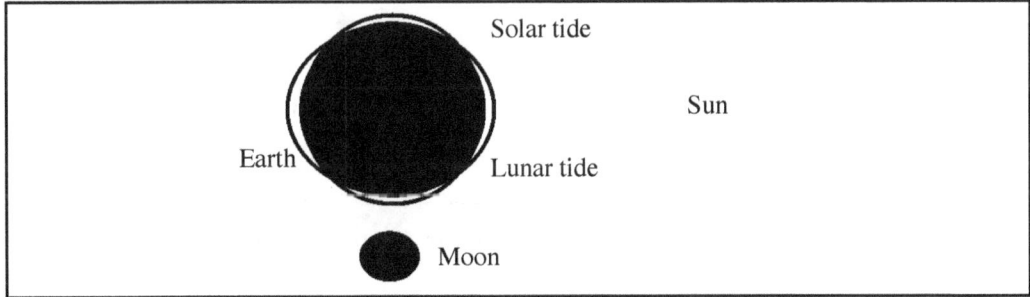

Fig. 138 : Neap tide

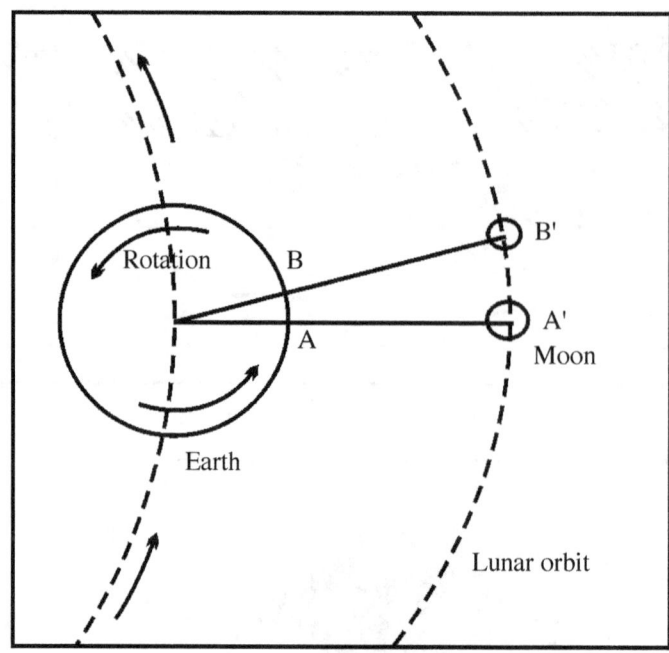

Fig. 139 : Daily lag in high tide

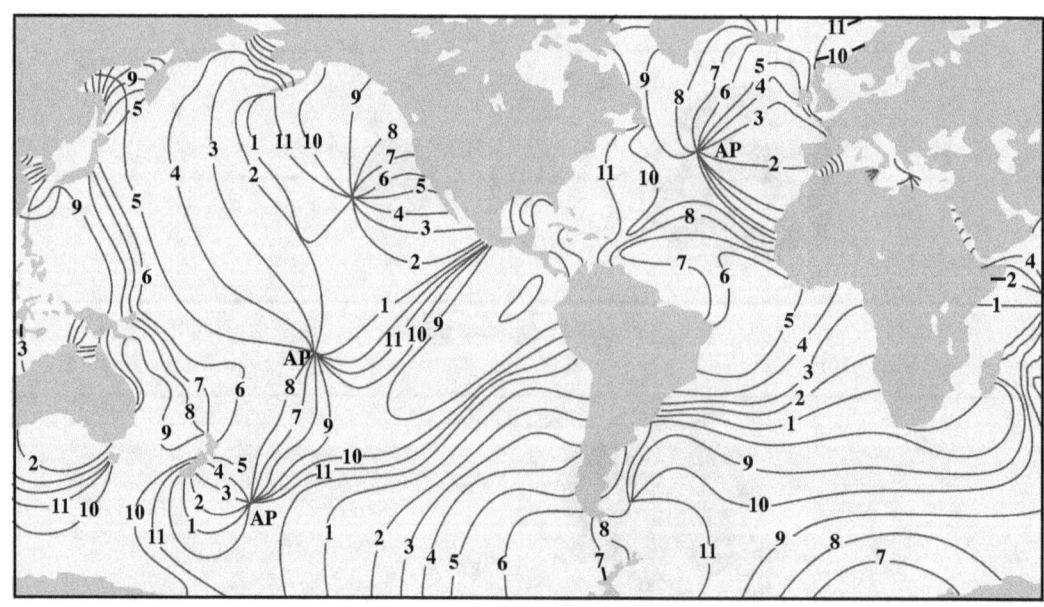

Fig. 140 : Amphidromic Points and Cotidal Lines

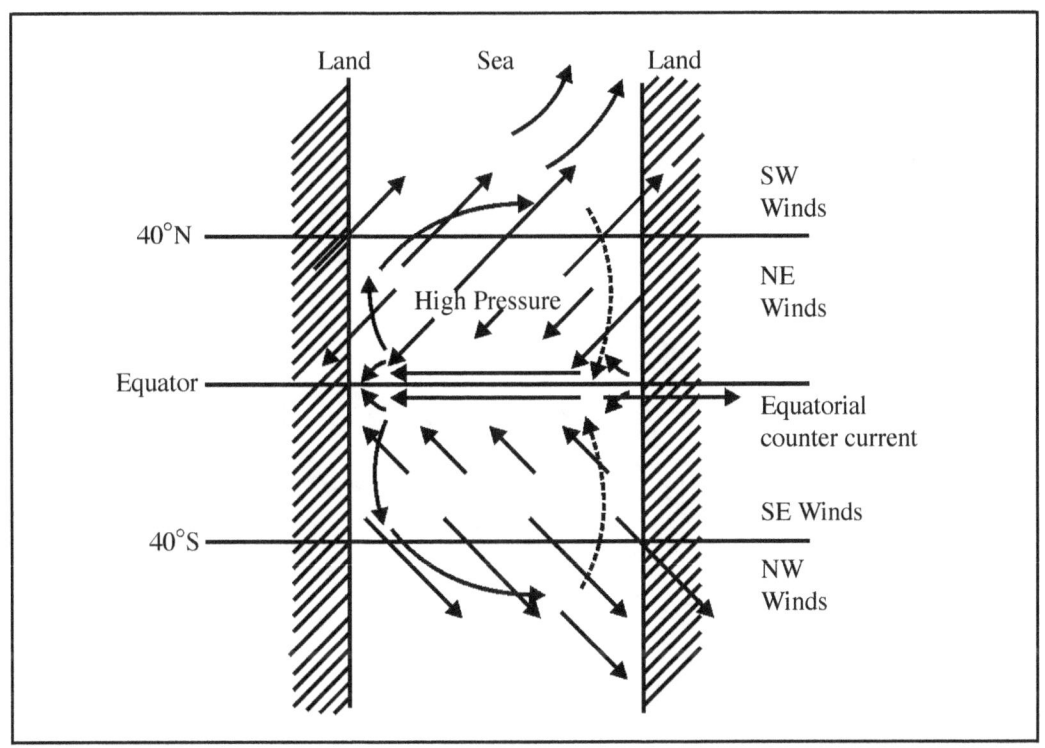

Fig. 141 : Planetary winds and ocean currents

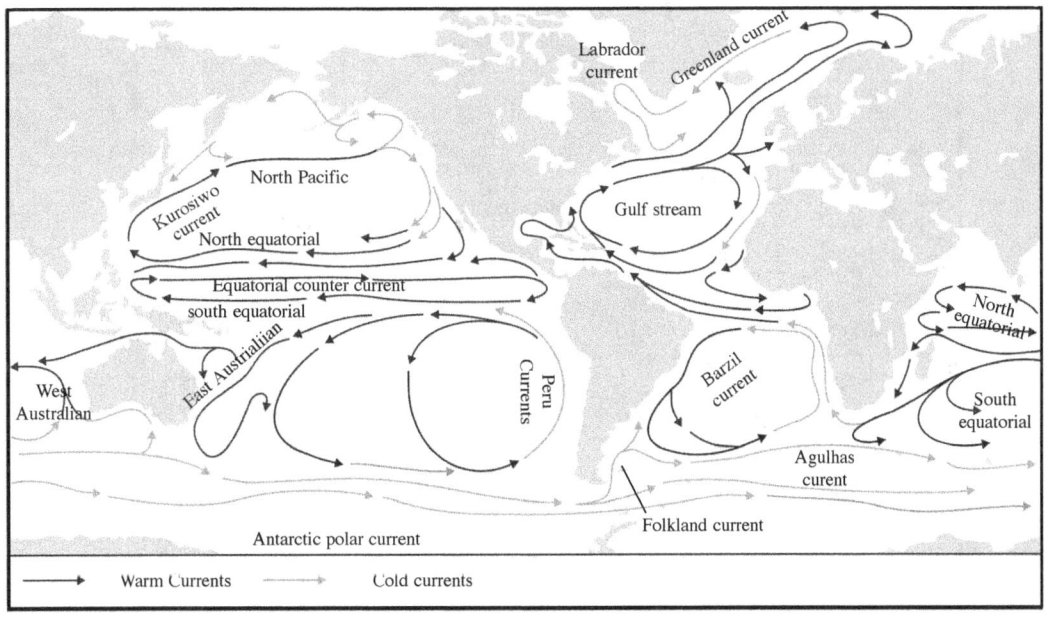

Fig. 142 : Ocean Currents

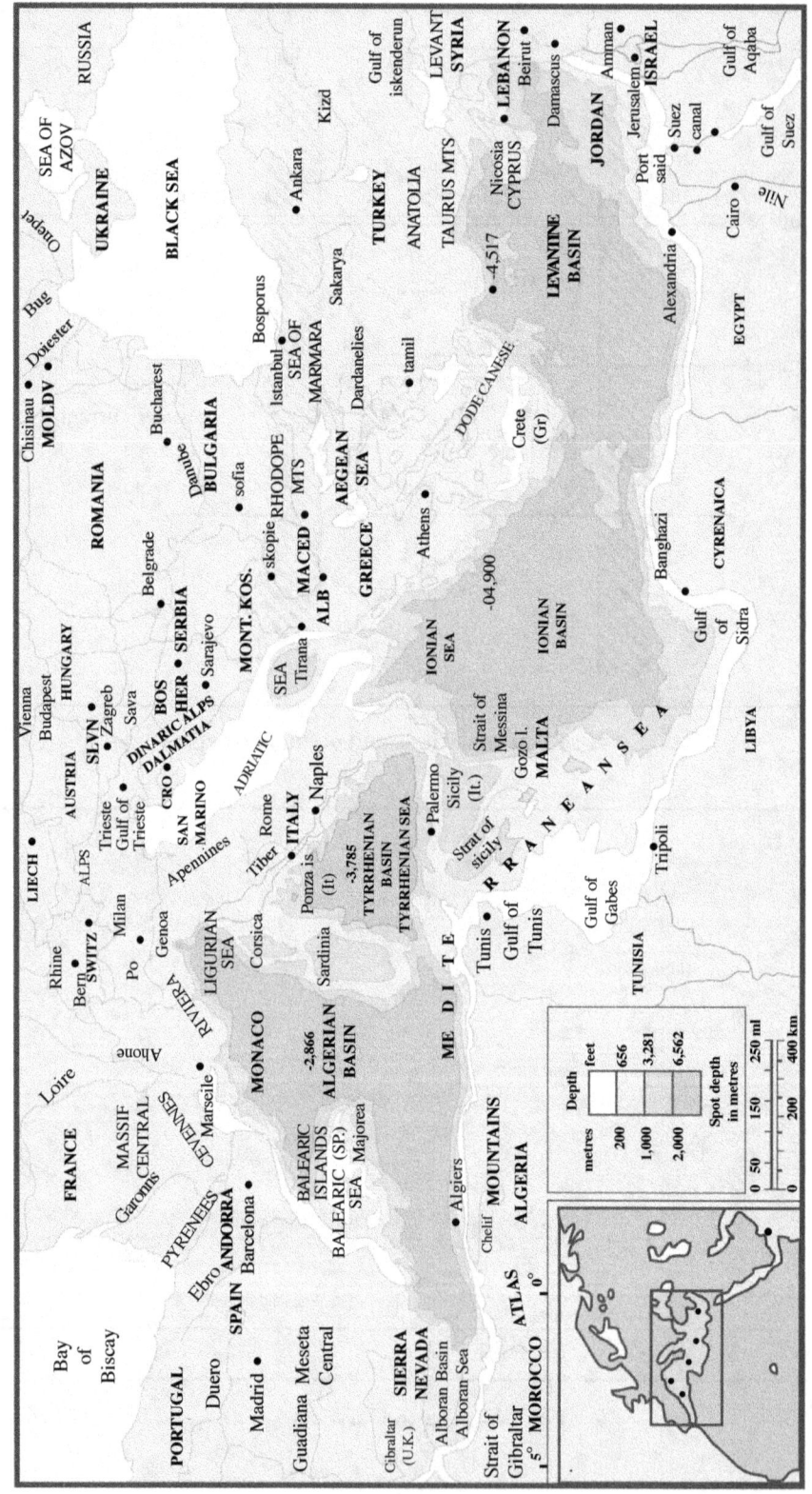

Fig. 143 : Mediterranean Sea

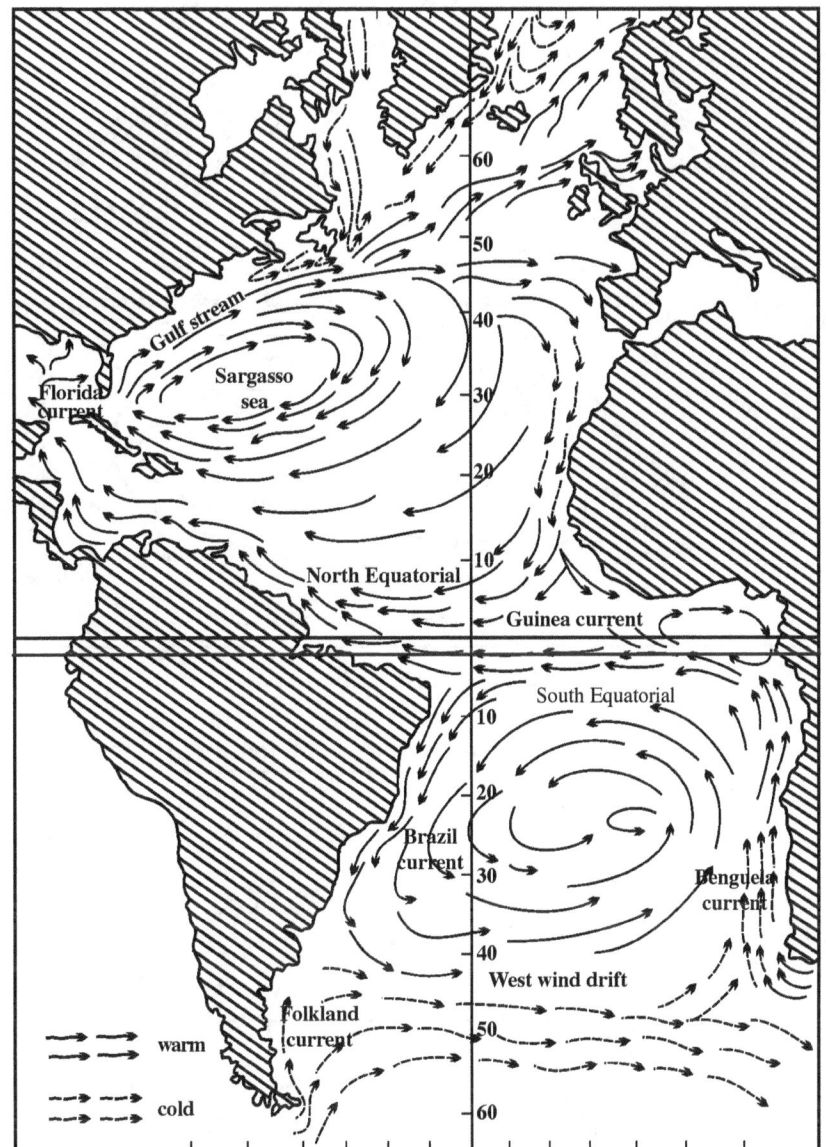

Fig. 144 : Currents in Atlantic Ocean

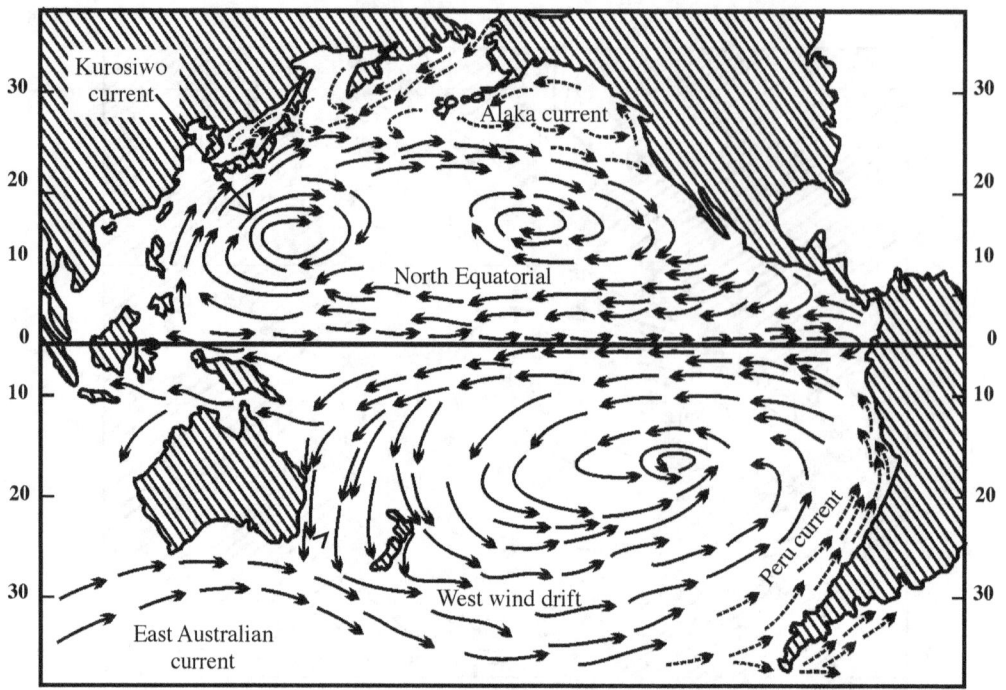

Fig. 145 : Current in Pacific Ocean

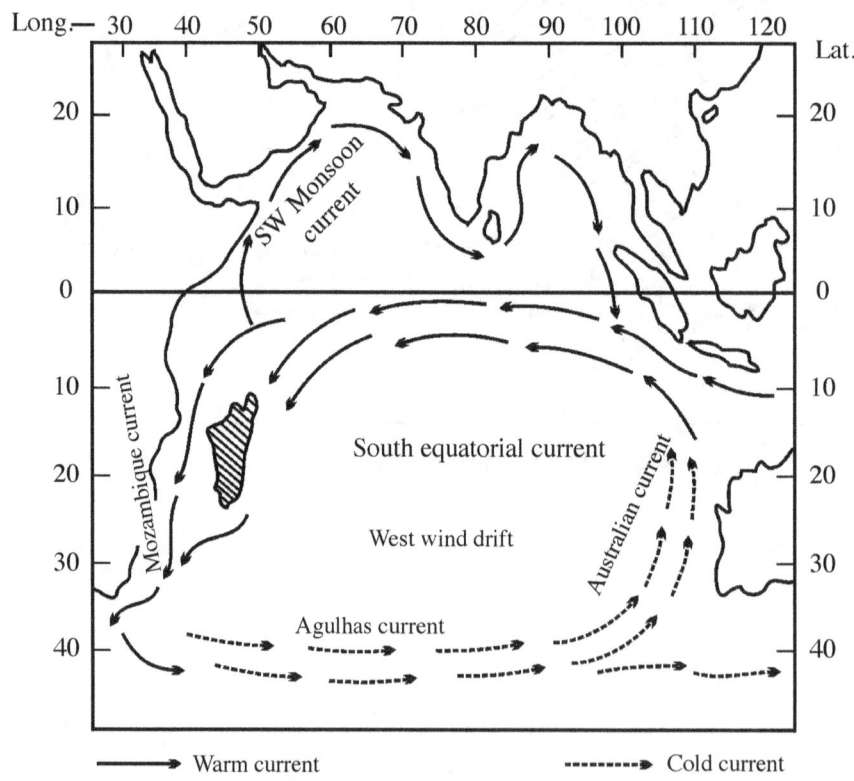

──────▶ Warm current   ------------▶ Cold current

Fig. 146 : Currents in Indian Ocean

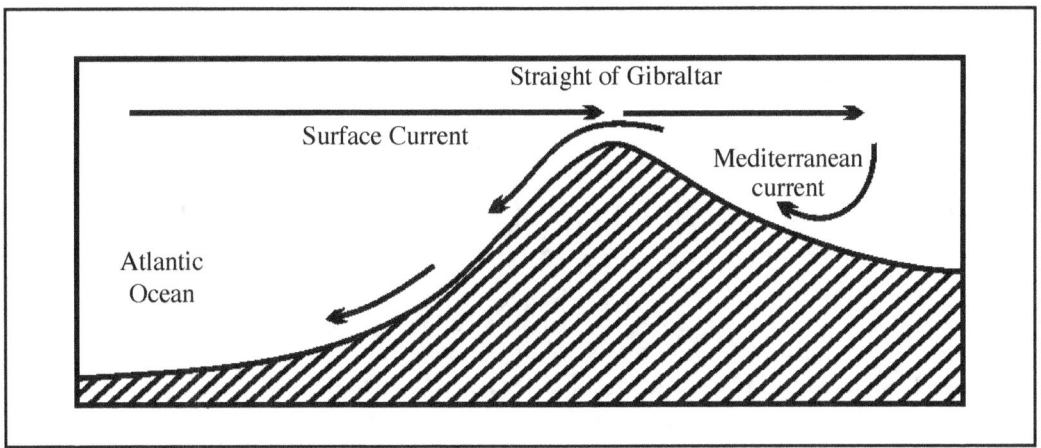

Fig. 147 : Salinity of Partially Enclosed Sea

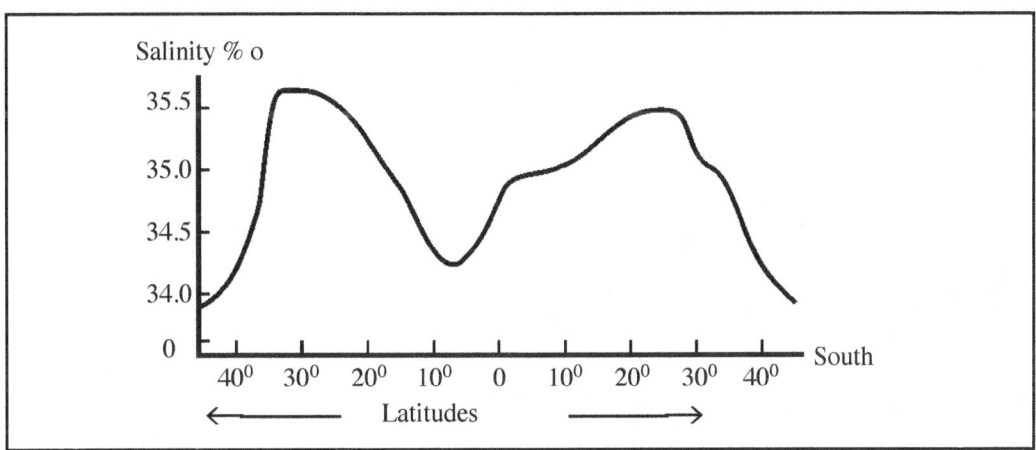

Fig. 148 : Latitudinal Variation in Salinity

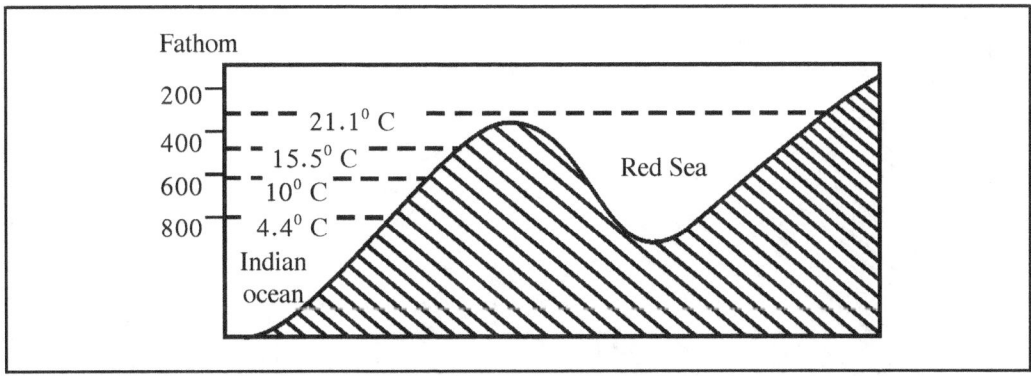

Fig. 149 : Variation in the salinity of open and land locked seas

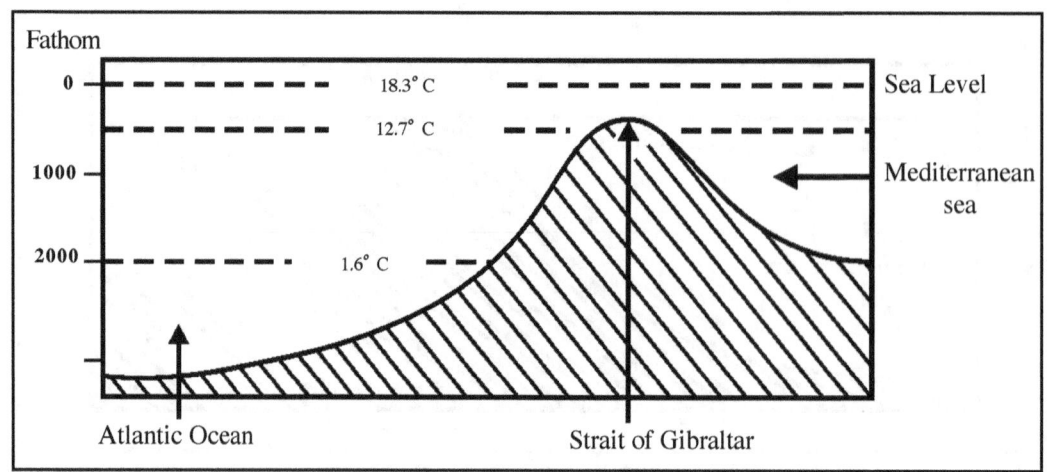

Fig. 150 : Temperature Variation in Atlantic Ocean and Mediterranean Sea

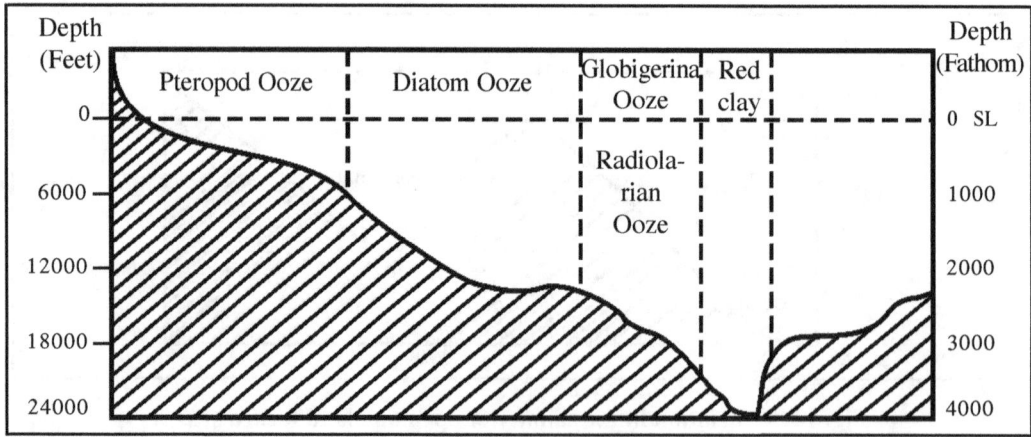

Fig. 151 : Distribution of Terrigeneous deposits

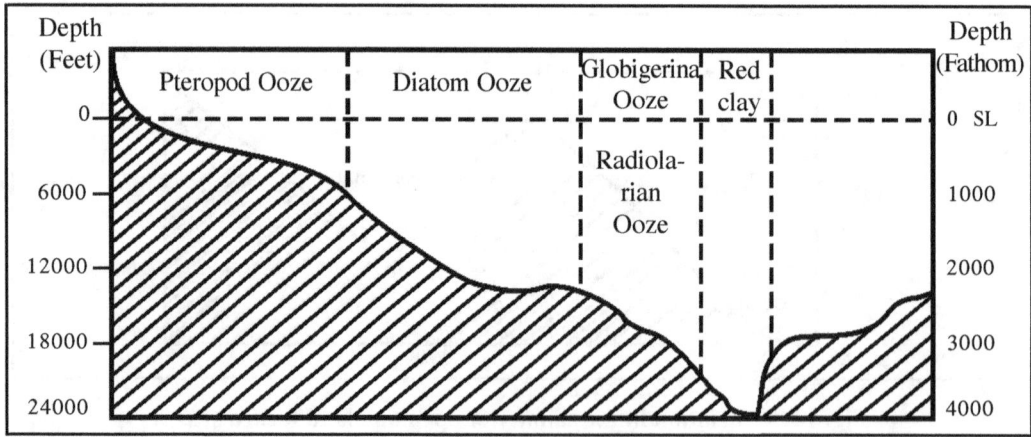

Fig. 152 : Pelagic Ooze

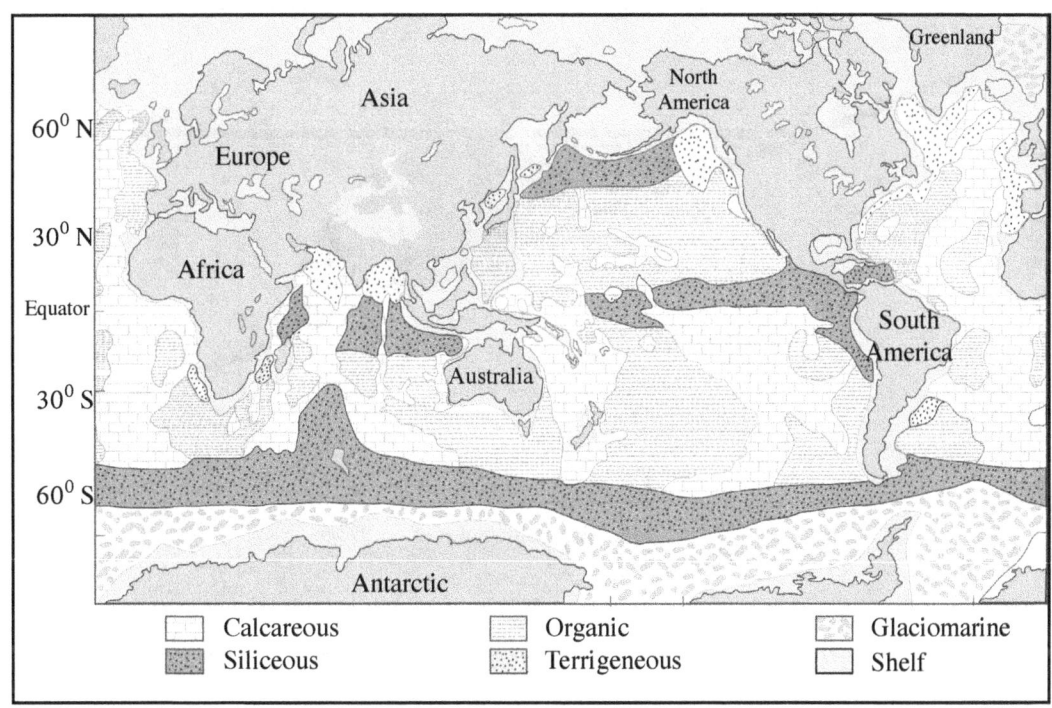

Fig. 153 : Distribution of Marine Deposits

Calcareous	Organic	Glaciomarine
Siliceous	Terrigeneous	Shelf

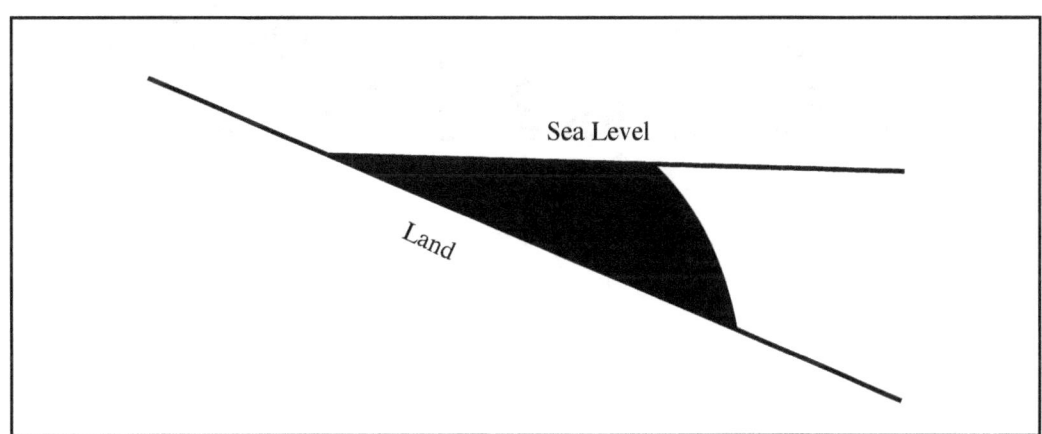

Fig. 154 : Fringing reef

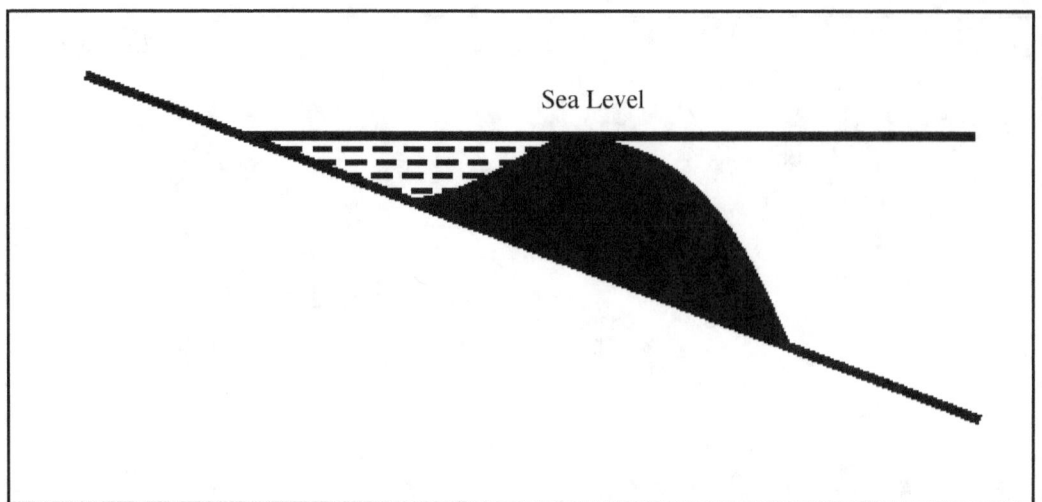

Fig. 155 : Barrier reef

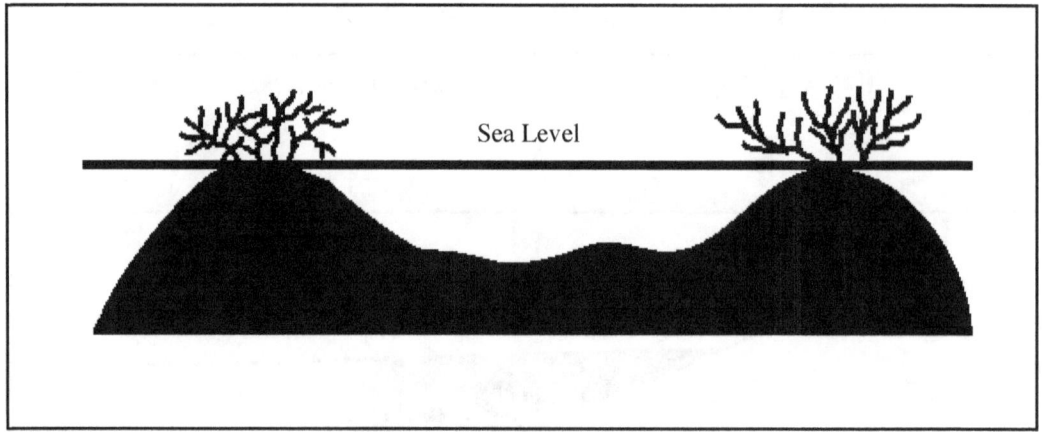

Fig. 156 : Atoll

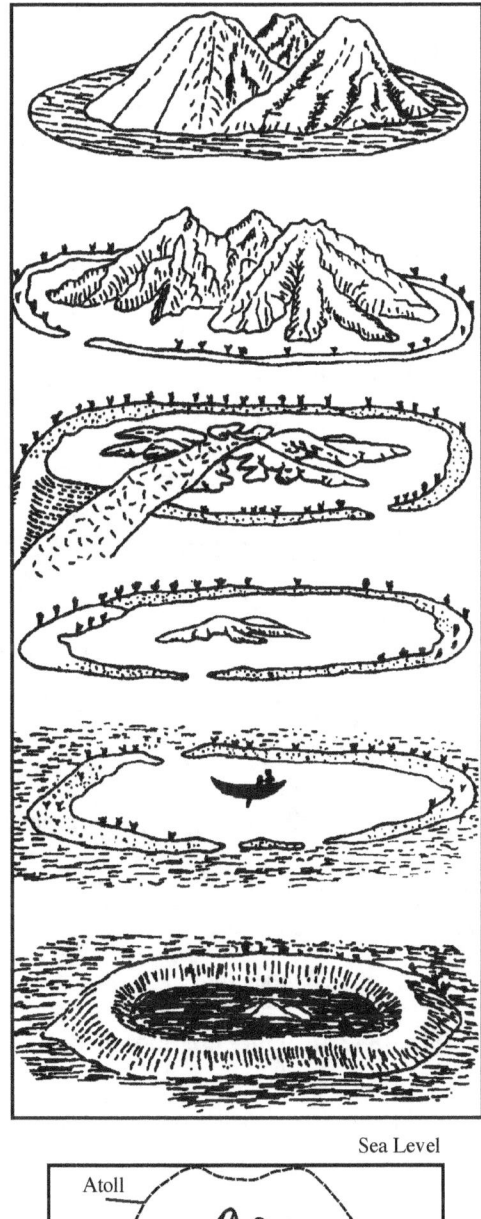

Sea Level

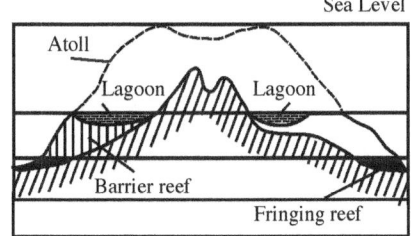

Fig. 157 : Formation of Atolls by slow subsidence

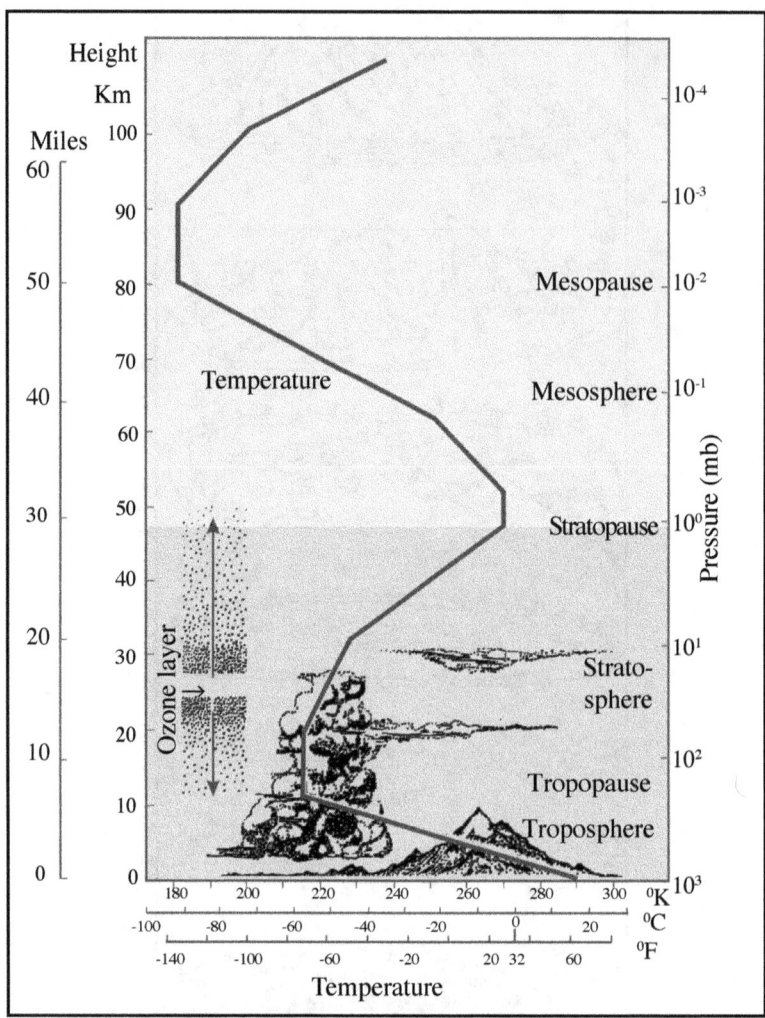

Fig. 158 : Structure of atmosphere

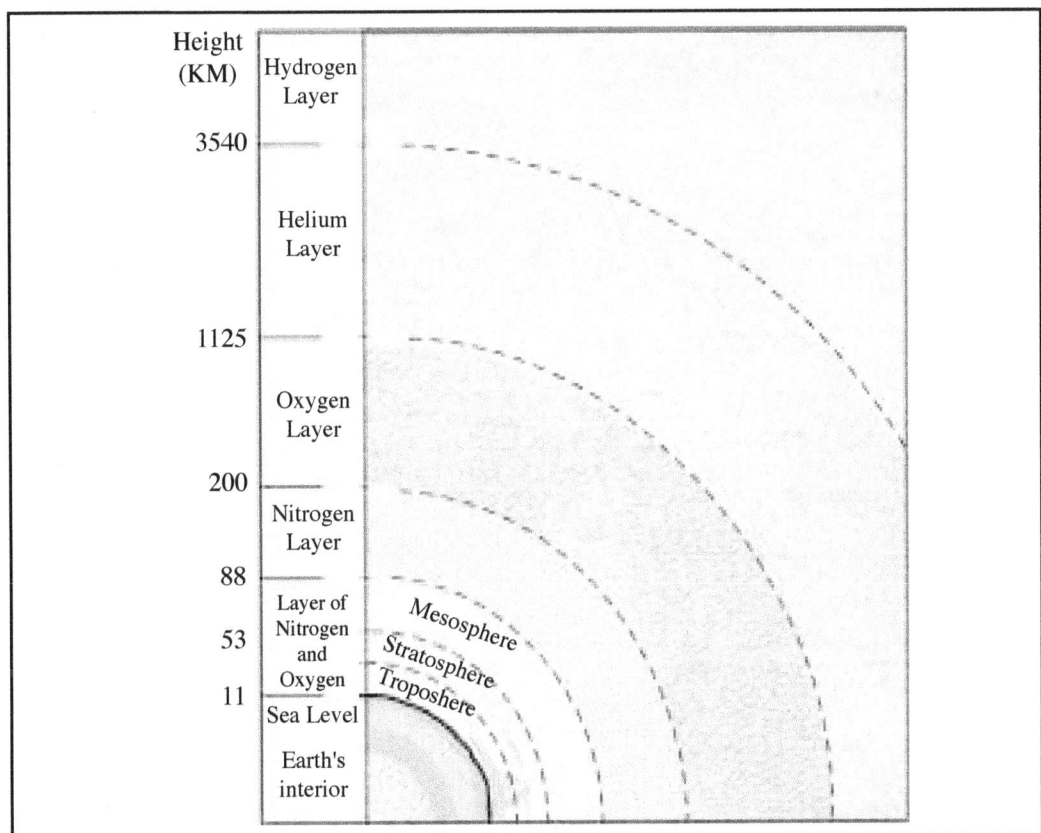

Fig. 159 : Chemical Zones in the atmosphere

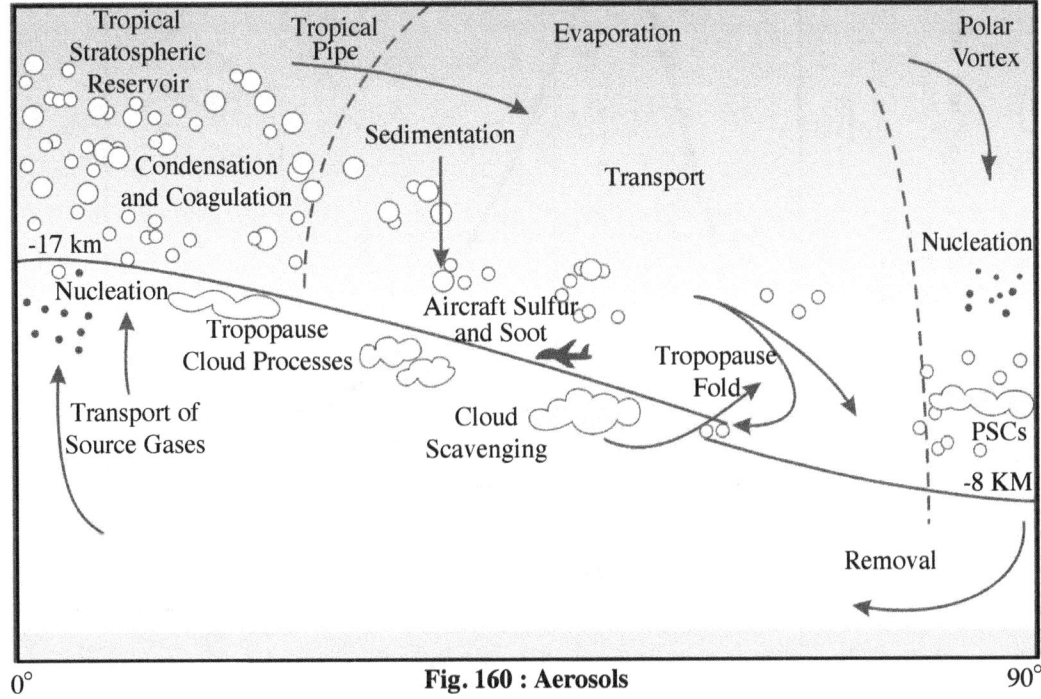

Fig. 160 : Aerosols

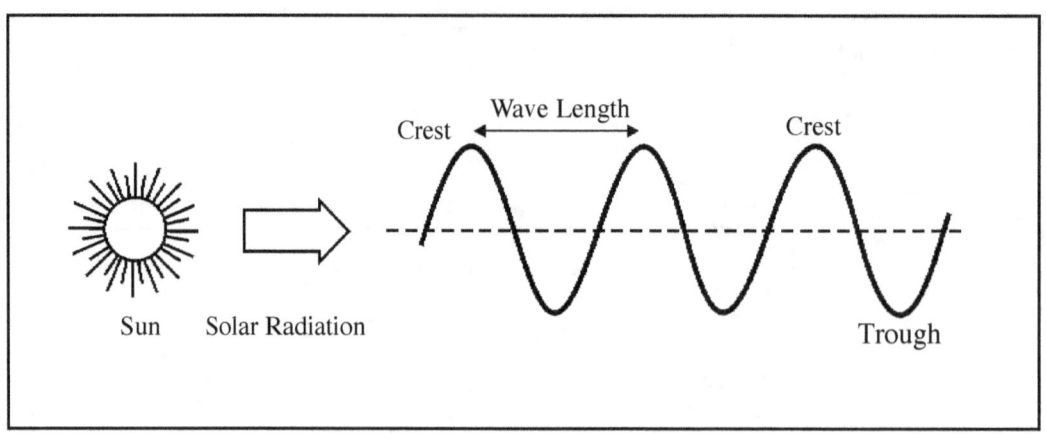

Fig. 161 : Electro Magnetic Wave

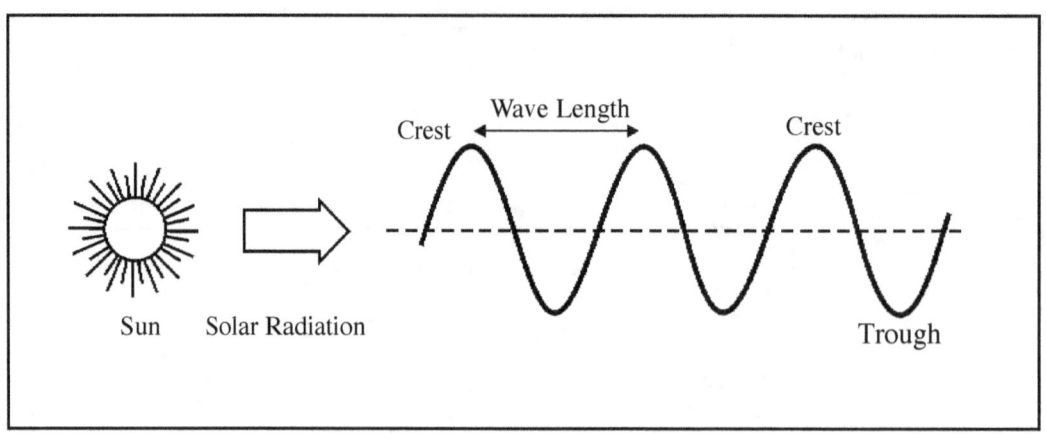

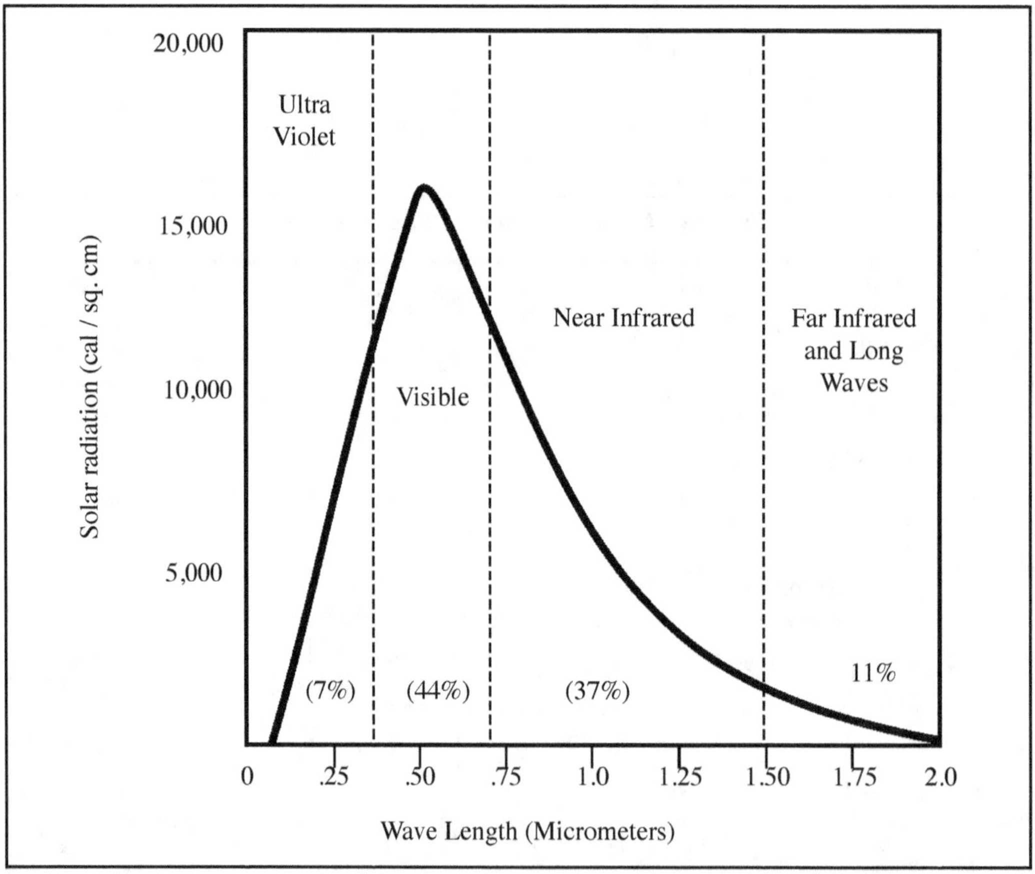

Fig. 162 : Regions of Electromagnetic Spectrum

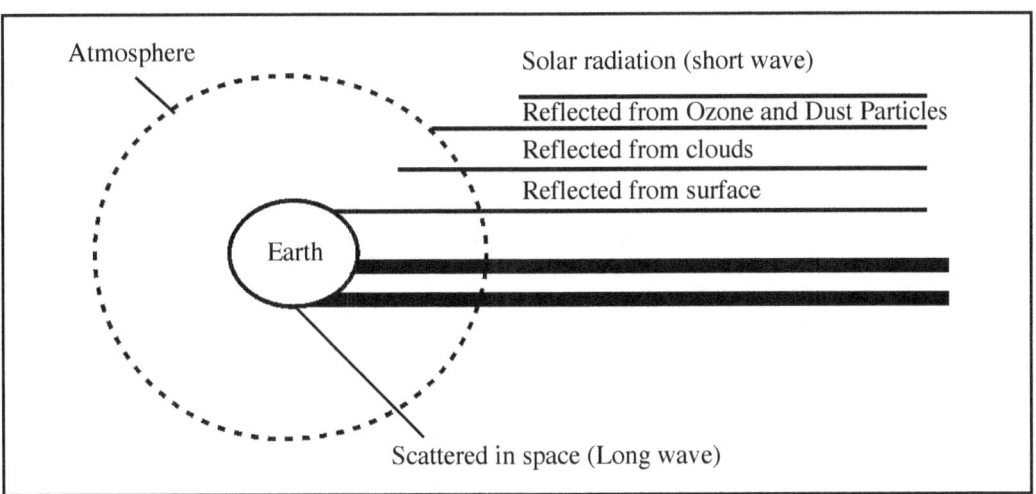

Fig. 163 : Distribution of Solar Radiation

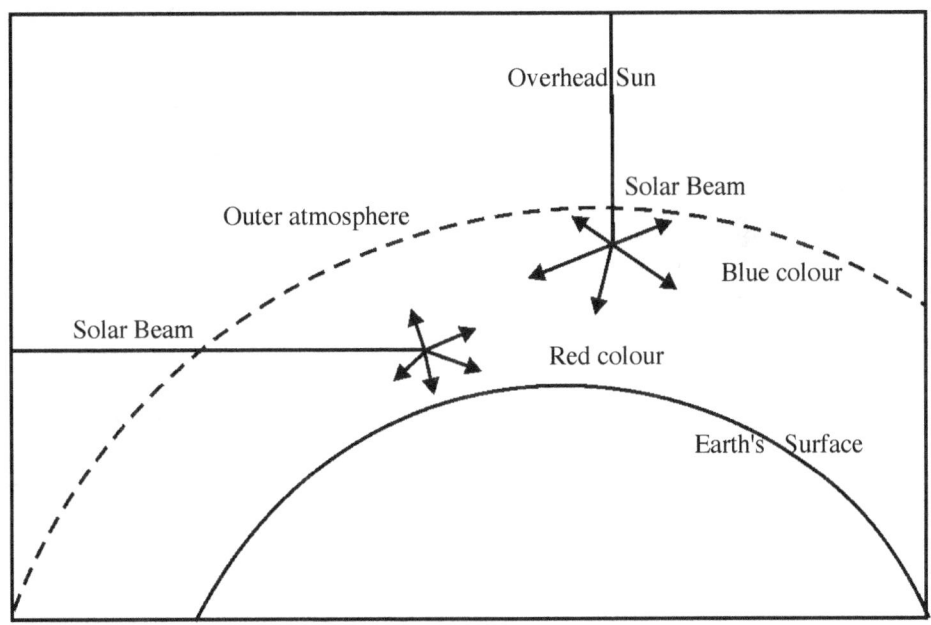

Fig. 164 : Solar Radiation and sky colour

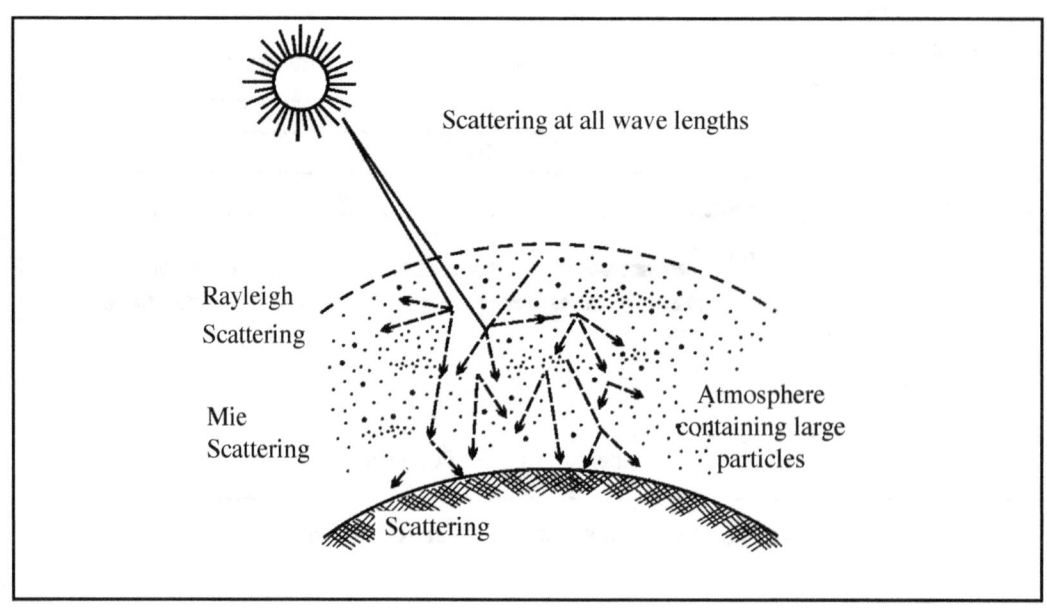

Fig. 165 : Scattering

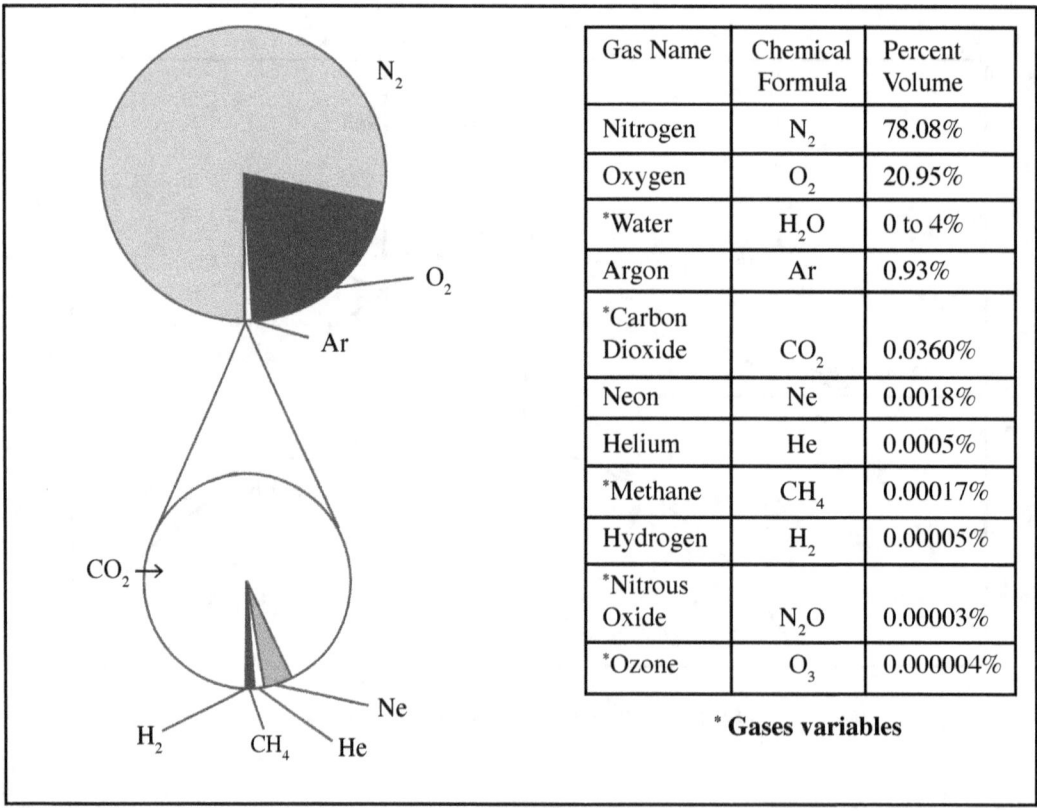

Gas Name	Chemical Formula	Percent Volume
Nitrogen	N_2	78.08%
Oxygen	O_2	20.95%
*Water	H_2O	0 to 4%
Argon	Ar	0.93%
*Carbon Dioxide	CO_2	0.0360%
Neon	Ne	0.0018%
Helium	He	0.0005%
*Methane	CH_4	0.00017%
Hydrogen	H_2	0.00005%
*Nitrous Oxide	N_2O	0.00003%
*Ozone	O_3	0.000004%

* Gases variables

Fig. 166 : Composition of Atmosphere

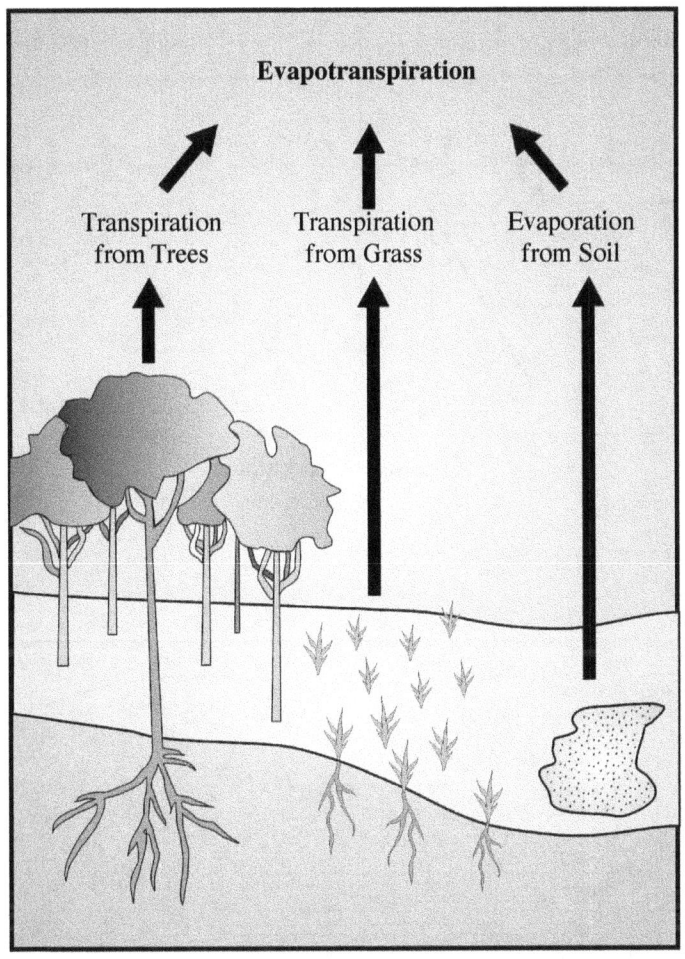

Fig. 167 : Evapotranspiration

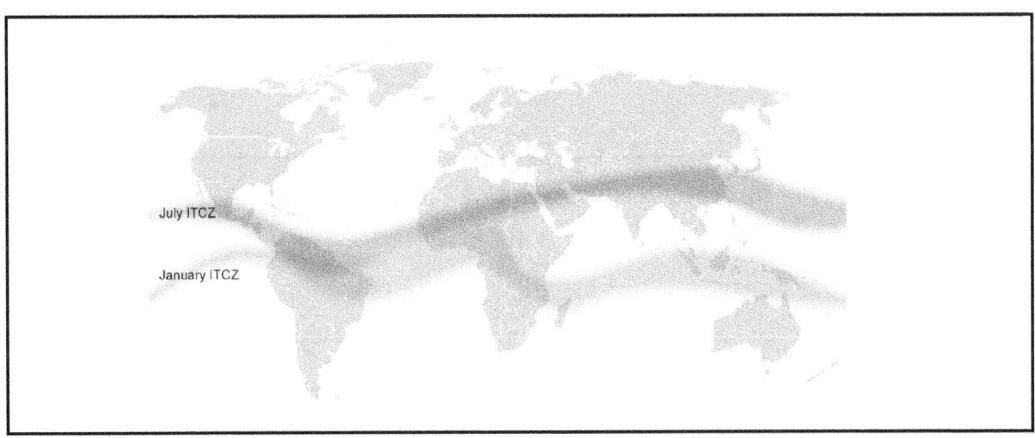

July ITCZ

January ITCZ

Fig. 168 : Intertropical Convergence Zone

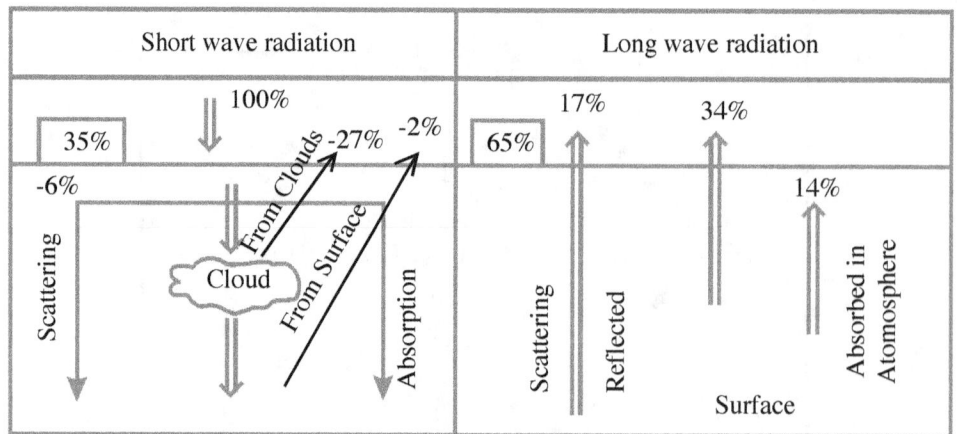

Fig. 169 : Heat balance

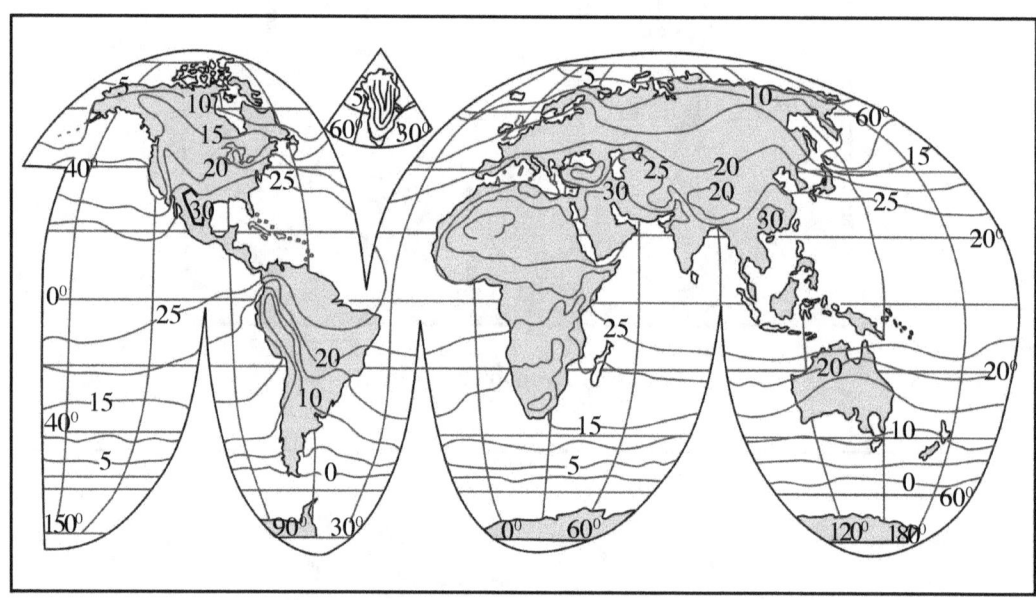

Fig. 170 : Distribution of average July Temperatures (Degree C⁰)

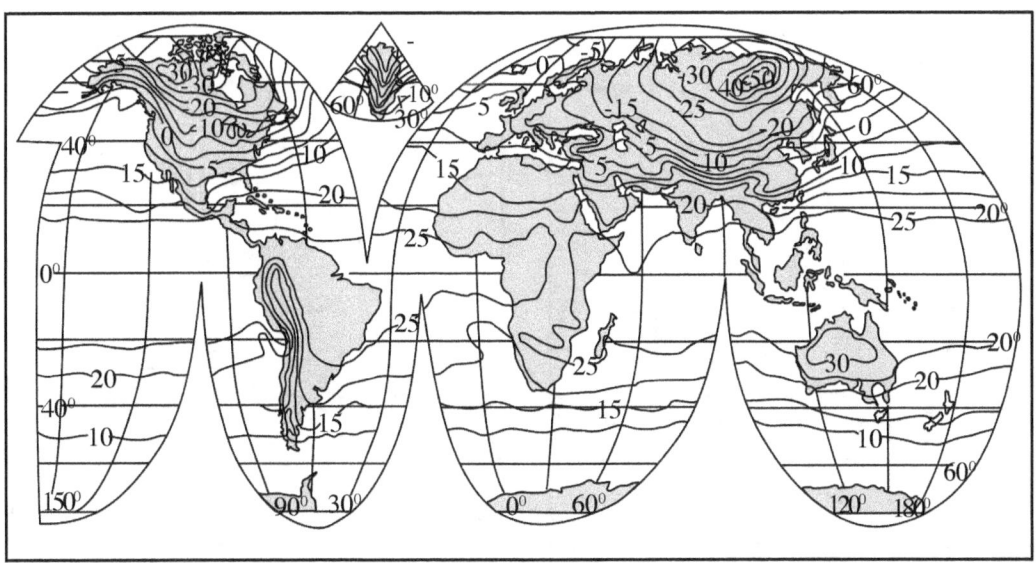

Fig. 171 : Distribution of average January Temperatures (Degree C⁰)

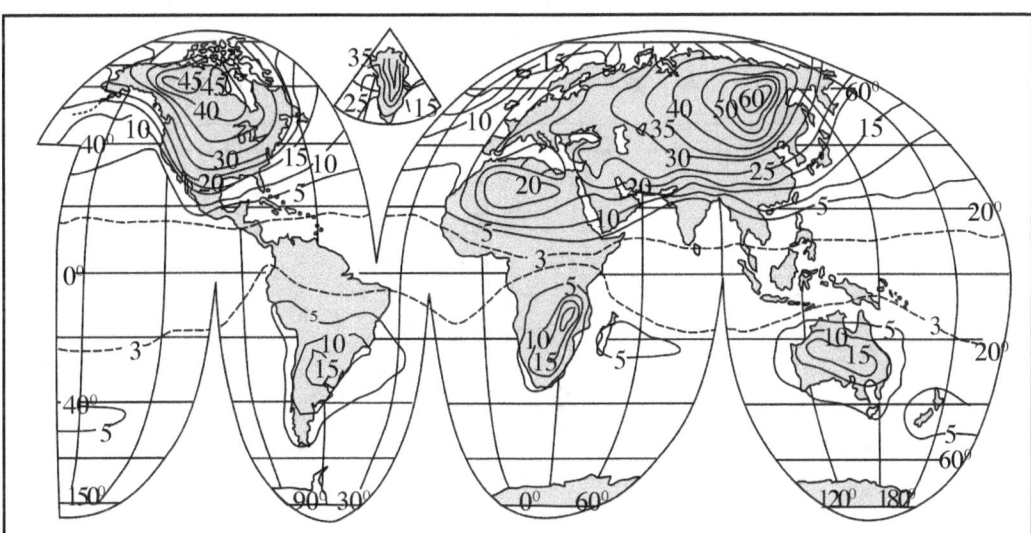

Fig. 172 : Distribution of mean annual average of Temperatures (C⁰)

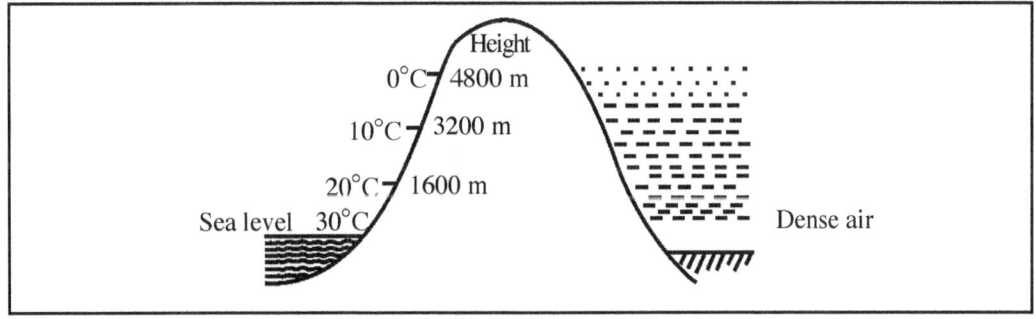

Fig. 173 : Altitude and Temperature

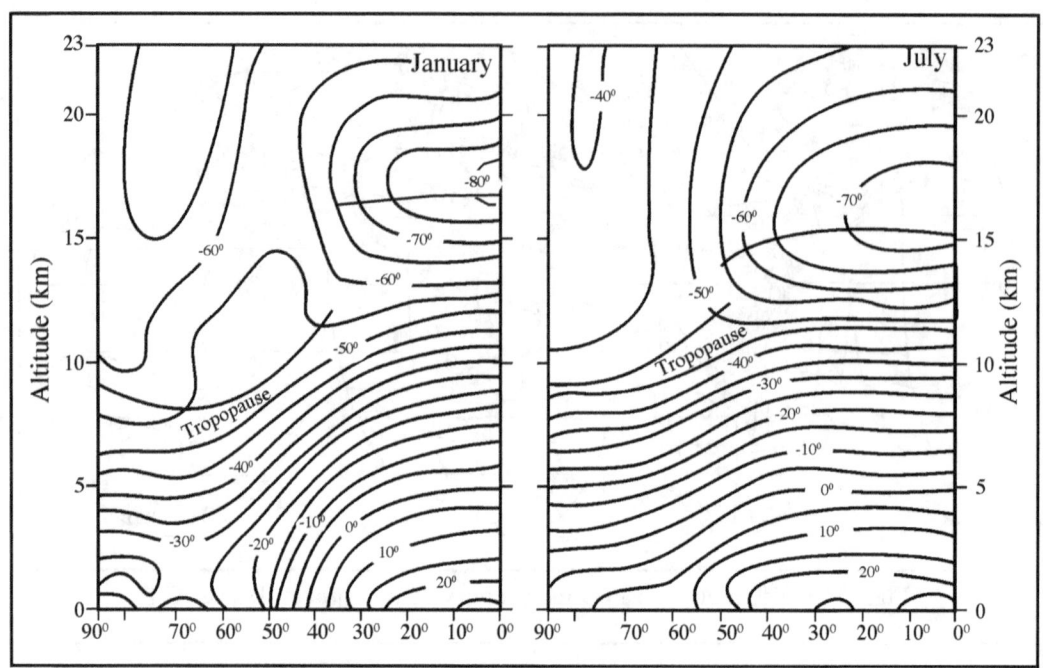

Fig. 174 : Altitudinal Change in temperature (Northern Hemisphere)

Fig. 175 : Foehn or Chinook Winds

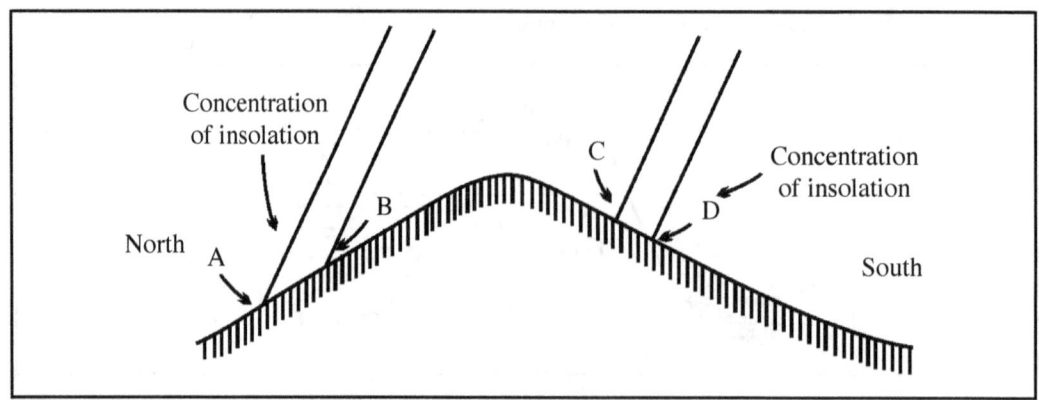

Fig. 176 : Slope and Temperature

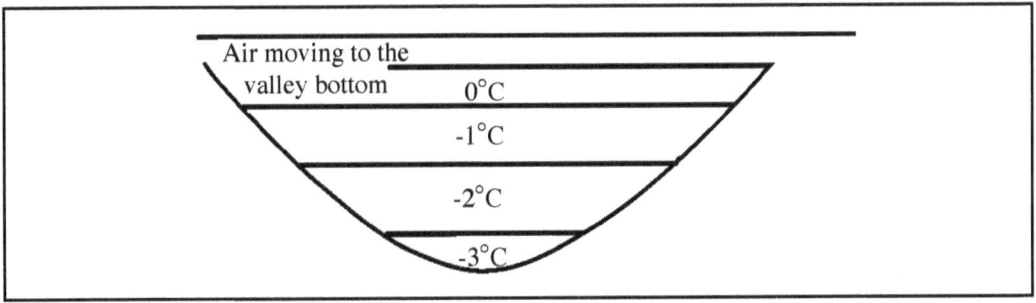

Fig. 177 : Inversion of Temperature

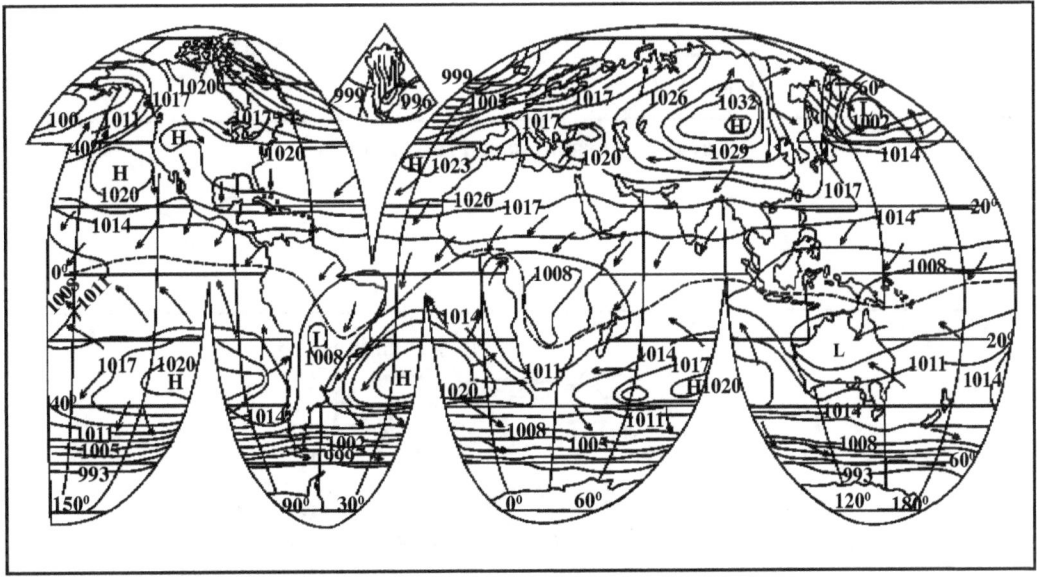

Fig. 178 : Mean sea level pressure in January (Millibars)

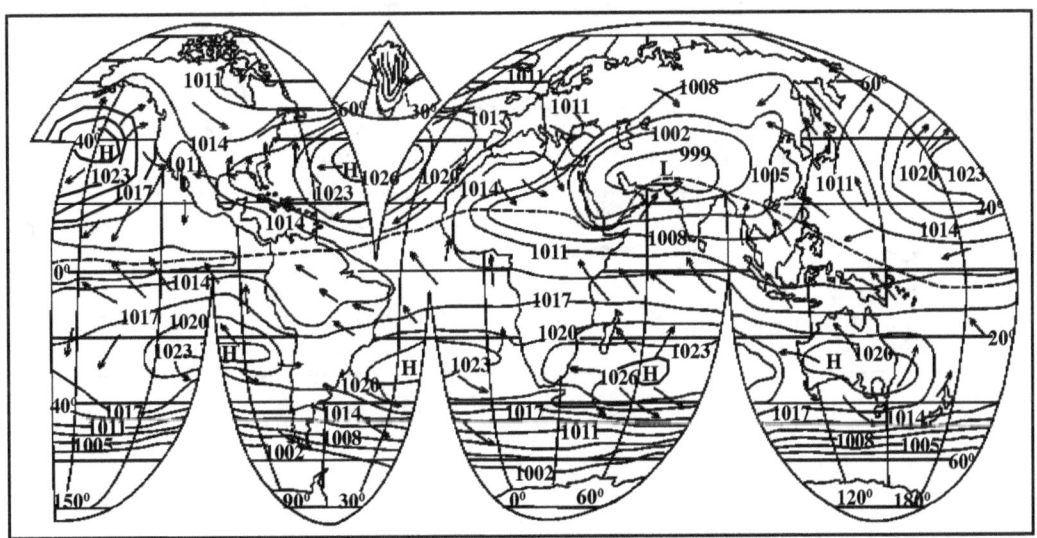

Fig. 179 : Mean sea level pressure in July (Millibars)

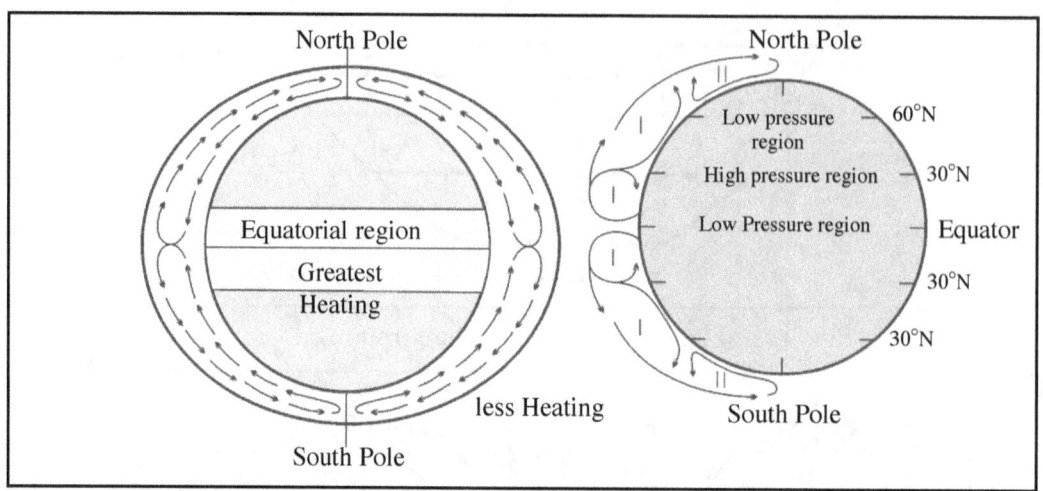

Fig. 180 : Formation of Pressure belts

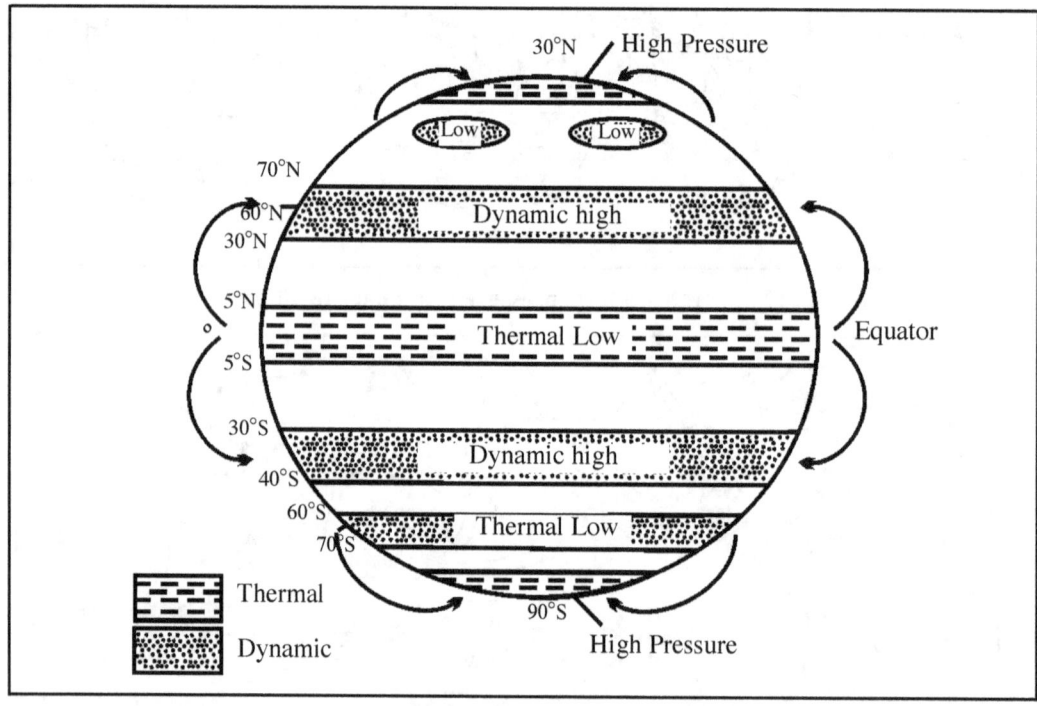

Fig. 181 : Pressure belts on Earth

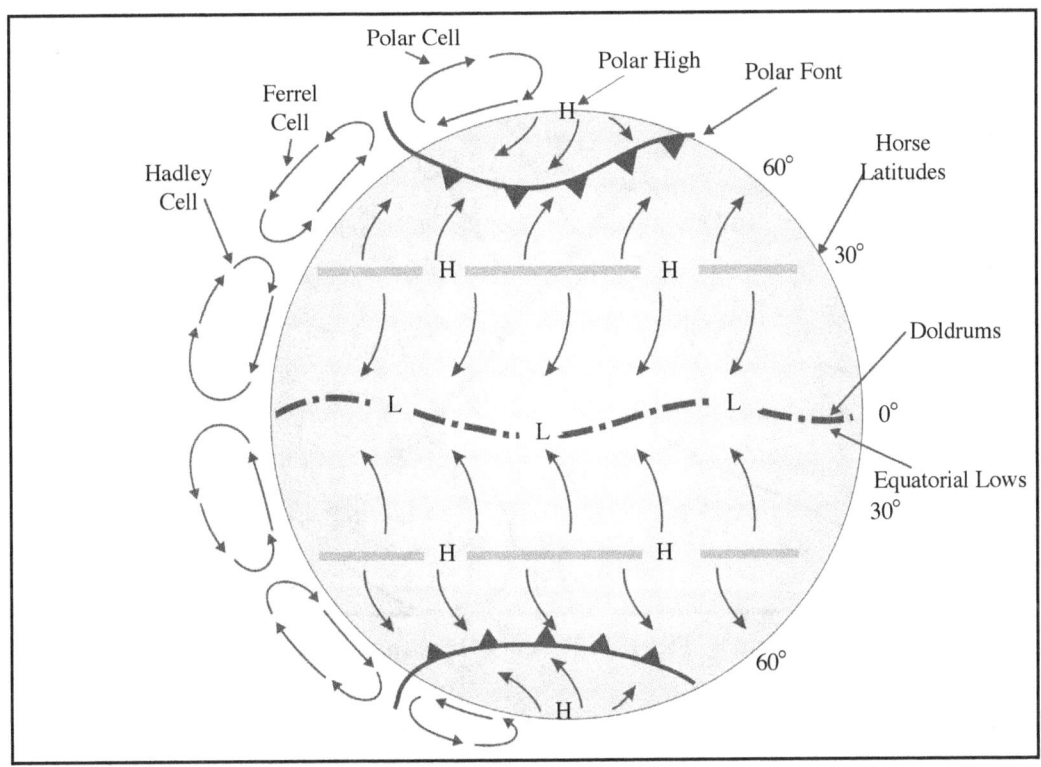

Fig. 182 : Hadley and Ferrel Cell

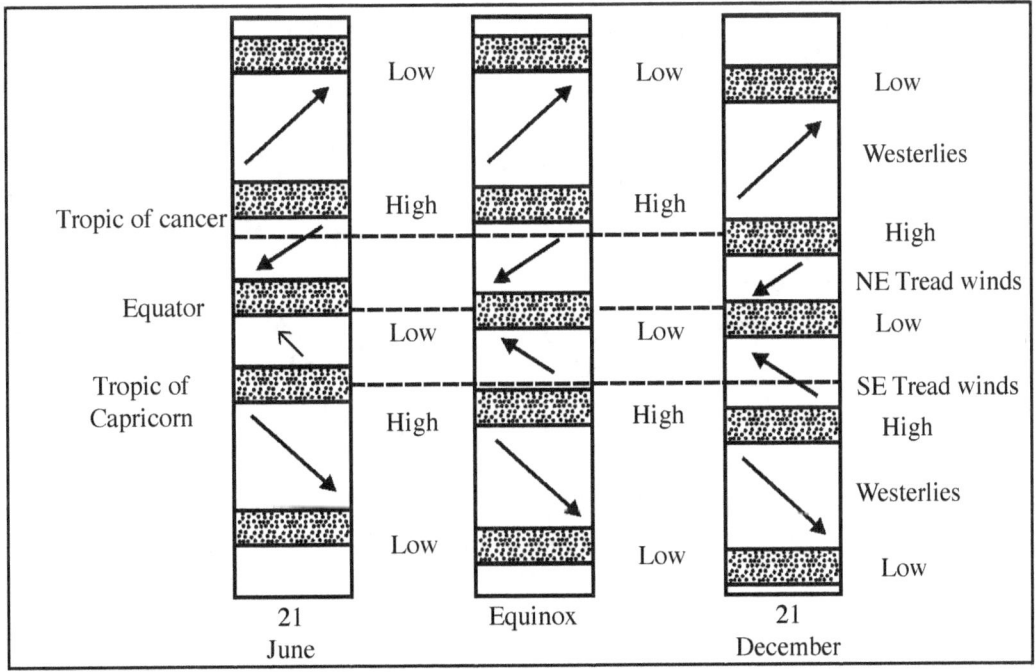

Fig. 183 : Shifting of Pressure belts

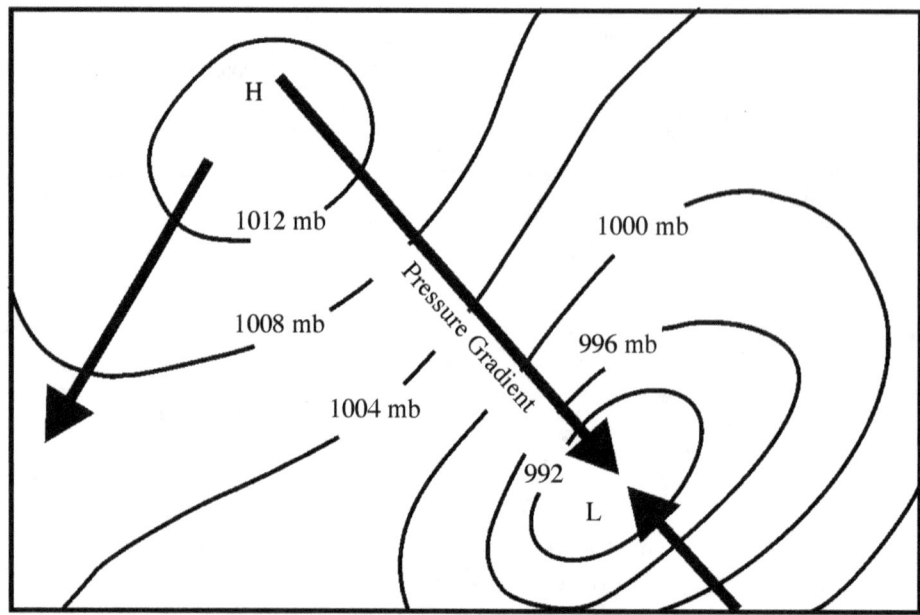

Fig. 184 : Pressure Gradient

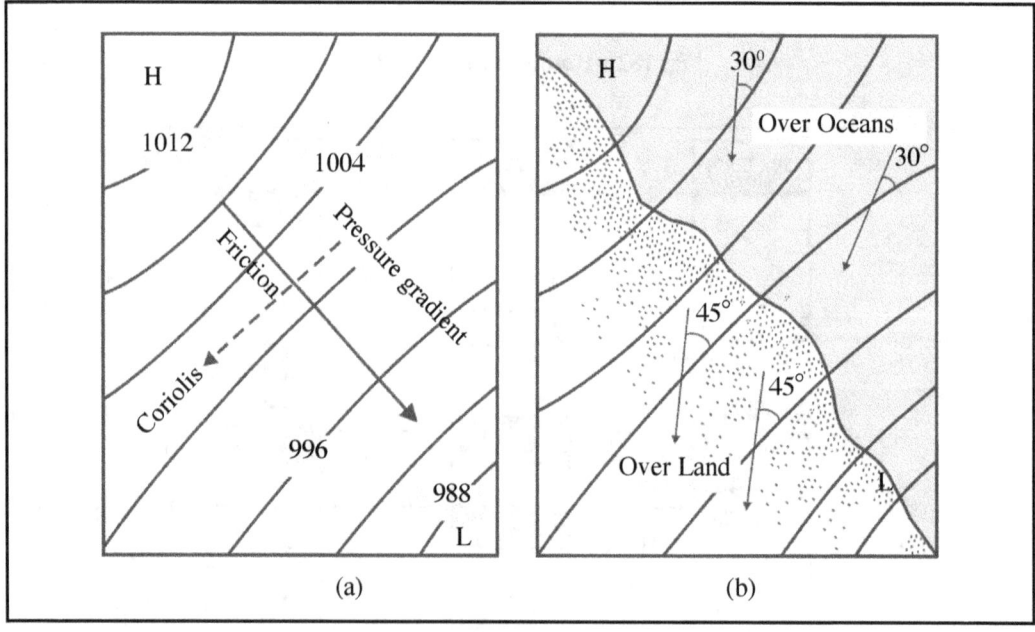

FIg. 185 : Winds on Land and Sea

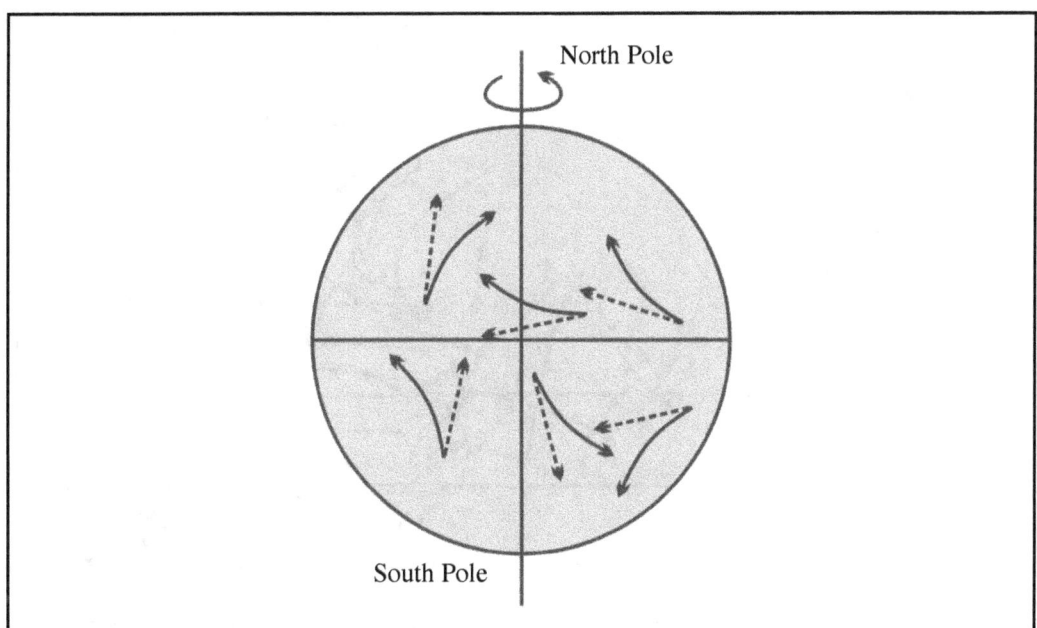

Fig. 186 : Coriolis effect

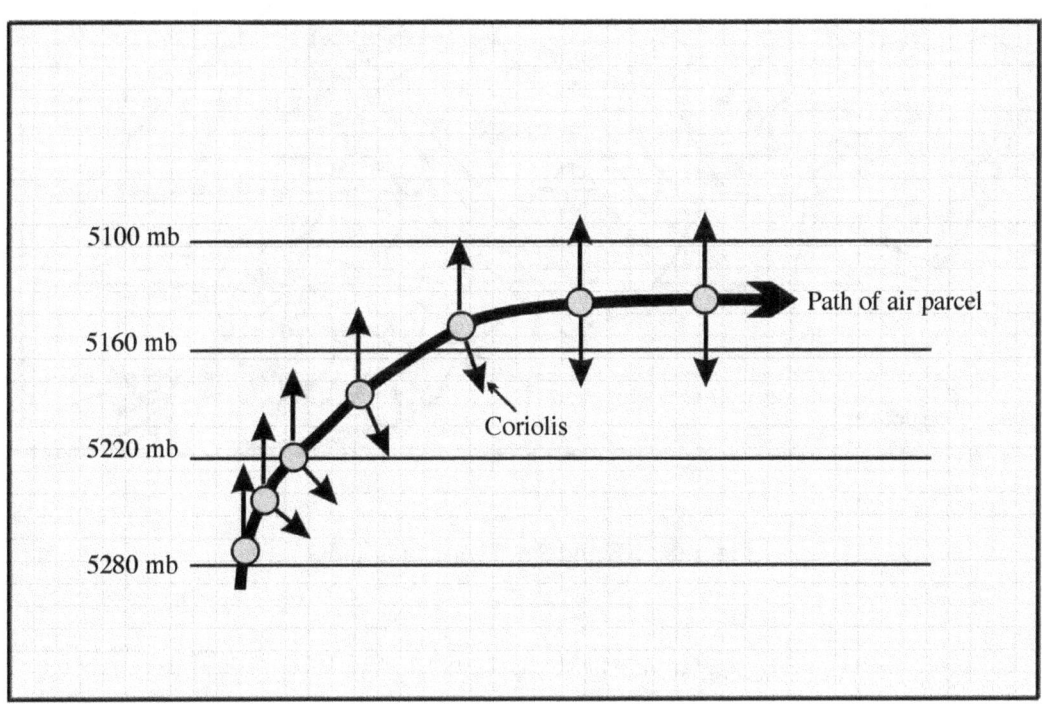

Fig. 187 : Geostrophic Wind

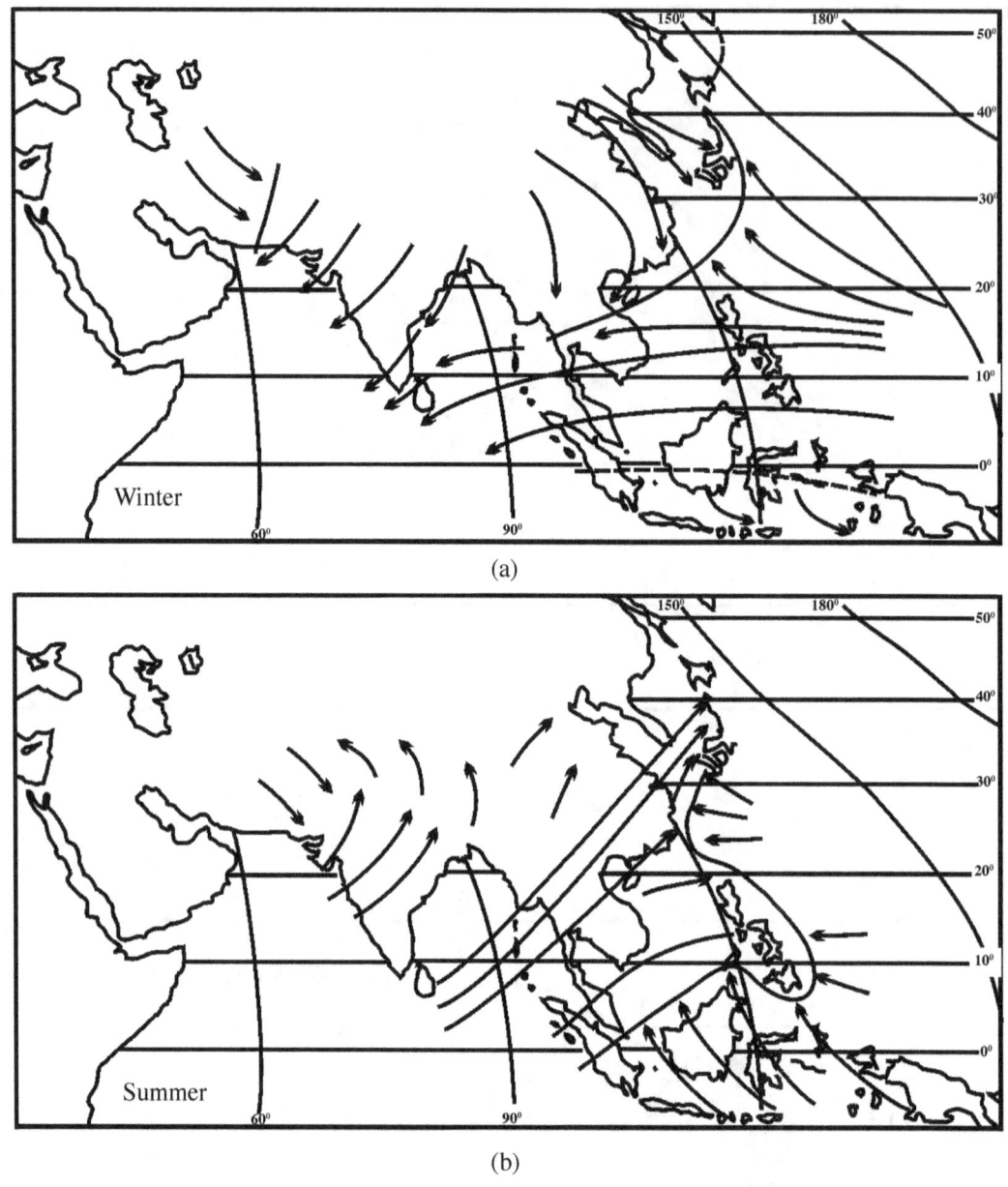

(a)

(b)

Fig. 188 : NE and SW Monsoon in India

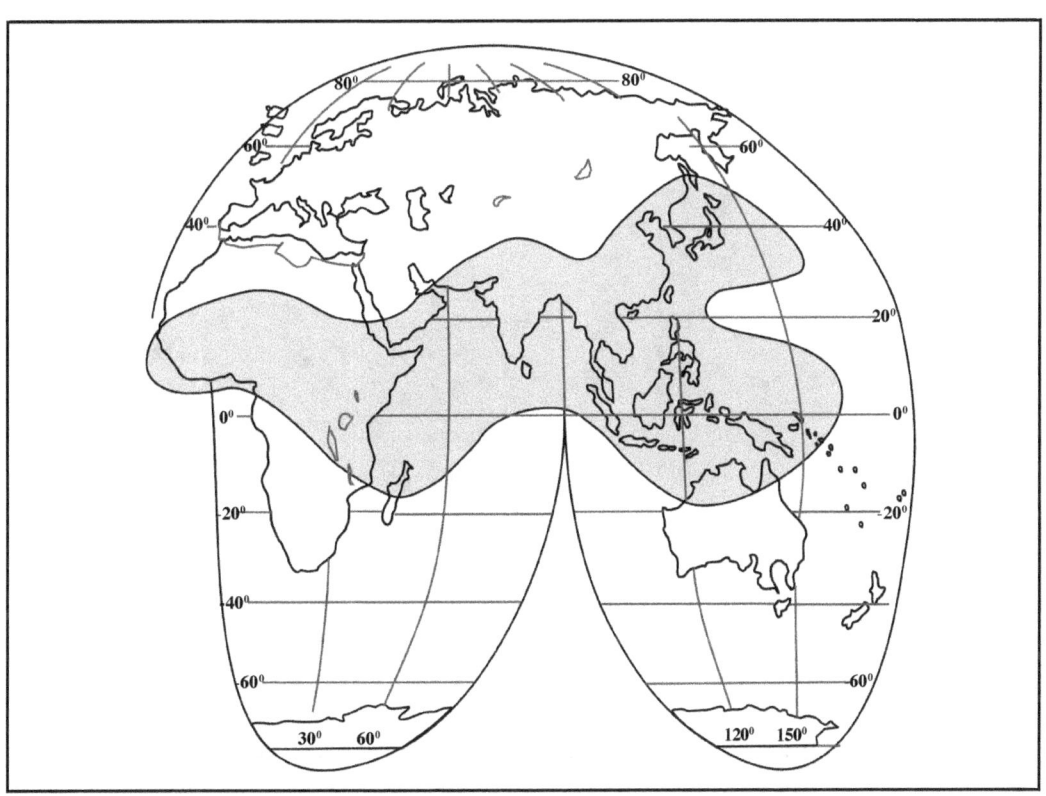

Fig. 189 : Monsoon Over Africa and Asia

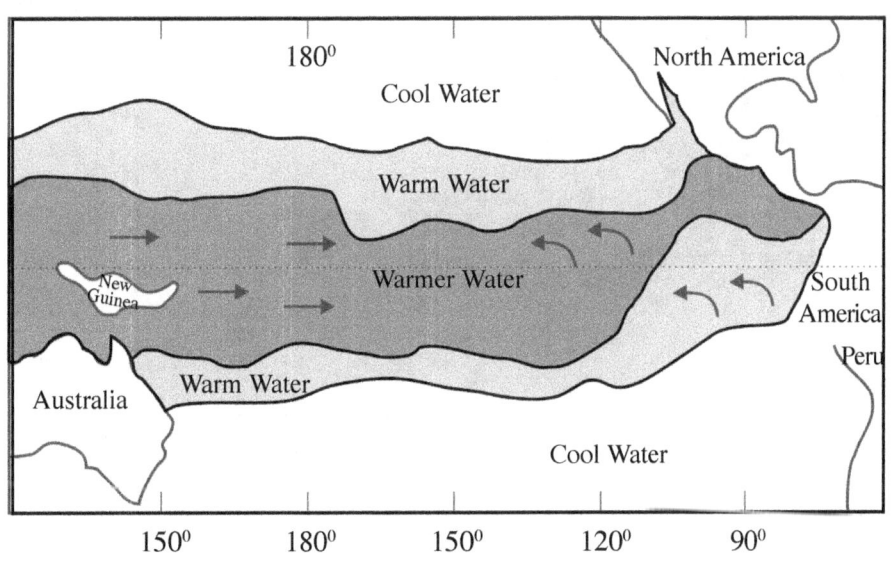

Fig. 190 : Circulation during El Nino

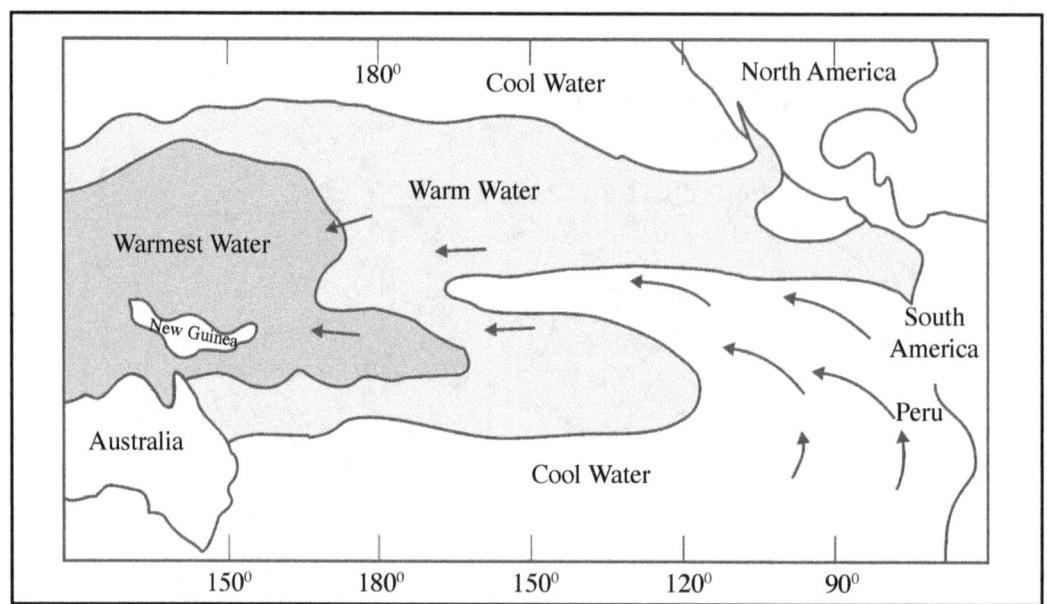

Fig. 191 : Circulation during La Nina

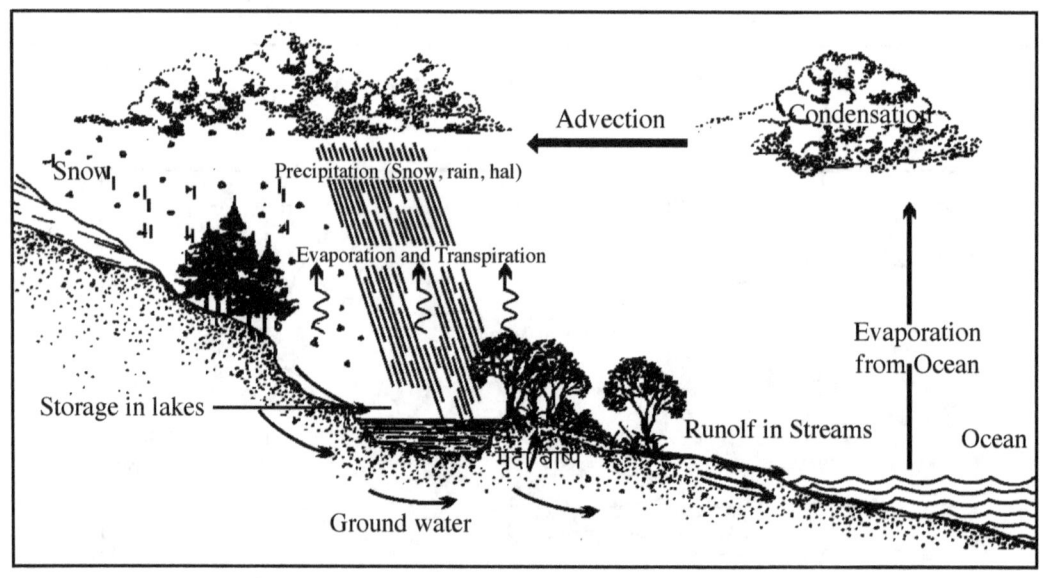

Fig. 192 : The Hydrologic Cycle

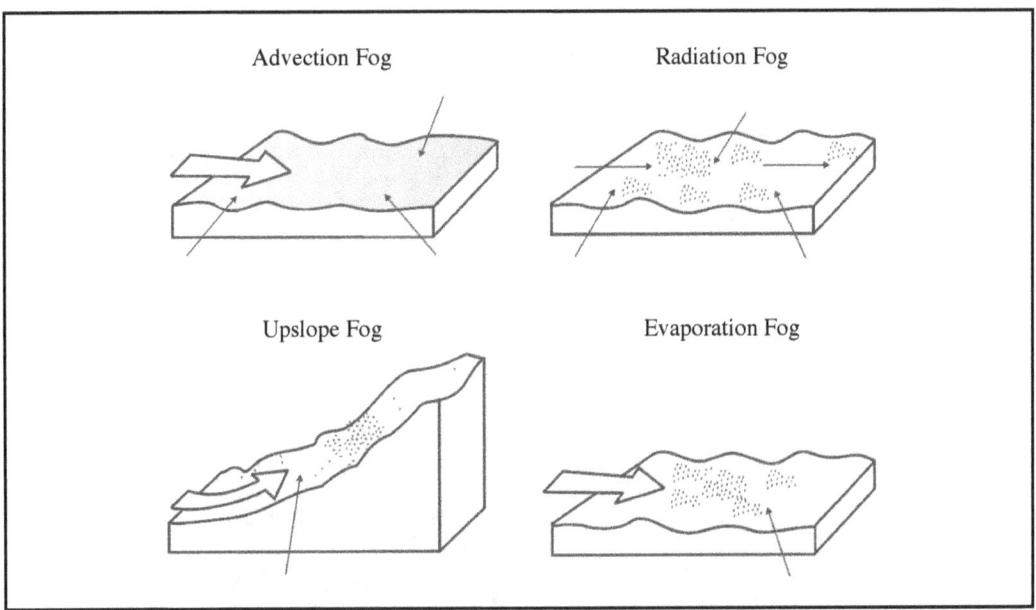

Advection Fog

Radiation Fog

Upslope Fog

Evaporation Fog

Fig. 193 : Types of Fog

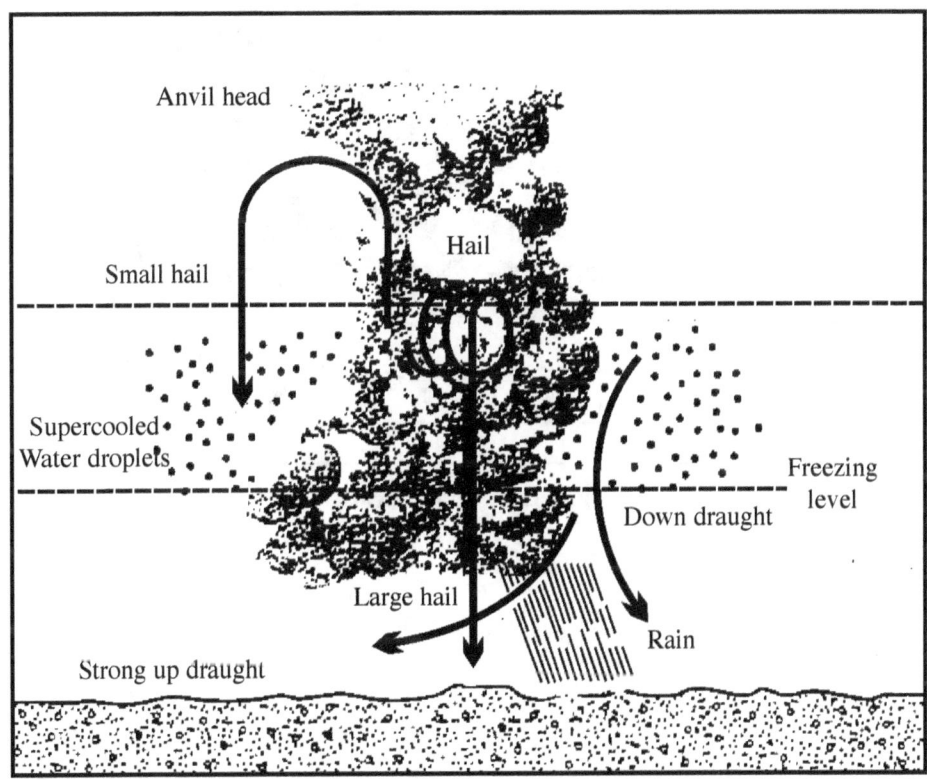

Anvil head

Hail

Small hail

Supercooled
Water droplets

Freezing
level

Down draught

Large hail

Rain

Strong up draught

Fig. 194 : Formation of hail in cumulus clouds

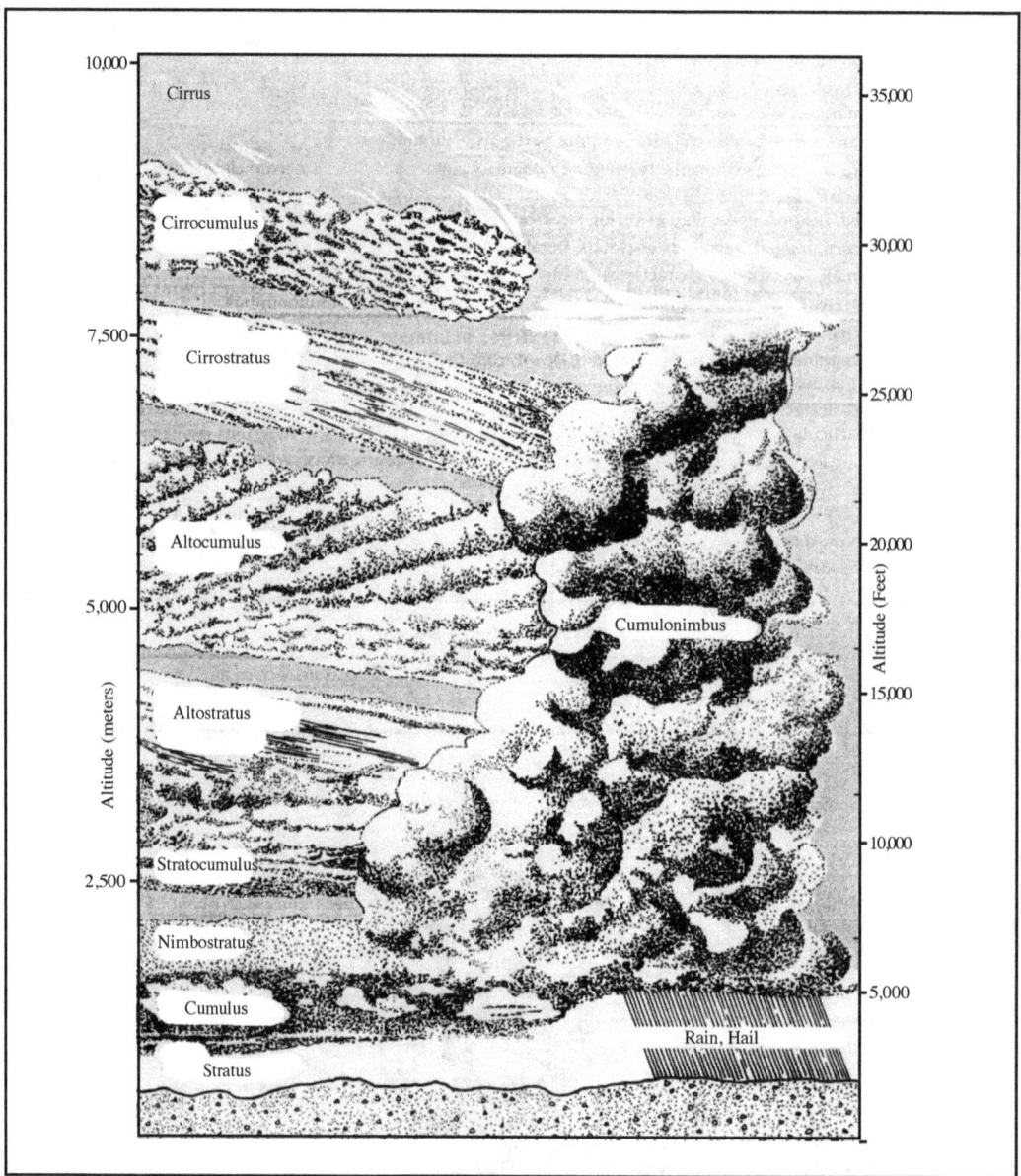

10,000 — Cirrus

Cirrocumulus — 30,000

7,500 — Cirrostratus — 25,000

Altocumulus — 20,000

5,000 — Cumulonimbus — 15,000

Altostratus

Altitude (meters)

Stratocumulus — 10,000

2,500 —

Nimbostratus — 5,000

Cumulus

Rain, Hail

Stratus

35,000

Altitude (Feet)

Fig. 195 : Colud forms

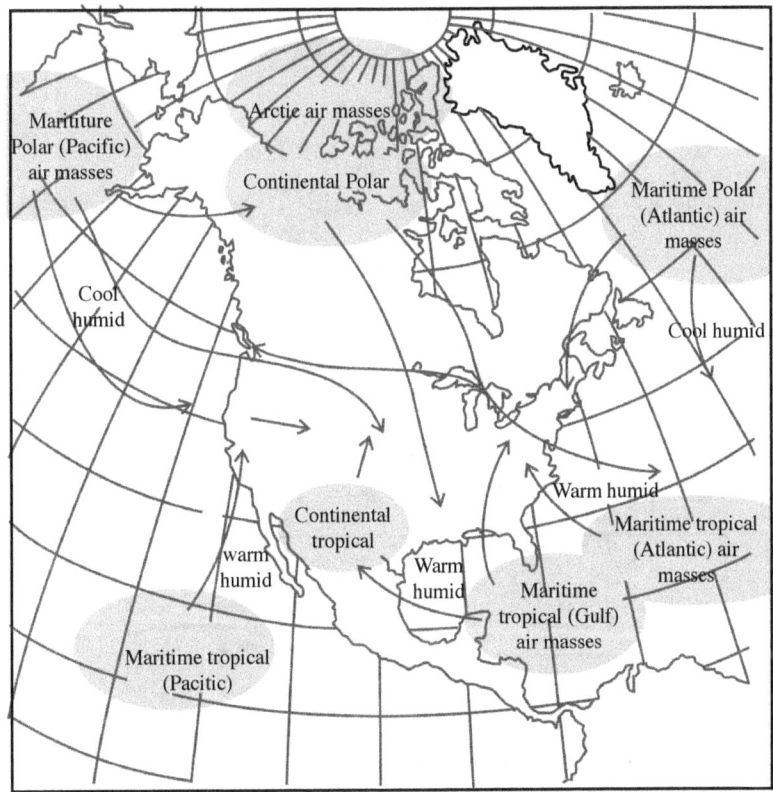

Fig. 196 : Air mass source regions (North America)

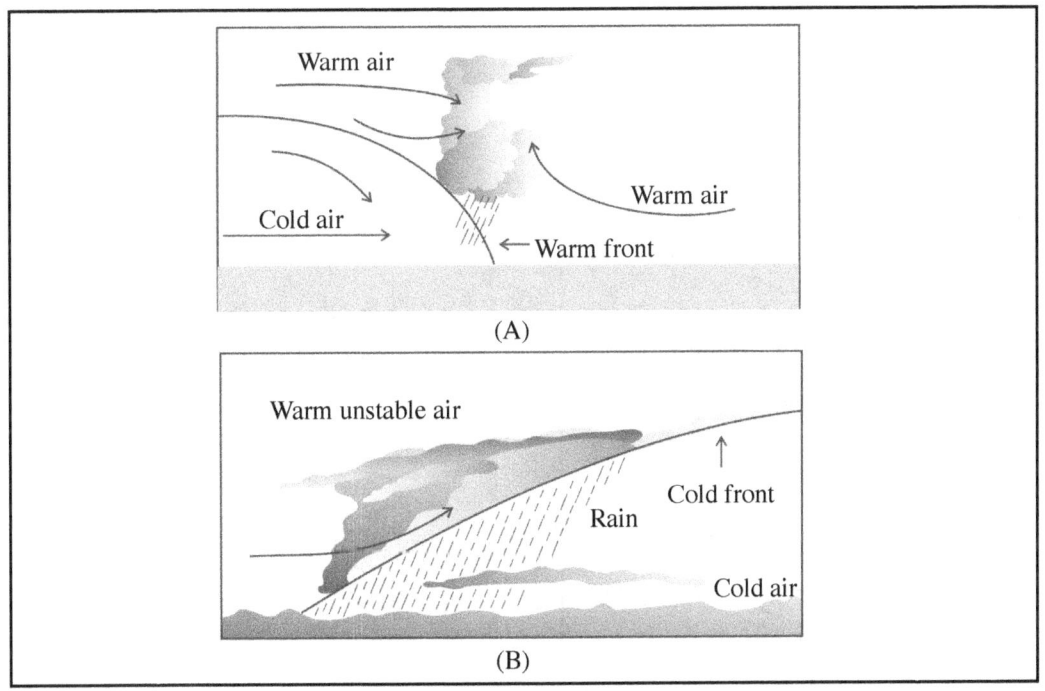

Fig. 197 : Frontal Movements

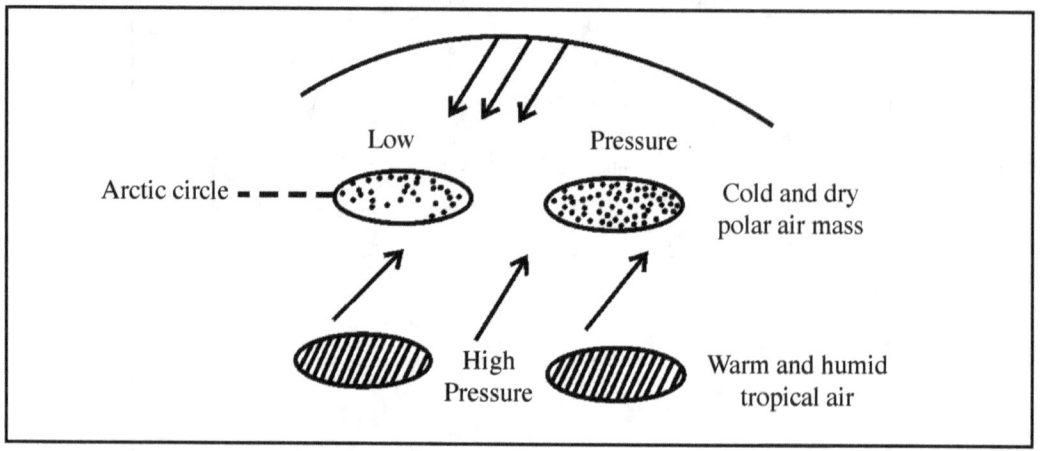

Fig. 198 : Mid Latitude Cyclones (Northern hemisphere)

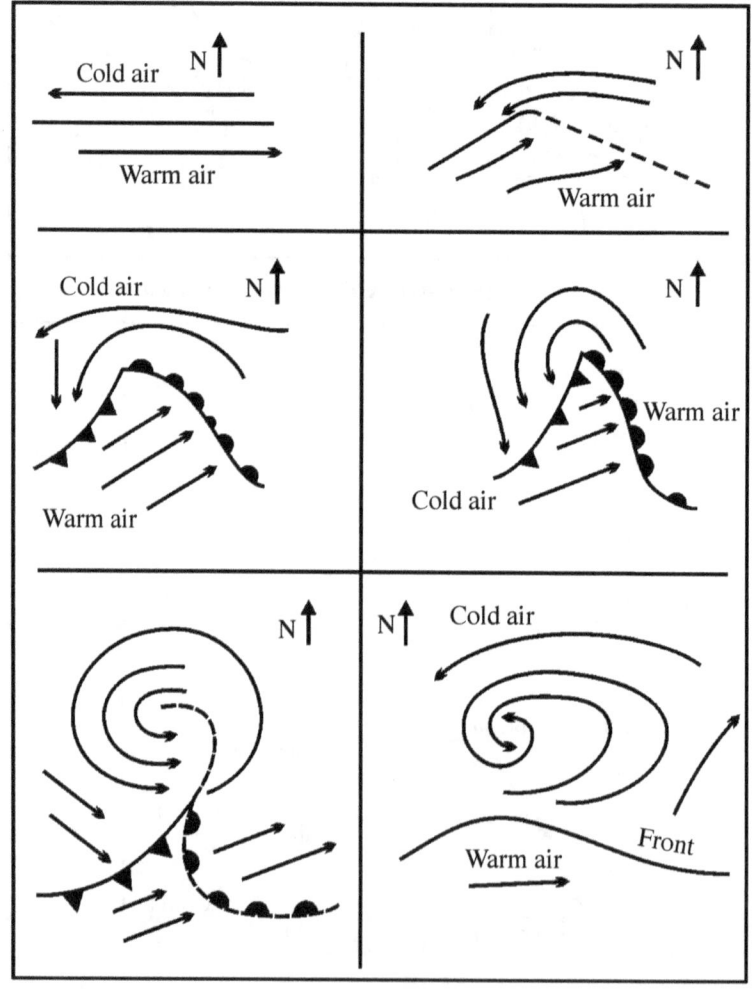

Fig. 199 : Life Cycle of a frontal cyclone

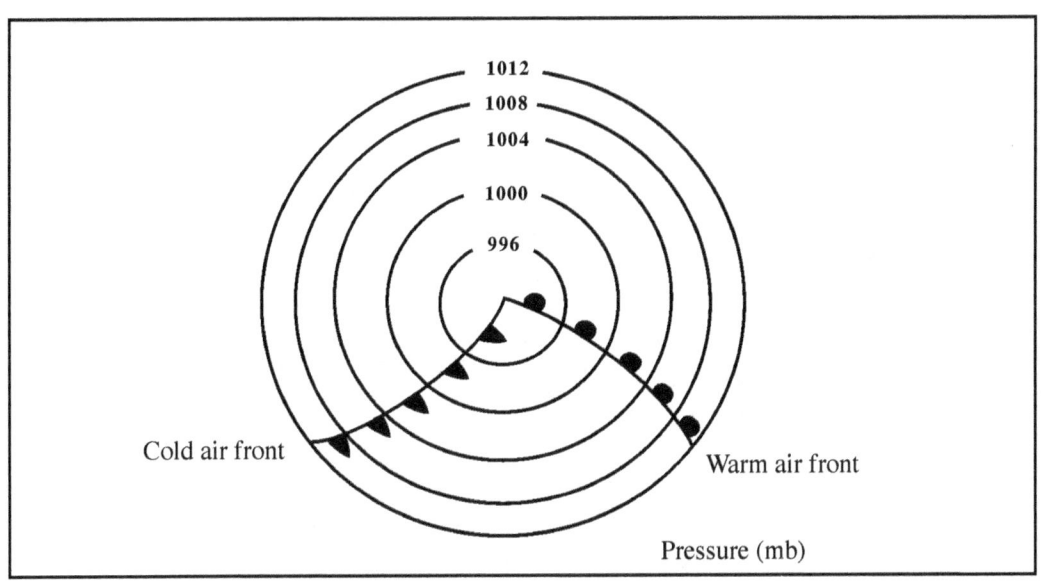

Fig. 200 : Mid latitude Cyclone

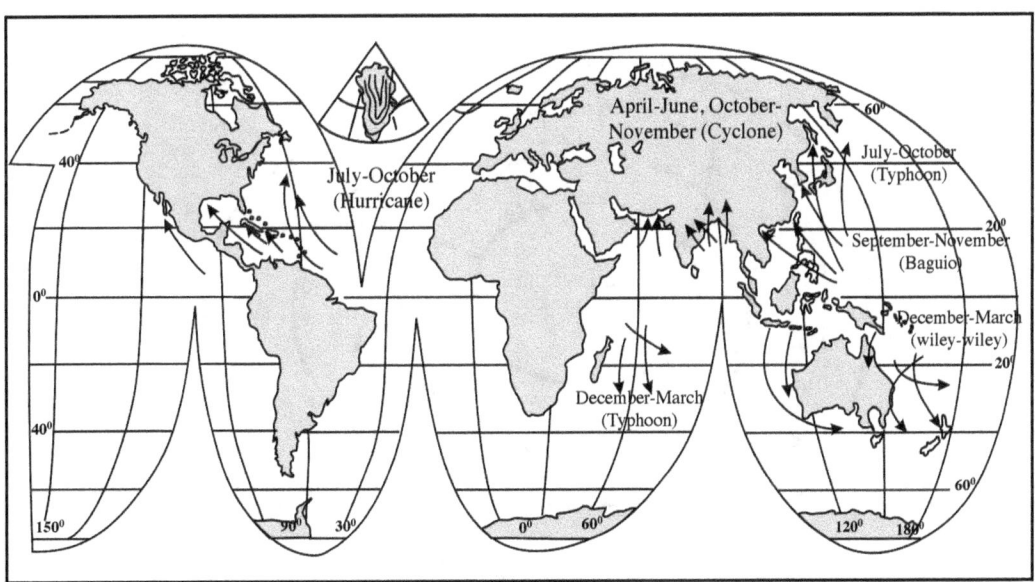

Fig. 201 : Tropical Cyclones

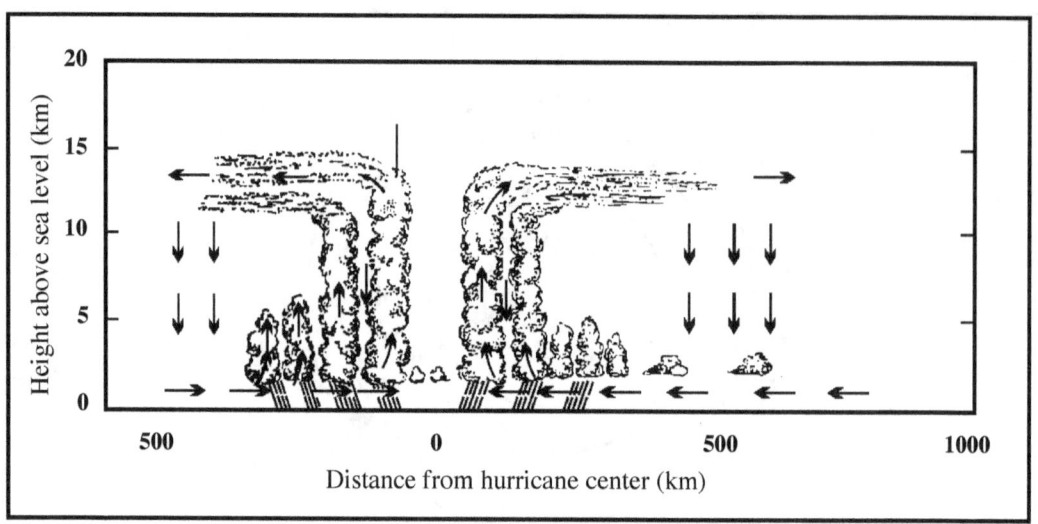

Fig 202 : Structure of a hurricane

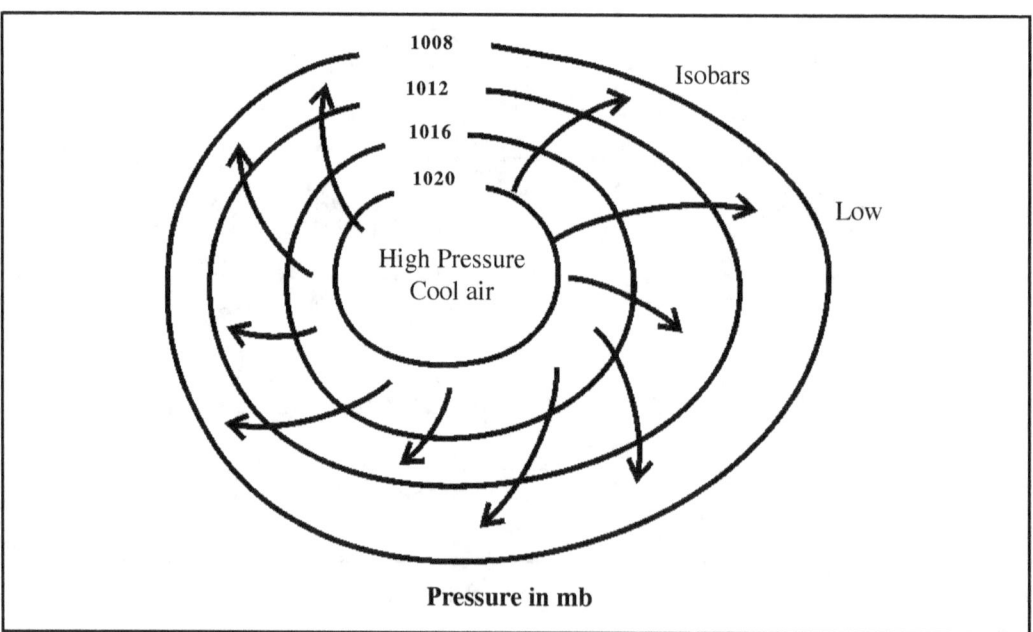

Fig 203 : Anticyclone

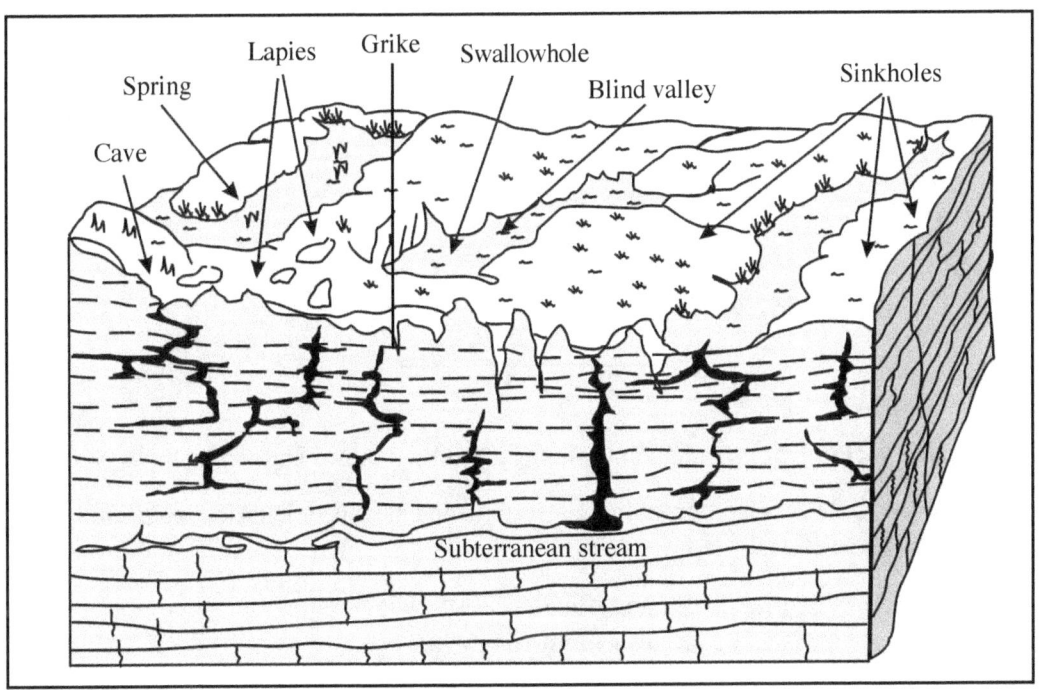

Fig. 204 : Blind valley in Karst

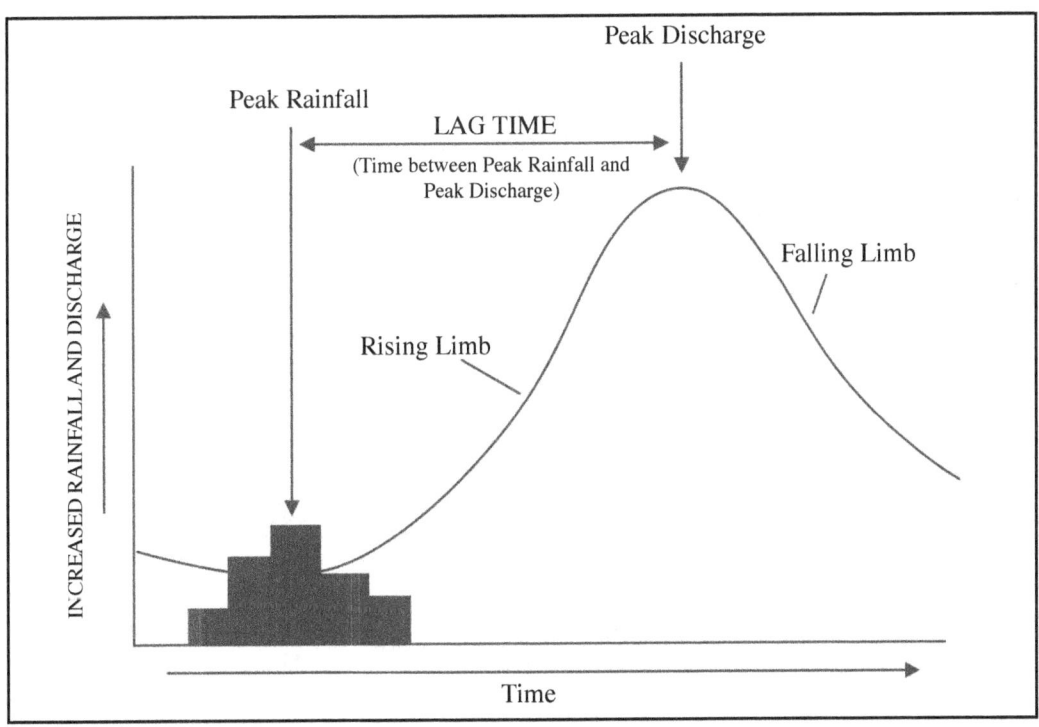

Fig. 205 : Flood Hydrograph

References

Birkeland, P.W. 1999. Soils and geomorphology, 3rd Ed. Oxford University Press; 430 p.

Bloom, Arthur L. 1997. Geomorphology: a systematic analysis of late Cenozoic landforms, 3rd Ed. Prentice Hall.

Boothroyd, J.C., Friedrich, N.E., and McGinn, S.R. 1985. Geology of microtidal coastal lagoons: Rhode Island. Marine Geology 63:35-76.

Davis, R.A. 1994. Barrier island systems - a geologic overview. P. 1-46. *In:* Davis, R.A. ed.) 1994. Geology of Holocene barrier island systems. Springer-Verlag, New York.

Lancaster, N. 1995. Geomorphology of desert dunes. Routledge, New York, NY. 209 p.

Osterkamp W.R. (2008) : Annotated definitions of selected terms and related terms of Hydrology, Sedimentology, Soil Science and Ecology, (Virginia ,open file report 2008 – 1217, pp 49)

Ritter, D.F., Kochel, R.C., and Miller, J.R. 1995. Process geomorphology, 3rd Ed. Brown Publ.; Dubuque, IA; 539 p.

Schumm, S.A. 1977. The fluvial system. John Wiley & Sons., Inc., New York, NY; 338 p.

Schumm, S.A. 1987. Experimental fluvial geomorphology. John Wiley & Sons, Inc., New York, NY; 413 p.

Selby, M.J. 1993. Hillslope materials and processes, 2nd Ed. Oxford University Press Inc., New York; 451 p.

Strahler, A.N. and Strahler, A.H. 1989. Elements of physical geography, 4th Ed. John Wiley & Sons, Inc., New York, NY.

Trewartha, G.T., Robinson, A.H., Hammond, E.H., and Horn, A.T. 1976. Fundamentals of physical geography, 3rd Ed. McGraw-Hill, New York, NY.; 384 p.

U.S.D.A. Glossary of selected Geomorphic and Geologic terms, U.S.D.A., Soil conservation service, Portland

About the Author

Dr Shrikant Karlekar (M.Sc., Ph.D)

- Formerly Honourary Prof. and Head, Dept. of Earth Sciences, Tilak Maharashtra Vidyapeeth, Pune and Prof. and Head, Dept. of Geography at Sir Parushurambhau College, Pune.

- Awarded Ph.D. in Geomorphology by University of Pune in 1981 on "A Geomorphic Study of South Konkan".

- Worked as a Professor in Geography, at University of Pune in 2004-2005.

- 17 Students have received their Ph.D. degree and 7 M.Phil, under the author's supervision.

- About 60 research papers published in various National and International Research Journals.

- 25 academic books (text and reference) published till year 2013.

- Worked as a Principal Investigator in many UGC and ICSSR funded projects.

- Received training in 'Photogrammetry' at Indian Remote Sensing Institute, Dehradun, in 1978.